DALE BROWN
AND
JIM DeFELICE

STRIKE ZONE
A DREAMLAND THRILLER

HARPER

An Imprint of HarperCollinsPublishers

This is a work of fiction. Names, characters, places, and incidents are products of the author's imagination or are used fictitiously and are not to be construed as real. Any resemblance to actual events, locales, organizations, or persons, living or dead, is entirely coincidental.

HARPER

An Imprint of HarperCollins*Publishers*
10 East 53rd Street
New York, New York 10022-5299

Copyright © 2004 by Air Battle Force, Inc.
Excerpt from *Raven Strike* copyright © 2011 by Air Battle Force, Inc.
ISBN 978-0-06-208784-3

First Harper premium printing: February 2012
First Avon Books mass market printing: January 2004

Printed in the United States of America

Visit Harper paperbacks on the World Wide Web at
www.harpercollins.com

10 9 8 7 6 5 4 3 2 1

STRIKE ZONE

I

GHOST CLONE

———

Bright Memorial Hospital, Honolulu
3 September 1997
0302 (all times local)

IT LOOKED LIKE AN ARROW AS SHE TURNED TO GET AWAY from it. Breanna pushed hard on her control stick, but the plane barely responded. Caught with little forward momentum, the Megafortress waddled in the air, finally managing to jerk its nose back to the right just in time to avoid the missile.

A second and third homed in. Breanna Stockard put her hand on the throttle slide, desperate to get more speed from the power plants.

It was too late. She could see one of the missiles coming at her right wing, riding the air like a hawk. Bree had ECMs, flares, tinsel—every defensive measure the experienced Megafortress pilot could muster was in play, and still the hawk came on, talons out.

And then, just as it was about to strike the fuselage in front of the starboard wing root, it changed. The slim body of the Russian-designed Alamo missile thickened. Wings grew from the middle, and the steering fins at the rear changed shape. Breanna was being tracked by an American Flighthawk, not a missile. For a moment, she felt relief.

Then the robot plane slammed into the wing.

* * *

BREANNA SHOOK HERSELF AWAKE. THE PALE GREEN light of the hospital room threw ghost shadows across her face; she could hear the machine monitoring her heartbeat stuttering.

"Damn drugs," she said.

They'd given her a sedative to help her sleep, fearful that her injuries would keep her from resting for yet another night. Breanna had bruised ribs, a concussion, a sprained knee, and a twisted neck; she was also suffering from dehydration and the effects of more than twelve hours' exposure to a bitter Pacific storm. But the physical injuries paled beside what really ached inside her—the loss of four members of her crew, including her longtime copilot Chris Ferris and Dreamland's number two Flighthawk pilot, Kevin Fentress.

Breanna rolled onto her back and shoved her elbows under her to sit up in the bed. She was angry with herself for not flying better, for not avoiding the Chinese missile that had taken her down. The fact that she had sacrificed her plane to rescue others was besides the point. The fact that the Piranha mission had been a stunning success, averting war between China and India, mattered nothing to her, at least not now, not in the room lit only by hospital monitors.

She should've saved her people.

Her father would have. Her husband would have.

She ached to have them both here with her. But her father, Colonel Tecumseh "Dog" Bastian, and her husband, Major Jeff "Zen" Stockard, had been called back to Dreamland, to deal with problems brewing there. She was sentenced to sit in this bed until her injuries healed.

"Damn drugs," she muttered again, reaching for the control at the side of the bed to raise it.

What the hell had that stupid dream been about? She'd been taken down by a missile, not a Flighthawk. The Flighthawks were U.S. weapons, not Chinese.

But as they were going down, before she gave the order to abandon ship, Torbin Dolk had said something about a Flighthawk. What the hell had he said?

"I have a U/MF at long range."

Those were his words, but they had to be wrong. Their own Flighthawks had been lost, and there were no other Megafortresses with their robot scout fighters nearby.

What the hell did he say? Had she got it wrong?

The confusion and static and storm of the shootdown returned. She closed her eyes, wishing she hadn't failed.

"Damn drugs," she said, playing with the bed control in a fruitless effort to make herself more comfortable.

Outside Taipei, Taiwan
1700

CHEN LEE WAITED UNTIL THE CHIME OF THE ANTIQUE grandfather clock at the far end of his office ended, then rose slowly from his desk, following a ritual he had started many years before. His movements were weighted by eighty years of exertion, and so it took longer for him to cross the large office than it once had, but the familiarity of the afternoon ritual filled him with pleasure. He had long ago realized that, no matter how much wealth one had—and he had a great deal—the more important things, the things that gave life meaning and value, were less tangible: family affection and respect, dreams and ambitions, ritual.

Chen Lee went to the chest at the right side of his large office and took the bottle from the top, carefully pouring two fingers' worth of Scotch in the glass tumbler. He had developed a taste for single-malt Scotch as a young man during the last days of the war with the communists when he'd been sent to London as part of a delegation working to persuade the Western allies that Mao must be stopped at all costs. The mission had been a failure; worn out by the World War, the British couldn't stop their own empire from slipping through their fingers, let alone send an army to help Chiang Kai-shek and the rightful rulers of the great Chinese nation. Not even the Americans were willing to help them until the communist treachery was made obvious in Korea. Even then, the only assistance they would begrudgingly afford was to prevent the invasion of Taiwan by the mongrel bastards who had marched among the peasants, pretending moral superiority when all along practicing opportunism.

The tingle of Scotch as he took his first sip reminded Chen Lee of his bitterness, and he welcomed it wholeheartedly. For it was only by acknowledging the past that he could look toward the future.

Much had changed in the nearly fifty years that

had passed since his stay in London. Chen Lee had left the government to become a man of business; he had started humbly, as little more than a junk man. He took discarded items, first from the Japanese, then from Europe and the U.S., and turned them into useful materials. Metals first, then gradually electronics and chemicals and even, eventually, nuclear materials. He had made a fortune, and then lost much of it—a loss he blamed on the treachery of the Japanese he was forced to deal with in the early 1980s. But this loss had tempered him; he would not willingly wish it upon anyone else, but he had managed to overcome it, and applied its lessons well.

His assets now totaled close to a billion dollars U.S.; he owned pieces large and small of businesses throughout the world as well as the Republic of China—Taiwan to the outside world. In fact, his wealth was so extensive he needed two of his three grandsons—his only son had died more than a decade before—to manage it. They were given relatively free hands, as long as they did not break his cardinal rules: no investment in Japan, and no dealings with the communist mongrels under any circumstances.

Others on the island were not so fastidious, and in their eagerness to enrich themselves had prepared the nation for the ultimate treachery—surrender to the communists.

It was coming. Several months before, the provinces had clashed. At first, the Americans had seemed to help them; Mainland bases were bombed in a spectacular campaign referred to by the media as "Fatal Terrain." Had the war proceeded then, reunification might have been possible. But the Americans had proven themselves interested only in preserving the status quo. Worse, the government on Taiwan—the rightful representatives of all China, in Chen Lee's view—lost face and gave way to a group of men who could only be called appeasers. In a matter of weeks, the president was due to fly to Beijing for talks with the mongrels who had usurped the homeland.

The meeting would be the first of many.

Chen Lee was determined not to let it take place. He was willing, in fact, to spend his entire fortune to stop it.

He was willing to go further. He would give his own life so that his grandchildren's children might once more live freely in their homeland.

Was he willing to give their lives as well?

The Scotch burned the sides of his tongue.

He was willing to let them die, yes. Even his favorite grandchild, Chen Lo Fann. Indeed, Fann had volunteered to do so many times already.

Would he give up the lives of his great-grandchildren, the sweet little ones?

As he asked the question, he saw the faces of the little ones, whose ages ranged from two to ten.

No, he would not wish any harm to them, boy or girl. That was why he must act immediately.

The Americans had interfered, preventing what should have been a war between the communists and India—a war he had clandestinely encouraged.

Chen Lee took another sip of his drink. He had to encourage a wider war, one that would involve all of South Asia and the mongrels. Even if the war did not lead to conquest of the stolen provinces, it would at least halt the present slide toward accommodation.

It might yet yield conquest, thanks to the weapons he had developed and secreted away. But he felt he could not share them with the present government, headed as it was by traitors. He would have to follow his own path.

Chen Lee was bitterly disappointed in the Americans, whose ill-considered attempts at imposing peace merely made the world safe for the mongrel usurpers. During the course of his life, Chen Lee had had many dealings with Americans; he admired them in many ways. But ultimately, he found them weak and undisciplined.

He knew too that their aims were not his aims. They protected the Republic of China only when it suited them.

So be it. If the Americans intervened again, their blood would flow.

Air Force High Technology Center/ Whiplash Complex (aka Dreamland) 4 September 1997 0700

JENNIFER GLEASON PUSHED BACK A STRAND OF HER long hair and leaned forward, her nose nearly against the large flat panel of the computer display, as if close proximity to the line of code might reveal more detail.

The line itself was abstract and seemingly meaningless:

AAA488570c6633cD2222222222BCD354777

But to the computer expert, the gibberish told an ominous tale. She picked up the pencil she had laid on the desk nearby, twirling it in her finger before copying the line on a yellow pad nearby.

"Pad and pencil—never a good sign," said an acerbic voice behind her.

"Hi, Ray," she said before double-checking her copy against the screen.

"Well?" Dreamland's senior scientist Ray Rubeo stood over her, squinting down at the screen.

"Our compression algorithm."

"Yes," said Rubeo.

"It doesn't prove anything. The algorithm itself could have come from a bunch of places."

Instead of answering, Rubeo stooped to the workstation next to her, quickly tapping a pair of keys and bringing up a small snippet of video. A gray shadow of an aircraft banked and turned away in the screen.

The image had been built from a fleeting radar contact made several days before in the South China Sea, during a bloody battle between the Chinese and Indian navies. A Dreamland Megafortress called *Quicksilver* had tried to stop the conflict, and in the process had been shot down. Four of the six crew members aboard had died.

Quicksilver, with the help of other Dreamland air and ground assets known collectively as Whiplash, had forestalled a nuclear confrontation between the two Asian powers and saved millions of lives. Four lives for a million. Most people would think that a worthwhile trade-off.

The equation was difficult when it involved people you knew. Jennifer, one of the top scientists at the facility, knew all of them very well. She was thankful at least that the pilot, Breanna Stockard, had been spared. Bree was her lover's daughter, and while the two women had never gotten along particularly well themselves, Jennifer could not have borne the hurt Bree's death would have caused the colonel.

Jennifer watched as the three-dimensional blob reappeared in the right-hand corner of Rubeo's screen, commanded to reappear by Dreamland's senior scientist. It twisted and jerked left, then down and over to the opposite corner of the screen. The simulation multiplied real time by a factor of twenty, so that the blob stayed on screen for an entire minute, rather than the three seconds it had appeared on the original radar.

Those three seconds, along with the five seconds' worth of radio transmission Jennifer was study- ing on her own terminal, were enough to have cost both her and Rubeo several days' worth of sleep. For together they meant there had been another unmanned robot plane in the air about seventy-five miles from the Megafortress when it was shot down.

And not just an ordinary "robot," or unmanned aerial vehicle, commonly known as a UAV. The ex- perts interpreted the poor quality of the radar re- turns to indicate that the tiny aircraft was faceted much the way first-generation Stealth fighters were;

the blanks in the simulation that made the plane jerk across the screen were a function of weak or missing radar returns. The experts had also determined that the craft had been going somewhere around 400 knots and took a turn sharp enough to pull close to ten g's.

Designing and building a small aircraft—its wingspan appeared to be under ten feet—was certainly difficult, but the real achievement was controlling the robot. To make it fly and maneuver in real time took considerable skill, skill that until now had resided only at Dreamland. While there was a variety of UAVs around, most flew preprogrammed courses or went relatively slowly. Only the U/MF-3 Flighthawks developed at Dreamland were capable of high-speed maneuvers and aerial combat.

Imitation might be the highest form of flattery, but in this case it could also be deadly. Properly handled, the U/MF-3s were almost impervious to American defenses. If the ghost clone—one of the techies had named it that while reviewing the radar and telemetry intercepts—was armed, no part of the country would be safe.

"So whose is it?" asked Rubeo, voicing the question of the hour.

"Could be a Russian project," offered Jennifer.

"Yes," murmured Rubeo. "It's possible."

"And they stole it two years ago."

"The intelligence assessments would have shown this," said Rubeo. Dreamland had been rocked two years earlier when a deeply planted Russian spy was exposed. He had compromised some of the facility's top projects, and in many ways Dreamland had never been the same. But he had no access to the Flighthawk project, as an extensive investigation had proven.

So if the technology had been stolen, someone else had done it.

Someone still working at the base.

Rubeo stood back from the screen.

"Our code or not?"

"Very close," said Jennifer. "It uses similar theories and compression schemes."

"So what does it mean?"

Jennifer pointed to the first few integers. The code was in base sixteen. "It's detecting the radar, giving a position, tagging the type, and then I think this part confirms a maneuver it's already started on its own."

"Still think it's a coincidence?" Rubeo asked her.

"Mmm," she said. "It could be."

"The memorial service is in half an hour," he told her. Then he walked from the room.

COLONEL TECUMSEH "DOG" BASTIAN LOOKED OUT AT the apron in front of Dreamland Hangar Two. A half-dozen temporary bleachers had been erected in front of the building; augmented by a sea of folding chairs, they held a good portion of the men and women he oversaw at the high-tech developmental base in the wastelands near Glass Mountain, Nevada. In front of the bleachers was a podium; off to the side, a short row of folding chairs. In a few minutes, an honor guard would appear from the building for a ceremony commemorating a recently concluded operation in the Pacific. Some of the people back at the Pentagon called the action "the Piranha Incident" because of the undersea surveillance weapon Dreamland had used during it; to Dog, the nickname was appropriate for its bloody connotation—the operation had been a man killer. Five members of Dreamland had lost their lives during it: four when a Megafortress was shot down by an errant Chinese missile; the fifth had stepped on a mine during a support operation.

Ostensibly, the ceremony that was about to kick off would honor the living—the President had issued a special, albeit secret, unit commendation to Dreamland, which would be read by the President's representative, NSC assistant director for technology, Jed Barclay. But for Dog and most of the people attending, the ceremony was mostly about the men who had lost their lives.

It was something of a cliché to refer to military commands and bases as families. In many cases, it wasn't a very accurate description—thousands and thousands of men and women might work at a typical base. The majority would have little contact with one another outside of their assignment area. But Dreamland was different. Ostensibly part of Elliott Air Force Base, the home of the High Technology Aerospace Weapons Center, Dog's command was an ultra-secret and relatively small unit contained at facilities adjacent to the main base. Dreamland didn't just make the country's next-generation weapons; they tested them in combat under an ops program known as Whiplash, which answered to the President through the National Security Council. Whiplash was Dog's brainchild.

Only a few hundred people worked here, and the majority lived here as well. Not only did civilian experts mix freely with military personnel, service people of all ranks worked together in as close to harmony as the high-pressure, creative atmosphere would allow. The cafeterias, lounges, and rec areas were "all ranks," open to everyone who worked at Dreamland, from Dog all the way to the kitchen help. Pilots still ruled the roost—it was, after all, an Air Force operation—but, with a few notable exceptions, the zippersuits kept their egos well in check.

Partly, that was a function of whom they worked alongside. Everyone here was the best of the best. The ordies loading missiles to be tested on a plane were likely to have helped design and build the weapon. And partly, it was a reflection of Dog's own personality, and his desire to run a cutting-edge operation that made a difference, not just for America, but for the world.

Dreamland had done that, as Piranha proved. But it had also paid a terrible price.

The loudspeaker near the side of the bleacher blared with a solemn martial tune. The colonel stiffened, waiting for the honor guard that just now emerged from the building. He glanced at the bleachers, where everyone had suddenly snapped to attention. Despite the solemnity of the occasion, the scene brought a smile to his lips—not only were all of Dreamland's military personnel wearing freshly starched uniforms, but the civilian scientists, engineers, and other technical experts were wearing their own Sunday best—suits and dresses.

Dresses!

Ties!

These were as rare a sight at the top-secret base as any Dog could imagine.

The colonel fell in, his legs a little rusty as he marched to his place at the front. He was joined by the Reverend Madison Dell, Dreamland's chaplain, and two other members of his staff: Major Natalie Catsman, who had just been named second in command at the facility, replacing Nancy Cheshire, who had recently been given new responsibilities integrating the Megafortress in the regular Air Force; and Captain Danny Freah, who besides being the head of base security also commanded the Whiplash ops team, the ground force charged with providing security and ground intervention in connection with Dreamland deployments.

After a brief prayer, Dog stepped forward. He'd worked on his speech for several hours the night before, carefully revising and rewriting it over and over again. But now as he walked to the microphone, he decided not to take it from his pocket.

"I don't have a lot to tell you," he said simply. "You've done a good job, and I know you know that. I also know that, like me, you're hurting today, because of our friends who aren't here. Unfortunately, that's part of our business—it's part of our lives. I hate it myself . . ."

CAPTAIN DANNY FREAH STARED INTO THE DISTANCE AS Dog began to read the President's commendation. He was thinking of the man he'd lost to a booby trap, Sergeant Perse "Powder" Talcom. Powder was a hell of a team sergeant, a hell of a serviceman, a hell of a hero. The two men had been together since Bosnia, coming under fire several times. Like any good officer, Danny drew a line between command and friendship, duty and camaraderie. And yet, Powder's loss affected him in ways he couldn't fully explain. Dog had offered him the chance to talk at the ceremony; Danny had begged off, claiming he wasn't much of a talker.

The real reason was that he could never have hidden the tremor in his voice, or stopped the tears from falling.

Powder's death had convinced him that he should take an offer to run for Congress back in New York, where his wife lived. To do that, he'd have to leave the Air Force.

Dog had asked him to stay on for a short while. The ghost clone business had to be investigated by someone the colonel trusted, and the job naturally fell to Danny.

But he would quit when it was done.

Quit? Was he walking away?

No. His time was up; he'd done his duty. He could leave.

Quit.

The reverend stepped forward and gave a reading from Isaiah, his text the famous line about beating swords into plowshares. It was appropriate in a way—Dreamland's efforts had saved many lives, and given the diplomats a shot at turning China and India from their warlike ways. But Danny couldn't help thinking that no text about peace would ever be truly appropriate for a warrior, certainly not a member of the Whiplash team. Peace was an unfulfilled promise, a mirage that sucked you in. As soon as you dropped your guard, disaster would strike.

As it had with Powder, stepping on the mine.

My fault, thought Danny. My inattention cost my man his life.

My fault.

A solitary tear slipped from the corner of his eye.

As the minister ended his sermon, recorded music began to play through the speakers. As it grew louder, a slightly discordant bass note could be heard rising over the violins like an extended rap note coming from far away. A Dreamland formation suddenly appeared from the desert floor, seeming to rise from the mountains themselves.

The first plane over was an EB-52—black, huge, and thunderous, a Megafortress similar to the one Dreamland had lost in the South China Sea. Born as a Boeing B-52 Stratofortress, the airframe had pounded communists in Indochina and stood alerts against Soviet bomber strikes, then gone on to serve a long and respected career as a testbed, launching drones and missiles.

Just when it seemed ready to retire, the Dreamland wizards had tapped the thirty-year-old soldier for refurbishment. It had been taken into a large hangar and stripped naked, most of its parts dismantled. New wings made of ultra-strong composite were added; the rear tail and stabilizer assembly was replaced with a V-shaped unit affording more maneuverability and somewhat less radar profile. The eight power plants were replaced with four Dreamland-tuned monsters that could drive the aircraft nearly to the speed of sound in level flight, yet were as easy on gas as a well-tuned Honda.

The wires and circuit boards that had made up its avionics systems were salvaged and recycled for other B-52s; their replacements were fiber optic and gallium-arsenic, silicone, and in several cases custom-grown crystal circuitry. Besides the equipment that helped the pilot fly the aircraft through a hostile-fire zone, this particular EB-52— nicknamed *Raven*—was stocked with an electronics suite that would have made an NSA officer's eyes water. It could capture a wide array of electronics signals, everything from encoded radio transmission to missile telemetry and even, as some of the Dreamland wags put it, the odd leak from a microwave oven. Besides monitoring those signals, *Raven* could use its on-board circuits to confuse and baffle a wide range of radars, providing cover for a fleet of other aircraft.

Raven's bomb bay had been overhauled so that its rotating dispenser could launch (or drop) a variety of smart weapons—not just bombs and air-to-ground missiles, but AMRAAM-plus antiaircraft missiles. At its tail, the four 12.7 or 50-caliber machine guns had been replaced by a Stinger airmine gun, which could pepper the sky behind the plane with exploding shards of tungsten, just the thing to shred a jet engine and ruin a pursuing fighter pilot's day. While no match for a frontline American interceptor, the Megafortress could hold her own when attacked by most enemies—as this one had done on several occasions.

Next over the Dreamland apron area was a heavily customized C-17, the product of an intense collaboration between Dreamland and the highly skilled engineers at McDonnell Douglas further enhancing its already impressive heavy-hauling and short-runway abilities. Dubbed the MC-17D/W-2, the black-skinned aircraft sported two belly blisters, which in time would be filled by specially designed howitzers. According to the concept, the aircraft would be able to drop two companies of Marines and then provide fire support à la the AC-130, combining two functions in the same aircraft. The weapons had not yet been fitted to the plane; they were due to be tested in about two weeks. The guns, as awesome as they were, were just a start—a team was hard at work trying to make enough adjustments to the Razor antiaircraft laser so that it could be used in place of the howitzers.

As the big plane came over, she dipped her left wing, a nod to the fallen comrades being honored at the ceremony below. Not far behind the MC-17 came an F-22. Like every aircraft at the high-tech developmental center, the Raptor's airframe had undergone extensive revamping. Now longer, it sported a delta-shaped airfoil and saber-toothed tiger strakes at the front; the design was being studied for possible use as an F-15E replacement.

Last but not least in the Dreamland formation was a B-1B, the swing-wing, Mach + attack craft that had once been seen as the B-52's replacement, though the versatile Stratofortress had refused to be pushed aside. The big wings of the Lancer—sometimes dubbed the "Bone" by her crew, a pun on B-One— were fully extended, allowing the aircraft to parade over the grounds at a low and solemn speed.

This aircraft had been used to test some concepts for the Unmanned Bomber project; its four GE F101 engines had only recently been returned to their place under the wing roots and fuselage, reclaiming their position from hydrogen-powered prototypes that would be the main impetus for the UMB. Immediately after the ceremony, the B-1 would head for Underground Hangar Five, where she would begin a new phase, testing a concept as an advanced penetrator/weasel equipped with antiradar HARM missiles and a multiple mini-bomb launcher.

As the B-1 climbed away, a second group of aircraft, these much smaller, appeared from the right. Four U/MF-3 Flighthawks thundered by in a diamond pattern. Just as they reached the center of the viewing area in front of the stands, one of the aircraft peeled off; the others circled around the field, commemorating the loss of Dreamland's fallen comrades. Smoke canisters under the fuselages of the remaining aircraft ignited, and the sky turned red, white, and blue. The Dreamland audience rose to their feet as one, saluting their comrades and pledging themselves once more to the cause of keeping America free and the world safe.

Danny stared into the distance, back teeth tightly clenched.

Dreamland Commander's Office
1407

SOMETIMES IT SEEMED LIKE DOG'S WHOLE LIFE CAME down to paper. Reams of it sat on Colonel Bastian's desk—reports, folders, notices. The computer at the corner held even more—emails, various attachments, all marked urgent, more urgent, or impossibly urgent. Dreamland's command structure was perhaps the most streamlined in the military, yet it still killed more trees than Dog could count.

There was a familiar knock on the door. Fearing that it meant Chief Master Sergeant Terrence "Ax" Gibbs was bringing yet another wagonload of paper for him to process, Dog growled "come" in a voice that would have sent anyone else into retreat.

Ax, however, walked calmly into the room. He had taken the precaution of arming himself with a fresh carafe of coffee.

"Thought you could use a refill," said the chief.

"Thanks," said Dog, his mood lifting slightly.

"Jed Barclay's on line four over there," he added, pointing to the lit button on the black scrambled phone. "He's got an off-the-record heads-up for you."

"Just great," said Dog, his mood once again diving into the depths.

He took a sip of the coffee, then punched the button. Ax thumbed through some of the paperwork on the desk, retrieving several items he needed, then left.

"Jed? What can I do for you?" asked Dog.

"Colonel. Um, this is, uh, un-unofficial," said Barclay.

Barclay was the National Security Council assistant director for technology and the right-hand man of the NSC advisor, Philip Freeman. Jed's responsibilities included acting as the de facto liaison between the White House and Dreamland. Though only in his early twenties, he'd been involved in several Dreamland missions and had proven that, despite his pimples, he could hang in there with the best of them.

It was a very bad sign, however, that he was stuttering. He usually only did that when a situation was red-lining.

"Uh, I'm calling off the r-record," he said.

"Jed, I know it's bad news, so don't sugarcoat it," Dog told him.

"I wasn't going to, Colonel. I wouldn't sugarcoat anything."

"Don't bullshit me either."

"Yes, sir."

"So?"

"The NSC and the Joint Chiefs, they put their heads together in a way—well, you know how Admiral Balboa is, and what they want is an outsider. We cut them off a bit and got a compromise but—"

"Who's investigating?" asked Dog, deciding to cut to the quick. Balboa was the head of the Joint Chiefs and a general pain in the butt when it came to anything concerning Dreamland.

"Air Force Office of Special Investigations," said Jed. "They're sending a woman out this afternoon. Her name is Cortend, and she's a bitch with wings. Um, pardon my French."

"Didn't sound very French to me, Jed." Dog sighed and took another sip of his coffee. "Who is she?"

"Full-bird colonel. She's, uh, she's going to answer to the chief of the Air Force directly because—uh, do you want all the political interplay, or just the shorthand?"

"Shorthand's fine."

"They want to make sure this isn't a replay of the Russian situation a few years ago," said Barclay, making an oblique reference to the spy scandal that had preceded Dog's arrival at the base. "Defense Secretary Chastain got Balboa to sign off on her because she did the, uh, she found the fraud at J&D on the propulsion contract last year, and the Chinese spy at the Alaska contractor. She's tough. But even so, this is just like a preliminary, unofficial, I mean, she has full powers, but it's—"

"Thanks, Jed. I get the picture," said Dog. Basically, they were sending someone there with the power to turn the base upside down, but because she was only coming on an informal or unofficial basis, she wouldn't have to play by any of the rules meant to keep things fair.

So be it.

"There's a couple of people who want your scalp," added the NSC official. "Uh, I know you don't care for the politics but, uh—"

"I don't."

"They may, uh—you have to watch the way you handle it," said Barclay. "Because they have their knives out."

"I appreciate the warning, Jed. Really. It's all

right. I can take care of myself. So can the rest of the people here."

"There was something else," added Jed.

"Fire away."

"The President wants to talk to you personally. He's concerned about China. You probably ought to expect his call around midnight our time. You know how he burns the midnight oil."

"Thanks for the warning."

"Yes, sir."

Dog hung up the phone. The President had personally ordered Dreamland to intervene between China and India. The unit's stock—and Dog's—were extremely high with the White House. But if a spy had delivered Flighthawk technology to the Russians or Chinese or anyone else, that would change quicker than the stock market had on Black Tuesday.

If a spy had penetrated the U/MF project, he or she was undoubtedly still at Dreamland. Dog didn't think it possible.

Then again, General Brad Elliott, the last commander of Dreamland, probably didn't think any of his people had been spies either. And he'd been proven wrong.

General Elliott. God rest his soul. He had given his life to stop China from taking over Taiwan and engulfing the U.S. in a major war. A true American hero.

Dog took another sip of the strong black coffee. He gave himself thirty seconds to enjoy it, and then went back on the offensive, tackling the paper before him.

Dreamland Ground Range Three
1500

DANNY FREAH NODDED AT THE TWELVE MEN DRESSED IN full combat gear, then began his short speech.

"It's live fire. I don't want anyone hurt. Sergeant Liu will go over the objectives. You've all been through the Army Special Forces Q Course, so I don't think you'll have any trouble with this."

Freah glanced at Liu, who was suppressing a smirk. The exercise had been designed with the help of two Army SF veterans with the express intention of making it much more difficult than the SF qualifying exercise, no picnic in itself. It wasn't really a matter of physical exertion. The men would be slogging nearly thirty miles in the next twenty-four hours with full rucks, addressing a number of objectives that ranged from taking out a machine-gun post to helping a little girl find her doll. (This was a particularly perverse exercise: The girl was in the middle of a simulated minefield. Once rescued, the doll contained a radio-activated bomb that had to be disarmed. Throwing it away was not an acceptable solution, since it would set off all the mines.)

The difficult aspect of the exercise was the fact that it was impossible to succeed. Everyone in the exercise—everyone—would wash out at some point. That was when the true test began.

The men here were in excellent physical shape. Most had worked as PJs, members of the illustrious "pararescuer" community that had saved countless Air Force and civilian lives. Several had jumped behind enemy lines in Iraq during the Gulf War to direct close combat support. All were volunteers, and in fact Danny had chosen them all as part of the elite security force that kept Dreamland safe. The final cut—a trooper to replace Sergeant Powder on the Whiplash action team—would be made by the present members of the deployment squad themselves.

The recruits were divided into four three-man teams, each matched with a Whiplash trooper, who would rotate to a new group after six hours. Liu, as team sergeant, would move between the teams.

"All right. You have your orders," said Danny. "Sergeant Liu."

Liu stepped forward. At five-six and maybe 140 pounds, he hardly seemed the typical hard-assed special operations soldier. Indeed, most of the men in front of him outweighed him by a hundred pounds. But he could have taken any of them with one hand tied behind his back, even the three men who, like Liu, had black belts in Tae Kwon Do.

"Team One up," said Liu.

As he did, he pressed a button on the remote control in his pocket. An M/V-22 Osprey gunship revved from the other end of the range, bullets spilling from the pair of Avenger Gatling guns in its belly.

As bullets began splashing twenty yards away, the first team joined up with Sergeant Kevin Bison and began running toward a helicopter that had been set up to simulate a hostage rescue situation. Danny was pleased to see that none of the men flinched as the massive shells from the guns landed.

That would no doubt change by the end of the

day, but it was good to see that they were starting well.

Dreamland
2010

COLONEL VICTORIA MARGARET CORTEND FOLDED HER arms impatiently as the Dolphin transport helicopter strode in toward its landing dock at the top-secret base, a series of automated landing and auxiliary lights popping on. Nearby, an I-HAWK or Improved HAWK surface-to-air missile battery swung around, keeping the approaching aircraft well in its sights; Cortend suspected that the missile had been situated primarily to impress visitors, as any intruder would have been blasted out of the sky by the more sophisticated laser defenses at the base perimeter.

Bozos. Just the sort of arrogant waste of resources she detested. It was typical in the special commands. Weeding out the problems here would be a pleasure.

Cortend waited until the chopper settled down on the cement, then with a brisk snap undid her restraint and climbed out of the helicopter. A staff sergeant grabbed at the door. She stared at him until he finally stood back and snapped into a salute. Returning it, she walked toward the pair of Air Force security personnel posted nearby. The men had the good sense to challenge her, and after a very proper exchange she was cleared to proceed to the Jimmy with its flashing blue light a short distance away.

The same sergeant who had held the door earlier ran to grab her bag; Cortend dismissed him with a glare and proceeded to the SUV. She had long ago learned that it was a serious mistake to allow anyone—*anyone*—to touch her things. She did not ask for assistance, nor did she accept it. While being a colonel brought with it certain prerogatives of rank, having a slouch-man—her term—was one she could do without.

If all colonels, and generals, followed her example, the military would be a much leaner and meaner organization. As it should be.

"Colonel Cortend," said the driver, stepping from the car. His salute was sloppy, but recognizable.

"Is that a question, Sergeant?"

"Oh, no, ma'am. I just, uh—I'm here to take you to your quarters."

"I'm not going to my quarters. Take me to the commander's office."

"The Taj?"

"Young man, if you don't know where the commander's office is, why were you assigned as my driver?"

"Um, I do know, ma'am. I mean, uh—"

He tried to open the door for her but she was too annoyed to allow it.

Dreamland had a certain reputation back East. Obviously it was overinflated.

The airman got into the truck and began driving away from the Dolphin portal.

"The Taj? As in the Taj Mahal?" said Cortend, suddenly understanding what the airman had said.

"Well, uh, yes, ma'am. Officially, it's Administrative Building Two, but uh, everyone just kinda calls it the Taj."

"Everyone except me. Take me there," said Cortend.

"COME," SAID DOG, HEARING THE KNOCK ON HIS DOOR. Thinking it was Ax or maybe one of the scientists, he continued scribbling the last thread of his thoughts about the project he'd just reviewed. It involved further testing of a space-based laser weapon; while Dog was all for the weapon, the tests would cost several hundred million dollars at least, money that he frankly thought would be better spent on next-generation UAVs. But that wasn't his call; he said the tests were a reasonable step if money could be found.

"Lieutenant Colonel Bastian."

Dog put down the pen. Colonel Cortend was standing in the doorway; the sergeant assigned as her escort shifted nervously behind her.

"Colonel Cortend," Dog said, rising. "Welcome to Dreamland."

Cortend stood in the doorway, frowning. The frown deepened as he extended his hand; she looked at it as if it contained a dead fish, then extended her own. She grabbed about halfway and squeezed—an old Pentagon trick, Dog knew, to make a firm grasp seem life-threatening.

Frankly, Cortend didn't look as if she needed any tricks. She had shoulders that would cow an NFL linebacker.

"Are your quarters satisfactory?" said Dog, trying

to break the ice as Cortend surveyed the boat of a desk and the matching cherry bookcases that graced his office. He'd inherited the furniture from General Elliott, who had paid for it himself.

"I expect they will be," said Cortend.

The frost in her voice removed any last doubt Dog might have had about how pleasant the colonel's stay might be. He put on his Pentagon face and told her that she was welcome to go where she wanted, and that everyone at the base would fully cooperate in any way possible.

Cortend's scowl deepened. "I'll see the computer labs and the Flighthawk hangar first. Then I want an office. My staff will be arriving at 0800."

It was rather late for a tour, but Dog didn't bother arguing with her. "Security detail will take you around. Chief Gibbs has already set everything up and will personally make sure that you're squared away in the morning. We've allocated a pair of rooms on the first level of the building. There's a conference room as well. The chief has a handle on the badges, phones, computers, everything you need. Ax is really incredible. You'll be impressed."

"Ax?"

"That would be Chief Gibbs. One of the best, believe me."

Dog ignored her scowl and rose, intending that as her cue to clear out. She didn't take it.

"I'm afraid I've been away," said Dog. "And I have a few things to attend to before turning in."

"I see." Cortend frowned, but didn't move as Dog sat back down.

"Colonel?" he asked.

"Are you going to get this Chief Ax, or should I locate him myself?"

"Uh, it's a little late in the day—"

"You, Lieutenant Colonel, are working. Why is your staff not?"

Dog stifled his instinctive response, trying to turn it into a joke. "I don't like paying overtime," he told her.

"Hmph," said Cortend.

"Would you like some advice?" Dog asked. He ignored her frown and continued anyway. "You have to remember, Colonel, Dreamland is not like most other military commands. There are a lot of civilians here. A lot of scientist types. And we don't have the sort of bureaucratic infrastructure that a lot of the military has. I'm not critcizing other commands at all; I'd love the personnel slots, believe me. But we're a bit different. And because of that, the atmosphere takes a little getting used to."

"You seem to have adjusted."

"You mean that as a compliment or a criticism?"

Dog had controlled his temper for a remarkably long time, but the implied slur on the people who worked for him was simply too much.

"Take it as you wish," said Colonel Cortend, not giving an inch. "Now let me give you some advice, *Lieutenant* Colonel. I'm here informally, but if anyone interferes with my work—you especially—"

Dog's anger had built to such a level that even he would have been unable to stifle an outburst had the phone not rung.

"I'm afraid I have to take this behind closed doors.

The security detail will see to your needs," he told Cortend, struggling to keep his voice neutral. "The sergeant will give you access to your quarters and to your office; the phone lines, computers, they're all ready to go. Believe me, when Chief Gibbs sets something up, it works. And that goes for everyone here. Now you'll have to excuse me."

Cortend frowned, but stepped into the outer office, closing the door behind her.

"Bastian," said Dog, picking up the encrypted phone.

"Colonel, it's Jed Barclay. Stand by for the President."

President Kevin Martindale's voice practically jumped through the phone when the connection finally went through.

"Tecumseh, I'm sorry I couldn't come out there myself for your ceremony."

"Thank you, sir."

"You did a fine job in the Pacific. A very good job. The Navy's jealous. You should see Admiral Balboa. Just about apoplectic." The President laughed, but his tone changed quickly. "We've spent a bit of time reviewing the situation in South Asia. The consensus seems to be that the Chinese will leave the Indians alone for a while."

"I hope so."

"Makes two of us, Tecumseh. Now tell me about the Flighthawk you discovered. Whose is it?"

"Sir, we're not sure it's a Flighthawk. We have only a few seconds' worth of intercepts and a minuscule amount of radar on it. But it's highly capable, probably as advanced as our own aircraft."

"I understand there's some sort of computer coding that is the same?"

Dog gave the President a brief overview of the latest analysis. "Very similar," he concluded. There was no sense being anything less than candid.

The President said nothing for a few moments. "I'm also told that there's a chance that your gear was mistaken. The information came from the aircraft that was shot down."

"Yes, sir. But we believe the data was very good."

"How is your daughter?" asked the President, changing the subject.

"She's doing very well. Should be out of the hospital any day now."

"If she's anything like her father, she'll be back on active duty in a week," said the President.

Dog smiled. In fact, he had talked to Breanna earlier in the day, and she insisted she would be back home next week.

Home being Dreamland, of course.

"I want you to get to the bottom of the situation right away," the President said. "I want you to find out who has the other aircraft. Given the volatility of Asia right now, a weapon such as the Flighthawk would greatly complicate the chances for peace."

"Yes, sir."

"I realize there's a possibility the design was stolen," said Martindale. "That has to be explored as well."

Dog nodded silently to himself. The President was being tactful, but nonetheless making it clear that he was on top of the situation. Dog admired that—even though the implications might not be pleasant.

"We will, sir."

"You've done well, Tecumseh. We've spent much of the evening reviewing your work in the South China Sea. Another home run. No matter what the Navy says. I won't forget. But let's get this other matter straightened out."

"Thank you, sir," Dog told the President, but Martindale had already hung up.

Dreamland Lecture Center Two
5 September 1997
0845

MAJOR JEFF "ZEN" STOCKARD ROLLED HIS WHEEL-chair next to the free console in the small auditorium, trying not to spill his coffee. He was surprised and relieved that he wasn't late. While he didn't have to worry about getting a place—the station was specially designed for a wheelchair, and he was the only one on the base in one—he hated having everyone stare as he wheeled himself in.

"Hey, Zen," said Major Alou, one of the Megafortress pilots. "How's Bree?"

"Claims she'll be home next week," said Zen.

"Yeah, what's she doing? Soaking sun on the beach."

"That and taking hula lessons," said Zen.

Alou laughed and sat down.

Breanna had told Zen last night that she was ready to come home but the doctors wouldn't release her. Doctors meaning her mother, who by some bad fortune happened to be a muckety-muck on the hospital surgical staff. Worse—much worse—said mother was taking a position at Medici Hospital just outside Las Vegas, which would put her within interference range of her favorite—and only—daughter.

It wasn't that Zen had a bad relationship with his mother-in-law. He had no relationship, and would have preferred it that way. It was bad enough that Breanna's father ran Dreamland. Now he was going to have her mother looking over his other shoulder.

Not that the Dog was a bad commander, or that he interfered with their personal lives. It was just—claustrophobic.

Ray Rubeo and Jennifer Gleason entered the room wearing deep frowns. Rubeo scowled habitually; the muscles in his face refused to unclench even when he ate. Jennifer, though, could be counted on for a cheery smile even after working for sixty straight hours. The appearance of the "ghost clone"—and the implications that someone had sold Flighthawk secrets to a foreign government—obviously had her deeply troubled. The scientists took seats at the consoles a row down from him, Jennifer forcing a smile as she sat.

Colonel Bastian entered, trailed by Danny Freah and Mark Stoner, a CIA officer who had worked with Dreamland during the Piranha deployment.

Zen didn't particularly like Stoner. He had to fight to prevent a frown from clouding his face as the spook looked at him and nodded. He managed to nod back, then took another sip of coffee, hoping the caffeine would chase off his bad mood.

"And you must be Major Stockard."

Zen spun his head around and found a tall, thick-shouldered woman eyeing him. She wore a visitor's badge on her uniform and stood so straight he could almost see the broomstick extruding from her behind—obviously the colonel from the Air Force Office of Special Investigations.

"People call me Zen," he told her.

"Yes," said Colonel Cortend, her tone implying that there were a large number of insane idiots in the world that couldn't be accounted for. "I'd like to speak to you after this conference a little later. My inquiries are informal, though cooperation is advised. Strongly advised."

"Not a problem."

"I understand you're the project officer on the Flighthawks?"

"That's correct," answered Zen, meeting her icy tone with one of his own.

"I've been reviewing the personnel attached to the project," she told him. "Quite a collection."

It was clear she didn't mean it as a compliment.

"You bet your ass it is," said Zen. He turned his attention to the front of the room.

"THE SIMULATION YOU'VE JUST SEEN REPRESENTS OUR best guess as to the capabilities and configuration of the ghost clone," said Dog. "As you can see, it's very, very similar to a first-generation Flighthawk. As such, it could be used for a variety of purposes. Air-launched from a bomber, or even a civilian transport, it could attack an urban area with a variety of weapons. It would be difficult to see on radar."

Dog hit the remote control to restore the lighting. "We have two tasks. We have to find the clone, figure out who's operating it and what its actual capabilities are. And number two, we have to determine if our own security has been breached. We'll have help," said Dog, brushing past the implication that a traitor was among them. "Most of you are familiar with Mr. Stoner, who is an expert on Asian technology and high-tech deployment. He was responsible for identifying the Indian sub-launched weapons."

Dog turned toward Colonel Cortend, who was beaming laser animosity from both eyes.

"And Colonel Cortend has joined us from the Air Force Office of Special Investigations. For those of you who haven't dealt with OSI before, they're a thorough, professional group," said Dog.

The flattery, of course, only deepened her glare.

"I expect everyone will cooperate to the fullest of their ability," added Dog, looking toward Rubeo. The scientist had already lodged a complaint about the investigator, who apparently had arrived unannounced at his quarters at 0700 for an interview.

"Questions?" said the colonel, knowing his tone would ward any off. He gave them three seconds, then dismissed them.

**Dreamland Computer Lab One
1100**

"SO YOU ALONE ARE RESPONSIBLE FOR THE CODING?"

Jennifer flicked the hair back behind her ear. "Of

course not," she told Cortend. The colonel had two bleary-eyed technical experts and a pair of bright-faced lieutenants standing behind her, but none of them had uttered a peep.

"I work with a team of people," said Jennifer. "Depending on which project and what we're talking about, the team could have a dozen or more people. Six people handled the compression routines for C^3."

"C^3 is?"

"The computer system that helps fly the Flight-hawks. The communication sequences have to—"

"And any of these six people could have given the secrets away."

"No one gave the secrets away," said Jennifer.

"Someone did, my dear. Someone."

"Let me explain how the compression works. See, the algorithms themselves aren't necessarily secret—"

"Everything you work on is secret," said Cortend. She rose. "I think we have enough for now. We'll be back."

"Peachy," muttered Jennifer beneath her breath.

MAJOR MACK "THE KNIFE" SMITH ADJUSTED HIS swagger as a quintet of officers came out of the computer lab. Mack had recently returned to Dreamland after a series of temporary assignments had failed to get him the squadron command he so ardently desired—and, in his unprejudiced opinion, deeply deserved. He accepted a position as temporary test officer for a project dubbed Micro-Mite, a twenty-first century fleet of interceptors no larger than cruise missiles that would use energy beam weapons to bring down their opponents.

Or maybe lasers, or railguns, or some as-yet un-perfected Flash Gordon zap weapon. That was the beauty of the assignment—four weeks of blue-sky imagining with a bunch of pizza-eating eggheads, who would spit out sci-fi concepts for him to con-sider as they worked feverishly over their laptops on simulations. They were all recent grads of MIT, RPI, and Berkeley—or was it Cal Tech? In any event, the pimple-faced pizza eaters looked to him as the voice of reality and experience. With his combat experience and superior flying and fight-ing skills, he was their god, and they bowed down before him.

Figuratively, of course. Which was the way he wanted it. For alas, while there were six females among the chosen, the eggheads' bodies were no match for their brains. Even mixing and matching their best attributes would still leave the composite far short of Jennifer Gleason, Dreamland's resident brain babe. He was in fact on his way to see her now, hoping she might be available to give his acolytes a few pointers about the value of working with the military. They really didn't need to hear another pep talk—he had that under control himself—but it would give Mack an excuse to admire her assets—er, abilities—for a good twenty minutes or more.

Mack had tried several times to steer her into his quarters for an up-close examination of her charms. Of late, though, he'd had to settle for watching from afar. Jennifer was seeing the base commander, and even Mack knew better than to cross the boss, especially when he required Dog's connections and good word to help steer him toward the command he deserved. With any luck, Dog would come through and deliver him a tasty squadron post in the next week or so. The colonel's star was rising in Washington, and surely he owed Mack a bit of largesse.

"Halt," said a tall, rather striking if formal woman at the rear of a three-man formation that had buzzed into the hallway.

She had been speaking to the drones behind her, but Mack momentarily thought the command was meant for him. Taken by surprise, he stopped and gazed at the woman, realizing with his connoisseur's eye that, if properly undressed, this frame and face might be fittingly attractive. It was tall for a woman, with shoulders that were admittedly manly. But the starched trousers sheathed long, undoubtedly athletic legs, and there was no hiding the voluptuous breasts standing guard above the slim waist.

"Can we help you?" barked the breasts' owner.

"You must be from OSI," said Mack. He extended his hand. "Mack Smith."

"Major."

The drones hovered, unsure whether their master was being greeted or attacked.

Mack gave them nods—lieutenants, mere children—then turned toward their leader.

"I'm available for background," Mack told her. "I've been here awhile. I know where the bodies are buried."

"I see."

She looked him over. Mack pushed his shoulders back.

"Perhaps we'll arrange something," said the officer, turning to go.

"What was your name?" he asked.

"It's Colonel Cortend," whispered one of the underlings.

"First name?" said Mack.

Cortend whirled around. "Why would you need to know my first name?"

"For future reference," said Mack.

The colonel frowned in his direction, then turned and set off so quickly that her minions had difficulty keeping up.

Mack felt his face flush. By the time he started moving again, his palms were so sweaty that he had to wipe them on his pants, and he was so obsessed with Cortend that he forgot what he'd come to see Jennifer about.

Dreamland, Flighthawk Hangar Offices
1300

"No way this is a Chinese project," Stoner told Zen as the briefing session broke up. "No way."

"Why not?"

"Because I'd know about it."

Zen, Rubeo, and several of the other civilian experts involved in the Flighthawk project had just finished giving Stoner a comprehensive briefing on the technologies involved in the U/MF-3. They had emphasized three areas—materials, propulsion, and communications—which until the discovery of the clone had appeared to be Dreamland monopolies.

"I've dealt with the Chinese," said Zen. "They're pretty damn competent. I wouldn't underestimate them."

"I'm not underestimating them. I just don't think they did this. Consider their aircraft technology. Their most advanced aircraft is the Shenyang F-8IIM. It's basically a very large MiG-21. If they were able to construct lightweight carbon fiber wings, for example, they'd be building something closer to the F-22."

"So who? The Russians?"

"They're much more capable than anyone gives them credit for," said Stoner. "I wouldn't rule out the Indians either. You saw their sub-launched cruise missile. That was a pretty serious weapon."

"The technology here is more advanced," said Zen.

"In some ways, certainly." Stoner folded his arms. "What about the Japanese?"

"The Japanese?"

"Forget the technology a minute," said Stoner. "Look at the way the craft was used. It wasn't taking part in the battle. It was watching what was going on. It was a spy plane. It stayed far away from the action."

"That doesn't rule China out," said Zen.

"Sure it does. If the Chinese had this weapon, wouldn't they have been using it to scout the Indian forces?"

"Maybe they did and we didn't see it. The Flighthawks are very difficult to pick up on radar," said Zen.

"You think this thing flew over the Navy task force without being detected?"

Zen shrugged. He didn't, but he didn't feel like admitting it to Stoner.

"My guess is it's a third-party player," said Stoner. "Japan, Russia—someone interested, but not directly involved."

"My money's still on China," said Zen. "I don't trust them."

"And they don't trust us," said Stoner. "But that's good."

"Why?"

"Makes them predictable."

FOR AN EGGHEAD NERD, RUBEO SET A GOOD CLIP, AND Stoner had trouble catching up with him as he cleared through the underground maze back toward his laboratories.

"Doc, can I talk to you?"

"You seem to be making an effort to do so," said Rubeo, not pausing.

"Who really could develop this?"

Rubeo stopped at a locked door and put in his card. The door clicked and buzzed, but didn't open.

"Your ID," said Rubeo. "In the slot."

Stoner complied. The door opened. Rubeo stepped through and resumed his pace.

"We can. The Japanese maybe. The Chinese. Not the Russians."

"That's it?"

The scientist stopped outside one of the lab doors. Despite his high clearance, Stoner was not allowed into the room, which contained the terminals used for work on the Flighthawk control computers, as well as a myriad of other projects. Rubeo frowned at him, then touched his earring. He seemed to be trying to figure out exactly what to tell him. Stoner wasn't sure whether he was trying to translate complicated scientific data into layman's terms—or if he just didn't trust him.

"Plenty of countries have unmanned vehicles, don't they?" prompted Stoner.

"Forget the mechanical aspects," said Rubeo. He glanced down the hallway, making sure they were alone. "It's the computers that are important. Yes, anyone can build a UMV—we could go to Radio Shack and buy a radio-controlled model that's about ninety percent as advanced as Predator."

"Ninety percent?"

"Well, eighty-five." Rubeo smirked. "Building the aircraft is not the difficult part. The problem is to transfer data quickly enough to control the plane in aggressive flight. This craft seems to have done that. And if it's used as a spy plane—well, then you have an enormous data flow, don't you? Bandwidth—you understand what I'm talking about."

Stoner nodded. The scientists had emphasized earlier that massive amounts of data flowed back and forth very quickly between the Flighthawks and their mother ships. To be honest, Stoner didn't completely get it—what was the big deal about some video and flying instructions? But it was enough to know that they said it was significant.

"All of that is going to take custom-designed chips, both for the communications and for the onboard computer. Because it will have to have an onboard computer," said Rubeo. "That's what you have to look for. That's the defining characteristic."

"Okay, so who could do that?" said Stoner.

Rubeo shook his head. "Weren't you paying attention? We can. The Japanese. The Chinese. Not the Russians."

"No one else?"

Rubeo fingered his earring again. "Maybe India. Some of the Europeans, possibly. There are good fab plants in Germany. They've done memory work there as well. The processor, though."

Rubeo seemed to be having a conversation with himself that Stoner couldn't hear. He segued into contract factories or fabs that fabricated chips for custom applications. A small number of concerns could manufacture specially designed chips. They needed special clean rooms and elaborate tools, but if there was enough money, existing machinery could be adapted.

"What if I look for those?" Stoner asked Rubeo.

"You don't really suppose they're going to tell you what they're doing, do you?"

"I'm in the business of gathering information," said Stoner.

Rubeo made a noise that sounded a bit like the snort of a horse. "There are several facilities in America that could do the work. More than two dozen that I can think of off the top of my head. Any of them would be willing to design the proper chips for a foreign government if the price were right."

"I'll check them first," said Stoner. "Unless they're already doing work for us."

"Why would that be a limiting factor?" said Rubeo, the cynical tone in his voice implying that greed would motivate any number of people to sell out their country.

Dreamland Ground Range Three
2100

SERGEANT BEN "BOSTON" ROCKLAND GOT TO HIS FEET slowly. The rest of his team lay around him, officially "dead." Their objective—carrying a small amount of radioactive soil back from enemy lines for testing—had not been met.

Boston—as the nickname suggested, the sergeant was a Beantown native—picked up the ruck containing the soil. The desert before him was dotted with small rubber balls with nails sticking out from them—simulated cluster bomblets, representing air-dropped antipersonnel mines with proximity fuses. The little suckers worked too—as soon as you got within five feet, an ear-piercing siren sounded, and the range monitor proclaimed you were dead.

Not dead, actually. Just maimed. The range monitor seemed to take a perverse joy in announcing which particular body part it was that had been blown off.

There seemed to be no way across the minefield. Yet to get to the objective—a small orange cone about a quarter mile away—he had to cross it.

As Boston stared, he heard the roar of the returning Osprey gunship. Sergeant Liu had explained earlier that the aircraft was programmed to orbit the test range randomly. He'd also warned that the massive Gatlings were firing live ammunition.

The Osprey swung forward in a wide arc, hunting for a target. Boston had seen from the exercises earlier that it would home in on small reflectors that the people running the exercise had planted around the field. It wasn't clear to him whether the red disks had some circuitry inside, or if the weapons directors on the M/V-22 could actually home in on the glints of light. Whichever it was, flinging the little disks drove the gear batty, as one of the Whiplash team members had proven yesterday when morale had started to sag.

Maybe he hadn't flung the disk as a joke, thought Boston. Maybe he was hinting at the solution.

Boston threw himself back down as the Osprey approached. The computers controlling the guns were programmed to avoid hitting anyone, but they didn't miss by much. As the guns began to fire, the tilt-rotor aircraft seemed to jump upward in the sky.

The burst lasted no more than three-quarters of a second. When it stopped, the Osprey settled back down and flew in a semicircle close to the ground.

Eight feet off the surface.

That wasn't all that high.

Boston watched as the Osprey flew toward the hangar area, still skimming low over the terrain.

That was the solution. It had to be.

As soon as the tilt-rotor craft had gone, he began grabbing the disks.

CAPTAIN DANNY FREAH WATCHED IN AMAZEMENT AS the Osprey whirled around, hoodwinked by the flashing reflectors. It fired, then settled back down into a hover just at the edge of the minefield.

"I think he figured out how to control it," said Liu, who was next to Danny.

"Or at least confuse it," answered Danny.

"If he uses the Osprey to blast a path through the minefield, the computer simulators won't understand," said Liu. "He'll still be blown up by the proximity fuses. But you'd have to give him points for figuring it out."

"Sure, but that's not what he's doing," said Danny as Boston began running toward the rear of the Osprey.

"Holy shit," said Liu.

Boston leaped into the air and caught the rear tail of the variable-rotor aircraft. His legs pitched forward and his ruck hung off his back, but the sergeant managed to hang on.

EVEN THOUGH THE MASSIVE ROTORS WERE LOCKED above the aircraft, they still kicked up a hurricane around the aircraft. Boston shook like the last leaf on a maple tree in a nor'easter blizzard as the aircraft pushed ahead toward the apron area beyond the minefield.

The trooper felt his fingers numbing as the MV-22 moved ahead. They were cold, frozen even—his right pinkie began to slip, then his ring finger, then his thumb.

He leaned his head down, trying to see exactly where he was.

Not even halfway across.

Hang on, he told himself.

The aircraft bucked upward. Boston realized he'd miscalculated about how close to the ground it flew once it cleared the minefield—from where he'd stood, it didn't seem as if it rose at all, but now he realized it must go up at least a few feet, and a few feet were going to make a very big difference when he jumped.

He could get it to dip again by tossing one of the reflectors. But to toss one—he had two more in his pocket—he'd have to hold on with one hand.

Could he?

No.

Besides, the shock of the guns would easily throw him off.

The Osprey began turning to the left. The shift in momentum was simply too much, and Boston lost his grip. He tried to relax his legs so he could roll when he landed, but it happened too fast; his heels hit the ground and he fell back hard. His backpack took a little of the sting out of the fall, probably just enough to prevent a concussion as it slipped upward on his back. He rolled and flipped over, then hunkered against the hard surface of the ancient lakebed, anticipating the screech and growl of the simulated mine.

But he heard nothing. Boston raised his head. Shit, he thought, I blew my eardrums out.

Then he heard the Osprey thumping in the distance. He saw one of the spiked balls lying about fifteen feet away—just far enough not to go off.

Slowly, Boston pushed up to his knees. He rubbed some of the grit from his eyes, then stood, trying to get his bearings.

The cone was ten feet away. He took a breath, and walked slowly toward it.

I could use some water, he thought as he put the ruck containing the soil sample next to the cone.

BY THE TIME SERGEANT LIU APPEARED, BOSTON HAD stretched out on the ground, his body hovering just this side of consciousness.

"Yo," said Liu. He turned and started walking away.

Boston rose and fell in behind, his limbs sore not just from the fall but from the last twenty-four hours. He managed to lean forward and break into a rough trot, catching up.

"What's next?" he asked.

"Nothing for you," said Liu.

"Shit," said Boston, but he couldn't figure out where he had screwed up.

The Osprey? But how else was he supposed to get across the minefield? He'd have had to leave the range, and even then, the entire cone was surrounded.

Liu didn't explain. A GMC Jimmy, blue light flashing, appeared in the distance, kicking up dust as it sped across the open landscape. It whipped to a stop a few feet from him. Liu pulled open the front passenger door, waiting for Boston to get in.

There was no driver. Boston was only slightly surprised to see that—as the Whiplash veterans were fond of saying, *This is Dreamland*. Nor was he particularly surprised when Liu didn't climb in after him.

As soon as the door was shut, the vehicle started up again, slowly at first, then gradually picking up speed. It drove to a small building just beyond the old bone yard—a storage area for old planes at the eastern end of the base. Boston got out; when the door was shut, the vehicle backed up and drove away.

Captain Danny Freah was waiting inside. Like Boston, Freah was of African descent, though it was clear from his demeanor that any appeal to ethnic roots was *not* going to cut it.

Maybe, Boston thought, he could appeal to his mother's side of the family. She was Sicilian. He could hint at a mafia connection.

Probably wouldn't cut it either.

"Who told you you could climb *on* the aircraft?" demanded Captain Freah.

"Sir." Boston snapped out the word, but he was too worn down at this point to play rogue warrior. "Uh, no one. I just did it."

"You know how much that aircraft costs?"

Visions of living on bread and water well into his retirement suddenly filled Boston's head. He had heard stories about the military taking the cost of high-tech gear out of soldier's pay, but had never believed they were true. Now he suddenly realized that they might be.

"Um, I didn't think I'd do any harm to it."

"You didn't *think*?" barked Freah.

Boston winced; he had given the classic— *classic!*—bad answer.

"I thought incorrectly, sir," said the sergeant. "I was focused on the objective, to the exclusion of other factors."

He could practically feel the heat coming off Freah's face. From the corner of his eye, he saw another member of the Whiplash team joining them in the building—Sergeant Liu. Behind him came the other Whiplash veterans.

Great, thought Boston, they're all here for the hanging.

"You only thought of the objective?" said the captain.

"Yes, sir, I'm afraid I did. I'm sorry."

One of the Whiplash troopers—Bison—started to laugh.

"Hang him by his toes," said Egg Reagan.

Boston felt the blood rushing to his face.

"Are you blushing, Sergeant?" asked the captain.

"I, uh . . ."

"Jeez, if I'd known he was a blusher, I woulda never voted for him," said Bison.

"Me neither," said Egg.

"We need a blusher," said Liu.

It was only then that Boston realized he was in.

Dreamland Flighthawk Simulation Hangar
6 September 1997
0245

ZEN KNEW HE WOULDN'T BE ABLE TO SLEEP, AND SO didn't even bother going home. He and Breanna had a small apartment—more like a dorm room with a kitchenette—on the base where he could crash when he ran out of energy. But that figured to be a long way off.

He sat in one of the simulation blocks, playing a loop the programmers had designed to mimic the engagement in which his wife and her plane had been shot down. The simulation was a subset of their normal tactical simulations, used not only to train pilots but to help refine the combat library that was an integral part of the Flighthawks' control computer, C^3. By jiggling the parameters a bit, the techies had given Zen a Flighthawk clone that could fly to within seventy-five miles of the Megafortress before being detected.

Actually, depending on the altitude, atmospheric conditions, and the orientation of the planes, it could make it to within fifty miles.

But that was as close as it could get. That meant that the ghost clone couldn't target the Megafortress. That also meant it couldn't possibly get much more information about the Megafortress than a standard aircraft would; in fact, almost certainly less.

Which meant that *Quicksilver* hadn't been the target. Nor, from the configurations of the battle forces, were the Indians.

That left the Chinese.

So maybe the Indians were using it to spy on the Chinese.

Or attack them?

Zen played the simulation again. This time, he took control of the ghost clone and flew directly over the Chinese fleet. Antiair missiles flashed on, but he was able to drive his attack home. He rolled his wing at twenty thousand feet, slapping his nose down on a direct line for the flight deck on one of the two pocket Chinese carriers.

The mach indicator clicked upward; he nudged

the stick and got the bridge in his pipper, fat in the gun sights.

Blam. No more bridge, no more radar, no more flight operations. The clone skipped away unharmed, tucking right as a simulated Chinese MiG launched a pair of heat-seekers in a belated and desperate attempt to exact revenge.

Zen stopped the program. If the clone was an Indian aircraft, then surely it wasn't outfitted with a weapon. Even simply crashing it into the bridge would have dramatically altered the battle.

So the clone couldn't have been an Indian plane.

Maybe it was Russian.

"Or maybe the Chinese spying on themselves," he said aloud in derision, frustrated that he couldn't figure out what was going on.

"Possible, actually, though unlikely."

Zen jerked away from the controls. Stoner walked down the long ramp at the far end toward him.

Zen wheeled his chair around. "What's up?"

"Want to get a beer or something?"

"No."

The CIA officer pulled out the chair from the main programmer's station and sat on it, rolling it forward as Zen approached.

"You don't like me, Major," said Stoner.

"Is that relevant?"

"Probably not."

Stoner and Breanna had lashed themselves together after bailing out, and it was probably because of that that they survived the fierce storm that had swallowed most of the rest of the crew. Zen didn't begrudge Stoner that.

If anything, he should be grateful.

And yet.

And yet.

He just didn't like him.

"I don't think it's Chinese," said Stoner. "Is that the flight where we got shot down?"

"More or less."

"Can I see it?"

"You're not in the picture," said Zen, but he rolled back anyway.

The simulation area duplicated a Flighthawk control deck aboard an EB-52, with a double set of configurable displays and dedicated systems readouts. It wasn't a perfect match—some of the equipment on the side racks was omitted, the floor was cement rather than metal mesh, and most importantly, the station never reacted to turbulence. The simulator that did, located down the hall, required at least one techie to run.

"We didn't go in like that," said Stoner, watching the screen that showed *Quicksilver*. "Breanna— your wife—held us up and got us away from danger before telling us to bail. There was some other stuff, self-destruct routines."

"We skip that. We're not really interested in the accident, just the ghost clone."

"Where is it?"

Zen slapped at the keyboard. The sitrep showed it at seventy-five miles, to the northeast of the Chinese fleet.

"It's got to be spying on the Chinese," said Stoner. "But it doesn't really make sense that the Indians would send it that far around, does it?"

"No," said Zen.

"It could be another Chinese unit," Stoner said. "The admiral in charge of this fleet, Xiam, is not well-liked. But I still don't think they have the technology."

"They spy on themselves?"

"Sometimes."

"I know how we can settle it," said Zen. "We go back, buzz their coast, see if it comes out."

Stoner shrugged. "Maybe."

Zen had thought of the idea earlier and been ready to reject it because it didn't seem as if the clone could be Chinese. But if what Stoner was saying was true—that one unit might spy on another—then the clone's location made perfect sense.

"We fly over their coast, try to get them to come out. If it's Chinese, eventually they'll come and take a look. In the meantime, we can adjust our Elint gear to look for their transmissions," added Zen. "Now that we know what we're looking for, our range will be wider. They won't know it."

"I guess."

"You have a better idea?" Zen asked.

"Actually, I came down to suggest it myself."

Dreamland Perimeter
0525

JENNIFER GLEASON TOOK THE LAST TURN AND BROKE into a sprint as she headed up the hill back toward the low-slung building that housed her small apartment. As she ran, she glanced in the direction of

Dog's small bungalow, hoping he might appear. The fact that he didn't probably meant he was already over at his office. She channeled her disappointment into her legs, pushing out long strides as she finished her daily run.

One brief warm-down and shower later, she grabbed breakfast from her tiny refrigerator—strawberry-banana yogurt—then headed over to the computer labs located below the main Megafortress hangars. Jennifer liked the feel of the empty lab around her early in the morning; she generally had the large underground complex to herself for at least a few hours and could walk around talking to herself as she figured out problems. That would be especially important today; she had an idea on how they might be able to break into the ghost clone's coding and take it over, assuming they could get close to it again.

Jennifer got off the elevator and punched her card into the reader next to the door, fingers slipping to the side to hit the number combination to clear the lock while she stared down the retina scan. Inside, she got a pot of coffee going, then went back to kick her computers on so they'd be ready when the coffee was.

Except nothing came up.

Jennifer stared at the blank screens, then reached down to the keyboards and gave her access codes again, directing the terminals to boot into the main system housed in a shielded bunker two floors below. The coffee hissed at her from the bench at the side of the room. She hit Enter and went back for a cup, expecting the screens to be blinking their hellos when she returned. But they were still blank.

Kneeling at her station, she keyed her passwords one letter and number at a time. The system allowed only three tries, so she had to get it right.

She did.

But there was still nothing.

The computers were operating—there was a cursor on the fifteen-inch network screen, and the two larger CRTs had their indicator lights on.

The bungled attempts at signing on locked her out as a user, but not as system administrator. She went to the network bench, where the operating system—which she had helped tweak—was controlled. The monitor flashed to life, reported that the system was in perfect shape—and then refused her password.

"You get up early," said Ray Rubeo, coming into the lab.

"Something's wrong with the system," said Jennifer.

"Hardly. Miss Spanish Inquisition has temporarily locked us out of the system."

"What?"

Rubeo went to the coffeemaker and poured himself a cup. He drank the whole cup, black and steaming, in two gulps, then poured himself another one.

"We're under suspicion of being spies," said Rubeo.

"No, that's not true," said Danny Freah, entering the room. Cortend was right behind him.

"Danny, did you lock me out of the system?"

"I did it," said Rubeo. "We're all out."

"We're just following standard procedure," said Freah. "Just until we can go through some more interviews."

"I thought this was an informal inquiry," said Jennifer.

Danny didn't answer.

"When is this lockout going to end?" asked Jennifer.

"When you pass a lie detector test," said Cortend.

"What?"

"Are you refusing?" said Cortend.

Jennifer had taken several lie detector tests before, but the implication of it—that she was suspected of being a traitor—floored her. She felt as if she'd been kicked in the stomach.

"You don't have to take the test if you don't want, Jen," said Danny.

"Oh, please," said Rubeo. "If we don't take the test, we won't be restored to the system. And you'll consider pulling our clearance permanently."

"Not necessarily," said Danny.

Cortend said nothing. Jennifer thought she saw the faintest outline of a grin at the sides of the colonel's lips.

Where was Dog in all this?

No wonder he hadn't run with her this morning. Danny wouldn't have gone ahead with all this unless he'd cleared it with the colonel first.

What, did he think she was a traitor too?

How could he?

She clamped her mouth shut, stifling a string of curses. But her anger had to come out somehow—

she batted her coffee cup to the floor, sending the hot liquid streaming onto the industrial carpeting.

"Jen, where are you going?" asked Danny as she brushed past.

"I'm going to go get some breakfast. Then I'll take your fucking lie detector test. What a bunch of bullshit."

Taj
0800

STONER COULD FEEL HIS EYES DROOPING AS HE stepped off the elevator and headed for the commander's suite. He'd pulled an all-nighter, working out a plan with Zen to provoke whoever was flying the ghost clone into appearing again. The Air Force officer clearly didn't like him, but Stoner admired him even so. Zen had lost the use of his legs in a flying accident; rather than dropping out he'd fought his way back into the Air Force and actually onto the front lines.

Stoner would have liked to think that he'd have done the same thing—but he was smart enough to realize he would more likely have succumbed to the inherent bitterness of the situation. While Zen did seem to approach the world with a chip on his shoulder, he didn't let the chip keep him from getting things done.

That alone made him worth watching.

Chief Master Sergeant Terrence "Ax" Gibbs popped up from a desk near the side of the room as Stoner entered.

"Stoner, right?" asked the chief.

"Yes, sir."

"Jackie, go get Mr. Stoner some coffee. He likes it on the weak side. Grab some sticky buns too. The cinnamon ones." The chief master sergeant turned to him and grinned. "It's okay, Mr. Stoner, one or two buns isn't going to hurt your girlish figure."

Stoner had never met him, much less told him what he liked to eat or drink, but somehow the chief had nailed it.

"Thanks, Chief Gibbs," he said.

"We take care of people here. Zen's inside already, along with the colonel. You call me Ax," added the chief. "You need something around here, you get ahold of me. You got that?"

Ax reached back to his desk and hit an intercom buzzer, then stepped up to the door.

"We all know what you did to save Captain Stockard," said Ax. "We appreciate it."

"She saved me as much as I saved her," said Stoner.

The chief smiled and pointed at him, then opened the door.

DOG NODDED AS THE CIA OFFICER ENTERED HIS OFFICE, listening to Zen as he continued laying out the game plan—two Megafortresses, one to act as agent provocateur and the other hanging back to gather information. When the clone showed itself, Flight-hawks from the second EB-52 would come forward. Operating at the far end of their range, they would gather information on the clone without its being able to detect them.

"We could even turn them loose," said Zen. "We could program them to home in on their own, gather whatever information they can get, then return."

"No—too risky," said Dog. "I don't want to chance losing one. But otherwise, this makes sense."

"We need a remote base," said Stoner. "I'd recommend the FOA in the Philippines we used last month."

"It's a good distance from the area you two have mapped out," said Dog.

"We're not quite sure where exactly the clone is flying from," said Stoner. "If it's China, this is far. But if it's Thailand, say, or even off a ship—"

"The Philippines also limits our exposure," said Zen. "We've been there already. And in terms of the operating radius, it's the same."

"Still a stretch," said Dog.

"Better than locating in a country that has the clone," said Stoner.

"As unlikely as that may be," said Zen.

"Start working on a detailed deployment plan," said Dog, ignoring the bite in Zen's voice. "I'll talk to Jed and get the wheels in motion. It may take a while to get approval."

"This may not work," said Stoner.

"Don't be a pessimist," said Zen. He wheeled himself backward and spun toward the door at the right side of Dog's office, which had been widened so his wheelchair could easily fit through.

"I'm just being realistic," said Stoner, standing.

He went to open the door for Zen, but the major had already gotten it himself.

"Play nice, boys," said Dog as they disappeared.

**Dreamland Visiting VIP Office Two
1350**

"Name."

"Minnie Mouse."

The technician handling the lie detector suppressed a grin.

"Name," repeated Colonel Cortend.

"Jennifer Gleason."

"Age?"

"What's yours?"

"Age?"

"Twenty-five."

"Um—" said the technician, raising his finger.

"I'll be twenty-five next month."

"The needle was okay, but I saw the, I mean I knew the answer was wrong," said the technician.

Cortend folded her arms. "Continue."

"This needn't be an adversary procedure," said Danny, standing near Cortend.

"Thank you for your advice, Captain. Miss Gleason—"

"Ms. Gleason."

"Miss Gleason, how long have you been at Dreamland?"

"You could at least call her by her proper name," hissed Rubeo. "She's a doctor. Her Ph.D. was a brilliant piece of work. Classified need-to-know, I might add."

Rubeo had passed his own lie detector test earlier, which obviously had put Cortend in a bad mood. The colonel ignored him.

"Miss Gleason," insisted Cortend, "how long have you been at Dreamland?"

Jennifer realized that Cortend was trying to rattle her. She also knew the best thing to do was simply answer the questions and get on with her life. But something inside wouldn't let her do that. She was just so put out, so angry with it all, that she had to fight back somehow.

"I've been here too long, obviously," she said. Then she answered the question, remembering the day in 1993 when as a freshly minted computer Ph.D.—she would go on to get another degree in applied micro circuitry, her weaker discipline—she had come off the Dolphin transport. General Brad Elliott had taken time from his schedule to show her around some of the base, and it was his tour that had cinched her decision to come here.

Poor General Elliott. A brave man, a true hero.

He'd been persecuted by people like Cortend. He was honored in the end, but it was too late for him by then—the brass had kicked him out.

The brass and people like Cortend.

"I asked, what is your specialty?" said Cortend.

"Long or short version?"

"Short."

"Just the unclassified portions, Jen," said Danny, clearly trying to play nice guy. "Just sum it up."

"Computers. Mostly software, but on occasion I do hardware. I could have gotten around the lock-out easily. If I were a scumbag traitor."

"Just answer the questions, Miss Gleason."

"I'm trying."

Cortend asked a short series of questions regarding Jennifer's education background and her contributions to the Flighthawk program. The questions skipped around, but none was particularly difficult, and in fact Jennifer had answered all or almost all the day before for one of the technical people assigned to Cortend's team. But yesterday they had seemed informational; now even the simplest question felt like an accusation.

"June 7, 1993," said Cortend.

"Excuse me?" asked Jennifer.

"June 7, 1993. What does that date mean to you?"

Jennifer shook her head. "Should it mean something?"

"Where were you that day?"

"Here?" said Jennifer.

"Let me refresh your memory," said Cortend. She walked over to the side of the room and returned with a folder. "You were in Hong Kong."

"A conference?" Jennifer stared at Cortend.

"Are you asking me or telling me?"

"I honestly can't remember where I was."

"Your memory seems very convenient."

"It's not."

Cortend made a snorting sound, a kind of animal chuckle that seemed to signify some sort of personal victory. "You don't remember attending a conference in Hong Kong in June 1993?"

"I've attended many conferences."

"How about September 1994?"

Jennifer turned to Danny. He had a worried look on his face.

"Another conference?" asked Jennifer.

"Did you obtain permission to attend those conferences?" asked Cortend.

"She doesn't *need* permission," snapped Rubeo.

"Did you register with the Department of Defense and your superiors here that you were attending those conferences?"

Jennifer saw Rubeo muttering under his breath.

"This interview is completely voluntary," said Danny.

"I don't really remember," said Jennifer.

"So you didn't," said Cortend. "You're best off being honest with me, Miss Gleason."

"Ms."

"Oh, yes. Mizz Gleason. Excuse me. Let's be precise. Where were you that day? And what did you do?"

"I don't remember. I know that sounds lame," Jennifer added, realizing immediately that saying that only made her sound even lamer.

Cortend seemed to grin ever so slightly before continuing.

White House
1703

JED BARCLAY TOOK HIS PLACE IN THE OVAL OFFICE nervously, sitting between Arthur Chastain, the secretary of defense, and Jeffrey Hartman, the secretary of state. Jed had been here dozens of times, but today felt different. Not because of the subject matter; the appearance of the UAV Dreamland had dubbed the ghost clone had enormous implications, true, but Jed thought the plan for drawing it out that Colonel Bastian had outlined to him made a lot of sense. He also felt that it was unlikely another spy was at the base, though admittedly the fact that he knew most of the important players there might be blinding him.

What was bothering him was the fact that he was at the meeting in place of his boss, Philip Freeman, the national security director, who had been hospitalized with pneumonia.

Jed would have been at the meeting even if Freeman was well; Dreamland was his portfolio. He might even be sitting in this chair. But somehow, being here *officially* as Freeman's replacement— temporary as it was—unnerved him.

He stuttered as he said hello to the President. Martindale smiled and started talking about a football game the week before that Yale, Jed's alma mater, had lost.

Jed smiled and tried to say something along the lines of "can't win them all." But what came out was "k-k-k-k."

The President laughed, maybe thinking he was joking, and moved on to start the meeting. Jed reached into his briefcase and passed out the executive summary of the Dreamland plan, then fired up his laptop for a PowerPoint presentation, which he planned to present on the twenty-one-inch flat screen he'd brought with him. But the President stopped him.

"No slides, Jed," said Martindale, who put more stock in honest opinions than zippy pie charts. "Tell us why this is important."

"Well, um—" started Jed.

"If the Chinese have robot aircraft as capable as the Flighthawks," said Admiral George Balboa, the head of the Joint Chiefs of Staff, "they could conceivably use them to achieve first-strike capability in a war against Taiwan and even us. The UAVs are very difficult to detect unless you're looking for them, and even then they can be close enough to initiate an attack before the defenses are alerted."

Ordinarily, Jed might have bristled at Balboa's taking over his presentation. But now he was grateful. In any event, the admiral was merely stating one of Jed's own arguments.

"Yes," said Jed. He didn't stutter, a major victory.

Maybe he'd get through this after all. Why was he so unnerved? His boss would be back in a few days.

"The problem with this plan," said Balboa, "is that it doesn't go far enough. We need the Navy involved—if there is a UAV we have to take it out. Right away."

"That m-m-might be premature," said Jed.

"Nonsense."

"Provoking the Chinese at this point is risky business," said the secretary of state. "The meeting with the Taiwanese is set for two weeks from now. The rapprochement should take priority."

"Why?" said Balboa bluntly. "Why is it in our interests?"

Hartman's face turned beet red. "Peace is always in our interest."

"It depends on what the terms are," said Chastain.

If Freeman were here, Jed thought, he would be mediating between the blustery Balboa and the more reticent Hartman. He'd also be pointing out that finding the UAV and dealing with it need not interfere with the summit between the two Chinas.

So why didn't he say that?

He should.

Jed opened his mouth, but nothing came out.

"What do you think, Jed?" asked the President.

"I, well—if the operation is run exactly the way Colonel Bastian outlined it, sir, it won't provoke the Chinese any more than any routine mission would." Jed took a breath and then pressed his fingers together, one of the tricks he had learned in high school when the stutter first became an issue. If he didn't think about it, it wouldn't be a problem.

The trick was not to think about it.

"I don't think that, um, that the secretary of state is proposing that we stop gathering intelligence on the Chinese, or that we leave Asia," said Jed.

"Of course not," said the secretary of state.

"So this—if it were, say, wrapped up in routine maneuvers, in an exercise that they would be interested in, or that anyone who might have the ghost clone was interested in, I would think that would work."

Jed glanced up and saw that Martindale was looking directly at him. He floundered, turning his eyes back down to the floor before continuing.

"The, uh, the ASEAN, the ASEAN exercises are set to begin in two days. My thinking was that the Dr-Dreamland plan might fold into that, or we could use the maneuvers as a cover somehow."

"The Navy was ordered to take a low profile. We've only allocated a frigate." Balboa cleared his throat, obviously warming to the idea. While as the head of the JCS, Balboa was technically in charge of all the services, rare was the operation he didn't believe should be spearheaded by the Navy. "We could get some assets there, a carrier, have some patrol craft. Yes. A P-3 in an Elint role, and we have two Vikings that have just been overhauled precisely for this sort of mission."

"Why don't we just send the fleet?" said Chastain.

"We could do that," said Balboa, somehow missing the sarcasm in the defense secretary's voice.

"Jed?" prompted the President.

"I did some checking and, um, there was originally a request for B-52s in the exercises," Jed told them. "So we could grant it and, uh, the Megafortresses could go in their place."

"There is a bit of an issue with the Dreamland people," said Balboa. "Some folks feel Colonel Bastian and his people are cowboys who need to be reined in."

"That's not fair," snapped Jed.

Balboa turned and stared at him. Jed realized that his dislike of Dreamland, born from a general prejudice against anything connected with the Air Force, had been fanned into a virulent hatred because of the Piranha affair. While the Navy had played an important role in preventing war, the Dreamland people were the ones actually taking the bullets, and for some reason that bugged him.

"I didn't say it was fair, young man. I'm just

saying it's the view." Balboa shifted in his seat, turning back toward the President. "We still haven't reached a decision on where the command should be located. Technically, Colonel Bastian doesn't answer to anyone at the moment. Except, of course, to the commander-in-chief."

"I haven't reached a decision," said the President.

He smiled, as if apologizing for telling a fib. Jed knew that the ambiguous situation served Martindale very well and was therefore likely to continue indefinitely. Under the present arrangement, Dreamland's Whiplash special operations team, its cutting-edge aircraft, and all its whiz-bang weapons answered directly to the President, with only one NSC staffer in between—Jed. All military personnel ultimately answered to the President as commander-in-chief, of course, but the chain of command could be torturous. As things presently stood, Martindale could use the Dreamland people as his own attack squadron, sending them to hot spots around the globe with a direct phone call.

"This plan calls for them to be based in the Philippines again," said Hartman, changing the subject. "The government there is still upset over the handling of the guerrillas we encountered. We need an alternative base."

"The, uh, uh—" Jed wanted to protest about the alleged guerrillas, who had turned out to be simply displaced villagers, but his tongue tripped and he couldn't get it out. The Dreamland people had insisted on protecting them until their identities could be proven; they were catching grief for doing the right thing.

"All right," said the President. "Where else? Taiwan?"

"Not Taiwan," said Hartman. "Far too provocative. What about Brunei?"

"Brunei?" asked Chastain.

"The sultan is looking for signs of friendship and pushing for access to more weapons," said the secretary of state. "This might be a good gesture."

Jed started to object. "It's f-far from—"

"It is far from China," said the President. "But according to the CIA, China may not be the country operating the clone at all. Besides, I'd like to show our friend the sultan that we value his alliance."

The President's tone suggested that the meeting had come to an end. He glanced around the room, then looked back at Jed.

"Jed, set this up. I want Dreamland deployed as part of the ASEAN exercises—give it a cloak of respectability."

"Yes, sir," said Barclay

"We'll supply a liaison," said the secretary of state. "There are important protocols. The sultan has to be handled with a certain amount of—"

The secretary stopped, glancing at Balboa. Jed realized that he was going to say "tact," then realized that might imply that Colonel Bastian had none.

Obviously, he didn't want to give Balboa the satisfaction.

"Protocol," he said instead.

"Fine," said the President, rising to end the meeting.

Dreamland Personnel Building Two
1805

DOG DECIDED TO SWING AROUND TO JENNIFER'S APART-
ment on his way back to Taj. He hadn't seen much
of her since getting back from Hawaii, and felt
guilty about it; while he'd been in Honolulu he'd
learned that his ex-wife was planning on moving to
Las Vegas. He knew he had to tell Jennifer about
it, let her know that however awkward it might be,
it was only that—awkward. Dog didn't hate his ex-
wife. The truth was he had never really hated her,
even when she asked for a divorce. Whether he'd
ever loved her or not—well, that was a question best
contemplated over a very long set of drinks.

He did love Jennifer. He was sure of that.

Dog jogged down the short set of steps to the
hallway leading to the apartments, which spread out
right and left. As he started down the hallway, he
saw two members of his Whiplash team standing
guard in front of Jennifer's door, Sergeant Liu and
Sergeant Bison.

"What's the story here?" the colonel asked.

"We're under orders not to let anyone in or out,"
said Liu.

"Whose orders?" asked Dog.

"Colonel Cortend," said Liu.

"Since when do you take orders from Cortend?"
Dog asked him.

"Sir, Captain Freah told us to stand guard here.
The colonel—Colonel Cortend is sending over a
detail to inspect the quarters, and it's to be secured
until then."

"What?" said Dog. "What the hell is going on here, Sergeant?"

"Sir, Captain Freah didn't explain."

The sergeant wasn't being disrespectful, but it was clear from his demeanor that he wasn't going to yield.

"Is Ms. Gleason inside?" Dog asked.

"No, sir."

Dog controlled his anger—though just barely. "Do you know where she is?"

"No, sir."

"Carry on, Sergeant," he said, turning on his heel. He walked back to the entrance of the building, resisting the temptation—again just barely—to grab a radio from one of the security detail and radio Freah. He walked outside and started toward Taj when he saw two black SUVs approaching with their blue lights flashing. Danny was in the lead truck—sitting behind Cortend.

"Captain Freah," said Dog as the door to the truck opened. "A word."

Dog took two steps away from the walk and turned.

"Why are Jennifer's quarters under guard?" asked Dog.

"She, uh, the investigation turned up some questions." Danny spoke as if he'd just been to the dentist to have a pair of wisdom teeth pulled—and needed to go back the next day to have the other set removed. "Apparently, there were some conferences arranged by the Department of Energy that Jennifer neglected to fill out the proper forms on."

"What?"

"I looked through the records myself."

"That's what this inquisition is about? Paper-work?"

"Technically, it's a violation. At least. I have to check into it—"

"Do so," snapped Dog, turning angrily toward the building.

Danny grabbed his arm.

"What the hell, Captain?"

"Colonel, we go back a bit, and I have a lot of respect for you. Tremendous respect, sir."

Dog looked down at Danny's hand, which was still grasped around his shirt.

"You can't interfere," said Danny. "You can't—you can't do anything that will look like favoritism."

Dog continued to stare at his captain's hand.

"You can't interfere, Colonel. I'm talking to you man to man. Right now—if there's a security break."

"There wasn't."

"That's really not for you to say at this point. Don't you see?" Danny finally let go. "You can't interfere, especially where Jennifer is concerned. You're only going to make it seem as if there's some-thing to hide. It'll be worse for her."

"Worse than what?"

"Just worse."

"Where is she?"

"Being interviewed."

Part of him knew Danny was right. He couldn't interfere—and hell, he didn't want to. There was no need to. Contact violations—well, they couldn't be ignored, certainly not. But undoubtedly there would be a good explanation. Jennifer was not a traitor.

No way.

"You asked me to investigate," said Danny. "I am."

"It's not you I'm worried about, it's Cortend," said Dog.

"Colonel, with respect, sir—a remark like that really could be misinterpreted, especially by someone who was looking to misinterpret it."

"I hate that tone of voice, Captain. I hate it."

Danny stared at him. Dog couldn't think of anything else to say. Danny was right; he had to consider how things looked—not because it might be bad for him, but because it might be bad for Dreamland. The last scandal here had nearly closed the place down.

And what would have happened to America if that had happened?

"All right, Danny. I wasn't going to interfere with the investigation," said Dog finally.

"I know you weren't."

A black Jimmy with a blue flashing light charged across the base, kicking up twin tornadoes of dust behind it. Dog and Danny turned and watched it approach.

"Got to be Ax," said Danny.

"Yeah," said Dog, folding his arms. Sure enough, Chief Master Sergeant Gibbs rolled down the window as the SUV slammed to a stop a few feet away.

"Colonel, Jed Barclay on the scrambled phone for ya," said the chief, hanging out the window. "Real important."

Dreamland Visiting VIP Office Two
1820

JENNIFER LEANED BACK AGAINST THE CHAIR, WAITING while the captain questioning her sorted through his notes.

Her head felt as if it had begun to tilt sideways. She hadn't eaten dinner, and lunch had been half of a chicken sandwich. Except for two trips to the restroom—escorted, though at least the security people had the decency to stay outside—she'd been in the room for nearly six hours. At least she wasn't hooked up to the lie detector anymore.

She felt as if she'd fallen down the rabbit hole in *Alice in Wonderland*. Cortend was the Queen, yelling, "Off with her head, off with her head."

Jennifer rubbed her arms, trying to get some circulation going. She needed to stretch—she needed to run, just get the hell out of this rabbit hole, where everything she said was turned upside down.

"You could make things easier," said the captain.

"Excuse me?"

"Cooperate."

"I *am* cooperating," Jennifer told him.

"Why would you help the Chinese?"

"I wouldn't."

"Don't get mad. I'm trying to help you."

"You're not." Jennifer sat up straight in her seat. "You think I'm a traitor, don't you?"

The captain didn't answer at first. "I think you might need help," he said finally.

"Oh, so you're going to be my friend, right?"

He made a show of sighing, as if she were the one being unreasonable.

"I'm not a traitor," she said.

The word sounded so odd, so foreign, that Jennifer had to say it again.

"I am not a traitor."

Until that point, tired and hungry, she'd been sustained mostly by anger. But now that foundation too slipped away. Jennifer Gleason had proven herself several times under fire, but this was something more fierce, more deadly. She'd never felt brave before—she'd just done what she had to do. It was easy almost, because she knew she could do it. She knew who she was—Jennifer Gleason, Dreamland scientist. And everyone at the base, everyone knew who she was. They trusted her, they liked her, and, in one case at least, loved her.

But the look in this man's eyes told her that trust was gone. She felt her whole identity slipping through a crack in her ribs.

Jennifer Gleason: traitor.

She wasn't. She knew she wasn't. But she worried that no matter what she did, she'd never convince anyone else of that again.

Not her friends. Not even Dog.

"So, when you were in college," said the captain, putting his papers down. "Tell me about your friends."

"My friends?"

"You had friends?"

"What does that have to do with anything?"

The captain pursed his lips.

"I don't remember who my friends were," she said honestly. "At this point, I don't know if I have any friends at all."

Dreamland Commander's Office
1850

"THERE'S A JOINT EXERCISE BETWEEN ASEAN ASSETS planned in the South China Sea, covering about a thousand square miles. More a goodwill exercise than actual combat training," Jed explained. "B-52s were requested. You'll go instead."

"All right," said Dog, listening as Jed filled him in on the arrangements for Brunei. A State Department rep was already en route to help smooth over any protocol matters. It had been suggested that an officer on his staff be appointed to liaison with the government.

"Brunei is not ideal," Dog told him. "It's a long way to operate it."

"Yeah," said Jed, who obviously agreed. "The President wanted you to locate there. It kind of interfaced with some State Department initiatives."

"What would those be? Making nice to Brunei?"

Jed gave him an embarrassed laugh.

"All right. If we have to go there, we will," said Dog.

"Listen, by the way, the Navy's still kind of pissed at you. There's a joke going around that an admiral has offered a reward for anyone who accidentally shoots down a Dreamland aircraft. At least I think it's a joke."

"Look, Jed, I have a lot going on over here."

"I'm sorry. The, uh, the President authorized this ASAP, so he wants you there, uh, right away. The exercises actually start tomorrow."

"Tomorrow?"

"Well, the time difference, it's like fifteen hours and that makes tomorrow today here—"

"We'll get there," said Dog, hanging up.

The phone no sooner hit the cradle than Rubeo walked in.

"The entire situation is piffle," said the scientist between his teeth.

"Which piffle?"

"The Colonel Cortend show. Piffle. It's a witch hunt. They hate scientists," continued Rubeo. "I've seen this before. They railroaded Oppenheimer on trumped-up charges that he was a communist." Rubeo snorted. "The man wins the war for them and they cashier him."

Dog didn't know the particulars about the Oppenheimer case, and he certainly wasn't going to ask about them now.

"No one's getting railroaded," he said.

Rubeo shook his head, flustered by his anger. The scientist's emotion had a strangely calming effect on Dog, as if Rubeo had somehow taken charge of being mad.

"You know they're questioning Jennifer Gleason," said Rubeo. "Questioning her. Her."

"I'd heard some scuttlebutt," said Dog.

"You're supposed to register when you attend a scientific conference where outside government agents may be. They've lost the paperwork, and they're hanging her for it."

"They lost the paperwork, or it wasn't done?"

"What does it matter?"

"It'll make a difference," said Dog.

"Then it was lost. Probably on purpose."

Dog leaned back in his seat. Rubeo showed exactly how right Danny had been—going off half-cocked made the scientist look like a crazoid, and did nothing for Jennifer.

"They questioned her for hours, and took away her clearance," said Rubeo.

Dog sighed. "I'm sure Captain Freah is just following procedure."

"Oh please."

"Did Jennifer answer their questions?"

"Of course."

"Tell me about the conferences."

Rubeo waved his hand in the air as if brushing away a fly. Then he sighed and began explaining in some detail the two scientific exchanges. One was on artificial intelligence and was rather broad; the other had to do with compression systems used in communications. The latter would inevitably have had applications for encryption and been subject to special scrutiny, though Rubeo thought it was more the fact that Jennifer might have come into contact with Chinese agents or spies that Cortend was focusing on.

"Chinese?" asked Dog.

"She asked specifically about Chinese. There

were five hundred people at one of the conferencs—
it'd be news if the Chinese weren't there. It's all
piffle, Colonel. It's a witch hunt."

Outside Dreamland Personnel Building Two
1805

MACK SMITH WAS HEADED TOWARD HIS BASE QUAR-
ters after a game of tennis when he spotted Colonel
Cortend heading toward her SUV, trailed by her
flock of lackeys. He'd had a good session, demol-
ishing a maintenance officer in straight sets. While
Mack had played masterfully, his victory had taken
a few minutes too long—he'd just missed inviting
the women on the court next to him to dinner.

Their loss, obviously.

Cortend turned in his direction as he approached.
Ordinarily he liked his women a little shorter, but
she was definitely worth the climb.

"Hello, Colonel," he said. "How goes the hunt?"

Cortend stopped. Her brown eyes focused on
him with all the intensity of a Sidewinder homing
in on a hot tailpipe.

"You are?"

"Smith—Mack. Remember? Hey, my friends call
me Knife."

She'd do for dinner.

"You like Vegas?" he asked.

"Las Vegas?"

"City of sin. Listen, I'm just on my way to hit
a shower, then I'm going to split for dinner in the
capital of sin. Come on with me and I'll show you

around. I know some clubs that'll blow you away. The food is fantastic. You like to gamble?"

"Mack Smith," said Cortend. She pronounced each consonant in his name.

"That's me. Call me Knife. Kind of a nickname."

She turned to one of her captains. "Is he on the list?"

"Yes, ma'am."

"In the truck, Smith. We have some questions for you."

Mack laughed. Cortend didn't.

"Yeah, well, maybe another time," he said, shaking his head. But as he took a step toward the building, he found two of the lackeys blocking his way. At the same time, two of the security men got out of one of the SUVs.

"What's the story here, sugar?" Mack said.

Cortend walked over to Mack. They were about the same height—but suddenly Cortend seemed to tower over him.

"The story, sugar, is that I have some questions for you to answer, and you will answer them now. Got it?"

"But I'm kind of busy."

"You're refusing to cooperate on a purely voluntary basis?"

The way she said the words made it clear to Mack that talking with her was about as voluntary as income tax. Still, he wasn't going to let some good-looking but hard-ass colonel screw up his night off.

"I wanted to take a shower," he said.

"I doubt it will make you smell any better," said Cortend, heading back toward her vehicle.

Outside Taipei, Taiwan
7 September
1100 (2000 Dreamland, 6 September)

CHEN LO FANN WAITED ON THE BENCH IN THE ANTE-chamber, soothing his troubled mind by staring at his surroundings. He had spent considerable time here as a boy, racing through his grandfather Chen Lee's house; under ordinary circumstances, those memories would soothe him.

They failed to now. In fact, the more he stared, the further those days became, faded pages from a discarded book.

Chen Lo Fann had failed in his mission to provoke a war between China and India. The weight of that failure sat heavily on him, blocks of iron pressing him from every direction. Fann might believe in the endless surging of the universe, but it offered little consolation, for he must now face the one man he loved and feared above all others, and admit his failure.

Time passed; he did not note it.

One of Chen Lee's secretaries stood before him. Without saying anything, Chen Lo Fann rose and followed the man through the hallway to the office where Chen Lee waited.

The old man stood gazing out the window. Taipei sat in the distance, a dirty gem in the rough land the old man had helped make prosperous. The old clock in the corner of the office ticked, slowly counting to itself as Chen Lo Fann waited for his grandfather to speak.

"Your mission failed," said Chen Lee finally.

"Yes, Grandfather," said Fann.

"History is a terrible force," said the older man, still looking through the window. "It cares for no individual. It is like the ocean wave in that way. And yet it can be turned."

Chen Lo Fann gazed at the back of his grandfather's white head. The old man had given him many lessons here, allowed him to watch and listen. Fann's education in America was nothing compared to those lessons.

"I have a second plan," said Chen Lo Fann. "The ASEAN exercises can be disrupted."

Chen Lee had clearly thought of this already, because he answered without his usual pause to consider.

"Simply disrupting them will not be enough. An attack must be provoked."

"If the Americans participate," said Chen Lo Fann, "I will succeed."

The old man said nothing. Chen Lo Fann realized he had made the same promise in the matter of war between the communists and India.

"If the meeting is not canceled, we shall have to take graver action," said Chen Lee. "Be prepared."

He turned back to the window.

"Yes, Grandfather," said Chen Lo Fann. He bowed, then left the room.

Dreamland Commander's Office
2050

ZEN ROLLED HIMSELF INSIDE THE OFFICE, SURPRISED TO find that everyone else was already there. Stoner had started the brief on the mission without him.

Zen banged against an empty chair getting in; no one seemed to notice.

"Major Stockard can give you the hard details," said Stoner, nodding toward him. "Basically, we get their attention by flying near their territory, and then make like we're testing a new weapon. The weapon is just a Hellfire missile with an ELF transmitter, but it's different enough to attract attention. So if the clone is a spy plane, it'll be worth checking out. You want to take over, Zen?"

"You're doing fine."

Stoner ticked off a list of areas to probe, starting with China and then moving to Vietnam—it was possible the Russians were using that country as a base. The ASEAN exercises were taking place about two hundred miles to the east of northern Vietnam.

"We're going to locate in Brunei," interrupted Colonel Bastian. "I realize it'll be a haul, but the facilities are first-rate. There's no doubt about that," said the colonel.

Dog added by way of explanation that Dreamland would be fulfilling a secondary diplomatic mission by being located in Brunei. It was clear to Zen that Dog didn't particularly like that part of the assignment, but he soldiered on with it, noting that the kingdom was constructing a new military air base near the international airport in the capital. The facilities would be made available to Dreamland, carte blanche. The sultan was rolling out the red carpet, a gracious host.

"The State Department is sending a babysitter,"

added the colonel. "There's some protocol crap we have to deal with. It won't get in your way, I promise."

The colonel ran down a tentative schedule on deployment—first thing tomorrow morning.

Really first thing: 0400.

Everyone in the room was used to dealing with rapid deployments, but 0400 was going to be tight, and Zen watched the concern rise on Major Alou's face. Alou, who would be in charge of the Megafortresses, had to round up full crews for two aircraft, get support people in place, move supplies, fuel.

"Major Alou, problem?" asked Dog.

"What the hell language do they speak in Brunei, anyway?"

Everyone laughed.

"Malay and English," said Stoner. "You'll be able to get by very well with English."

"Zen, problem?" asked Dog, turning to him. "I know you were looking for a deployment next week."

Zen shrugged. He'd already told two of his best Flighthawk trainee pilots to stand by. Rounding up the maintainers and other technical people would be a pain—but not particularly out of the ordinary. Most of the key people wore pagers when they were off campus, for just such a contingency.

"We can do it," said Zen. "We just have to hustle."

"I know it's impossibly short notice, but those are our orders," said Dog. "I'm going on the mission myself, and will serve as one of the Megafortress pilots. Major Catsman will stay here and take care of the farm. Questions?"

The colonel paused for his usual quarter of a

second before slapping his hand on the desk and rising.

"Let's do it, then."

"Colonel, what's the story with Jennifer Gleason?" asked Major Alou. "Is she under arrest or something?"

"Jennifer?" said Zen, taken by surprise.

Dog turned to Danny Freah.

"Jen is being questioned about possible security violations," said Danny.

"What violations?" asked Zen.

"I can't get into details," said Danny. "Look, my advice for everyone is to simply cooperate and answer whatever questions that come up. It's just an informal inquiry, not an investigation."

"That's bullshit," said Zen. He turned to Dog. "Jennifer? A spy? Shit."

Dog started to say something, but Danny interrupted. "Colonel Bastian can't comment on anything in any way that would be considered prejudicial."

"That's bullshit," said Zen.

Dog put up his hand. "All right. Obviously, because of what we do we're under special scrutiny. All of us, not just Jennifer."

"I wanted her along to handle the computers and whatnot," said Zen. Technical staff often accompanied the Dreamland team on missions, even those in combat zones.

"You better find someone else," said Danny. "At least for a couple of days."

"Colonel?"

"Is she essential for the deployment?" asked Dog.

"Not essential. But—"

"At this point, I think Danny's right. Once Colonel Cortend is finished talking to her I'm sure she'll be fine to come back."

TWO HOURS LATER, DOG FINALLY FINISHED SQUARING away everything that needed to be squared away before he left with the rest of the team for Brunei. He needed to get sleep—if takeoff time didn't slip, he'd be briefing his flight in a couple of hours. But more important than sleep, he wanted to talk to Jennifer.

He wanted to call her. In theory, there was no reason not to.

It might not look good, however, not if there had been a real violation of security protocols. As unit commander, he would eventually have to deal with the matter.

He could recuse himself, of course. Probably he had to.

Or just put an end to the whole thing.

No doubt if he did that, Dreamland's enemies would seize on it as ammunition for *something*— what exactly, he wasn't sure.

He reached for the phone. No harm in calling her, for cryin' out loud.

He dialed the lab but then remembered that she had no computer access; Danny had had to cut it off as soon as he learned about the possible security breach, as minor as it was. He paused, trying to remember her apartment number without going to the directory.

When he dialed it, her voice mail answered.

Maybe she was taking this harder than he thought.

Or maybe she was out partying.

Before Dog could leave a message, there was a knock on the door. He looked up and saw Colonel Cortend spreading her frown across the threshhold, trailed by a Dreamland security team and several of her aides. He put down the phone and waved her inside.

"Captain Freah said you'd be here," said Cortend, sitting in the chair nearest his desk.

"I often am," said Dog. "I understand you've been questioning my people."

"I've questioned several of your people, yes. On an informal basis. They've all volunteered to cooperate."

Dog let that particular fiction pass.

"Let's get to the marrow on this," said Cortend. "There's no need for fencing."

"I'm a right-to-the-marrow guy myself," said Dog. He slid back in his seat, knowing that Cortend had come to ask about Jennifer.

And perhaps exactly because that thought occurred to him, he glanced toward the door and saw her standing behind Cortend's aides, frozen, as if she'd taken a step inside before spotting them.

Was she really there? Or was it some strange trick of his imagination.

"Lieutenant Colonel Bastian," snapped Cortend.

"Excuse me a second," said Dog, rising. He turned his attention to Cortend for just a moment as he got up, and by the time he looked back at the door she was gone.

Gone?

Dog walked out into the outer office, past the reception area and then into the hall.

It was empty. The elevator was open.

Hallucination?

No, she'd definitely been here. Somewhere.

Jen would have taken the stairs. She'd seen Cortend's people or the back of her head, and split.

Wise move, really. Too bad he couldn't do that.

Dog walked back to his office. This time he pulled the door closed behind him.

"Sorry about that. Where were we?"

"You are seeing Ms. Gleason, are you not?"

"I don't think that's any of your business."

"Colonel, let me remind you—"

"I'm not denying that I see her. But for the record, my personal life is my personal life."

"Ms. Gleason is a civilian employee under your supervision," said Cortend. "As a matter of law and regulation, it would be possible for her to charge you with sexual harassment."

"Has she?" said Dog.

"She has not."

"You don't really think she's a spy, do you?" he said, tiring of her games. His voice was considerably more level than he felt.

"I try not to form judgments before I finish my job," said Cortend. "I understand the situation might be difficult for you."

"And?"

"I have a number of technical questions that I'd like answered," said Cortend, completely changing the subject.

Capitulation?

Or another one of her tactics?

"They have to do with compartmented areas, and I need to know what can be broached and what can't be," Cortend continued. "If you wish, it can wait until morning."

She didn't get up, and it was clear she wouldn't until he answered the questions.

"I have orders from the President. We're deploying at 0400."

If Cortend was impressed, she gave no hint.

"We'll discuss it informally first," she told him. "Then I can bring my people in. I want to be careful to delineate the areas, as my report will be read by—"

A knock at the door interrupted her.

"Come," said Dog.

Mack Smith opened the door. The major looked a little tired, walking rather than bounding as he normally did. When he saw Cortend he blanched.

"You wanted to see me, Colonel?"

"Yes, come in, Mack. Colonel, this will only take a minute."

"Of course," said Cortend, getting up. As she left, she gave Mack the look one might use to dismiss a whipped dog.

"Watch her, Colonel," said Mack as the door was closed. "She's evil."

"I'm sure she's just doing her job," Dog said.

"No."

Mack didn't offer any other explanation. Dog decided it wasn't worth pursuing—it was pretty clear that Cortend got off on intimidating people. Smith ordinarily wasn't easy to intimidate; maybe he'd ask her for some pointers when she came back in.

That would be the day.

"I need a political officer," Dog told Mack. "A liaison, actually."

"How's that?" asked Mack.

"We're deploying to Brunei, first thing in the morning," Dog told him. "I'll go into details if you're in. Otherwise, good night."

"Colonel, is she coming?"

"Colonel Cortend? No. Her investigation's here."

"Sign me up," said Mack, so relieved he looked as if he'd won the lottery.

"We have to leave at 0400."

"Whatever. I'll scrub toilets if you need it. Just take me with you."

Dreamland Personnel Building Two
2105

BY THE TIME SHE GOT BACK TO HER APARTMENT, JENnifer's hands were shaking so badly that she had trouble with the lock. Inside, she dropped her glass as she filled it with water from the faucet in the kitchenette; fortunately, it was plastic and didn't break, rebounding instead across the room.

The expression on his face when he saw her—anger and surprise . . .

Hate?

No, he couldn't hate her. He couldn't.

Did he think she was a traitor? How could he think that?

What had Dog been doing with that she-bitch Cortend? Had he put her up to this?

Dog?

It couldn't possibly be. There was no way. No way.

But Cortend was in his office.

Of course she was. Dog was the base commander; there were a million reasons for her to be there.

Dog, everyone, thought she was a traitor.

She was just tired, overwrought.

The bitch Cortend was playing with her mind.

Her hands wouldn't stop shaking.

She wasn't a traitor. She wasn't.

That had to be what they were thinking. Even Dog?

Even him.

The phone rang. Jennifer took a step toward it, then stopped.

What if it was Cortend, asking for more questions?

God no, she told herself. No more. Not tonight.

She let the phone ring until it stopped. As she stared at it, she realized her hand and shirt were wet, and so was the floor, but she couldn't remember why.

II

PARADISE

——

II

PARADISE

"A COUPLE OF HOURS IN PARADISE AND ALREADY you're sleeping late," Zen told Lieutenant Kirk "Starship" Andrews as the young Flighthawk pilot sat down at the table across from him. Starship's breakfast tray contained two large cups of coffee and nothing else.

"My body's still back in Dreamland," mumbled Starship.

"You sure it's not with the hospitality people?" said Lieutenant James "Kick" Colby, the other Flighthawk pilot Zen had taken on the deployment.

"It wants to be," said Starship.

"Natives are off-limits," said Zen. "You can look but you cannot touch. Got that? And be careful how you talk to them."

"How about the State Department liaison?" asked Kick. "She's hot."

"Out of your league," said Zen.

"Mack Smith's eyeing her already," said Starship.

"Oh there's serious competition," said Kick.

"I'll take one of the waitress babes," said Starship, lifting his gaze toward the buffet at the front of the room. Six of the most gorgeous women in

Asia stood at attention behind the table. Zen had his back to them, but he could practically feel the warmth of their smiles beaming across the room.

The Dreamland pilots and crew were being housed at a hotel just outside the airfield where they'd set up operations. "Mess" consisted of a lavishly appointed private room—thick tablecloths, hand-woven silk rugs, paint that seemed to contain speckles of gold—on the ground floor of the hotel. The room was part of a restaurant that back in the States would rate four stars—the wine list was a little too restricted to make five.

For breakfast, the Dreamland personnel—crew dogs and officers alike—had sorted through an all-you-can eat array of various meats, cooked-to-order eggs and omelets, a pyramid of exotic fruits, and enough donuts, rolls, and pastries to make a small town diabetic.

Zen had chosen his usual oatmeal and bananas, though he had made a concession to local tastes by sampling the pinkish-green juice. It was sweet, but tomorrow he'd go for the orange.

The coffee, however, was a real keeper. He might have to arrange for a pipeline back home when the mission ended.

"So are all the deployments like this?" asked Kick. He'd come to Dreamland from an assignment as a Hog "driver," piloting A-10As. The story went that his nickname came from early flight training, when he needed a kick to get going; if so, that need had long since disappeared.

"What do you mean?" asked Zen. "In terms of food?"

"The hotel rooms, the women. Everything."

"Usually it's cots and tents," said Zen. "Brunei's just a special place."

Starship and Kick had been with the program only a short time; neither man had logged a hundred hours with the robot aircraft. But Fentress had been the only other pilot with real experience. While the two youngsters had their drawbacks, both could handle a single plane reasonably well, and consistently scored high in the simulations and exercises. It was time for them to take the next step.

"Paradise," mumbled Starship.

"You have a hangover, Lieutenant?" asked Zen.

"Uh, no, sir. Whacked on the time difference, though. My body thinks it's yesterday."

"Tomorrow," said Kick. "Nine o'clock is five o'clock last night tomorrow."

"Huh?" asked Starship.

"I'll give you an example. 2200 here is 0600 at Dreamland, same day. 0900 here would be 1700 there—but they're back a day. So while we're out on a day patrol, they're sleeping. 1200 is 2000 yesterday there. Or 2300 in Washington, D.C."

Starship blinked at him. "You do weather and traffic, too?"

"Fifteen hours' difference. Would be sixteen, except the States are on Daylight Saving Time," said Kick. "You know it's Saving, not Savings?"

"Eat hardy, gentlemen," Zen said, pushing away from the table. "We brief at 1000, and we're in the air at 1300. And watch the alcohol, Starship. Those clubs are not officially sanctioned. No matter what Mack Smith says."

Brunei IAP, Field Seven
0910

BOSTON SLID HIS HAND ALONG HIS M-16A3 AND ROLLED his head on his neck. He figured he didn't hate guard duty any more than the next guy—but that meant he hated it pretty bad.

From what the others on the Whiplash team were telling him, guard duty was about all he was going to be doing for the next six months. He hoped they were just busting his chops because he was the team nugget, or new guy. He'd clearly drawn the worst assignment—he'd been standing out here since four A.M. local, and had another hour to go.

And when that was over, he wouldn't be hitting the sack—he was supposed to report to the Whiplash trailer, known as Mobile Command, and get himself educated on the high-tech communications gear they used. Whiplash team members were expected to act as communications specialists during the deployment.

All that SF training, and basically he was a radio operator and a guard dog.

In fact, he wasn't even a guard dog. The real sentries were high-tech sensor arrays placed at the edge of the field where they were assigned. The arrays were monitored in the trailer (at the moment, Egg Reagan had the con). A special computer screened video, infrared, motion, and sound detectors. Those inputs could be piped into Boston's Smart Helmet, supplementing the helmet's own infrared, short-range radar, and optical sensors.

The thing was, the helmet was pretty damn heavy and hot besides. Fortunately, Egg had told him it wasn't necessary to wear it; he'd alert him to any problem. The helmet was clipped to his belt.

Boston wasn't the only flesh-and-blood sentry. A battalion of Brunei soldiers blocked access to the area Dreamland had been assigned. There was also an honor guard—a mixed unit built around British Gurkhas, a storied unit of foreign troops that had originated in Nepal—which conducted a ceremonial changing of the guard on the apron twenty yards away every fifteen minutes, or so it seemed.

"Yo, Boston, trucks coming," said Egg in his earbud.

"Another ceremony?" asked Boston. His mike was clipped to the top of his carbon-boron bulletproof vest; it was sensitive enough so that he could whisper and be heard over the Dreamland com system.

"Negative," said Egg. "These are customized SUVs. Not military."

"I hear them," said Boston. He brought his gun up, though there was no way any intruder could get by the Brunei soldiers, whose weapons included several antitank missiles.

Unless, of course, they stood back and let the trucks pass.

"What's this?" Egg said in his ear.

The first truck—a large black Chevy Suburban with a block of lights across the top and enough chrome to make a drug dealer jealous—roared straight toward Boston.

"If he doesn't stop, I'm taking him out."

"Careful. I think they're VIPs," said Egg.

"If he doesn't stop, I'm taking him out," repeated Boston. He drew back, squaring as if to fire.

The driver of the SUV slammed on his brakes and swerved, stopping a few yards away. Two other SUVs pulled in alongside.

The doors of the vehicles flew open together. Men in lightweight civilian suits emerged from the trucks. Bruisers all, they were clearly bodyguards, with vests under their jackets.

"No weapons," said Egg, giving him the read from the monitor.

"If you say so," said Boston.

A short, slightly paunchy man stepped forward from the other side of the middle vehicle. He was obviously a local, and was wearing what seemed to be relatively expensive clothes.

"Hello," said the man with a jovial smile.

"I'm sorry," said Boston, his voice hard enough to make it clear that was a lie. "No one is allowed past this point. No one."

The man laughed.

"Sir, no one is allowed past this point," said Boston. "Not even the sultan."

"Oh well," laughed the man. "I'm just his nephew."

Thoroughly confused, Boston had the man covered. Someone else got out of the SUV from the other side.

"Colonel Bastian is on his way," said Egg. "Oh, I see now—that's Mack Smith."

"Who's Smith?" Boston said.

"Major Smith—he's ours. The guy getting out of the SUV. Colonel Bastian brought him as a political officer."

The somewhat bedraggled man came out from around the truck and approached Mack.

"It's all right," he told Boston. "They're with me."

"Sorry, sir," said Boston. "I have very strict orders. No one gets past me. I'm authorized to shoot," he added, as Mack continued to within a few feet of him.

Smith squinted at him. "You know who this is?"

"The sultan's nephew, sir."

"A prince," said Mack. "His Royal Highness Pehin bin Awg. Very, very important man in Brunei."

"I don't doubt it, sir. But he's not coming past unless my orders change."

"You really going to shoot?" asked Mack, taking another step forward.

"Bet your ass. Sir."

"Jeez."

Bin Awg laughed. "No need for an upset, Mack. We can come back another time."

"Colonel Bastian's at the gate," said Egg.

"Sir, my colonel is on his way," Boston told bin Awg. "I apologize, but my orders are very explicit."

"Let's have breakfast, then come back," the prince said, turning back to his vehicle. "Come on, Mack."

Smith frowned. Boston caught a whiff of perfume, stale cigarettes, and even staler alcohol as the major walked back to the SUV.

"That was really Smith?" asked Boston.

"The one and only."

Aboard EB-52 *Pennsylvania*, South China Sea
Near the Vietnamese coast
10 September 1997
1430

"ACTION AT DA NANG," THE EB-52'S COPILOT, KEVIN McNamara, said over the interphone, the Megafortress's onboard communications system. "We have two MiG-21s taking off. We're tracking. You have the data."

Starship felt his throat constrict. His hand involuntarily tightened on the control yoke, even though he didn't have control of the plane yet.

"Hawk leader copies," said Zen. "They have two more coming, huh?"

"Looks like it."

"Should we go ahead with the handoff?" asked Starship, sitting next to Zen on the Flighthawk control deck. They had just begun the prehandoff checklist before the MiGs scrambled from the Vietnamese airfield about a hundred miles to the northeast.

"Absolutely," said Zen. "You all right?"

Five minutes earlier, Starship would have told him that he'd never felt better in his life. Aspirin and the Brunei coffee had helped him get over the banger of a headache he'd had this morning, a hangover obtained courtesy of a few whiskey sours with Major Smith after the official reception.

But with McNamara's warning, his headache had returned. His muscles were twitching and his mouth felt dry.

Nothing a shot couldn't cure, but that wasn't possible here.

"Let's do it," he told Zen, forcing enthusiasm into his voice.

The Flighthawk commander gave verbal authorization. Starship acceded. Zen hit the keys on his panel and gave up control of the bird.

"Authorization Zed Zed Stockard," said Zen as the computer asked for final confirmation. C^3 buzzed in Starship's ear, turning over the helm.

"Handoff complete," said Starship. "On course."

He read off his bearing, altitude, and course speed—a prissy bit of the procedure in his opinion, though no one was asking—then worked through a full instrument check with the computer. Starship went by the book, aware that not only Zen but Kick were watching everything he did, ready to point out the slightest deviation from Major Stockard's prescriptions.

While ostensibly designed to familiarize the crew with the area and procedures for communicating with the ASEAN task force, Starship sensed that today's mission was really a tryout. Major Stockard had said during the preflight that he hadn't decided who was going to take the U/MF-3 on the decoy flight tomorrow, and it didn't take a rocket scientist to figure out that today's flight would help determine who got the glory and who sat on his thumbs in the fold-down rumble seat at the back of the compartment.

Starship liked Kick as a person, but he'd never be able to stomach playing number two to the other lieutenant. Kick had *never* been a top jock. Heck, he'd been a Hog driver, flying A-10As before coming over to Dreamland, and everyone knew the A-10As were basically cannon fodder.

Granted, he was a hard worker and a decent guy, but he wasn't first-team material. If he were, he'd've been in Eagles like Starship before transferring here.

"Be advised there are now two MiG-21s off Da Nang, bearing at three-one-five," said McNamara. The Megafortress copilot customarily kept the crew apprised of the location of other players on the field. "Climbing through eight thousand feet, accelerating—looks like they want to come say hello."

Like many of the members of Dreamland's Megafortress fleet, the *Pennsylvania* was named for a famous battleship, in this case the venerable battlewagon *Pennsylvania*, a member of the Iowa class that had served after World War II. She was equipped with a powerful AWACS-style radar, which rotated in a fuselage bulge around the wing root; augmented by a phased array unit in her nose and a host of other antennas and sensors, *Penn* could sniff out targets five hundred miles away. She and her sisters were intended as replacements for the venerable and considerably more vulnerable E-3 AWACS Sentry, though more mods and updates were planned before the type went operational with the "regular" Air Force.

Like Zen, Starship used a special control helmet to help him fly the robot plane; while heavier than the brain bucket he would have donned for an F-15 flight, it seemed more intuitive than the panels at the control station where he was sitting, which could also be used if he wished. Infinitely configurable, the display screen in the helmet could be divided into several panels. This allowed the pilot to simultaneously see what was in front of him, glance down at a "sitrep" of the area fed from the EB-52's sensors, and a full array of instrument readings. Though he wasn't yet rated to handle multiple planes, the helmet could in theory control up to four Flighthawks at a time, switching its views, sensor, and instrument data between them by voice command or keyboard toggle. Most times, Starship used a standard screen view that provided a nose camera shot in the top screen, with a sitrep at the lower left and various flight info on the right.

The MiGs blinked in the sitrep, two red triangles flying above the gray-shadowed coastline toward the light blue ocean. *Penn* was about two hundred miles east of them. If they were headed here, it was because of the ground radar and a controller; their own radars were far too limited to see the Megafortress.

And the Flighthawk was invisible to just about everybody, with the exception of *Penn*.

On the far right of the sitrep, a green-hued rectangle bore the tag YUBARI. If Starship asked for the information, C^3 would have looked into its memory banks and announced that *Yubari* was a Japanese patrol ship, carrying some surface-to-air missiles but primarily intended for antisubmarine work. She was sailing roughly a hundred miles to the east, part of the ASEAN exercises. The ship was working with an Australian cruiser, which was temporarily off the screen further east.

"Those suckers got to be thirty years old," said Kick, wearing a headset and standing behind him. He was referring to the MiGs, which indeed had been built before any of the men on the Flighthawk had been born.

"The sucker we're flying in is close to fifty," said Zen.

"I meant it in a good way," said the other pilot.

"The ground radars picked up the Megafortress and scrambled these guys to take a look," Zen added, using a voice that sounded to Starship like the one his Philosophy 101 professor used to explain Plato's theory that humans saw reality like shadows on a cave. "The MiGs are still picking up speed, but they're not going to come on too much faster or they'll end up with fuel issues. C^3 has already figured out an intercept. See it Kick, on the dedicated screen?"

"Got it."

"Obviously, it relies on you to know the ROEs," said Zen, referring to the rules of engagement that governed when—and if—force could be used. "As far as the computer is concerned, war is always in order."

"As it should be," said Kick.

Brown nose.

"Still coming at us," said Starship. He'd told Zen he'd gotten the nickname because of his first name—Kirk, as in James T. Kirk, the commander of the starship *Enterprise*. That was partly true—his parents had been serious Trekkies, and had the show in mind when they named him. But he'd actually earned the nickname during flight training for rashly predicting that he would pilot the space shuttle or its successor someday.

A prediction he meant to make good on.

"Mission commander's call on how to proceed," said Zen, still in instructor mode. "On a typical radar mission, the profile we're following, your job is going to be to run interference. But the pilot of the EB-52 is going to have to balance the situation. Let's say you have two bandits. If they're hostile and coming at you, he may be under orders to get the hell out of there. Never mind that a Flighthawk could take them in a snap."

Zen paused. Starship knew the major was speaking from experience—he had a lot of notches on his belt.

"What you don't want to do is put the Flighthawks in a position where they're going to get deadheaded," said Zen. "So you keep with what the EB-52 is doing."

Deadheaded meant that the command link had been severed. When that happened, the Flighthawk would revert to a preprogrammed mode and fly back toward the mother ship. It happened just beyond twenty-five miles, depending on the flight conditions. Because the U/MFs were so maneuverable and the EB-52 was flying its own course, it could happen relatively easily in combat.

But loss of a connection was the ultimate spanking, and Starship meant to avoid it. He was currently fifteen miles ahead of *Penn*, accelerating slightly.

"Zen, they're going to afterburners," said Major Merce Alou, the *Penn*'s pilot. The pilot's decision to communicate the information signaled that he was concerned about the situation.

"Roger that. I think we can hold on course," Zen told him. "We're plotting an intercept."

"Roger that. We're monitoring them up here. They're not targeting us at this time."

"You get all that?" Zen asked Starship.

"Yup," said Starship. He had the Flighthawk at 27,000 feet on a direct line toward the lead MiG; they were now closing to fifty miles. "If this were an F-15, I could take them out in sixty seconds."

"Yeah, what's a little court-martial for creating an international incident?" said Kick.

"What do you think of what the computer is suggesting?" asked Zen.

"It has me slashing down and getting that lead plane, then whipping back for the second in one swoop," said Starship. "Awful optimistic with a cannon."

"Yeah, especially for you," said Kick.

"Hey, I've seen you on the range, Mr. Marksman," snapped Starship. "They put you in a Hog so the bullets would be big enough that you couldn't miss."

"It is optimistic. The computer thinks it never misses. It's almost right," added Zen. "But the thing here is that it's figuring that the MiGs will stay on course. You can tell it to anticipate what they'll do, and it'll give you more options."

"I thought I shouldn't do that because we're not in attack mode," said Starship. He also felt that he was a bit beyond taking combat cues from a computer. That was okay for Kick, whose cockpit time had been spent largely in a ground-attack plane. Starship's entire training had been for air-to-air combat, and he'd flown against MiG-21s in numerous exercises.

Of course, he'd never gotten this close to *real* enemy fighters in an F-15.

Not that the Vietnamese MiGs were the enemy. They had as much right to be here as he did.

Starship checked his airspeed and heading carefully, trying to will away the dry taste in his mouth. He could feel Kick hovering over his shoulder, waiting for the chance to jump in.

"They're not acknowledging," said Alou after he hailed them, first in English, then with the help of the translation module in the EB-52's computer. He tried again, giving the MiGs his bearing and location, emphasizing that he was in international waters and on a peaceful mission.

The MiGs still didn't respond.

"Let's give them a Dreamland welcome," Zen told Starship.

Starship took a breath, then flicked the control stick left. The U/MF tipped its wing and whipped downward, its speed ramping toward Mach 1.

The odd thing was the feel. Rather than having his stomach pushing against his rib cage, it stayed perfectly calm and centered in the middle of his body. The disjunction between the Flighthawk and the Megafortress was one of the hardest things for the pilot to get used to.

Zen had warned him about that.

"Flares," said the Flighthawk pilot. He kicked out flares normally intended for dekeing heat-seeking missiles, making himself clearly visible to the Vietnamese fighters, who were now roughly two miles away.

The Vietnamese pilots reacted immediately,

turning together to the north, possibly convinced they were seeing UFOs or the fiery manifestation of a Buddhist god.

"Stay on your game plan," coached Zen.

Starship realized he'd started to pull up a little too sharply. He easily compensated, but he felt apprehensive nonetheless; Kick was standing behind him, after all, taking mental notes.

Even an F-15C Eagle would have had trouble climbing back and turning as tightly as Starship's Flighthawk as he whipped his plane onto the tail of the opposing flight, aiming to paint the enemy cockpit with his shadow.

Not enemy. Not enemy, he reminded himself. Relax.

"How long do you want me to sit here?" he asked Zen.

"Break off once they turn," said Zen. "There you go," he added as the first MiG changed direction. "Come on back to Penn. They look homeward bound."

"Roger that."

Aboard the *Dragon Prince*, South China Sea 1506

PROFESSOR AI HIRA BAI MONITORED THE COMMUNIST MiGs as they circled northward, away from the American Megafortress. The planes were more than one hundred miles from his own UAV, the *Dragon*, well out of range of its onboard sensors. To see them, he would ordinarily have had to rely on the limited data fed from the buoy network that helped guide the small robot plane, but the ASEAN maneuvers provided better opportunities.

The ships involved in the exercise were testing links that allowed data from one ship to be shared among the entire task force over a wide area. Since Professor Ai had been able to tap into an Australian frigate's communications system, he too had a full data set that included wide-ranging radar coverage courtesy of two Japanese Aegis-equipped destroyers.

Ai watched the screen with fascination. He was interested in the performance of the Flighthawk, though this was difficult to ascertain from the radar data, even as the robot plane passed almost directly overhead of one of the ships. The craft was clearly faster and more maneuverable than his own plane. Its data flow with the mother ship, of course, was extremely rich—he'd known that since their long-range intercepts of the signals. He would have given much to be able to decode the information that passed between them.

On the other hand, his own invention was not without its advantages. The buoy and satellite system that relayed its control signals allowed him to fly the aircraft far beyond its remote station— although in some circumstances there was a noticeable lag as the commands were transmitted. And his plane was not only stealthier, but its signal carrier included what he called a "mocking device" that could spit back bits of intercepted code to confuse a nearby Elint gatherer.

"Should we engage?" asked Kuo, who was helping fly the UAV.

"No," said Professor Ai. "Not today. Let us simply observe and see what our friends do. We may have only one chance, and we must choose it wisely."

Aboard *Penn*, South China Sea
1538

STARSHIP HAD JUST TRADED PLACES WITH KICK WHEN the pair of Chinese fighters appeared. These were Shenyang J-8IIs, more formidable than the ancient MiGs the Vietnamese had sent, but they too made a rather pedestrian and predictable approach, flying a routine intercept about fifty miles east of Guangdong.

"Same routine as Brother Starship," Zen told Kick.

Starship tensed, even though he knew Zen meant it as a joke.

Kick started his move about six thousand feet above the interceptors, rolling into a banking turn that would take him across their course. But they broke before he went for his flares, apparently in response to the Megafortress pilot's hail. Kick held on to his disposables and began to climb again, intending to circle back close to the Megafortress until it was clear what the Chinese were doing.

Conservative move, Starship thought. He would have tucked back toward them and hit the gas.

"They're looking for you," Zen told the two lieutenants. "They know the Megafortresses fly with U/MF escorts. They want to draw you out."

"What should I do?" Kick asked.

"Give me the controls," said Starship without missing a beat.

"Fuck off."

"Wait until they come out of that turn," said Zen. "They aren't particularly maneuverable, and it'll be obvious where they intend to go. You've got good position."

One of the J-8s—in some respects it was a supersized J-7, itself a kind of new and improved MiG-21—swung into a wide arc, trying to get nose on nose for the Megafortress, which the computer's dotted line showed would happen at about sixty miles away. The other plane ducked down toward the waves heading in the opposite direction.

"Trying to get lost in the clutter," suggested Starship. "Ain't gonna happen."

The powerful gear aboard *Penn* could track him right to the water, and probably a few fathoms below.

"So what should Kick do?" Zen asked.

"I'd go for the snake, get in his nose, show him there's no hope," said Kick.

"I wouldn't," offered Starship.

"Why not?" asked Zen.

"Because first of all, dropping down like that, he's going to have an impossible climb before he can deal with us," said Starship. He pointed over at Zen's screen. "Even if he goes to his afterburner when he's in position, he's going to be way gonzo in front there. You can splash number one, then come for number two."

"We're not splashing anyone today," said Zen. "Just remember that."

Starship felt his face redden.

"I think Starship's right," Kick told Zen.

"Well then make sure the Megafortress knows what you're doing," said Zen, implicitly agreeing.

ZEN WATCHED KICK SLASH ACROSS THE CHINESE pilot's nose, timing his maneuver to match a jink east by *Penn*. It came off well, the Chinese interceptor turning to the right—an instinctive move that widened the gap between him and his ostensible target.

"Okay, so how'd we know he was going to go right?" Zen asked.

"We didn't," said Kick.

"Well, most pilots do," said Starship.

"Western pilots, maybe," said Zen, still playing teacher. "But you have something to go on beyond that."

"He moved that way earlier," said Starship. "Plus it takes him closer to his base."

"Yeah," said Kick, getting it.

Zen said nothing as the Flighthawk pilot brought his plane around to intercept the second J-8, which as predicted was climbing off the deck, throttle nailed to the afterburner slot. He'd turned into him a little too soon, probably nervous about retaining his connection to *Pennsylvania*, which of course was moving in the opposite direction.

It wasn't exactly a huge mistake, but it was enough to convince Zen that he'd put Starship in the pilot's seat tomorrow. Lieutenant Andrews was a somewhat better pilot and had better tactical instincts as well—possibly a function of his time in Eagles. The difference between the two men would probably disappear in a few weeks' time, but for now it was enough to make Starship the clear choice.

As the second J-8 jock pulled off, *Pennsylvania* cut to the south, having reached the end of its practice search track. Zen watched as Kick rode the Flighthawk up through the clouds toward the mother ship.

"Not too quick. Hang back between the Megafortress and the J-8s," Zen told Kick.

"I know," snapped the pilot.

"Relax, Kick," said Zen.

A warning tone bleeped in the headsets.

"RWR," said Kick. "Wow—they're trying to spike us."

Zen's screen showed that the Chinese planes had activated their targeting radars. The planes carried PL-7A homers—semiactive radar missiles—but they had almost no hope of hitting the Flighthawk at what was now close to fifty miles. Nor were they in position to fire on the Megafortress.

Maybe they were newbies too.

"That's a hostile act," said Starship. "I'd splash him."

"You can't splash someone because they turn their radar on you," said Kick.

"That's not an air traffic control radar," said Starship. "That's weapons, baby. Hostile act, per ROE."

"Radar's off," said Zen.

"What was he doing?" asked Kick.

"Busting your chops," said Zen.

"Why?" asked Starship.

Zen laughed.

"We could've spun around, targeted him ourselves." The lieutenant seemed indignant. "I could have shot him down."

"Well, from his point of view, he could have shot you down," said Zen. "The Chinese pilots like to push things to the limit. I've dealt with these jokers before. Believe me, that's nothing. They'll do a lot worse tomorrow."

"How will I know whether they're serious or not?" asked Starship.

"My call as mission commander. No matter who is flying the Flighthawk," Zen added, emphasizing that he hadn't made his decision yet.

Or at least not announced it.

"Good time to tank?" asked Kick.

"Yup. You think you can do better than Starship?"

"I made it on the first try."

"There's always room for improvement," said Zen.

Brunei
1900

DOG STARED OUT THE WINDOW OF THE MERCEDES LIMO as the caravan approached the gates of the sultan's palace of Istana. Part of a large and modern government complex, the Istana Nurul Iman sat on a rise above the city. A golden globe sat to the left, shimmering with the reflected glare of floodlights. A web of white steel rose in the shape of an airy roof from the main gate, sheltering the procession past an honor guard to the entrance of the ceremonial hall, which sat just beyond the sultan's personal home and government offices.

Colonel Bastian had spent most of the day with members of the Brunei armed forces, trying to get the protocol crap out of the way so he could join the patrols tomorrow. He was now on his way to a state dinner being thrown in his honor; if he survived that, he figured he'd be done with the diplomatic BS for at least a few days.

Things had been so hectic he hadn't even had a chance to call Jennifer and see how she was. He thought of her as the cars started through the gate; if she were here she'd have some smart-alecky thing to say about the fancy buildings and frou-frou trees lining the grounds. She'd laugh about how uptight he was.

She'd also be wearing a pretty dress. He could do with that.

"The tie, Colonel. The tie."

Dog turned to Brenda Kelly, the State Department protocol officer who was sitting next to him in the back of the limo.

"Your tie," she repeated as the car stopped.

"Oh yeah."

Dog made the adjustment just as the door snapped open. Dog unfolded himself from the back of the car, then turned and put his hand out for Miss Kelly, who had dressed in a long, traditional sari with a scarf to cover her head, showing respect. With Kelly on his arm, Dog began walking down a red carpet toward a set of steps. It was a long walk, and he had to pause every ten feet or so, as a different contingent of the honor guards snapped to in anticipation of a formal salute.

"I feel like we're at a Hollywood premiere," Dog whispered when they reached the set of steps just below the main entrance. A group of soldiers barred their way, aiming a pair of flags at them.

"Wait until we get inside," said Kelly.

"I don't have to salute inside, right?" asked Dog. "Or are the rules different here?"

"Bow when the sultan comes," said Kelly, who had told him to do this at least a dozen times.

Dog remembered, bending stiffly with as much grace and solemnity that he could muster. The sultan, a congenial man who managed to seem both casual and regal at the same time, stepped up and put his arm around Colonel Bastian as if they were old friends.

"We are glad you are here," he told Dog.

"My pleasure. Absolutely my pleasure."

"Major Smith has regaled us with your achievements," said the sultan. "You are quite a hero."

"Not really, Your Highness."

"No need for modesty among friends," said the sultan, leading him from the large reception room. They walked down a hall, Miss Kelly and other dignitaries falling in behind them. The sultan pointed out some artworks and a letter from King George— it wasn't clear which one—as they walked.

"I thought of being a pilot in my younger days," said the ruler as they entered a room that looked somewhat like a fancy English club. It was filled with people, including Mack Smith, who nodded at Dog from the side. "But flying is a job for a young man."

"You're still young enough to fly," said Dog. He hadn't meant it as flattery; the ruler seemed about his own age.

The sultan smiled, then began introducing him to some of his government ministers, members of the legislative council who advised him on important matters. He and most of the country's elite spoke English perfectly; Brunei was part of the Commonwealth, and had in fact spent much of the twentieth century under British rule. While Malay was the official language, a good number of the 336,000 people who lived in the country spoke English, and no member of the kingdom would consider himself educated if he didn't.

Dog shook hands and nodded for nearly a half hour, continuing to do so even as the sultan stepped away to confer with one of his sons. Miss Kelly stepped up and whispered in Dog's ear, identifying whom he was greeting—the British ambassador, the head of the British Army Gurkhas battalion stationed in the kingdom, and a number of prominent businessmen.

Waiters appeared carrying plates laden with food. Everyone seemed to stand back on some invisible signal. Dog realized they were watching him anxiously.

"You have to try the food first," whispered Miss Kelly. "Manners."

"I'm not hungry."

"It doesn't matter," said the State Department rep. "You're the guest. Go."

Dog took a fork and small plate from the nearest server. The hors d'oeuvre tasted somewhere between a pepperoni and an anchovy (it was a specially pickled shrimp), but Dog figured he would survive.

"This one," said Miss Kelly.

"More?" he whispered.

"Smile, Colonel."

"What is it?"

"Some sort of jellied curry fruit. I think."

"You think?"

Dog speared the thick green curlicue. He'd just about gotten it into his mouth when Mack Smith appeared at his elbow.

"Hey, Colonel," said Mack. "Try the monkey brains yet?"

"Mack. Where the hell have you been since last night?"

"You told me to make nice with the political types. I have been. Me and the sultan's nephew are like that."

He twisted his fingers together.

"Which nephew?" asked Dog.

"Unofficial head of the air force. Catch up with you in a bit," said Mack, sliding away. Colonel Bastian started to take a step after him, but Miss Kelly grabbed him.

Not particularly gently, either.

"Eat," she whispered.

"You and my grandmother have a lot in common," said Dog.

"I hope that's a compliment."

Dog smiled at the latest waiter, taking a plate from him. This time the intricate creation—it was a collection of fruit in a tiny cup made from rice—tasted so delicious he actually wanted another. But apparently the protocol didn't allow for seconds; he needed to try as many dishes as possible.

"You're doing great, Colonel," said Miss Kelly.

"If I don't like it, what happens?"

"They chop off the cook's head," she said.

Dog thought it was a joke, but he wasn't positive.

"I have someone you have to meet, Colonel," said Mack, tugging slightly at his arm.

Dog turned. A youngish, slightly paunchy man wearing a perfectly tailored suit smiled and bowed his head. Dog bowed back, noticing the man's large black opal pinkie ring and his thick Rolex.

"His Royal Highness Pehin bin Awg," whispered Miss Kelly, a second before Mack could. "The sultan's nephew. Unofficial head of the air force."

"Your Highness," said Dog.

"Colonel Bastian. We have heard much about you and your squadron," said bin Awg. "We are extremely impressed, and deeply honored to have you in our kingdom."

"The pleasure's ours, I assure you," Dog told him. "I'm glad that we could assist in the ASEAN exercises."

"Most delightful," said bin Awg.

"Pehin's a collector," said Mack.

Dog saw Miss Kelly stiffen. She had explained yesterday that "Pehin" wasn't a name but rather an honorific used by important members of the government. But bin Awg ignored the faux pas, smiling and tilting his head.

"I have a few old airplanes," said bin Awg. "It's a hobby."

"I see," said Dog. "What sort of airplanes?"

"You'll have to come see for yourself."

"I hope to," said Dog.

"Hell, Colonel, Pehin's got two MiG-19s, a MiG-21 from Yugoslavia, a Mirage III—piece of shit, take it from me—and, get this, a Badger. A Badger, Colonel."

"Nice," said Dog. He could practically feel the killer stare Miss Kelly was laying on Mack.

"I have been fortunate in finding old wrecks and restoring them," said bin Awg modestly. "I also have a Catalina flying boat. A handsome aircraft as built, and I have added a few modern amenities. I've offered Major Smith the chance to fly some of my fleet," added the prince. "Perhaps you would care to as well."

"I'd love to," said Dog. "When I get a chance. You really have an old MiG-19?"

"Yes, yes. The North Koreans will sell anything for food these days. It was in reasonable repair— if one overlooks the fact that it did not have an engine."

"I told the prince he and his uncle could come up in a Megafortress for a spin tomorrow," said Mack. "They're psyched."

It took every ounce of Dog's restraint not to slap his erstwhile political officer across the face.

"Mack, let's talk for a second," he told Smith. "Excuse us, Your Highness."

He took two steps backward. Miss Kelly stepped forward to chat with the prince, who sampled some of the food in Dog's place.

"Are you out of your mind?" Dog asked Mack.

"Why?"

"We're not here as part of a carnival show. We have a mission."

"Yeah, but Miss State Department Bombshell says we're supposed to make nice," said Mack. "That's what I'm doing."

"Bin Awg is head of the air force?"

"Unofficially," said Mack. "He's more a consultant. See, the sultan is the head of the military forces. Then there are the professional officers and whatnot. My buddy Pehin is kinda between them and his uncle. Haven't seen him fly yet. Great guy. Knows where the best clubs are. Doesn't drink— that's his only flaw."

"Mack, you're supposed to improve relations, not threaten them."

"I am. So what do you say? We take him up for a spin in the morning? Morning's around noon here, if you get my drift."

"Both planes are taking off at 0700 tomorrow," Dog told Mack. "There's no time for a demonstration flight tomorrow."

"Next day then," said Mack. "Hey, Zen brought his nuggets with him. Hey, boys."

As Mack walked off, Dog reminded himself that he had personally tagged the major to come along. While he'd made the choice largely because Mack was one of the few officers at Dreamland he could actually spare for a do-nothing job, it was nonetheless a decision that could not be cited as one of his best. Smith was an excellent pilot, but outside of the cockpit, he was a class-one boob.

Dog turned back to find bin Awg talking up Miss Kelly, who was flashing her full smile on him.

"We are very much in the mind frame of expanding our air force," said the prince. "At present we have the Hawk 100s and 200s but, well, without disparaging our British friends—I fear the ambassador is within earshot—we are certainly in the market for upgrades."

"We use a version of the Hawk ourselves," said Dog. "It's a competent aircraft."

"Yes, the Goshawk T-45A, as a trainer for the Navy," said bin Awg. "Very suitable in that role. But as compared to an F/A-18 or a Mikoyan MiG-29 . . . Well, Colonel, I leave the judgment to you."

"You're thinking of buying Russian planes?" asked Miss Kelly.

Bin Awg smiled apologetically. "They are so desperate for hard currency these days that the price can be very attractive."

"I'd think there'd be no comparison between the F/A-18 and a MiG-29," said Dog.

Again, the prince flashed his apologetic smile. "The difficulty is perhaps with the export regulations. Sometimes these are not easily overcome."

"Have you considered F-16s?" asked Miss Kelly.

"An admirable design," said the prince.

"Better than the MiG," said Dog.

"Yes," said bin Awg. "To be candid with you, Colonel, our true desire is for an aircraft with much longer range. The F-15; that would be most desirable."

"It is a good aircraft," said Dog.

It was also a difficult one to obtain; Congress didn't relish the idea of the country's frontline fighter serving under other flags. Only the Japanese,

Israelis, and Saudis had been allowed to buy it, and in each case the decision involved considerable political wrangling.

"We are very much in the market for aircraft," said bin Awg. "Perhaps we can talk tomorrow, when we are aboard the Megafortress."

"I'm afraid we're not going to be available for a flight tomorrow," said Dog as apologetically as he could. "We have orders from Washington to have both aircraft in the exercises. I'm sorry."

The barest flicker of displeasure passed over the prince's face.

"I'm afraid Major Smith made the commitment without checking with me," added Dog.

"A raincheck perhaps," said the prince.

"Definitely," said Dog. "Definitely.

ZEN LISTENED TO THE AUSTRALIAN AMBASSADOR lecturing on the weakness of China.

"A few cruisers and a pair of submarines could hold the communists at bay," said the diplomat. "They're a shadow of themselves. A shadow of a shadow. That's why they're willing to talk to Taiwan. Their day is over."

Zen had everything he could do to keep from rolling his eyes. Granted, Mainland China had suffered some reverses over the past few months; the country remained a potent military force. Forget the ghost clone: It had several hundred more aircraft than the ambassador's country, along with several new pocket aircraft carriers capable of projecting power throughout the region. Toss in cruise missiles, nuclear submarines, and undoubtedly a long-range bomber or two that the intelligence boys hadn't caught on to yet, and you had a serious military power.

Not quite in America's class, but nasty nonetheless.

Shadow indeed.

Stoner, standing across from Zen, nodded like a metronome as the ambassador continued.

Finally, Zen could take no more and wheeled himself away.

He found Kick standing by himself at the edge of one of the tables.

"Hello, Lieutenant," he said to the Flighthawk pilot. "Where's your partner in crime? Did he leave to catch up on his beauty rest?"

"Yeah right," said Kick.

"You don't like Lieutenant Starship?" asked Zen.

"He's all right," said Kick. "I think he headed out with Mack."

Zen asked for a fruit drink from the waiter behind the table. There was no alcohol at the event; Brunei was an Islamic nation, and the sultan was a devout believer who would not have countenanced a violation of his religious principles.

"You sore because Starship is going to take the decoy flight tomorrow?" asked Zen.

"No, sir."

Zen smiled at the obvious lie.

"It's all right to be pissed," he told the lieutenant. "If I were in your shoes, I'd be mad too. Come to think of it, I have been in your shoes. And I was pissed."

Kick seemed surprised by Zen's response and

looked at him as if trying to figure out whether he was being tested. "Starship's background with the F-15s means he has a little more experience. Right?"

"Just a little. You'll catch up."

Zen took a sip of his drink. Maybe, he thought, there was something more, something in their personalities. It seemed to him Kick was trying hard to be nice. He wouldn't have.

Maybe that was all for show. Make nice to the boss.

"How's your wife?" asked the lieutenant, trying to change the subject.

"Don't know. She's sleeping every time I call her," said Zen.

"How's the punch?" asked Stoner, coming over.

"It's punch," said Zen. "You agree with that crap the Australian was putting out?"

"Of course not," said Stoner, taking a drink for himself.

"You didn't argue with him," said Zen.

"You think I could have changed his mind?"

Zen shrugged, though of course he didn't.

"If I don't listen to what people tell me, I won't know what they're thinking," said Stoner. "It's useful."

"Man, I could never be a spy," said Zen.

"Some of us are just born slimy," said Stoner, his voice deadpan. "Right, Lieutenant?"

"I wouldn't know, sir."

Stoner looked down at Zen, smirking. Despite the fact that he still didn't like the SOB, even Zen had to laugh along with him.

Dreamland
0500

JENNIFER LAY ON THE COUCH, WATCHING AS THE CHAN-
nels on her television clicked by, a mélange of in-
fomercials, talking heads, and crashes filling the
screen. She had been here for an hour or so, unable
to sleep, not really up to leaving the apartment for
her usual early-morning run. She was still locked
out of her computers, and it seemed pointless to go
anywhere or do anything.

Finally she saw the start of an old Warner Bros.
Bugs Bunny cartoon and stopped. She observed sci-
entifically as Bugs made his way out of the hole and
began tormenting Elmer Fudd.

Wabbits. He sounded a bit like Ray.

But at least Rubeo had been fighting for her.
He'd told Cortend exactly what he thought. More
than she could say about any of her other so-called
friends.

The phone rang.

Maybe it was Dog, calling to see how she was. If
it was, did she want to talk to him? Why should she?
What could he possibly say?

The phone stopped. She waited a minute, then
picked it up and checked her voice mail system.

No message.

Jennifer turned back to the TV just in time to see
Fudd blast himself with his own shotgun.

She felt so sorry for him she started to cry.

Brunei IAP, Field Seven
Dreamland Mobile Command Post
11 September 1997
0710

DOG, ZEN, ALOU, AND STONER PREVIEWED THE MIS-sion together, reviewing the latest intelligence from the States as well as Dreamland and the ASEAN flag staff. Two dozen ASEAN ships, mostly frigates and destroyers, would track the progress of a pair of Australian submarines across a swatch of ocean nearly twelve hundred miles wide over the course of the next few days. The exercises today were being conducted in an area two hundred miles east of the Vietnamese coast; besides the allied vessels, the Chinese had two trawler-type spy ships in the vicinity, as well as a submarine. Further to the north but still in the open sea, the Russians were expected to fly a long-range surveillance aircraft; they had done so yesterday, following the progress of the exercises. There were also a number of civilian flights and merchant vessels that would routinely ply the area.

"Flight plan is basic. We come up, rendezvous with the frigates, then keep going. Stop short of Hainan, we do a square out and catch the clone in the flat," said Zen. "*Penn* rides just to our half of the international side of the property line to make sure we have their attention. *Raven* and the Flighthawk with the passive sensor set are out in the flat, waiting for the lateral here to the West."

"Who's got the blitz?" asked Dog.

"We audible that at the line," said Alou, not missing a beat.

"The Chinese may or may not pick up the U/MF that launches from *Penn* on their radar," said Zen, getting the hint and dropping the football metaphors. He pointed to the radar installation on the southern tip of the island. "Starship will pull around here and throw off some chaff so he's visible on radar. Once they know he's there, he heads southeast and launches the dummied-up Hellfire. It transmits and you track it a bit, Colonel. Basically orbit around for an hour, which should give them time to get the clone over in our direction."

"They may send fighters if you get this close," warned Stoner. "The Chinese aren't known for subtlety."

"I've gone through it with my guys. They know to ignore the fighters," said Zen. They were standing in the main room of the Whiplash security trailer, which doubled as a home-away-from-home sit room. Live connections to Dreamland, and from there to the rest of the world, were just a hot key away. "Only way we're going to get their attention is if we're obnoxious."

"If it's Chinese, yes," said Stoner.

"Only one way to find out," said Dog. "Are you sure your guys can handle the decoy?" he asked Zen. Neither of the new Flighthawk pilots had ever seen combat.

"All they have to do is fire the missile and hang on. We're starting them off slow," said Zen.

"Slow to us, but not the Chinese," said Stoner.

"Hainan is part of their country. It would be like going over Staten Island."

"Worse case, Starship puts the Flighthawk on automatic and follows *Raven* home. Merce'll kick them in the butt if they screw up," added Zen, nodding to Major Alou.

"I don't think I'll have to," said Alou.

"I'll be watching from *Raven*. All they have to do is yell for help."

Dog looked over the charts. Hainan was a large island below the Chinese Mainland across from northern Vietnam; its western shores edged the Gulf of Tonkin. The clone had appeared to the southeast of Hainan on the earlier mission. Zen and Stoner were theorizing that the clone was based northeast of there, and so its flight path would inevitably cross close to *Raven*.

The techies had made a few small tweaks to *Raven*'s Elint gear to optimize gathering in the frequencies the clone appeared to use. *Raven* should be able to detect and record transmissions at about two hundred miles, which would allow it to get plenty of data without having to go over Chinese territory. Of course, there was no real way of knowing how far its net would truly extend until the clone appeared.

Dog looked down at the charts, sorting out possible bases. Southern China was regularly covered by a variety of systems, from optical satellites to RC-135 launcher trackers. How could a UAV base be missed or overlooked?

"What if this came off a ship?" he said.

"The Chinese carriers were under surveillance the whole time," said Zen.

"Not a carrier," said Dog. He leaned over the map, practically putting his face on it. "There were plenty of ships that would be within range."

"Their destroyers, their patrol ships—everything was covered," said Zen. "The Navy wouldn't miss something like that."

"What if you launched from a civilian ship?" asked Dog. "Is it possible?"

"You tell me," said Stoner.

"You'd need some sort of catapult system," said Zen. "Even then, it might be hard. One of the reasons the Flighthawks are air-launched is the stealthy characteristics would make it difficult for them to get airborne in a short distance. Besides, those other ships are not Chinese."

"Maybe it's not Chinese," said Stoner.

"You could overcome the launch limitations," said Dog. "Part of the reason the Flighthawks are air-launched has to do with their mission, working with EB-52s. There are other ways to go."

"Sure," said Zen. "Hell, anything's possible, at least until we see what we're dealing with."

"Well, hopefully that happens today. You coming with us?" Dog asked Stoner.

"I have some people to talk to here," said Stoner. "Zen said he didn't need me."

"I got it covered."

Zen and Stoner still weren't getting along, although to their credit they hadn't let whatever personal animosity was between them get in the way of the mission.

Yet.

Colonel Bastian checked his watch. It wasn't quite seven-thirty A.M. here, which would make it about 1530 or three-thirty in the afternoon the day before back home. He needed to check in with a whole roster of people back at Dreamland—Major Catsman, Ax, Danny Freah, and Rubeo—before the flight briefings. He was also supposed to update Jed Barclay, though that could wait until he was aboard *Raven*.

He also wanted to give Jennifer another try. She hadn't answered any of his calls.

"Are we set?" Zen asked.

Dog took another look at the map. It bothered him that he had an inexperienced man running the Flighthawk that would cross over Chinese territory, but tracking the clone definitely called for someone of Zen's skill. And the EB-52s had different specialties, so they couldn't be easily swapped.

The thing to do, Colonel Bastian realized, was to switch places with Alou. This way, if things got too hairy with the Chinese in the early going, he'd be there to take care of it.

Made sense. He ought to be the guy with his neck on the line.

"I'm going to take *Penn*," he told Alou. "We'll swap seats. I want my neck on the line up there if we're flying that close to China."

"Your call, Colonel," said Alou. "One way or the other's fine with me."

Dog nodded. Alou was typical of a certain type of officer common in the Air Force. Easygoing and generally quiet, they were pros who tended to do their jobs without much flash or complaint. They didn't have the balls-out aggressive manner of a Mack Smith or a Zen before his accident—or even a Colonel Bastian, for that matter. But their steady approach and calm demeanor would generally carry the day when the mud hit the fan. Most of them, certainly Alou, didn't lack for personal courage; they just didn't strut about it.

"All right," Dog said. "I have to go talk to the folks at home. I'll see you in a half hour or so."

Aboard the *Dragon Prince*, South China Sea
0806

CHEN LO FANN GRIPPED THE SIDE OF THE SEAT AS THE small helicopter pivoted toward the fantail of the trawler. The Messerschmidt-Bölkow-Blohm 108 settled into a hover about a foot and a half above the deck of the ship. Chen Lo Fann nodded to the pilot, then undid his seat belt and opened the door, holding himself precariously as the wash from the overhead blades beat the salty air against him. It was just a bit too high to step down comfortably; with as much patience as he could muster, Chen Lo Fann took hold of the side of the plane and lowered himself carefully to the deck. He ducked away; the pilot in the aircraft waited until one of the crew members waved, then he revved the rotor, lifting and speeding off, flying back in the direction he had come.

The captain of the ship met Chen Lo Fann with a salute, though Fann had told him many times that was unnecessary. After a brief report that basically repeated everything he had already been told, Fann followed the captain downstairs to the command post for the robot plane.

Professor Ai met him at the door.

"Commander," said the professor. Despite his age, his manner was humble, a sign of respect not for Chen Lo Fann himself, but for his grandfather. Chen Lo Fann knew this and accepted it as proper.

"There is news?"

"Much," said Ai. He explained what he had observed from the encounter between the communists and the Megafortress the day before.

"They are due in a few hours," said Ai. "The Australians were checking a position with another ship. The communist dogs will react again. One of their patrols will come south. If their instruments are confused, an accident is inevitable," Ai said. "If we use the repeater devices aboard the UAV to blind and confuse the mongrels, it may be possible—"

"An accident will not give us the provocation we need," said Chen Lo Fann. "The Americans must attack the Chinese, or vice versa. Both must be convinced that the other started the conflict. It must be done quickly."

"That will not be easy."

"Whether it is easy or not, it will be done."

"Yes," said Professor Ai.

Brunei IAP
1000

MACK SMITH THOUGHT BIN AWG WAS A BIT OF A blowhard—albeit a rich one who didn't mind spending his money—but his opinion changed the moment he stood under the nose of the Tu-16 Badger C.

At that moment, he became convinced that the prince was one of the most generous and wonderful human beings on the planet, with a connoisseur's eye for vintage aircraft.

A one-time member of the Aviatsiya Voenno-Morskovo Flota—the Soviet naval aviation branch—the aircraft had had a rather checkered history after being decommissioned sometime in the 1980s. It had flown briefly with the Polish air force, put in a few months in East Germany (where it had allegedly worked as a weather plane, according to the somewhat unbelievable records supplies to bin Awg; more likely it was some sort of spy plane), and finally been "loaned" to Indonesia as part of a program by the Soviets to convince that country to purchase updates for its twenty-two-member fleet of Badger Bs. When the loan period ended, a series of complicated financial dealings resulted in the plane being deeded to the Indonesian air force, which then put it up for sale as surplus material.

It was at that point that bin Awg had obtained it, and after considerable time and expense restored it to 1961 condition. Though technically part of the Brunei Air Force—it had military insignia—it was in fact one of the prince's private airplanes, and not included in the regular chain of command or inventory.

The design of the Tu-16 dated to the early 1950s, and in fact some elements owed their origin to the Tu-4, a Russian knockoff of the American B-29 Superfortress, the famous aircraft that had helped win World War II. Though only a little more than half the size of a Megafortress, the plane was *large*—its wings spanned a nudge over 108 feet, and a tape measure pegged from nose to cannon tip at the tail would notch over 114 feet. (Before being refurbished as a Megafortress, a B-52 spanned 185 feet and measured 160; Megafortresses typically added ten to the length but shaved off an even two with the composite wings. The real difference was in potential weight at takeoff; a Badger might tip the scales—and just make it off the ground—at 167,110 pounds; a B-52 could get up with over 500,000 and an EB-52 with even more, though it rarely was configured with that much weight. The Tu-16 might be more favorably compared to a B-47, another Cold War veteran that served as a medium bomber in the American order of battle.)

Mack didn't particularly like the Megafortress and had turned down an offer to become a pilot in the program. But that didn't mean that he didn't appreciate old birds, and standing beneath the Russian Cold War bomber, he felt something like love.

Lust, really, since Miss Kelly was coming along for the flight. She had a nice hourglass thing going on with khaki pants and a button-down shirt that might have been just a size too small.

"Look at those engines," said Mack, belatedly turning away to pat the air intake cowling of the Mikulin RD-3M turbo. "This sucker is a serious hot rod."

"It does look big," said Miss Kelly doubtfully.

"Come on, let's go up inside her," said Mack.

"Shouldn't we wait for the prince?"

"He'll catch up. Come on. We won't break anything."

The boarding ladder extended just in front of the forward landing gear, opening into a typically barebones Soviet-era cockpit. There were three seats on the flight deck—a swivel seat belonging to the forward gunner was mounted in front of the electronic gear racks at the rear of the deck—with a station for a radar navigator-bombardier in the nose.

At the center of the flight deck was an observation roof or "astrodome." Behind this on the upper fuselage sat a pair of 23mm cannons; two other sets of the antiair guns were included in turrets in the belly and tail. The original model included another cannon in the nose—it wasn't clear whether the designers had intended this for strafing or dogfighting, neither of which the plane would have been very good at. Bin Awg's modifications had removed it; the space was needed for the updated avionics and radar gear.

Had the Badger been left completely stock, the nav's seat up front in the nose would have seemed more than a little claustrophobic. Not only did he have to squeeze under the pilot and copilot to get into the compartment, but in the C model the forward-looking radar blocked off the view. But the prince's updates enabled a different radar to be used and installed in the chin area; to replace it in the nose he had purchased a glass house from the Chinese, who were still making their own version of the plane, dubbed the Xian H-6. The navigator thus had the best seat in the house.

Mack pointed this out and eagerly helped Miss Kelly slide down and into the seat. She had just gotten snugged in when the prince climbed aboard, dressed in his flight gear; he wore a G suit despite the fact that the cabin was completely pressurized.

"Major, very good. And you have our guest installed."

"Your Highness," said Mack. "Ready to rock?"

"Yes," said the prince, his tone slightly distant. He moved forward and took the pilot's seat—a slight disappointment for Mack, who nonetheless slid into the copilot's slot. The sultan's nephew pulled out a clipboard and began working through an extremely lengthy checklist.

And working. And working. He didn't merely turn a switch on; he found it, touched it, double-checked it against the list, made sure he knew all the positions, tentatively checked to see that all the selectable positions were indeed selectable, consulted the list, put the switch into the proper detent, re-checked it, went back to the list, nodded to himself, then penciled it off before proceeding.

Understandable for a complex dial, perhaps, but a bit much for a simple two-way toggle. Especially given the thick sheaf of procedures he had to work through.

"Can't beat these old planes," said Mack, hoping to hurry him along.

The prince smiled indulgently.

"We taking off soon?"

"In good time, Major. We plan the flight, then fly the plan."

"Well, sure."

They'd done that earlier, actually, but the prince saw fit to do it again. He was a demon of a partier, but when it came to aircraft, there was not a more careful or conservative man in the world. Mack tried to get involved in the checklist as an ordinary copilot—though his intention really was to hurry the procedure along—but the prince considered it mostly a solo act. Mack had everything he could do to keep from nodding off until the engines finally spooled up.

As the old red dog nudged along the runway, Mack felt his pulse rate start to climb. It didn't hurt that Miss Kelly chose that moment to twist back toward the flight deck, exposing a good portion of cleavage.

"This is it," she said giddily.

"Yeah," said Mack. "It really is."

Aboard *Raven*, over the South China Sea
1153

ZEN SAT BACK IN HIS SEAT ABOARD *RAVEN*, WATCHING the diagnostics screen fly by as the prelaunch checklist for the U/MF-3 Flighthawk continued. The words HAWK ONE READY flashed on his screen. By convention, the robot aircraft was dubbed "*Hawk One.*" Each U/MF in the air was called "Hawk" and numbered by the computer system, generally by launch sequence. The green color-coded screen told Zen that everything was optimum and routine.

But not for him. For Zen was actually sitting in an aircraft twenty miles from the plane preparing to launch *Hawk One.* The robot's mother ship was

Penn; its pilot was Starship, who had just finished the preflight check without help from Zen. Zen felt a bit like an anxious father, watching his son take his bike out for the first time without training wheels.

Zen still wasn't quite used to watching while others flew the Flighthawks. He'd never be used to it, to be honest.

Even worse, he'd lost his last protégé, Captain Kevin Fentress, over this very ocean not two weeks before.

Fentress was good, too good to lose. Zen had ridden him hard, much harder than Starship and Kick. He wanted to think it had made a difference.

Had it, though?

Maybe. Part of the reason he'd ridden him, and he had to be honest with himself about it, was that he was jealous of the kid—Fentress could get up and walk away at the end of a flight, something he'd never be able to do again.

He was jealous of Stoner too, for the same reason.

"*Hawk One* away," said Starship.

"Roger that," said Zen, watching the optical feed. The computer showed the aircraft in good mettle, systems in the green, course perfect.

"Looking good, *Hawk One*," he told Starship.

"Thanks, big guy."

Aboard *Penn*, over the South China Sea
1213

WEATHER WAS CLEAR, VISIBILITY UNLIMITED. HE DIDN'T even have a hangover. Starship couldn't be happier.

Well, Kick could be back home or in the other plane. That would make him happier.

"*Hawk One*, be advised we have a pair of Chinese Sukhois, that would be J-11s similar to Su-27s, coming south toward the task force," said the plane's copilot, Captain McNamara. He gave their bearing, altitude, and approximate speed; the figures were duped on the display. If he changed course slightly he could intercept them in roughly five minutes.

"Hold your present course, *Hawk One*," said Zen from the other plane, as if reading his mind.

Starship acknowledged, though he chafed a bit. He really didn't appreciate having a babysitter.

"Looks like they want to see how low the Aussies can track them," said Kick. The J-11 pilots had tickled their afterburners and plunged toward the waves, riding down in an extremely low-level track; so low, in fact, that Starship wasn't entirely sure the Russian-made fighters weren't skipping on the water.

HMAS *Maryborough* was one of Australia's finest destroyers, an American-built ship of the Oliver Hazard Perry class. Outfitted very close to the American standard, the *Maryborough* packed a competent Mk 13 SAM system; its SM-1MR missiles could take out a target at twenty-five nautical miles, but was arguably better at defending against medium- and high-altitude attacks than the wave-top dash the Sukhois were attempting. While it was academic—the Australians weren't about to fire at the Chinese planes—it did make for an interesting few minutes.

"I'm amazed they're not flaming out," said Kick,

monitoring the Chinese hot dogs from his screen. "The radar says they're six feet above the water. They're going to slam into the hulls of the ship if they're not careful."

"They'll pull up, watch," said Starship. They did—though a little later than he thought, the lead plane ripping so close to the *Maryborough*'s antenna mast that it undoubtedly wobbled in the wake.

"They're out of their minds," said Kick.

"Typical Chinese bullshit," said Zen from *Raven*.

"Gentlemen, let me remind you we are supposed to be flying silent com," said Colonel Bastian from the pilot's seat of the *Pennsylvania*. "Please keep unnecessary chatter to a minimum. We have twenty-five minutes to the start of the show."

**Aboard Brunei Badger 01,
over the South China Sea
1230**

THEY WERE WITHIN VISUAL RANGE OF THE ASEAN TASK force—cleared to fly above courtesy of the prince's rank and their theoretical status as members of the Brunei air force—before Mack got a chance to take the helm, but as soon as he did he started making up for lost time. After a bit of straight and level to get the feel of the plane—sucker flew like a big ol' Caddy, fins and all—Mack decided to see how good a job the riveters had done lashing the Soviet metal together.

"Hang on," he said, and he tipped his right wing and slid the big Russian bomber downward. It didn't quite knife through the air—the action was a bit more like an ax head hurtling down a slope—but after the relatively placid flight north it felt like a roller coaster. Mack rode the plane down through fifteen thousand feet before rocking level.

His nose started to float up as he tried to put her into a hard turn—it was a big plane, and the hydraulic controls felt very different from the fly-by-wire gear he spent most of his time with. But a sigh from Miss Kelly over the interphone circuit chased off any hint of doubt; Mack tensed his biceps and the big plane moved smartly through the sky, right where he wanted her.

"That boat looks so small," said Miss Kelly. "What a view."

Mack's view—both of the ocean and of Miss Kelly—was not nearly as expansive as he would have liked, but it would do. The Thai destroyer she admired was off his right wing, bow nudging away the swells.

"We are in an exercise area," said the prince. "We must be careful."

"Not a problem," said Mack. "You think we can make it through a roll?"

And without waiting for an answer, he flicked the stick—well, more like leaned on the old-fashioned wheel yoke that served as a stick—and pushed the big old bomber through an invert.

**Aboard *Raven*, over the South China Sea
1233**

ZEN DOUBLE-CHECKED THEIR POSITIONS ON THE SITREP in his flight helmet, then flipped the main view back to the feed from the nose of *Hawk Two*, the Flighthawk still sitting under *Raven*'s wing. The computer had finished the prelaunch check and was holding.

"Hawk leader, we're ready when you are," radioed Dog from the *Pennsylvania*.

"Hawk leader copies," said Zen. "*Hawk One*? Status?"

"On course. Twenty minutes from alpha point," said Starship. Alpha was an arbitrary spot sixty seconds from Chinese territorial water where Starship would start his dance.

"Hawk leader copies. *Raven*?"

"*Raven* is ready. We'll initiate launch maneuver at your command."

"Hawk leader copies."

A quick glance at the instrument panel. Green, green, green. You could write a tech manual using these readings.

"Initiate launch maneuver."

"*Raven*," said Major Alou, piloting the plane. The mother ship began a gentle dive, which increased the separation forces as the Flighthawk was launched. Zen turned over control to C^3, authorizing the launch—standard practice—and waited as the EB-52 nosed downward, picking up momentum.

And then he was in the air, speeding away, going through a system check, nudging the Flighthawk out ahead of the EB-52. He climbed upward, the blue bulb of heaven spreading out around him. Major Stockard was sitting in a seat in the bay of the massive Megafortress, but his mind soared through thirty thousand feet, climbing up over the shimmering Pacific, looking down at the world as God looked down on His universe.

Upstairs on the flight deck, the Megafortress crew quickly ran through their own checks, making sure the electronics link between the two planes was at spec. The pod the Flighthawk carried was a shallow, rectangular box fitted under the fuselage area; it looked a bit like a sculpted pizza carrier. Most of what was in the pod were small but powerful amplifiers, tuned to work with a specific set of signals picked up by an antenna (actually a matrix of antennas generally spoken of as one) that would be cranked out of a second box that looked like a parachute pack at the rear of the small plane. The pack and antennas changed the flight characteristics of the aircraft, though C^3 had been programmed to compensate so well that Zen wouldn't "feel" a difference unless he put the small plane through some very hard maneuvers. The antenna and its filament mesh stretched nearly one hundred yards and could be jettisoned by verbal command.

A series of test tones shot back and forth as the techies upstairs took the measure of their gear. Satisfied that they had a good feed, Zen leveled his Flighthawk off at 39,573 feet and opened up the antenna. *Raven* began tracking slightly east, anticipating the Flighthawk's turn once it reached their target orbit.

"Hawk leader, we are zero-five from alpha," said Dog. "Looking for a go–no go."

"Roger that," said Zen.

He clicked the interphone and queried *Penn*'s radio operators to make sure they were set. Alou and his copilot, meanwhile, completed a weapons check, making sure they were prepared for the worst.

"*Hawk One* is at alpha," said Starship.

"Roger that," Zen acknowledged. "Colonel, we're go."

"Let's do it, gentlemen," said Dog. "*Raven*, you're silent com. Talk to you guys when we all get home."

**Aboard Brunei Badger 01,
over the South China Sea
1244**

"WELL, MAJOR, YOU'RE AN EXCELLENT PILOT," SAID THE prince as Mack finally relinquished the controls for the trek back. "I must say, you put this old plane through its paces."

"Ah, you should see me in an F-22," Mack told him. "But I like this old plane. Solid. Big. Solid."

He saw Miss Kelly looking back at him and smiling. He gave her a big Mack Smith smile, then checked his watch.

They'd be back just in time for cocktails at the club the prince had taken him to last night.

Delightful.

Mack took off his headset and loosened his restraints, thinking he'd stretch his legs a bit. But as he started to get up, the prince put his hand out.

"Wait, please," said bin Awg. The indulgent smile he had worn constantly since Mack met him had drained from his face. Mack slid back into his seat and grabbed his headset in time to hear a position and a vector.

"Chinese planes," explained the prince. "J-11 interceptors coming south toward the exercise area." He reached to the side and pulled up a flight board, handing it to Mack. "Major, please, if you could check our fuel situation. I believe sheet two would be appropriate," he added, referring to one of the matrixes that showed how much flying time the plane had left for different flight regimes. "I would like to show these Chinese pilots that the Brunei air force is not entirely without representation in the area."

"Sounds good to me," said Mack, snugging his seat belt.

Aboard *Penn*, over the South China Sea
1244

DOG GLANCED AT THE MULTIUSE DISPLAY ON HIS LEFT, which was set as a sitrep to show the position of the Megafortress and its Flighthawk, as well as any other aircraft nearby. The Flighthawk was about a quarter of a mile from Chinese airspace south of Yulin on Hainan, just completing a turn to the east after discharging a packet of electronic tinsel, or chaff, which could be easily detected on the Chinese radar. They'd launch the Hellfire in sixty seconds.

"J-11s are running south toward the Australian

frigate," said the copilot, Captain McNamara, relaying word from the radar operator. "Another one of their mock attacks."

"They'll have to fend for themselves," said Dog. "I'm more worried about that civilian," he added, referring to a small private plane flying at about twelve thousand feet on almost the exact path the Flighthawk was taking. "I don't want to hit him with the missile."

"Shouldn't come close," replied McNamara.

"*Hawk One*, this is *Penn*," Dog said. "Ready to make your run?"

"Yes, sir."

"You see that civilian?"

"Oh yeah."

"Delay your event for ninety seconds."

"*Hawk One*," acknowledged the pilot.

The RWR panel on the Megafortress buzzed as one of the self-defense units on the island switched on radar used to guide Hongqi-2B missiles, a Chinese surface-to-air missile that was essentially an upgraded version of the Russian V-75 SA-2. The weapons system was potent but fairly well understood by American analysts and easily defeated by the onboard ECMs, or electronic countermeasures, carried by *Penn*.

But that wasn't why they were here.

"Looks like we have their attention," said Dog. "Radio the flight information back to the ASEAN ships over the clear channel," he added. *Raven* was monitoring the frequency and would hear the information.

"I'm being tracked," said Starship. His voice

sounded less haughty than it customarily did—but only slightly.

"Steady as you go," said Dog. "Let's get that civilian out of the way, then fire your missile as planned. Be very careful of your position."

"Yes, sir."

Brunei
1245

STONER GOT INTO THE CAR AND GAVE THE DRIVER THE address, settling back in the seat as they headed toward the outskirts of the capital, Bandar Seri Begawan. The day had started steamy and was now as hot and muggy as a Finnish sauna; the Toyota's air-conditioner was cranked, but Stoner's white shirt was still pasted against his neck.

Oil had made the kingdom prosperous over the past decade or so, but in some respects Brunei remained unchanged. The spirit of the people was still generous and reverent; Islam gave the society an ordered and calm quality. Even in the city, the population was relatively small, especially for Asia; the crowds that were familiar in Hong Kong or Beijing, for instance, were missing here.

They turned up a road that bordered on the jungle and stopped in front of a large, white building. Stoner got out, told the driver that he would be back, and walked inside. The man at the security desk took his name, then made a phone call. His Malay was so quick and accented that Stoner couldn't follow what he was saying, though he assumed he was calling the man he'd come to see, John Conrad.

"You will wait," the man told him.

Stoner nodded. In a few minutes, a large Anglo with a very bright red face rushed into the reception area, nearly out of breath.

"Conrad," he said. "You're Stoner?"

The CIA officer nodded.

"Ah, good. Come with me. We're off."

"Off?"

"We've got to get to Kampung Ayer," he said in a thick and proper English accent. "That's where our acquaintance is."

A few minutes later, Stoner found himself in the stern of a small water taxi, speeding toward the floating island that lay in the mouth of the capital, an ancient tongue stuck in the ocean's shallow bay. Built largely on stilts, the water village, a maze of wooden promenades and buildings lashed together with thin ropes, was home to more than thirty thousand people. The air had a pungent odor; the water went from deep blue to an almost coppery red as they drew closer to the village.

Conrad gave the taxi operator a few directions and they began threading their way through a narrow lagoon. Two turns later, they stopped in front of a large white structure that looked like an American double-wide trailer. The rusted tin roof boasted two large satellite dishes at its apex.

"Off we go," said Conrad.

Stoner got out. The taxi backed up and sped off.

"We'll get another, don't worry, old chap. Plenty hereabouts."

The two men walked up the plankway to the building. Stoner was surprised to find a cool interior and a thick, new-looking carpet. A young man sat at a desk that could have been a reception area at a better doctor's office in the U.S.

"Cheese in?"

"Ah yes, Mr. Conrad. Please go."

Stoner followed Conrad through the door into what looked like a small den. A large TV screen filled one side; CNBC was on. Near the television a man in shorts and T-shirt sat on a leather couch, a phone at his ear. He had a pair of laptops out—one on the floor, one next to him on the couch. Conrad pushed over a large chair for Stoner, then got another for himself. The man on the phone—Cheese—continued to talk for a while, mentioning some sort of stock he wanted to short—then finally concluded the conversation.

"Listen, I got to go," he told whoever was on the other line. "I have MI6 and the CIA sitting in my office. Yeah, looks like I got big trouble."

He punched the phone, then rose, jabbing his hand toward Stoner. "James Milach. They call me Cheese because I made a killing in Kraft. No shit."

Stoner shook his hand. "Stoner."

"Beefeater told me. You figure it out yet?" he added, turning toward Conrad.

"Still working on it."

"Thinks he may be related to Conrad, the author. Except what he doesn't know is, Conrad was Polish," said Cheese, sitting back on his couch.

"There is a possibility I'm related," Conrad told Stoner. "And the author traveled through here. I, of course, was raised in London. Unlike Cheese, who is so obviously an American. Though he has settled in rather well."

Cheese wasn't paying attention. He looked at the laptop, then studied the stock screen at the bottom of the TV. "I hate these stinking time delays."

"I've been trying to come up with a list of chip fabricators," Stoner said. "Ones that are active in Asia, that have custom capabilities but would work quietly for another country. I've looked into official sites, but I'm told that—"

"Yeah, yeah, I know. Beefeater told me all about it. I can help. Hang tight a sec, okay?"

Cheese grabbed his phone and quickly punched a combination of numbers. "Hey, screw what I told you yesterday. Dump 'em. Yeah. I don't care. Buy IBM or Intel. Whatever. Just do it. Quick."

"Cheese spends an inordinate time thrashing about in the stock market," said Conrad.

"Why don't you just use your laptop and make your own trades?" Stoner asked.

"Oh, I do. But sometimes when you want to make certain moves, brokers are useful. You may have to spread things around. It's more a hobby these days. Then again, there's always hope I'll come up with something to beat Kraft and get a new nickname."

Conrad chuckled.

"So you can help?" said Stoner.

"Chip fabricators. Processor chips doing really high-grade stuff. Not a lot of them in Asia that aren't, you know, say, under a government's thumb. My bet would be Korea," said Cheese.

"Yes," said Stoner. Another officer had checked

on the Korean plants very extensively, and had assured him they weren't involved.

"All right, so forgetting Korea, what do we have, right?" continued Cheese. "We're talking very high-end processors and no questions asked. Right?"

Stoner nodded.

"I know of a factory in Thailand. I'd start there."

"Others?" asked Stoner.

"My assistant will get you a list. But forget it. If it isn't that Thai place, it isn't anywhere. Anything you need, they'll do. Of course, if you look at the customs records, what few there are, you'll see they only make chips for VCRs and TVs, that sort of thing. Don't believe it."

"Can they do memory chips and CPUs? Specialized work?"

"One of their partners was a Taiwan company owned by Chen Lee. You hear of him?"

"No."

Cheese smiled. "His company ever goes public, you want a piece of it. He's the king of salvage. Anyway, he withdrew his financing or something about a year ago. I don't know the whole deal. Supposedly it was a top operation, though why they located there, I wouldn't begin to guess."

"Maybe so nobody would come around asking questions."

Cheese shrugged. "Anyway, they'd make something for you. They're desperate. Or they were."

"Were?"

"I believe they're bankrupt, now that Chen cashed out." Cheese jumped up. "I got to hit the treadmill down the hall. You guys want to come or are we done? I got sweats if you want. Shower when you're done."

Stoner looked at Conrad. His red face had turned beet red at the prospect of exercise.

"I think we're done," said Stoner. "If I can get that list."

Aboard *Raven*, over the South China Sea
1245

"THEY'RE TELLING THE SUKHOIS TO THE SOUTH TO come home," said Captain Justin Gander, one of the intercept officers upstairs who was listening in via the Elint gear on the plane. A translation unit in the computer could give on-the-fly transcripts of voice messages.

Zen checked the counter in the screen on the left, noting that they were now about thirty seconds beyond the designated launch time for the dummied-up Hellfire. He wasn't sure why Starship had missed the launch.

"Sukhois are saying—having a little trouble with the translation—they're going to inspect another aircraft."

"What aircraft?" asked Zen. The Sukhois were a good seventy miles south and back further to the west.

"They're calling it a Xian. Hang on—all right, registry is Brunei, *uh*, Badger belonging to the air force. Has a utility role according to our index. Uh, looks like it's on a routine patrol, just kind of flying around but not an official part of the exercise. Oh— VIP plane. Prince bin Awg flies it. Sight-seeing."

"Great place for sight-seeing," said Zen. "Our ghost clone show yet?"

"Nada. Got a lot of traffic out near Taiwan. We're reading pretty far."

Zen grunted, preparing to bank the Flighthawk as they came to the end of their orbit.

"Zen, looks like they held off on the Hellfire launch because of civilian traffic," said Merce Alou, who was piloting the plane. "They're giving positions to the Australian frigate."

"Not a problem," said Zen. He dipped *Hawk Two* into a shallow bank. As he took the turn he watched the view from the rear-facing video cam, which was using a computer-enhanced mode to show the antenna, whose silvery metal was nearly invisible to the naked eye. The web crinkled a bit as the direction changed, but Zen was able to keep it stretched out by nudging downward a little more.

"Turn complete," he told Alou, who was timing his own maneuvers to the Flighthawk.

Aboard *Penn*, over the South China Sea
1246

STARSHIP SAW HIS POSITION DRIFT TOWARD THE CHI-nese border over the ocean. He applied light pressure to the stick but couldn't seem to master it, the nose of the small robot stubbornly edging northward.

"You're going over their line," said Kick.

"No shit."

Starship gave up on the light hand, jerking the aircraft sharply to get back on course. The Flight-hawk responded as it was programmed to do, veering sharply and changing course. The pilot cursed to himself but kept his cool, sliding back onto the dotted line provided by the computer.

"What are we doing, *Hawk One*?" asked Colonel Bastian.

"Controls getting a little twitchy," said Starship.

He swore he heard Kick chortling to himself.

"The controls or you?"

"Me, sir." Starship felt his cheeks burn.

"The Chinese are scrambling additional planes. We definitely have their attention," said Dog, his voice calm. "Resume the countdown on the Hellfire and launch when you're ready."

"Yes, sir. We're at thirty seconds."

Aboard Brunei Badger 01, over the South China Sea 1324

MACK COULD SEE THE IDIOT CHINESE PILOTS COMING toward them from the north, riding a quick burst from their Saturn AL-31FM turbos. The planes they were flying were license-built Sukhois Su-27s, known in China as J-11s and virtually identical to the Russian model, whose design dated to the late seventies and early eighties. Essentially an attempt to keep up to the frontline F-14 and F-15, the

Sukhoi was a very good and capable aircraft, but even gussied up with a glass cockpit and thrust vectoring tailpipe, it didn't impress Mack. Zen could nail one of those suckers with his little bitty robot planes, which as far as Major Smith was concerned, said it all.

The lead Chinese pilot challenged them, calling them "unidentified Xian H-6" and asking what unit they were with.

"Usual Chinese bullshit," grumbled Mack.

"What's going on, Major?" asked Miss Kelly.

"He's just jerking our chain," Mack told her. "Pretending to think we're a Chinese aircraft. It's a game. They make believe they don't know who we are, so they can fly up close and show off. Goes on all the time. Macho posturing. Don't be impressed."

The interceptors started a wide turn, obviously planning to swing around and come across their wings.

"The Chinese can be quite aggressive," said bin Awg. "They don't believe that Brunei should have an air force."

"They don't think *anyone* should have an air force," said Mack.

"They are precisely why we need an air force."

"You got that straight, Prince," said Mack. "Jerks. Don't let 'em push you around."

Bin Awg broadcast his ID, course, and added a friendly greeting, all in Mandarin.

The Chinese didn't bother acknowledging.

Mack pulled out his large map of the area, working out how far the planes had come. The Sukhois were large aircraft and could carry a decent amount of fuel; even so, he figured these two jokers must be out near bingo—they'd have to go home soon.

The J-11s had slowed considerably, and as Mack had predicted split wide so they could bracket the Badger. Painted in white, the double-finned planes were trimmed in blue. They had what appeared to be R-73 Russian-made heat-seekers tied to their wings. Known as Archers in the West, the short-range missiles were roughly comparable to Side-winders.

"Frick and Frack," said Mack as the planes pulled alongside.

Miss Kelly laughed.

The backseater in the J-11 on the right had a camera. Mack resisted the impulse to give him the finger—it would be posted on the Internet tomorrow if he did. No sense giving the Chinese jerks the satisfaction.

The Sukhoi on the right swung across the Badger's path, a few yards away. The prince struggled to hold his big, fussy aircraft steady and not hit the idiot. Bin Awg was a good pilot, but the J-11's bulky mass presented a case study in wake turbulence. Nor was the other commie giving him much room to work with.

The RWR bleeped on and off. The Chinese jocks were really pulling their chain, activating their radars as if intending to target them.

"They're lucky we don't have air-to-air missiles," grumbled the prince.

That gave Mack an idea. He threw off his restraints and climbed back to the gunner's station. It took a moment to get the hang of the gear, but though ancient it was straightforward enough that even a zippersuit could figure it out. Mack felt the gears chattering behind him as it turned. He put his face down into the old-fashioned viewer, surprised to find that it was actually a radar screen, not an optical feed. As he did so, the pilot had to push down to avoid the Sukhoi's tailpipe. Losing his balance, Mack grabbed for a handhold. His finger found the gun switch, and to his shock and surprise, a stream of bullets flew not just from the top guns but from all three of the antiair stations.

For one of the few times in his military career, Mack Smith was utterly speechless. He hadn't thought the weapons were loaded—bin Awg hadn't given any indication that they were. Nor would he have guessed that they could be fired so easily, or that all three weapons could be commanded from one station.

Of course, had he been trained as a weapons operator, a glance at the panel would have told him all this. But then if he'd been a real weapons operator, he wouldn't have been fooling around in the first place.

Actually, the same might be said for a pilot, or any officer of the U.S. Air Force, Navy, or Army, whose duty might reasonably be said to include restrictions against being a bonehead in a potential war zone.

Without saying anything, without breathing, Mack slid back into his copilot's seat, sure that his career in the U.S. Air Force had just ended.

At least he hadn't shot down the planes. The J-11s pulled off to the north, making tracks.

No one else said anything as he pulled on his headset. Mack glanced toward the prince. His face was red.

Probably, he couldn't be jailed for what was just a dumb-ass mistake. Court-martialed, sure.

But jailed?

If they did jail him, would it be in Brunei or the U.S.?

A communication came in from the Australian frigate.

Mack listened as the prince gave his position and intentions; they were homeward bound.

"Scared those buggers off, mate," said the Australian. "Good for you."

Obviously, it wasn't a flag officer talking. Bin Awg acknowledged with his ID, but said nothing else.

"I, uh, I—" started Mack. He intended to apologize, but apologies had never exactly been his strong suit. His tongue froze in his mouth.

"Major?" said the prince.

"Um."

"Major Mack Smith, you have just done something I wish I had the guts to do ten years ago. You sent the devils packing. This is a great moment. A very, very great moment."

If Mack had had trouble speaking a moment before, he was utterly speechless now. He wanted to tell the prince that, in all honesty, he was exaggerating by a country mile.

Then he thought he'd apologize, say he hadn't thought the gun was loaded, and throw himself on the mercy of the court. Maybe the prince might say a few words on his behalf.

But nothing came out of his mouth.

Bin Awg turned to him. "Well done. Well, well done."

"Uh, thanks," was all Mack could manage to get out of his mouth.

Aboard *Penn*, over the South China Sea
1424

DOG CHECKED THE SITREP. THEY HAD CHINESE J-11S to the south of them, J-11s to the west, a big ol' Russian Coot, and even a U.S. Navy P-3—but no ghost clone, at least not that they could see. He hoped *Raven* was having better luck.

"They're getting to be at bingo now, sir," said the copilot, whom Dog had asked to keep track of the Flighthawk status. "Bingo" in the Flighthawk referred to the point at which they had to refuel.

"*Hawk One*, this is *Penn*. How's your fuel state?" said Dog.

"Getting edgy," replied Starship.

"What's edgy?"

"Uh, we're getting there."

Dog shook his head. The nugget was like a kid who'd been swimming in a pool all afternoon and didn't want to get out even though his lips were chattering and his body was blue. As long as he didn't admit being cold, he wouldn't be.

Didn't work that way with jet fuel, though.

"*Hawk One*, have you discovered the secret to perpetual motion?" Dog asked.

"Um, excuse me, Colonel?"

"Time for you to refuel, no?"

"Yes, sir. I'm ready."

"All right, let's radio the fleet that we're breaking off and going home," Dog told the entire crew.

STARSHIP SLID BACK IN HIS SEAT AS THE COMPUTER took the Flighthawk in and began the refuel.

He was tired and more than a bit frustrated. All that flying and no sight of the ghost clone.

Not to mention the fact that the Chinese fighters had stayed well clear of him.

"Tired?" Kick asked.

"Nah," said Starship.

"Zen's probably tracking him right now."

"Yeah."

"You hear what happened with the Brunei Badger?"

"Something happened?" Starship had been too intent on his own mission to bother with anything that didn't concern him.

"Couple of J-11s buzzed them just about an hour ago. Mack Smith sent them packing with a burst of cannon fire across their bow."

"Live gunfire?"

"No shit," said Kick.

"Wow. He allowed to do that?" Starship's ROEs strictly forbade him from firing except in the most dire of circumstances, and if he had tried that Zen would have found a way to kick his butt back to Dreamland.

"Got away with it. Nobody's complaining."

"Those the planes we saw earlier?"

"Yup."

"They were probably just out of fuel," said Starship. "They were operating at the edge of their range."

"Yeah, well, that's not the way the Brunei prince sees it. They're sending airplanes out to escort them back to a hero's welcome. I'm not making this up."

"Man, I wish I had Mack Smith's life," said Starship as the computer buzzed him. The refuel complete, he took over from the electronic brain, ducking down and then zooming ahead of the *Pennsylvania* to lead her back to the base.

Dreamland
10 September 1997
2344

DANNY FREAH GOT UP FROM HIS DESK IN THE SECURITY office, his eyes so blurry that he couldn't read any of the papers on his desk. He'd been staring at computer reports along with summaries of regulations, laws, and previous investigations for over four hours.

For all that, he probably knew less now than when he'd started. As head of security at Dreamland, Danny had extraordinary powers to investigate possible espionage; he didn't even have to rely on Colonel Bastian's authority in most cases. Everyone who worked at the base had to sign long, complicated agreements that essentially stripped him of privacy and made Danny Freah Big Brother. If events warranted, he could tap their phones, read their mail, even enter their homes.

But what he needed in this sort of case was the ability to read people's minds. Because it just wasn't clear to him that anyone—Jennifer Gleason especially—had betrayed his country, knowingly or unknowingly.

Occasionally during the Cold War, technology theft was straight-out obvious—the Soviet Union produced a four-engine bomber based on a B-29 a few months after the plane landed in the country's Far East, for example. But much more often, the theft was considerably more subtle and nuanced.

The Soviet Tu-95 bomber, for example, had probably been influenced by American designs—yet it did not directly correspond to anything in the American inventory. Were similarities between American jets and advanced MiGs and Sukhois due to similar design requirements and constraints, or espionage? When was a copycat simply that—and when was it an act of treachery?

Danny needed more extensive data about the ghost clone before he could even decide whether there might be a case here. Even then, he'd need really, really hard evidence to take to Colonel Bastian—or to Bastian's superiors, if Danny decided the colonel couldn't be unbiased.

Cortend, on the other hand, worked on the premise that espionage had occurred, and therefore she would find it. She didn't really care what effect she had on the base, much less on the people she was grilling. And because she wasn't conducting an official investigation—not yet, anyway—she could ignore a lot of the standard rules and procedures designed to prevent abuses. She bullied people into cooperating "voluntarily" and then screwed them, or tried to.

Danny wasn't like that. He didn't nail people without damn good reason to do so.

Should he?

Maybe Jennifer did know something, or had done something really wrong. She was pretty antagonistic, and hadn't been acting particularly, well, innocent.

She'd answered all the questions, though. She claimed she didn't remember the conferences or the paperwork.

Probably that was true. He couldn't remember back a few years himself. And as for paperwork . . .

It was bullshit. The files were full of contact reports that no one ever looked at. Truth of it was, Jennifer Gleason rarely left the base, not even to go home, not even for a vacation. She was about as far away from being a spy as you could get. Knowledge, yes, but little opportunity, and dedication probably unmatched even at Dreamland.

Were his emotions getting in the way of his judgment? He liked Jennifer, and even more importantly, he liked Dog; if Jennifer were guilty, it would kill the colonel.

To his credit, Dog wasn't interfering. Clearly he didn't think Jen was guilty, but he wasn't interfering.

Danny glanced at his watch and decided he'd go catch some Z's. Maybe tomorrow one of the scientists here would come up with some new gizmo that would let him read minds.

* * *

UNABLE TO SLEEP, JENNIFER PUSHED HERSELF OUT OF bed. Her legs and neck felt numb. She folded her elbows against the sides of her chest, then bent at the waist, stretching her muscles. The numbness stayed with her.

She walked from the small bedroom to the slightly larger living room, which had a kitchenette at the side. She sat on the couch, staring at the TV on the wall near the door but not bothering to turn it on. Jennifer pulled her feet up onto the couch, looking at her toes.

The numbness affected even them.

Was she going to stay in this hole the rest of her life?

Jennifer jumped off the couch, pacing across the small room. Cortend, Danny, Dog—they were all against her, weren't they?

They were all against her.

Did she deserve that?

Maybe she did.

Jennifer found herself at the small sink. A large paring knife sat at the bottom, next to a coffee cup from a few days before.

Did she deserve that?

She picked the knife up and felt the blade with the edge of her thumb. Only when she pushed hard against it did the numbness dissipate.

Blood trickled from her finger. She stared at the red dots, watched the flow swell.

Slowly, she brought the knife upward toward her neck. She ran it up against her chin and then the cheek, the way a barber would drag a safety razor.

Was there no way to make the numbness go away?

With a jerk, she grabbed a bunch of her long hair between her fingers and the sharp blade of the knife. She tugged. The hair gave way.

Again.

Again.

Aboard *Raven*, over the South China Sea
1444

ZEN CHECKED HIS FUEL STATE, THEN HIT THE MIKE switch.

"I think we're just about wrapped up," he told Alou. "I won't jettison the antenna until we're ready to refuel," he added. "Looks like, oh, ten minutes?"

"Roger that, *Hawk Two*," said Alou. "Be advised we're intercepting communications now between a ground controller and a flight of Chinese F-8IIs—hang tight."

While the pilot and the officer handling the intercept data sorted through the radio traffic to figure out what was going on, Zen brought his Flighthawk south and began descending. He had to visually inspect the area where the antenna would fall to make certain it wouldn't hit anyone—or be retrieved before it sank.

"F-8s are coming out to say hello," Alou told Zen. "Going to afterburners. Apparently pissed off about something that happened south of us, over the ASEAN fleet. Let's go ahead with the refuel."

"Roger that. Preparing to drop trailing antenna," said Zen. He checked his screen, went to the sitrep, then let the computer take the bird, holding it at

8,500 feet when he gave the command to release the antenna. A puff of smoke rippled from the rear of the Flighthawk; a set of charges no larger than firecrackers blew the mesh into sections, destroying any value it might have for an enemy. The metal that didn't disintegrate settled in the water.

"J-8s are in radar range," said Alou.

"Roger that." Zen took back control of the Flighthawk, climbing upward. He passed through fifteen thousand feet going toward twenty-five, where *Raven* was waiting with its probe already out for the refuel. It took a few minutes to climb and line up correctly, moving in toward the waiting straw like a kid homing in on a root beer float in an old-fashioned ice cream shop. Zen throttled back, hit his computer-generated marks, then prepared to give up control to the computer, which would fly the actual refuel. But just then the RWR buzzed in his ear, warning him that the Chinese pilots had turned their radar into targeting mode, as if they were preparing to fire guided missiles at the EB-52.

"Coming at us hard," said Alou.

"Holding off on refuel," said Zen. He rolled out to defend his mother ship.

One F-8—still on afterburner—shot in from the northwest, riding about a quarter mile away from the EB-52 at nearly the exact same altitude.

Four hundred meters sounds like a lot, but it's not a particularly wide margin when one plane is doing 380 knots and the other is up well over 600. It was ridiculously close for the Shenyang F-8. While admittedly fast—the delta-shaped arrow could top Mach 2.2—the Chinese design had the turning radius of an eighteen-wheeler pulling three trailers and none of the finesse.

As it came across *Raven*'s bow, its pilot threw the plane into a hard turn north, probably surpassing nine g's. It was a wonder he didn't pass out.

Meanwhile, the other F-8 took a slightly more leisurely approach, backing off his throttle and trailing his partner by a good ten miles. He turned slightly and took a course that would take him directly beneath *Raven*.

By maybe two feet.

"Could be he needs some gas," said Alou.

"I wouldn't be surprised," said Zen. "I'm going to get in his face."

"Hang back. Better that he doesn't try turning and hit into us."

"All right. Look, I'm going to have to refuel."

"Yeah, roger that."

The second F-8 pilot, perhaps finally realizing that he couldn't share the same space as the EB-52, banked about five miles from *Raven*'s tail. Zen pushed back toward *Raven* as the Chinese planes pulled north.

"Let's do the refuel while they're running away," he said.

"Bring it on in."

But Zen had no sooner started up toward the boom when the F-8s turned back and headed toward the Megafortress.

"What's with our friends?" asked Zen.

"Who knows," said Alou. "Maybe they're looking for flying lessons."

"I'll give them some cheap. You want to refuel?"

"Go for it. Delaney's trying to talk to these idiots and see what they're up to."

About a mile from the back of *Raven*, one of the F-8s drove up near Zen's right wing, closing the distance from about a hundred yards, obviously curious about the U/MF. Zen didn't blame him, actually; the little plane looked more like a UFO than a conventional aircraft. He switched over to the frequency the Chinese aircraft were using.

"Get a look at the future, my friend," said Zen, broadcasting in the clear in English.

"You must be very small to fit inside," answered the Chinese pilot.

His English was a little difficult to make out, so Zen's laugh was delayed. It was obviously intended as a joke—the Chinese had had the opportunity to meet Flighthawks before.

"No, I just sawed off my legs," Zen answered.

He continued on his flight path into the refueling probe, which was jutting out the rear of the EB-52. Just as he got to within twenty yards, the F-8 jiggled in front of him. Apparently caught in the wind sheering off the Megafortress, the Chinese plane jerked down and then up, finally tipping on its right wing and swooping away. Zen had to slide back, afraid he was going to hit the idiot.

"Say, guys, no offense, but you have to stay clear, okay?" said Zen. "We're working here."

The lead F-8 took offense at his tone, telling him the sky belonged to everyone.

"Well, yeah," said Zen. "But if you want to stay

in it you better stand back. Even we haven't figured out a way to get two airplanes in the same place at the same time yet."

He brought his Flighthawk up, but before he even started to close, he got a proximity warning. The F-8 leader flew under the Flighthawk and crossed in front, missing both planes by no more than twenty yards.

That was just a prelude for the maneuver by his wingman, who took his F-8 close enough to the wing of the Megafortress that it looked like he was going to try docking on the Flighthawk cradle. He stayed under the big plane, making it impossible for Zen to refuel.

"I'm tempted to use the cannons," Zen said to Alou.

"Makes two of us. How's your fuel?"

"I can't do this all afternoon." The fuel panel showed that he was well into his reserves, with only ten minutes of flying time left.

"Should we be polite?" asked Alou.

"Give it a shot. If they don't move off, break left hard. I'll drop in and we'll hook up before they can get back."

As Alou asked the Chinese pilot in English and Mandarin Chinese to stand clear so they could refuel, the lead F-8 returned, taking up a position under the other wing. This ruled out Zen's plan.

"All right, that's it," said Zen. He pushed the slide on the throttle and whipped the Flighthawk forward, riding in between the F-8 on the right and the Megafortress. The Chinese pilot got the message and began to duck off to the right. But as he did, his flight leader lost his nerve and jinked downward as well—right into the other plane's wing.

A turbulent rumble of air shook all four aircraft. Zen thought he had hit the belly of the Megafortress—he'd been closest to the EB-52—and slammed the Flighthawk downward as quickly as he could.

For a long half second, he wasn't sure where anyone else was. He felt a disconnect between his mind and body—his eyes were plummeting with the Flighthawk while his chest was taking a few g's from the other direction, Alou trying to climb out of trouble.

By the time Zen pulled upward, Alou had steadied the Megafortress. It hadn't been hit.

"All right. I have to refuel," said Zen. "No more fooling around."

The warning tone was loud in his ear, the Flighthawk pleading for gas.

"Roger that," said Alou.

"Chinese aircraft are down," reported the copilot. "I see one, I have two chutes. Good chutes. Lucky bastards."

"Thank God for that," said Alou. "Even if they don't deserve it."

Aboard the *Dragon Prince*, South China Sea 1500

FROM THE AIR, THE SMALL TANKER LOOKED NO DIFFERent from the average commercial vessel plying the South China Sea. A small gray tarp, frayed at one edge, flapped in the wind on the starboard side; the masts were in disrepair and the paint near the waterline clearly needed to be scraped and reapplied. Anyone who followed the ship for any length of time would realize that the engines had a habit of spewing dark smoke at unpredictable intervals, but they would also notice that the crew, while relatively small, was motivated and disciplined. The flag that flew from the mast was Malaysian, though of course in these days of international shipping, any observer might guess that was more a matter of convenience than a clue to its ownership. The *Dragon* ship—its actual name was *Dragon Prince*, though few used it—was to all outward appearances just one more small merchant vessel trying to make a living in the difficult business of international shipping.

But as the old Chinese proverb put it, appearances were often meant to deceive.

Chen Lo Fann stood on the bridge of the *Dragon Prince*, waiting. An American satellite had just inconveniently passed overhead, delaying their launch. They had to wait another ninety seconds to make sure that it was well out of range.

Chen Lo Fann waited stoically, willing the time to pass. There was no doubt in his mind that their chance had passed by today; he hoped Fate would provide another tomorrow.

"Commander?"

Surprised, Chen Lo Fann turned. "Professor Ai, why are you on the bridge? Shouldn't you be with your controls?"

"You need to listen to this," said the gray-haired scientist.

Chen Lo Fann nodded, then followed as Professor Ai led the way below to the compartment where the intercepted information was compiled. He stepped quickly to the panel at the right and flipped a small toggle switch, allowing an intercepted radio transmission to be broadcast onto the deck.

The words were in Chinese.

A search-and-rescue operation.

One of the Communist planes had gone down!

"Two of the planes collided," said Professor Ai. "They will send a rescue craft, a Harbin flying boat. It is their usual procedure."

And so, thought Chen Lo Fann, there is such a thing as Fate.

"Yes," he said. "Let us refine our plan."

Aboard *Raven*
1503

ZEN COMPLETED HIS REFUEL AND PUSHED THE FLIGHThawk away from the belly of the big plane, looping over the wide expanse of water. The two Chinese aircraft had crashed roughly five miles from each other, the planes zigging away after the collision. One of the F-8s had lost its wing, and its jock had hit the silk within seconds of the mishap; the other pilot had stayed with his plane though a good hunk of tail fin had been sheered off. That pilot was just now hitting the water; Zen banked and approached him from the west.

The Chinese had shot down *Quicksilver*, killing four of Zen's friends and nearly killing his wife;

while the reviews showed that the attack was a mistake, Zen nonetheless held the Chinese responsible. If they hadn't been overly aggressive, his people would still be alive.

On the other hand, his duty was to help rescue these jerks.

"Do you have their exact position?" Zen asked Alou as he watched the first pilot hit the water.

"Negative. If you want to go over them and get some GPS readings, we can alert PRC rescue assets," said the pilot.

"Have they scrambled SAR units yet?" Zen asked.

"We're working to figure that out, Hawk leader."

Zen slowed the Flighthawk down as he took a wide bank to swing over one of the Chinese pilots, who was struggling with his gear. The air-to-ground attack mode on the Flighthawk's radar gave a precise reading of cursored objects as part of the data set; intended to target GPS-guided munitions in coordination with the Megafortress, it could also help in the SAR role. Zen told C^3 to find the pilot in the water; the computer popped a little red halo around his head and plotted his exact location.

"Got Idiot One," said Zen, uploading the information as he brought the Flighthawk back in the direction of the other pilot. At about two miles, he saw a yellow splotch appear on the waves—the pilot had inflated his life raft. "Idiot Two is alive and well."

"Hawk leader, be advised we have a pair of Chinese aircraft—uh, J-11s or license-built Su-27s—coming out in our direction," said Alou. "Looks like they've been tasked for search and rescue. We'll attempt to contact them; at present they're outside of radar range but we have some telemetry on them. Going to take them a bit to get down here."

Zen acknowledged. As he orbited back, he saw that the second Chinese pilot had not yet inflated his raft.

"Either one of our friends is having trouble with his gear, or he likes to swim," Zen told the others.

The pilot remained a small dot in the water as he approached. Zen tucked lower, easing down below five thousand feet to try and get a better look at the pilot. He was going about 220 knots and couldn't get much of a visual; he came back around, speed dropping through 200 and altitude bleeding away, but the cam caught only the top of the man's head. Just as he pulled off, Zen thought he saw the Chinese pilot's arm jerk up; if it hadn't been for that, he wouldn't have known he was alive.

"He's alive but definitely having trouble with the sea," said Zen. "Where are those SAR assets?"

"Still trying to get a direct line to the Chinese. They're not answering our hails. They're on your radar now."

"Yeah. More idiots. Can we get a helicopter up from one of the ASEAN frigates?" Zen asked.

"We're working on it, Zen. Looks like we're out of their chopper range. Hang tight."

Zen flew a racetrack orbit over the two men, a simple, lazy oval in the sky. *Raven* had already made two broadcasts over the international UHF Mayday frequency, using the Chinese planes' call signs, but had not received answers. Zen clicked into the SAR circuit himself and gave it a shot, telling the downed pilots he had their locations and help was on the way.

"Thank you," came a staticky reply. "Is Commander Won okay?"

"I'm not sure who is who," replied Zen. "I can see two men down. One of you is in a life raft. The other is just in the ocean."

The reply was garbled, but Zen made out the words "malfunction" and "problem."

"Get this," said McNamara, *Raven*'s copilot. "The Chinese are warning us off."

"Tell them to fuck themselves," Zen replied. He overheard Alou transmitting to the Chinese fighters personally, giving the location of the two downed planes and telling them that the planes had collided with each other. Alou added that they were standing by to assist.

The answer from the Chinese was rather emphatic.

"Their weapons radars are active. We are spiked," said McNamara, meaning that the radars had a lock on the Megafortress, and the interceptors' missiles could be launched at any time, though they were probably about ten miles outside their optimum range.

Ten miles equaled a bit less than a minute at their present course and speed.

"They are jerks, aren't they?" said Alou.

"Incredible," said Zen. He was tempted to tell Alou to open the bomb bay doors and target the PRC fighters with their AMRAAM-plus Scorpions. But it was no more than a quickly fleeting thought.

"I think we should tell them they're being assholes," Zen suggested. "And in the meantime, offer to pass on messages to their comrades. Give them IDs and stuff. We can break the ECMs on launch. If we don't shoot the idiots down."

"I concur. You want to talk with the pilot in the water?"

"Sounds good."

The Chinese pilot's name was Lieutenant Tzu— or something reasonably close. He gave his unit identification and the plane he'd been flying to Zen to pass on. At the same time, he asked again about his flight leader.

"He's definitely in the water, and he's moving around," Zen told him. "But his raft doesn't seem to be working."

The pilot said something that was overtaken by static. Zen thought he was asking if he could drop a life raft. That was impossible, since the EB-52 hadn't been rigged for rescue missions, and didn't carry gear that could be dropped out to pilots. The Flighthawks had no gear at all.

"We're sorry, but we don't have that kind of gear aboard. We'll keep an eye on him," Zen explained.

"Give me the direction," said the other pilot.

The two men were now about six miles apart; surely it would take several hours for Lieutenant Tzu to reach his comrade. But the idea was a noble one, and Zen gave the lieutenant the heading, circling around a few times to make sure he understood.

The J-11s, meanwhile, had decided to play nice. They'd turned off their weapons radar and were asking for vectors to their downed airmen. Alou and

McNamara used the computer's translator module to help communicate as they spoke with them; it turned out to be faster to go back and forth in Chinese than to struggle in English. A Harbin Z-5 seaplane was being scrambled and was en route.

Scrambled was a relative term—the aircraft was only now leaving its base, and at top speed—300 knots—would take an hour and a half to arrive. More than likely, it would be more than two.

The J-11s, meanwhile, were near bingo.

"The Chinese want to know if we can stay aloft over their pilots while they go and refuel," said Alou. "They're just about out of gas."

"Well, what the hell did they send them down here for if they didn't have enough fuel to do anything but spin around and go home?" asked Zen.

"You're asking me to explain the logic of the Chinese command system?"

"Do we have enough fuel ourselves?"

"Tight. We'll have to try and arrange a refuel as we head south," said Alou. "We can do it, though. Mission commander's call."

"Well let's not run out of fuel ourselves," said Zen. "But you better tell that Z-5 to get a move on—Commander Won doesn't look like much of a swimmer, even with his lifejacket on."

COLONEL BASTIAN WAS SEVERAL HUNDRED MILES AWAY, about to enter Brunei airspace, but his voice came through loud and clear on the *Raven*'s flight deck. Major Alou switched into the private Dreamland circuit, which used a dedicated satellite network to provide around-the-globe encrypted transmissions.

"*Raven* here. Major Alou."

"Bastian. What's the situation?"

Alou filled him in. The J-11s had taken a quick look and gone home; the Chinese rescue plane was still a good half hour off.

"We've asked Texaco to come up and stand by," Alou added, referring to a KC-10 tanker asset operating in Brunei with the Dreamland team. Its tanks were filled with a special Dreamland jet fuel; though the planes could use the ordinary J-8 blend, the tiny Flighthawks operated better with a slightly tweaked mixture, and whenever possible Dreamland used its own tankers and support crew.

"That's fine. You say you have video on the Chinese planes' collision?"

"Yes, sir. I've already downloaded it to Dream Command."

"Good," said Dog. "I'll talk to Major Catsman and Jed Barclay. We're about to land," he added. "Keep me informed. *Penn* out."

"*Raven*."

THE HARBIN Z-5 WAS A MONSTROUS FOUR-ENGINE seaplane, a big flying amphibian that had been designed as a replacement for the Russian Beriev Be-6. The Z-5 had no American equivalent; it looked a bit like a Consolidated PB2Y from the World War II era, with the fuselage lengthened and slimmed down and the wings set very far back. While slow and ponderous, it was well suited for long-range and tedious SAR missions over the ocean. It could stay aloft for at least fifteen hours, carried an eight-man crew, and had a pantry full of rescue gear.

By the time the Harbin made contact with *Raven*, the raftless Commander Won had managed to get his rescue radio working. Zen passed along a message that the pilot was tired but alive. When the Z-5 came in sight, Zen rode *Hawk Two* out to meet it, looping around and bird-dogging the big flying boat in toward the pilot. He pulled off and watched the lumbering plane touch down, splashing against the water as it came in. The ocean was as calm as a bird bath, and the airplane had no problem coasting near its man to facilitate the rescue.

"They're saying thank you, and they can take it from here," said Alou. "Our tanker's en route to the rendezvous. Good time to split."

"Well, at least the SAR guys know their manners," said Zen, climbing so they could tank and begin the long trek home.

Brunei
1630

BY THE TIME DOG RETURNED TO THE BASE, THE ADULA-tion for Mack Smith had reached comical proportions. The Brunei officials spoke in tones that suggested the major might have a national holiday named after him. Even Mack seemed a bit embarrassed by the reaction of the Brunei officials, though this hadn't stopped him from giving two interviews to the state-run media in a special lounge over in the international airport terminal.

"What happened, Mack?" said the colonel when the major finally managed to pull away from the horde of officials and bureaucrats trying to congratulate him.

"Colonel, you wouldn't believe me if I told you."

"Take your best shot."

Dog listened as Smith told him how the cannons had fired on their own when he turned the radar on.

"They fired on their own?" said Dog. "You didn't hit the armament panel and then push the trigger?"

"I don't believe that was the case, sir."

"Mack, you really don't expect me to believe that, do you? Didn't you know the weapons were loaded?" demanded Dog.

"No, sir. Not at all. I swear to God. I did not know they were loaded."

The last bit—but only the last bit—seemed sincere.

"You know what would have happened if you hit one of those planes?" Dog asked.

Mack held out his hands.

"This is a serious screw-up," said Dog.

"Prince bin Awg doesn't think so," said Mack. "He thinks I'm a hero. And Miss Kelly says it'll probably help the alliance."

"This is the sort of thing I'd expect out of a lieutenant," Dog told him. "A lieutenant who was maybe about to be bounced down to airman. Not a major. Not someone who has serious responsibilities and wants to command a squadron someday."

Mack's face blanched.

"Colonel, honest to God, I didn't know the cannons were loaded. I thought I'd just spin the gun around. I was, it was, I just thought—"

"What *did* you think?"

"It's hard to say what I was thinking now," said Mack. "It's hard even to say I was thinking at all."

"You got that right."

There was a knock on the door.

"No more interviews," Dog told him. "Don't say anything. Nothing. Not one word until I speak to Washington."

He turned and went to the door himself. He pulled it open, thinking he would find one of the local press people, but instead found bin Awg.

The sultan stood a few feet behind him.

"Your Highness," said Dog, bowing his head in respect.

"Colonel Bastian."

"Your Excellency, let me apologize," said Dog. "I deeply regret the trouble we've caused."

"Apologize?" said bin Awg.

The sultan put up his hand. "The Chinese have been taught a lesson," said the ruler. "There is no need for apology. I hope you and Major Smith will be our guests this evening for a private dinner."

As Dog started to say he couldn't, he saw Miss Kelly in the background. She was nodding her head emphatically.

"I um, I'll try, Your Excellency."

The sultan smiled. "Try very hard," he said before turning to leave.

Aboard *Raven*, over the South China Sea
1800

LIEUTENANT DECI GORDON STUDIED THE DISPLAYS ON his console, looking at a graphical representation of the many different electrical signals in the air around *Raven*. While the complex array of sensors lining the Megafortress's hull could pick up everything from rocket telemetry to cell phone conversations, the computer had been programmed to look for a very narrow band of transmissions in the same power range as that used by the Flighthawk. The graphical representation of the scan—custom-designed for the EB-52 and still being refined—looked something like an undulating sand dune, with narrow symmetrical lines formed by an unseen rake. His eyes hunted the ever-shifting sands for a blue triangle—the indicator that would show the ghost clone's broadcast. Though he had told the computer to alert him if it was detected, Gordon trusted his own mark-one eyeballs more than the computer. He stared at the screen and worked his equipment, changing different parameters and the capture patterns in hopes of finding something.

Trained as both an electronic warfare and Elint specialist—traditionally separate though linked roles *Raven* itself combined—Gordon was a next-generation whizzo, a backseater whose mastery of the radio waves allowed him to listen in on, confuse, or destroy transmitting devices from radars to cell phones and walkie-talkies. Typically, *Raven* carried two experts; generally in combat one would concentrate on radar intercepts and the other would work with enemy telemetry and communications. Deci's specialty was radar, but both he and his workmate, Lieutenant Wes Brown, were cross-trained. In this case, both men were using different sets of the gathering gear to look for the clone.

Deci flipped his scan back to an overall capture pattern, showing the active radio transmissions within a two-hundred-mile radius of *Raven*. Purple starbursts representing the Chinese SAR effort appeared at the top left, with ASEAN transmissions to the southwest below and the radioed instructions from the tanker they were to meet in five minutes a nice lime green at the right. The colors had been selected from a list of preferences Gordon himself had set; he'd already decided the choices needed a bit more work, but any refinement would have to wait until he got back to Dreamland.

Gordon couldn't wait for the refuel. A large submarine sandwich was waiting for him in *Raven*'s fridge, located in the galley area at the rear of the flight deck. He'd chow down as soon as they hooked up with Texaco.

He flipped back to the ghost clone monitoring screen, determined to take one last look. As he did, the computer sounded the "gotcha" tone in his ear.

It took a half second for him to spot the triangle, flickering at the very top edge of the screen. When he did, his finger shot toward it, tapping the touch-sensitive screen.

"Capture," he said, "capture."

"Crew, we're zero five from the rendezvous with Texaco," said Major Alou.

"Major, hold off! Hold off!" said Gordon, barely able to control his excitement. "I have something. I have it."

ZEN JERKED IN HIS SEAT. HE PULLED THE FLIGHTHAWK back north, waiting as the information on the intercepted data flashed onto the sitrep screen, sent there from the data link upstairs.

"Yeah, yeah, looks good. *Raven*, I think we have a hot one," said Zen.

"Hawk leader, our fuel state is getting toward critical," said Alou.

"How critical?" asked Zen. He was roughly six minutes away from the ghost clone.

"We can give you ten minutes, no more," said Alou. "Then we come back or we ask the Chinese for a link home."

"I'll take it."

"Roger that. Texaco's coming north with us, but even so, we're cutting it close."

Zen pushed the throttle slide up, increasing his speed. He shot a glance at his own fuel panel, just to double-check that he had enough petrol himself. The computer told him that at this speed he could go nearly fifteen more minutes before hitting his reserves.

Plenty of time, he told himself, nudging for more power.

**Aboard the *Dragon Prince*,
in the South China Sea
1806**

PROFESSOR AI HIRA BAI SAW THE COMMUNIST CHInese aircraft at the bottom of the viewscreen as he approached. It looked like a burning cockroach sprawled across the water, its white hull glowing in the reflected sun. He brought up his weapons screen, though he was still a good distance from his target.

Professor Ai did not like to think of himself as a vengeful man, but as he began to close on his target and his heart pounded harder, he did start to feel a certain satisfaction rising in his chest. He tried to push it away, realizing it was a distraction—all emotion was a distraction—and yet he could not.

He wanted to kill. There was no question about that. He wanted to kill the men in the aircraft as surely as he wanted to breathe. He wanted to kill all the mongrels on the Mainland.

He would settle for these communist dogs.

The pipper crawled toward its target. The H-5 was taxiing, moving in the water.

Suddenly, the radar aboard the robot sounded a warning—another plane was approaching.

Professor Ai ignored it, leaning forward in his control screen.

Aboard *Raven*, over the South China Sea
1808

ZEN SAW THE CHINESE RESCUE PLANE BEFORE HE SAW the ghost clone. The H-5 was just starting to move at the top left of his screen; the unmanned airplane had to be somewhere just to its right, but he couldn't see it yet on the visual.

Zen realized what was happening a second before McNamara alerted him from the flight deck.

"We have his radar," said McNamara. "They're targeting the Chinese plane!"

"Warn them," said Zen. "The AMRAAMs—can you target the clone?"

The interphone and radio circuits clogged as the pilots above tried to communicate with the Chinese plane and locate the clone at the same time. Zen continued on his course, powering up his own weapons. An upside-down W appeared on the left side of his screen, whitish-gray in the harsh light above the waves. It was the clone.

Zen pushed his stick hard, trying to get it into his aiming reticule.

He was too far. He'd never get to it before the clone opened fire.

"Can you jam his radar?" Zen asked.

McNamara didn't answer. Instead, C^3 gave a buzz indicating that *Raven*'s ECMs were being activated. This was followed by a proximity warning—the electronic fuzz eroded the communications link between the mother ship and the Flighthawk. Zen had to throttle back or risk losing the connection.

Which gave him an idea.

"Get north," he told Alou. "Get between the clone and its mother. Knock down its signal."

Again, the only answer from the bridge was nonverbal—a quick jerk in the air as the heavy bomber lurched northward, trying to follow Zen's directions.

Zen's targeting cue began blinking, its color changing to yellow. He was lined up for a shot but too far away, the computer was telling him. He needed to wait until the cue blinked red.

The clone danced up and down, weaving through the air. Then it exploded—

No, it was firing.

Zen pressed the Flighthawk trigger, though he was still well out of range. The W-shaped boogie split off to the right, climbing. Zen turned hard and hit the gas, immediately getting a proximity warning.

"Turn off the ECMs. I have to follow him."

"Zen, we're at bingo. We're beyond it—we have to refuel. We have to go back," said Alou.

His voice was so stern Zen didn't argue. He pulled around, looking in the direction of the H-5.

It was still on the water, taxiing he thought. Then the large tail seemed to fold backward, the massive airplane crumpled like a piece of origami caught in a tornado. Flames burst from the engines; in a matter of seconds, the entire aircraft had disappeared under the water.

"Oh shit," said Zen.

III

CHIPS

Brunei
11 September 1997
1829

DOG HAD JUST STRIPPED AND TURNED ON THE WATER to take a shower before dinner when his secure satellite phone buzzed. Thinking—hoping—it might be Jennifer, he grabbed it off the sink and looked at the LED window on the top, which was like a caller ID device indicating which node of the Dreamland secure system had originated the communications. He was surprised to find that the alphanumeric was Z-99—Zen.

"Bastian," he said, wrapping a towel around himself.

"Colonel, we have a problem. We found the ghost clone, but before we could get to it, it shot down the Chinese aircraft. It took off before we could apprehend it."

Dog reached back into the tub to turn off the shower as Zen continued, explaining what had happened.

"There's a merchant ship about twenty minutes away," Zen added. "He's en route. We can see debris on the water, but no survivors."

"No survivors?"

"We're still looking," said Zen.

He added that the Chinese had additional assets

en route. The final transmission from the H-5 was garbled, and it wasn't clear to them what happened.

"The Chinese know the plane is down?" asked Dog.

"Yes, sir. A J-8 was coming down to hook up with it and escort it home. The J-8 radioed us shortly after the shootdown when it didn't show on radar. We told them we were refueling but would come up and look for them. It wasn't a lie, exactly. We just left out some of the details."

There was a knock on his door. Dog ignored it. "What are you doing now?" he asked Zen.

"I'd like to stay around until the ship gets there at least."

"Any possibility of finding the clone?"

"We can try, but the trail's pretty cold. Alou won't complain, but his crew's been at it a pretty long time."

Whoever was at the door knocked again. Dog thought it must be Mack, who'd promised to give him a ride over to the palace.

"All right," Dog told him. "Stay aloft until the Chinese have the area covered. Offer whatever assistance you can. After that, head back. I'll meet you in the trailer."

"The Chinese are going to think we shot them down," said Zen.

"I know."

Dog hit the End button and pulled the towel tighter around his waist. But instead of Mack he found Miss Kelly.

"Colonel, you're not dressed yet," she said.

"I'm afraid there have been new developments,"

said Dog. He decided to give her a brief overview of what had happened.

"I have to check with Washington to see precisely how they want to handle this."

"It's not good," she said.

"No, it's not," said Dog. "I'm going to have to miss dinner with the sultan."

"You can't."

"This is much more important."

"Not showing up will be interpreted as an insult."

"I'm afraid it can't be helped."

"Colonel, you can't snub the sultan."

"I'm not snubbing him. I just don't have time for diplomatic bullshit," he told her. "You're the State Department. You fix it."

"But—"

He slammed the door before she could finish her sentence.

Aboard the *Dragon Prince*, South China Sea 1925

THE STORMCLOUD APPROACHED FROM THE EAST, rushing in like a tempest sent from the gods. Low to the water, riding in the thick band of the setting sun, it seemed to kick up fire and ash rather than steam as it came toward the *Dragon Prince*. Suddenly a black cloud furled from behind and it settled onto the waves, skimming the surface.

The *Dragon* had returned. The small robot plane taxied on its skis toward the ship, its speed steadily dropping. Professor Ai watched from the rail as the computer on the plane jettisoned the parachute it had used to slow and then spun the plane around the ship with its last bit of momentum, ready to be picked up. The skis that it rode on held it above the water, but just barely, and the recovery had to be completed quickly once the aircraft stopped moving.

Professor Ai had found that his presence on the deck helped the process, as the crew inevitably moved even faster. There was little danger that the craft would sink, but the longer it sat in the unfriendly salty water, the more maintenance it required. Already the coating of its composite hull and skin had to be reapplied every second or third flight.

Dragon Prince had lowered a boat earlier to help in the recovery. It approached the small robot plane now, helping as the hoist was secured to its fuselage. Within minutes, the crank on the edge of the ship began to groan.

Professor Ai had wanted to name the robot plane *Xi Wang Mu* after the goddess in Chinese mythology who was said to be the Queen Mother of the West. She was the patron of immortality, a beneficent figure.

To most. Professor Ai, however, knew that the earliest texts mentioning Xi Wang Mu referred to her as a monster—part human, part tiger. She ruled over demons and the plague answered her command. The kinder image had evolved over the centuries.

Ai Hira Bai's own history had drawn him to the story of Xi Wang Mu. It was not a coincidence that his middle name was Japanese—Ai had been born during the Japanese occupation of Manchuria during World War II. His father had died shortly after his birth—or at least that was what his mother had been told. A native of Shanghai, she had returned to the city after the war. But her neighbors and relatives considered her a collaborator and would have nothing to do with her; in her anguish she had fled the country after the war. She had worked hard to raise her son, though she had died before he reached twenty.

Ai wanted war not to liberate the stolen provinces, but as a measure of vengeance. Soon, he thought, he would have it.

As long as the communists reacted as they should, interpreting the destruction of the innocent SAR flight as a wanton act by the Americans. Professor Ai did not particularly care for the Americans either, though he did not hate them as he hated the Mainlanders.

"A successful mission," said Chen Lo Fann nearby.

The professor nodded to the young man. "Now it is up to the mongrels to play their role."

"Yes," said Chen Lo Fann.

Alexandria, Virginia, near Washington, D.C.
0640

JED BARCLAY HEARD THE PHONE RING AND REALIZED something big was up—it was his encrypted line, installed at the NSC director's request in his home office.

Since Jed lived in a one-room studio apartment, his home office was also his bedroom, family room, and dining area, so he didn't have to lean far from his foldout couch to grab it.

"Barclay," he said, not quite awake yet.

"Jed, the Chinese are claiming that we've shot down one of their planes," said his boss. "Get over to the White House right away."

"Shot down one of their planes?"

"Find out if it's true while you're at it. Call me back. I'm still confined to bed."

"Yes, sir."

AN HOUR LATER, JED WALKED THROUGH THE WEST Wing basement flanked by a pair of Secret Service agents. With the help of Colonel Bastian and briefings from the NSA and CIA, he had managed to pull together a pretty fair understanding of what had happened. Unfortunately, understanding the situation and being able to do something about it were two different things.

"Barclay," said Admiral Balboa, spotting him in the hallway outside the situation room. "What the hell is that cowboy Bastian up to now?"

"He's not up to anything," Jed told the head of the Joint Chiefs of Staff. "Whoever is operating the ghost clone shot down a Chinese flying boat while it was trying to make a rescue. They're trying to provoke a war."

"Gentlemen, let's discuss this in the situation room," said the defense secretary, coming in behind them. "Come on."

Balboa grimaced but said nothing. The secretary of state and the President were already inside, along with the other service chiefs and the head of the CIA. Balboa's broadside had a positive effect on Jed—he got through his quick overview of the situation with only a single stutter.

"The Chinese are on alert now. They're threatening to retaliate," he said, turning to Jeffrey Hartman, the secretary of state. "You might, uh, want to cover that."

"Actually, I have some fresh data on the Chinese units that are standing by," said General Victor Hayes, the Air Force chief of staff. "As well as ours."

Jed stole a glance at the President. Some months before, Kevin Martindale had threatened the Chinese with war over Taiwan. He'd backed the threat up with covert action, and only the Chinese really knew how close the world had come to a nuclear exchange. But that conflict seemed justifiable and even reasonable, the result of a series of aggressions and countermoves by America.

This was almost an accident—a crazy, chaotic accident.

Or not. Whoever was operating the ghost clone wanted war. World War III.

"How much do the Chinese know?" asked Martindale.

It took Jed a second before realizing the President was speaking to him.

"We don't think they know about the ghost clone at all. Circumstantially—we were there at the time. I, uh, uh, if it were me . . ." Jed's voice trailed off. His tongue was threatening to revolt again.

"Go on, Jed," said the President calmly.

"I would reach the same conclusion the Chinese did," said Jed. "B-b-because based on the evidence they have, we did it."

"Maybe we should add to their evidence," suggested Martindale.

"Tell them about the UAV?" asked Chastain.

"Why not?" said the President. "Jed, what do we have?"

"We have video of the c-c-collision itself, and of the shootdown. Radar stuff, sensor data. Uh, but, but—"

Jed felt them all staring at him.

"Very sensitive," he continued, managing to blurt out the words. "Giving them all the information we have would show the Flighthawks' capabilities. And, uh, the, uh, uh, *Raven's*, the Elint c-c-capable Megafortress."

"I doubt they'll believe us at this point anyway," said the secretary of state. "Or rather, that they'll admit that they believe it."

"My feeling is we should just ignore their threats," said Balboa. "They're just flexing their muscles. They won't move against us."

"Maybe, maybe not," said the President. "At the moment, I don't feel like taking a chance. Jed, prepare the data, minimize the exposure to our technology. They know we have good sensors; we won't give away the store by letting them see a blurry shot or two. Let Defense review it before it comes over to me. Once I have it, I'll decide whether to use it or not. Jeffrey, get the Chinese ambassador and have him meet me in my office. I'll clear all my other appointments."

The President rose and started to leave the room. But when he got to the door, he stopped and turned back.

"And Jed—tell Colonel Bastian he's past due on finding out who's operating this so-called ghost clone."

Dreamland Command Trailer, Brunei
2320

DOG STARED AT THE VIDEO SCREEN, WHERE A VERY tired Ray Rubeo updated the latest information from the team studying the *Raven*'s intercepts back at Dreamland. The members of the team had been able to sketch a tentative model based on the captured telemetry and video. The aircraft was roughly the length of a Flighthawk, but with a radically different airfoil; in fact, it looked closer to a Boeing design dating before the Flighthawks and originally intended as a one-off to test low-cost stealth concepts. The flight data suggested that the aircraft's top speed was slower than the Flighthawk's, but the analysis had concluded there were two cannons aboard, and the fuselage was wide enough to carriage a good-sized air-to-ground missile.

"The difference in the physical design should eliminate any suspicion of spying by the physical team," added Rubeo at the end of his brief. He seemed to be alone in the Dreamland Command Center, except for a skeleton crew. "Perhaps that will act as an enticement for our inquisitor to leave at least those people alone."

"Come now, Ray, Colonel Cortend can't be that bad," said Dog.

"The colonel has completely changed my opinion of the Spanish Inquisition," said Rubeo. "I now recognize it was a charitable organization."

"What's controlling it?" asked Zen, who was sitting next to Stoner behind Dog in the trailer's communications center. "Where's its control aircraft? We never saw it on the radar."

"That remains a mystery," said the scientist. "We are working on it, Major."

According to the information from Raven, the only aircraft that had been in the area were Chinese—and it didn't make sense that they had shot down their own plane.

"Ray, what's the possibility that the clone is being controlled from a ship?" asked Dog.

"At this point, I wouldn't rule anything out."

"The closest ship was that civilian vessel that searched the area of the crash," said Zen. "We overflew him. There's no way he launched the clone, let alone recovered it."

"We'll look into all of the ships that were in the area," said Rubeo. "But if they're controlling it from a vessel, they're using a system we don't know about."

No kidding, thought Dog. He started to ask if anyone else had anything when Stoner interrupted.

"Doc, getting back to the UAV for a second. You said it would have a lot of computing power aboard, right?"

"Yes, Mr. Stoner. Considerable computing power."

"Gallium-arsenide chips?" asked Stoner. "Custom-made?"

"Perhaps."

"I think I know where they were manufactured," said Stoner. "I'd like to check it out. I need some information on what to look for."

"You want a course in chip manufacturing?" said the scientist in a tone even more sour than usual.

"What the machines would look like, the plans, byproducts, that sort of stuff."

"Do you have six months? You're asking for a graduate seminar."

"I have a plant that supposedly manufactured chips used for VCRs. I want to see if it could have done anything else."

"VCRs," said Rubeo. "Might just as well look for vacuum tubes."

"Ray, maybe Jennifer can give Mr. Stoner a few pointers," said Dog.

"Jennifer is not available," said Rubeo. "She's confined herself to quarters. She says she's sick."

"What?"

"In any event, her security status is still in doubt. She's not allowed to use the computers, and she can't go into sensitive areas. Which would preclude her from using the command center."

"Is she all right?" asked Dog.

Rubeo put his lips together in one of his twisted scowls. Dog resisted the urge to press further—he didn't want to mix his personal concerns with business.

Still, it was difficult to keep quiet. The briefing dragged on a bit, with updates on the Chinese military—every unit was on standby alert, and there were threats from Beijing about war. The top leaders were all blaming America for the shootdown.

"At the moment, we're grounded," said Dog. "We don't want to incite the Chinese any further."

"I hope somebody's going to tell these jokers it wasn't us," said Zen.

"Washington will," the colonel told him. "But they have to be careful about how much information they can give the Chinese about our own systems. Too much and we may jeopardize future missions."

"Too little and these idiots will start shooting the next time they see us," said Zen.

"Yeah, right now all they're doing is trying to run into you," said Stoner.

The CIA officer was so deadpan it took a second for everyone to realize he meant it as black humor and start to laugh.

AFTER THE SESSION BROKE UP, DOG TRIED AGAIN TO get ahold of Jennifer. But she wasn't answering the phone, either at her apartment or at the lab. He decided not to bother leaving a message—with the investigation still under way, it was bound to be misinterpreted.

Most likely that was why she hadn't bothered emailing or leaving a message on his personal voice mail. Come to think of it, they usually didn't talk much during deployments anyway. She knew he was busy and didn't want to bother him.

Not that he considered talking to her a bother. Not at all.

Hell, he'd really like to hear from her right now.

Dog started to punch the numbers on the phone, thinking this time he'd leave a message and Cortend be damned, but then hung up.

Personal concerns came after duty. If he couldn't get his priorities straight, how could he expect anyone under him to?

Club Paradise, Brunei
12 September 1997
0023

"MACK SMITH."

"Colonel Bastian!" Mack nearly knocked over the table jumping to his feet, surprised—astounded— that Dog had tracked him to the small club on the outskirts of the city. He'd come with Stoner and was wearing civilian clothes.

"Boy, you missed a hell of a dinner," Mack told him.

"Thanks for filling in for me. Can Mr. Stoner and I sit down?"

"Colonel, of course. Ladies?" Mack gestured to the women who'd been fawning over him. As luck would have it, there were exactly three of them. Their eyes blinked as they did the math. One by one they took up positions.

"Actually, we'd like to be alone for a while," said Dog.

Mack feared that the colonel was about to lower the boom for his accidental firing of the Badger's machine gun. He told the women he'd see them later, then took a gulp of his drink as a final fortification against the inevitable onslaught.

"You just missed Prince bin Awg," said Mack, wishing he had left with his host.

"The prince approves of this?" said Dog.

"Oh sure."

"How about his uncle the sultan?" asked Stoner.

"Well, uncles, fathers, you know how that goes. Right, Colonel?"

Dog gave him a very disapproving frown.

"I don't know that I saw any alcohol touch the prince's lips," said Mack, sticking up for his host.

"Mack, I need you to do me a favor. Or rather, I need the prince to do me a favor, I want you to help me ask him."

"A favor?"

"We need to get to Thailand tomorrow, but not attract any attention," said Stoner. "Bin Awg has a fleet of aircraft at his disposal. We'd like to use one."

"Is that all? Hell, not a problem," said Mack.

Was that really it? Was that all the colonel had come for?

Mack felt as if he'd been plucked from a den of jackals and delivered back to paradise.

Paradise being Brunei, of course. There was no more beautiful spot on the planet, especially if you were considered a national hero.

"Can do, Colonel. How about the Badger? It's like driving an old Caddy, swear to God. Pickup's a little slack, but it'll remind you of the fifties. Not that you were around in the fifties, but if you were, I mean. It's a great plane."

"I don't want a Caddy," said Dog. "I understand he has a Beech King Air."

"Uh, I guess."

"That's the plane we'd like to borrow."

The Beech King Air—formally known as Beech Model 100 King Air B100—was an extremely reliable and sturdy workhorse, an excellent design that could carry fifteen passengers fifteen hundred miles or more. It was relatively cheap to operate, and testimony to the solid design and production skill of "small" American aviation companies.

It was also about as unspectacular a plane to fly as Mack Smith could imagine. A two-engined turboprop, the plane had been designed as a no-nonsense civilian flier, and that's what it was. It wasn't even a jet, for cryin' out loud.

"But, Colonel, I'm serious, you take the wheel of the Badger. You aren't going to . . ."

Mack's voice trailed off as he saw Dog's scowl.

"I'm sure it'll be fine. Should I ask now, or do you want to wait for morning?"

"Whatever's better," said Dog, rising. "We'll be at the airport at 0800."

Aboard Brunei King Air 2, over the Pacific
0854

IT HAD BEEN A WHILE SINCE DOG HAD PILOTED A CIVIL-
ian turboprop, and while he couldn't have asked for a more predictable and stable craft, his unfamiliarity with the plane did cross him up a bit. The King Air's maximum takeoff weight was perhaps

two percent of what the Megafortress could get off a runway with, and while there were clear advantages to the plane's small size—its ability to land on a small, unimproved runway was specifically important here—the cabin nonetheless felt like an overloaded canoe to him. Still, it was obvious why the army had chosen the type in the early seventies as a utility and reconnaissance craft, and the solid state of the aircraft showed why it remained in the Army's inventory when it could easily have been traded in for a newer model. The Garrett turboprops—fitted specially to the B100 model—hummed along in harmony as Dog and his team trekked northward across the ocean, their eventual destination a small airport in southern Thailand.

The strip lay about a half mile from the fab plant Stoner wanted to check out. Besides the CIA agent, Dog had brought along two members of the Whiplash security team, Sergeant Bison and Sergeant Rockland. The plant was in an area near the Cambodian border where rebels had been reported over the past six months. It wasn't even clear whether the plant was operating. Stoner had bought two small dirt bikes to use to get to the plant; they were stowed in the back of the plane.

Clear skies and a calm sea meant flying was a breeze, and Dog's hardest job was not getting too complacent at the wheel—or bored. There were only so many times he could check his instruments and look at the map to make sure he had the course nailed. Stoner, sitting next to him, wasn't very big on conversation. Inevitably, Dog began thinking of Jennifer, who still hadn't returned his calls.

Was she more upset over this investigation business than he'd thought? Cortend surely was a pain in the ass, but Jennifer ought to understand that the colonel's presence there was mostly a political thing; it wasn't directed at her and eventually would go away. Whatever minor violations of the rules she had committed—*if* she had committed any—would be outweighed by her value to the program. Any baboon would realize that.

Maybe he should just come out and tell her that.

Of course, that was the one thing he *couldn't* do as her commanding officer. It would be interfering with Danny, who had to have absolute autonomy, absolute authority to do the *real* investigation, Cortend be damned.

Dog checked his course, then looked at his watch. Bin Awg had modified the aircraft to increase the amount of fuel it could carry; in theory, they could have flown directly to the strip at Nanorpathet. But that would leave them with few contingencies, and so he had decided to refuel at Songkhla in the southern extension of Thailand on the Malay Peninsula. At 250 knots and better than eight hundred miles to go, it was going to be a long haul.

Maybe Mack had been right about taking the Badger.

Dreamland
11 September 1997
1800
(South China Sea, 12 September, 0900)

IT WAS SO OBVIOUS—SO PAINFULLY OBVIOUS—THAT
Rubeo very nearly smacked his head in derision as
he realized it.

Most of the intercepted code was nonsense.

Not nonsense, exactly—mirrored bits of their
own code, randomly sliced and diced, then spit back
to camouflage the actual transmissions.

And that made all the difference.

Rubeo got up from the computer bank and
walked to the counter where Mr. Coffee normally
kept at least a half carafe warm. The fact that there
was no coffee in the pot reminded him of Jennifer,
and that in turn reminded him of his stupidity.

Not that telling Cortend what he had just now realized would stop the Inquisition. Cortend was the
expression of a vast and infinitely stupid machine,
the dark enemy of knowledge. It had stripped Oppenheimer of his status and fame. It had pursued
Galileo; it had gotten Socrates to drink poison.
Cortend herself was a puny ant, a cog in the machine of ignorance.

A bad cog in a machine that couldn't even serve a
useful function, like making coffee.

Rubeo measured out some grains and filled Mr.
Coffee with water. As the liquid began to hiss downward, he went back to his secure phone and called
the Command Center, requesting to be put through
to Colonel Bastian. But Bastian wasn't immediately

available, according to the sergeant handling the communications system in the Whiplash trailer, aka Dreamland Mobile Command.

"I can get a patch through to his sat phone if you want," said the sergeant.

"Oh never mind. Tell him to call me when he lands."

"Here or there?"

"Whatever." The sergeant started to say something but Rubeo didn't have time for him; he killed the line and dialed Danny in the security office.

"I want to talk to Captain Freah. This is Rubeo."

"Uh, the captain's on another line and, uh, he's overdue at the handheld weapons lab to check out the updates to the Smart Helmets and some of the—"

"Tell him to see me when he's done playing with his toys," said the scientist, slamming down the phone.

AT THE VERY MOMENT RUBEO WAS SLAMMING DOWN the phone, Danny was fuming as well. He'd been on hold now for nearly five minutes, waiting for Jed Barclay to come back on the line. The NSC assistant had called Danny—then asked him to wait without saying another word.

"Sorry about that," said Jed, finally coming back on the line. "My boss has been sick and they're running me ragged. This China crap—they're crazy over there."

"What's up?" said Danny. He tried to be friendly but he knew there was a hard edge in his voice.

"Um, I wanted to tell you something, but, it's like, it's got to be off the record."

"Yeah?"

"The official channels'll come later."

"Let's go. What?"

"I talked to an FBI counterintelligence officer in charge of the Far East. Your scientist is off the hook."

"How's that?"

"Jennifer Gleason did follow procedure but her name was misspelled and reversed in the records. Dr. Rubeo figured it out. And she was a student on the date of the first conference and there wasn't even a formal requirement for her to register."

Danny wanted to reach through the phone and give Jed a high-five. But instead he gave the NSC official his standard security officer: "Are you absolutely sure about all this?"

"Yeah. Uh, like you'll get a paper report. I also told the FBI guy to contact Colonel Cortend. I figured she'd be really routing up people's butts."

"Thanks. Thanks a lot. Really. I really appreciate it," said Danny.

"Listen, I got to go—could you pass a message to, uh, Dr. Rubeo?"

"What'd he do, take your head off?" said Danny.

"He was going on about, um—well, you don't really want to hear it."

"Accused you of being part of the Inquisition?"

Jed laughed. "That part was a compliment compared to everything else. I, uh, really don't have time to uh, deal with him, but I need a favor. Not a favor really, but—"

"Tell me what you need, Jed, and I'll get it."

Jed explained that he needed yet another update

on the ghost clone for a meeting with the President scheduled in a half hour. Danny realized that, besides being angry about Jennifer, Rubeo was probably pissed that he had to keep updating Washington every few hours. But that was tough nuggies.

Besides, the news about Jennifer would put him in a better mood.

"He'll have to get me via sat phone. But I really need the latest. Really."

"Jed, I will personally make sure that Dr. Ray calls you. I will hold a gun to his head and make sure. I'm going right there now."

"Um, uh, that wouldn't, uh, be, uh—"

"It's a joke, Jed. He'll call."

Ten minutes later, Danny walked through the Megafortress hangar, down the long ramp that led to the elevators. He put his hand flat on the reader and waited for the car. When the door opened, Colonel Cortend and two of her lieutenants nearly flattened him.

"Colonel, just the person I wanted to talk to," said Danny. "Looks like Ms. Gleason is off the hook for those minor security violations."

"No security violation is minor," said Cortend.

Danny explained what had apparently happened, and told her that the FBI agent would be getting in touch with her.

"Good," said Cortend, in a tone so severe Danny momentarily regretted that he wasn't wearing body armor. She glanced at her minions, who snapped to and rushed to open the door ahead—even though it was operated by a motion detector.

Downstairs, Danny found Ray Rubeo talking to

himself as he pounded the keys on one of his computers.

"Hey, Doc," said Danny.

"Hmph," said Rubeo.

"I have good news about Jennifer," said Danny, summarizing what Jed had told him.

"Did you tell it to the hangman?"

Danny stifled a smirk. "If you're referring to Colonel Cortend, yes I did."

"Did she understand it?"

"What's to understand?"

"Precisely. *Precisely.*" Rubeo slashed at the computer keys, then hit a combination at the top to save his work. "You don't want to read this," he said, getting up.

"Top secret?"

"It's a letter to my congressman about idiots and numbskulls," said Rubeo.

"Present company excepted?"

"I tried to explain the significance of what's been found about the clone so far," said Rubeo. "I started with the very basics—completely different aircraft. I didn't even get to the transmission. Do you know what she told me? Do you know what she told me?"

"Uh, good job?"

"She told me that this was compartmentalized information, and she wasn't authorized to hear it. Not authorized to hear it! Not authorized to hear it!"

"Hey, uh, Doc, go easy, all right? I don't know how good my CPR is."

Rubeo shook his head. Volcanoes appeared calmer before eruptions.

"I believe in security too," he said. "You know

that. You understand that. You've been here—you know what kind of operation we run. But. But—"

"Sure," said Danny.

"This is obscene. This is harassment. I don't think she's coming back. She'll resign."

"Who? Cortend?"

"Jennifer Gleason." Rubeo's entire body shuddered.

"Look, Jennifer is off the hook for those meetings. The paperwork was misplaced. As for the rest of this, well, obviously we have to look very carefully, but—"

"Listen. I'm going to explain what they're doing. Just nod your head if you don't understand," said Rubeo. "Humor me. The reason the code is similar to ours is because it *is* ours—we're receiving a mirrored stream of data. Not all our data, just little bits. Their actual code uses an encryption that's twenty years old. They were using it when most of the scientists here were in diapers."

Before Danny could say anything, Rubeo marched over to a table lined with printouts. His fingers flew over them as he explained what he had found. Danny didn't quite catch it all—Rubeo made a big deal out of signal erosion curves and then somehow segued from that into how canon law made torture necessary during the Middle Ages because two eyewitnesses were always necessary for a conviction in the absence of a confession. But the bottom line was clear: No one at Dreamland was a traitor.

No one.

"The mirroring process is interesting in and of itself," continued Rubeo. "It's a real-time technique that uses a sampling sequence we haven't seen before. There have been only two papers published on it, and they're both several years old. Either the person behind the clone read those papers—or he wrote them."

"Great," said Danny. "Give me copies."

Rubeo blinked at him. "You understand what I'm saying?"

"No, but I get the gist. Can you get me those papers?"

"Gladly," said Rubeo. Somehow, his customary sarcasm seemed to lack the bite it had once had. It seemed almost—friendly. "You do read Chinese, don't you?"

"Chinese? As in the People's Republic of China?"

"No. As in Taiwan. The papers were written there by a man named Ai Hira Bai. If his name is any indication, he has both Chinese and Japanese ancestors, but he lived or lives on Taiwan. An adamant enemy of the communists. And a man who hasn't been heard from since shortly after the last paper was published. There are no academic listings of him anywhere."

"Interesting."

"Even more interesting is the fact that his expenses to the conference were paid by a company owned by a man named Chen Lee. A billionaire who hates the communists and who has access to a wide range of technology."

"How do you know this?"

"Well, if Colonel Cortend isn't going to investigate anything beyond her nose, don't you think someone better?"

White House, Washington, D.C.
2130

PRESIDENT MARTINDALE HAD A STATE DINNER SCHED-
uled to honor the ambassador from France, who
was retiring and returning to Paris after a decade's
worth of service in America. The President, whose
relations with France were as testy as that of any ad-
ministration since John Adams's, was only too happy
to throw a big party for the departing buffoon.

The dinner also allowed him the opportunity to
get off on a good foot with his successor, a Made-
moiselle Encoinurge. Encoinurge was an improvement in several respects, not least of all physically,
and the President found it necessary to engage in a
little personal diplomacy. This made it difficult for
him to sneak away as planned, and so Jed Barclay
and the others who were supposed to be meeting
with him were ushered upstairs to wait. The secretaries of defense and state had been at the meeting and were dressed in tuxedoes. Jed, wearing his
best pinstriped suit and a brand-new tie, felt under-
dressed. They were sitting in the dark and ornate
Treaty Room on the third floor, next to the Lincoln Bedroom. A massive chandelier hung down
from the center of the room like a beehive on fire.
Though sturdy, Jed's wooden chair creaked as he sat
in it; it was at least a hundred years old, and he worried that he might break it if he got up too quickly.

Nonetheless, he jumped to his feet as President
Martindale bounded into the room, several strides
ahead of two aides and Admiral Balboa, the head of
the Joint Chiefs of Staff.

"Gentlemen, Jed, good; we're all here then. I'm looking forward to better relations with France," the President told the secretary of state. "The ambassador actually seems to have a head on her shoulders."

"It'll make up for China," said Hartman.

"One step at a time. Would you like to brief us on the situation?"

"The Chinese are still officially blaming us for shooting down their aircraft," said the secretary of state. "But the premier was impressed that you called the ambassador and is willing to take your call on the matter sometime this afternoon. We're still working on the details. Jed's pictures helped."

Jed felt his face flush slightly.

"Good work, Jed," said the President. "Maybe we'll tell Mr. Freeman to stay in bed another week."

"Uh—"

"Philip is feeling much better," Martindale told the others. "I think he just didn't feel like having anything to do with France tonight. All right, back to China."

"The premier is in a conciliatory mood," said Hartman, picking up where he had left off. "Or at least he's prepared to be, if you say you're in favor of the summit between him and the president of Taiwan."

"I am."

"He'd like a sign of encouragement. He may suggest you attend."

"That's not going to happen," said Martindale.

"The vice president? He's in Japan."

The President frowned. "Let's think on that. Jed, what else do we know about the clone?"

"I have some data from Dreamland," said Jed. He reached for his briefcase. "I just have to boot up my laptop, and, uh—"

"No, let's skip the presentation," said Martindale. "Give us an overview. Quick one. I have to get back."

Until that moment, Jed hadn't thought about his stutter—and hadn't stuttered hardly at all. Now that he was on the spot, however, it came back with a vengeance.

"Well, um, we, uh, know from the wing configuration it's, uh, different than ours," he said. "The experts have some, uh, more, uh, more technical data to go through, and they still have a lot of questions. But at the moment it looks slower, like maybe 450 knots—"

"Whose is it?" asked the secretary of state.

Jed shook his head. "Dr-Dr-Dreamland is still working on it. We have Space Command and NSA r-reviewing sensor data in the area, and that's under way. But the first review of the earlier sighting didn't yield anything, so we're not sure what will come up."

He had to get rid of the damn stutter or no one would trust anything he said. It made him sound like too much of a jerk. Fortunately, Jed had some handouts summarizing the data Dreamland had compiled, and he passed them out.

"So it's not as capable as our craft?" asked Chastain.

"Well, it depends on your cr-criteria," said Jed. "The experts think it's not as f-f-fast. But it can carry a heavier load, which would mean a couple of things."

"Did the Chinese get all this information?" asked Balboa.

"No," said Hartman. "They know there was another craft involved. And that we're trying to track it."

"If they believe us," said the admiral, "and that's a big *if*, then we're in race with them to find this thing. Because if they grab it—"

"The Dreamland people will get there first," said Martindale. He rose. "Right, Jed?"

"They're getting closer."

"Close doesn't count," said Balboa. "We need results. Now."

Dreamland
1900

DANNY KNOCKED ON THE DOOR TO JENNIFER'S SMALL apartment twice without getting an answer. He turned and looked at the two airmen who had accompanied him, then reached into his pocket for the master key he'd brought along. He was just about to insert it in the door when a faint voice asked from inside who it was.

"Captain Freah," he told her. "Hey, it's Danny, Jen. Can I come in?"

She didn't answer.

"Jen?" he said.

He heard her footsteps and then her hand at the chain, pulling it open. She stood in the doorway wearing a bathrobe, though below it she had on jeans and a sweatshirt.

She'd cut her hair.

God, had she cut her hair—it looked as if she'd hacked it off with a knife.

Danny decided it was best to ignore it. He tried not to stare.

"Hey, you're off the hook. Completely," he told her. "Those conferences—we got information from the FBI and the security review at the time that clears you completely. Are you okay? Can I come in?"

She didn't answer, turning away instead. Danny glanced back at his men in the hall, then stepped inside by himself, closing the door behind him.

"Colonel Bastian's been trying to get ahold of you," he told her. "And Chief Gibbs. How come you don't return their calls?"

"How do you know I don't return their calls?" she said, twisting around in a fury. "Do you have a tap on my phone? You think you can just listen in to anything you want any time you want?"

Danny was authorized by the security regulations covering Dreamland to do just that, but this clearly wasn't the time to say so. "Of course not."

She pursed her lips. The lower one started to quiver.

"Jen, I know this has been tough for you. It's been tough for me," said Danny.

"You don't know what it's like to be considered a traitor," she said.

"You're right," he said. "It's got to suck."

"Yeah?"

"Yeah."

She frowned, but then she started to cry. Danny

found himself hugging her awkwardly, patting her back, telling her it would be okay.

Southeast Thailand
12 September 1997
1650

EVEN THOUGH HE HADN'T HAD MUCH SLEEP LAST NIGHT, Boston found it impossible to nap on the plane. While he had a special set of headphones to drown out the sound of the engines, the small plane shuffled up and down every so often, just enough to keep him awake. He spent his time leafing through a book he'd brought along and trading audio tapes with Bison, who unfortunately seemed to like the Grateful Dead considerably more than Boston would have thought possible.

Boston's adrenaline shot up as soon as Colonel Bastian announced that they were within sight of the airfield. He strapped his seat belt on and waited as the plane banked and then circled over the small strip. While they undoubtedly cleared the nearby jungle by a good margin, to Boston it seemed like the wingtip came perilously close to the top of the nearby trees. He struggled not to close his eyes as the airplane turned hard and legged down onto what looked more like an unkempt driveway than an airfield. The strip didn't have any lights or even a fence nearby; the only structures Boston saw as he stepped down the stairs were a telephone pole with a windsock and a two-story pillbox with a flat roof.

Boston put on his Smart Helmet and did a quick search of the area, using its composite view, which cobbled together IR, radar, and optical inputs to identify weapons and individuals. There was no one around.

"Yo, Boston, help me with the bikes," said Bison from inside. The sergeant went back and manhandled the small dirt bike out of the rear cabin, barely clearing past the seats. They had taken along several cans of gas as well as guns and radios. Everyone on the team wore civilian dress, authorized by the colonel because of the nature of the mission.

Colonel Bastian and Stoner met the two Whiplash ops on the hard-packed dirt.

"I want someone to stay here with me and watch the plane," said the colonel. "And let me emphasize, we show no military gear."

"I think we have to wear vests," said Stoner.

"All right," said Bastian. "Be as discreet as possible."

"Who's better at riding a motorbike?" said Stoner.

Boston looked at Bison, who looked at him. Both men shrugged. While riding a motorcycle was not part of the Whiplash job requirements, everyone on the squad had done so at one time.

"Flip a coin," said Dog.

Boston won the toss.

THE WIND WHIPPED HARD AGAINST STONER'S FACE AS he drove up the winding trail toward the fabrication plant. The sat photos he'd seen of it, part of a routine series covering the area, along with some background research provided by analysts back at the

CIA, indicated that it had been abandoned about six months before. Already the jungle had begun closing in. Nature's relentless march had broken up the edges of the road leading to the site; what two years ago had been a row of small, hastily built houses was now a collection of scavenged foundations.

Stoner would have preferred that the plant was still in operation. Getting information then would have been considerably easier—go in as a prospective client and look around, set up a tap into their computers, maybe even do a little B&E routine. Now all he could do was nose around and see what he could come up with. He had a digital camera and a chemical "sniffer" in his backpack, as well as a collection of programs on computer disks that would allow him to examine any computer he found. But as the building came into view, he realized he wasn't going to be finding much of anything.

The parking lot and helipad had been overgrown by vegetation, and the weeds were so thick that Stoner had to stop his bike about twenty yards from the front of the building. He got off and took the IR viewer from his backpack, using it to check around.

"We should cover the road," said Boston, who'd taken his MP-5 from his ruck.

"Anyone who's interested in us isn't going to use the road," said Stoner.

Built of cinderblocks, the one-story building had a row of windows at the front and side. Most of the windows were broken; the interior of the building had been stripped, not just of the valuable tools and machinery, but also of most of the sheetrock, ceiling tiles, and electrical wire. Stoner used his elbow to break enough of one of the windows so he could slip in easily.

A thick coat of reddish jungle clay covered the floor, swept in from the lot by the wind. There were tracks from another window at the side, but in the dim light Stoner couldn't tell how recent they might be. He took out his sniffer and started walking toward the back of the large open room, holding the long sensor wand ahead of him as he went.

The metal skeleton of a wall stood about twenty feet from the front. A jungle of twisted metal studs and beams lay beyond it, marking the actual fabrication areas. Much of the ductwork remained, though parts of it had been pulled out. Stoner followed the long runs as they snaked back into the bowels of the large plant. He nearly tripped over a row of pipes that jutted out of the cement floor, the last remains of a restroom. Pushing past a twisted wall brace, he entered a section of the plant that had been used as a clean room.

The sniffer picked up silicone and traces of gallium arsenide, along with a long menu of materials. There was no question the plant had been used to manufacture chips, and that its products were more advanced than the sort of circuitry needed to power a television or VCR.

WHEN BOSTON WAS A KID, HE'D LIVED IN A BAD SECTION of town, and he and his friends would sometimes wander through abandoned buildings about two blocks from where he lived. One building in particular held endless fascination for the nine- and ten-year-olds. Once a sewing factory, it was filled with ancient machines and all manner of pulleys and gears, many still hanging from the high ceiling. A mannequin sat in a shadowy corner; they liked to scare unsuspecting friends with it.

The afternoon visits ended abruptly when the building was taken over by crack smokers. Boston remembered them now as he worked through the skeletons of stripped walls, unsure exactly what they were looking for. He had his night-vision gear on, a special viewer designed by Dreamland that was much lighter than the normal-issue AN-PVS-7 and strapped on like a pair of swimming goggles. A light enhancer rather than an IR viewer, the device wasn't as powerful and versatile as the viewer integrated into the Whiplash Smart Helmet. But it provided more than enough light here.

Boston got a touch of the willies as a shadow passed along the metal struts where the wallboard had been removed. He knew it was just Stoner, but he couldn't rid himself of the tingle of fear bouncing in his chest. Then he heard something, or thought he heard something, outside.

Quickly, the Whiplash trooper retraced his steps out of the bowels of the building, pausing by a side window. He eased himself out of the opening and moved quietly toward the front of the factory. Sliding toward the bottom to peer around the corner at the overgrown parking area, he told himself he was being ridiculous; there was no one there.

Then he heard the bike engines kick to life.

STONER WAS JUST SCOOPING UP SOME SMALL BITS OF discarded chip material from one of the fab rooms when he heard the bike engine. Cursing, he stowed the sample and the sniffer in his ruck.

Boston had already gone outside.

He pulled out his pistol and ran to cover him.

THERE WERE THREE OF THEM, TWO ON ONE BIKE AND one on the other. Boston leaped to his feet, running toward them like a madman. He managed to grab one of the thieves by the back of the shirt and tossed him to the side, upending the other rider and the bike at the same time. A slap of MP-5 against the man's skull knocked him senseless. The would-be driver, meanwhile, scrambled in the dirt and managed to escape into the jungle.

Boston scooped up the motorbike, and reacting rather than thinking, he hopped on it and started to chase down the other thief.

Colonel Bastian had emphasized that they were not in enemy territory, and that their weapons were to be used only if their lives were threatened, and then only as a last resort. Did this situation qualify for deadly force?

Probably not.

Definitely not.

But Boston swore to himself that he'd upend the bastard and give him a good kick in the head when he caught him.

Just as he started to gain on the thief, the bike turned off a trail to his right. Boston skidded on the uneven surface, nearly losing the vehicle out from under him as he took the turn. He revved up the trail, came to a rise and found himself airborne; when he landed, the bike went one way and he went the other. By the time he got back to his feet, the thief was so far away Boston could barely hear the engine of the bike he'd taken.

BY THE TIME STONER GOT OUTSIDE, THE ONLY ONE IN the lot was a scrawny ninety-pounder, shaking like he was a puppy caught peeing on a rug. The kid looked to be about fourteen; whether he was Thai or Cambodian, Stoner couldn't tell.

"What's your story?" demanded Stoner. He repeated the question in Mandarin and then Cantonese Chinese, finally switching to standard Thai, a language he knew so little of that he could only ask what the man's name was and whether he could speak English.

The man said nothing in response to any of his questions, clearly frightened and probably believing he was going to die.

One of the motorbikes revved in the distance, returning. The CIA officer held on to the thief until he was sure that it was Boston on the bike, then threw the man down and told him, in English, to run. The man blinked at him.

"*Jàu hòi!*" Stoner said in Chinese. *Get away. Go.*

Finally the kid began crawling backward toward the jungle.

"Let's get the hell out of here," Stoner told Boston, climbing on the back of the bike.

"He a guerrilla?"

"I don't know. Probably just a thief. Come on. Let's get the hell out of here."

"You done inside?"

"For now. Go. Go!"

* * *

HISTORICALLY, THAILAND SAT AT THE CROSSROADS OF southeast Asia. The land had played host to various migrations for many thousands of years. This history had left a rich culture, but it had also greatly complicated the language situation. Thai was spoken by more than half of the country's population, but its various dialects and local accents made it difficult for a foreigner to understand, even when that foreigner was communicating with the help of a language expert who could listen in with the help of a small but powerful mike setup.

"I think what he's telling you is it's dangerous," said the Thai-Kadai language expert back in Dreamland as he tried to decipher the words Dog was repeating through his sat phone.

"Well, I kind of figured that," said Dog.

The man had arrived on bicycle after they'd been on the ground a half hour. He seemed to be a maintenance worker or caretaker; he had explained in heavily accented Thai that the administrator and staff had left some time before—though whether "some time" meant earlier in the day or weeks ago wasn't entirely clear.

"Why don't I let you talk to him directly?" Dog asked his translator.

"Sounds okay to me," said the man.

Dog had to coax the Thai worker into taking the phone. But he was soon chattering away, and Colonel Bastian thought he'd have a hard time getting the phone back.

"He says he hasn't been around too long," the translator told Dog. "He comes every day. The only other aircraft have been army helicopters. The Cambodian guerrillas hide when they come, but there are at least a few dozen armed insurgents nearby, and it sounds like they control the area. Most of the people who live in the jungle there are refugees, or were refugees and have just kind of squatted."

"Did he say anything about the factory?" Dog asked.

"Didn't know anything about it. Hard to tell how sincere he's being, Colonel. He may be scared of you and be telling you what he thinks you want to hear. Or he might be a guerrilla and be lying outright. Or he might just be telling the truth."

Dog looked at the middle-aged man. It seemed to him unlikely that the man was a guerrilla, but of course there was no way of knowing. The Thai government did not actively condone the guerrilla movement against the Cambodian government, but it didn't entirely discourage it either. The guerrillas were occasionally harassed, but the Thai government did not consider them a big enough threat to kick them out of the country. Historically, there had been plenty of animosity between Thailand and Cambodia, and if it weren't for the refugees who crowded their borders, the official line toward the guerrillas might have been openly encouraging.

"He offered to take you to his house for something to eat," added the Dreamland translator. "Pretty high honor."

"How do I say thanks but no thanks?" asked Dog. "We have to hit the road soon. Stoner should be just about wrapping up."

* * *

As THEY PASSED THE POINT WHERE THE THIEF HAD turned off, Boston saw something flash in the jungle on the opposite side of the road. He hunkered toward the handlebars, pushing the throttle for more speed though he already had the engine red-lined.

Stoner shifted on the bike behind him. Boston yelled at him to stop moving; he was afraid of losing his balance. But the CIA officer was oblivious, and Boston nearly lost the bike as the trail clambered across the side of a ravine before flattening out.

Someone was shooting at them.

Bullets flew on both sides of the road, dirt exploding in small wavelets.

And then there was a loud boom behind him.

Somehow, Boston managed to keep the bike upright. The small village near the airstrip lay just ahead.

STONER THUMBED THE TAPE OFF ANOTHER FLASH-BANG as they sped down the hill toward the village. The grenade he'd tossed off had temporarily slowed their pursuers, but he knew that it was just a matter of time before they closed in again. They had a jeep or something like a jeep as well as the other motorbike.

A group of children playing in the road ahead scattered as the bike approached. Stoner saw someone crouching near a building and realized he had a gun. Before he could do anything, he found himself flying through the air.

He realized he'd lost the M-84 stun grenade a half second before it exploded.

* * *

BOSTON HIT THE DIRT SO HARD HIS TEETH SLAMMED into his tongue. The pain made him scream; he jumped to his feet, head spinning in the dust. Someone grabbed him from behind, and he shoved his elbow hard into his side, fishing for his ruck and the submachine gun.

"Come on, come on," yelled the man who'd grabbed him. "The airport. Come on."

Stoner.

As Boston started to run, the bark of a heavy machine gun resonated off the nearby walls.

AS SOON AS DOG HEARD THE GUNFIRE AND EXPLOSIONS in the distance, he turned and ran back toward the airplane and Bison, who was standing guard near the wing.

"I'll get the engines going and turn around so we can take off," said Dog. "Get them aboard."

He didn't wait to hear an answer. He clambered into the cockpit, just barely patient enough to bring both engines on line before spinning the aircraft around. As he did, he caught sight of two figures running across the open field behind the blockhouse. Bison ran toward them, firing at something in the distance.

"Come on, damn it," Dog yelled.

The plane stuttered, its brakes barely holding it down.

"Move! Move!"

BOSTON TURNED AND SAW A JEEP BOUNCING ACROSS the edge of the road behind him. A machine gun had been mounted in the rear.

He leveled his MP-5 in the bastard's direction and emptied the clip. The front of the truck exploded and the vehicle flipped over, the gunner jumping out.

"In! Go!" Stoner yelled, pulling him toward the borrowed King Air.

Bison jumped up into the open rear doorway. Stoner yelled something, then threw himself inside the plane.

Boston took a look back. Two men were moving at the far end of the runway.

One was dragging a small sewer pipe with him.

No—he had a shoulder-launched missile.

The Whiplash trooper stopped, slapping a new magazine into his gun. By the time he had it ready to fire—no more than a few seconds later—the two men had disappeared.

There was a block building near the end of the runway.

The plane began moving behind him, but Boston couldn't worry about it now—he couldn't let the bastards shoot his people down. He heard the engines revving as he started toward the building.

Where'd the bastards go?

Ordinarily, he would have taken the corner slowly—ordinarily, he would have had a squad with him, flanked the SOBs, maybe used grenades and machine guns and every piece of ordnance known to modern man.

But there wasn't time for finesse.

Boston ran to the side of the building, finger edged against the trigger of his gun.

He saw them, the oversized blowpipe on the shoulder of the taller man.

Boston fired his MP-5 as the missile launcher exploded. For a moment, he saw everything stop; for a split second, he was part of the museum tableau, a display in Madame Tussaud's Wax Museum.

And then everything turned red. Then black.

DOG HAD ALREADY STARTED DOWN THE RUNWAY WHEN Bison yelled that Boston had gone back. He had too much momentum to stop; instead, he took the plane off the end of the runway, winging back quickly to land.

As he legged around, he saw smoke rise in a misshapen cloud, covering the building near the end of the runway.

He steeled himself for the worst as he touched down.

It took forever for Bison and Stoner to get out of the plane. When he saw they were out, Dog took off the brakes and trundled around once more, heart pounding—not because he worried that more guerrillas or whoever they were would appear, but because he dreaded having lost another man.

It was his fault. He could have worked with the Thai government. He should have.

He'd chosen not to because it would have involved politics and bullshit and delay.

His impatience had cost him a man.

Where the hell were the others?

"Go!" yelled Stoner finally, rushing into the forward cabin. "Go!"

"Boston?"

"Go!"

Bison appeared behind the CIA officer. "He's

okay. He just can't hear. The SA-7 flew into the side of the building and exploded. He shot the bastard just as he fired, and the missile went off course."

Dog punched off the brakes and slammed the engines to full power.

Brunei
1800

"AFTER YOU GET A LITTLE MORE EXPERIENCE UNDER your belt," Mack told Starship, "you'll see exactly what I'm talking about."

"I don't know, Major."

"Call me Mack, kid."

Mack smiled at the young pilot. Even though the kid had the bad luck to be working for Zen, Starship was all right. Balls-out Eagle jock, just like Mack.

Well, not quite as good a pilot. But who was?

"Single-malt Scotch," said Mack, raising his shot glass as he continued the young man's education. They were sitting in a reception room that was part of Prince bin Awg's lavish home. A butler had shown them here, and then vanished. "This is what real drinking is about."

"Guess I can't argue with that," said Starship, downing his glass.

"Sip. Sip," said Mack. "Like you're going to be doing it for a while."

"You sure we're allowed to be drinking his Scotch?"

"Why do you think they parked us in this room?" said Mack, refilling the glasses. "You don't understand Eastern hospitality, kid. It's subtle, but it's immense."

"Immense and subtle at the same time?"

"Drink up."

"There you are, Mack," said the sultan's nephew, entering the room. "And you've brought Lieutenant Andrews."

The prince ignored Mack's gesture toward the Scotch—he himself was an abstainer.

"The sultan wants you to attend dinner tonight," said bin Awg. "He has been thinking over things."

"Always up for dinner with the big guy. Right, Starship?"

"Um, I really have to get back."

"No, no, Lieutenant, you come along as well," said the prince. "Major Smith, His Majesty has a special surprise for you."

"What's that?" asked Mack.

"He's going to ask you to take charge of the air force."

"Which air force?" said Mack.

"Our kingdom's. We wish to modernize, and with a man of your stature, this could be easily accomplished."

Mack began to protest that he was happy as a member of the U.S. Air Force.

"But I'm sure we could make you happier," said the prince. "The sultan will be able to work things out with your government, of course. We would merely borrow you. I believe a somewhat similar arrangement was made with General MacArthur and the Philippines, prior to the World War. That might be the model."

MacArthur?

Head of the Brunei air force?

Why not?

"Well, it's an interesting idea," said Mack.

"Of course, you would be free to choose your own staff," said bin Awg.

"Starship can be chief of staff," said Mack.

"Um," said Starship.

"Please, there's much time to work on the arrangements directly," said the prince. "Your secretary of defense is an old friend of the sultan's. I'm sure he could arrange—what would you call it? A furlough?"

"I don't know," said Starship.

"And the arrangements would be quite generous," said bin Awg.

"Maybe I oughta talk to Colonel Bastian," said Starship.

"By all means. Mack?"

"Sign me up," said Mack, thinking of how many babes he might be able to get on staff.

Taipei, Taiwan
1900

HEADS TURNED AS CHEN LEE WALKED SLOWLY INTO the large reception hall. He smiled and nodded at the government dignitaries and businessmen, making his way slowly through the crowd.

His granddaughter's silk dress rustled against his leg as they walked. He did not actually need Kuan's support, but her presence was always a balm to him, making more palatable the false smiles and lies that he found it necessary to countenance. The fidelity of his family strengthened and comforted him; a mortal man could hope for no greater achievement than the unqualified love of his offspring, and the girl's willing presence at his side signified how truly rich he was.

"They are bowing to you, Grandfather," whispered Kuan. "They know you are a great man."

Chen Lee did not answer. He would not trouble the girl with the harsh reality that most of these men would be glad to see him pass on. They were appeasers, willing to sell their souls to the devil communists. For what? A few pennies and false promises. They were fools, and none so hardy as the president, who was holding court at the far end of the room, behind a phalanx of sycophants and bodyguards. Chen Lee waded in the other direction—let the president come to him, he decided.

Chen Lee had not heard from his grandson Chen Lo Fann, but he knew the young man's mission had failed. The Chinese had lost three aircraft—Fann's doing, no doubt—but aside from their usual hot-headed rhetoric, there had been no move against the United States, and no action to prevent the coming summit.

Chen Lee could not believe it. Had the generations that followed him become so weak, so puerile, that they did not recognize an act of war when they saw one? Did men wear dresses as well as false smiles now?

"Mr. Chen Lee, it is a great honor that you are here," said the British cultural attaché. The reception was ostensibly being held to commemorate the arrival of a British acting troupe in the capital, though of course it had many other purposes.

"You are too kind," Chen said humbly.

The attaché introduced him to another British citizen, Colonel Greene, who smiled benignly. Chen Lee turned and began to survey the crowd. Greene attempted to start a conversation by saying that the politics in the country had entered a difficult stage.

"Yes," said Chen Lee. It was necessary to be polite, but he did not want to encourage the foreigner.

"A shame so many people do not realize the danger of the situation," said Greene.

Chen Lee turned and looked at the colonel. He was dressed in civilian clothes, so it was impossible to tell if the title was honorary or not. The British seemed to be so overrun with retired colonels that they were exporting them to Asia by the planeload.

"Even the Americans seem blinded by the talk of peace," said Greene.

"The Americans have been allies for a long time," said Kuan. She had accompanied her grandfather to enough occasions such as this that she knew he wanted the foreigner drawn out.

"The Americans are endorsing the meeting in Beijing, and doing everything to keep it on schedule," said Greene.

"And how is that?" asked Kuan.

"They've told the communist pigs they were not responsible for the shooting down of the rescue aircraft in the South China Sea. They claim to be investigating and will present evidence that it was someone else. There are various rumors."

Kuan glanced at her grandfather. He did nothing—which she knew was a signal to continue.

"What sort of rumors?" she asked.

"The initial crash was an accident, yes," said Greene. "But the other plane—it seems doubtful."

"Who would have been involved?"

"Not Taiwan, I would think."

"We are not aggressors."

"Of course not."

"You are very well informed, Colonel Greene," Chen Lee said.

The colonel smiled. It was obvious now that he was part of British intelligence, though Chen Lee had never heard of him before.

"I am not so well informed as I would hope," said Greene. "But one hears rumors and has questions. And I for one would never trust the communists."

"Perhaps the British shot down the aircraft to disrupt the meeting in Beijing," said Chen Lee, staring into the colonel's eyes.

"Her Majesty's government is in favor of the meeting. Unfortunately."

Chen Lee smiled.

"So who would want to disrupt it?"

"It's not so much a question of whom," said the colonel, "but how. The Americans were the only ones in the area, from what I've heard."

"Then perhaps the Americans are better allies than I've been led to believe," said the old man.

Dreamland Command Trailer, Brunei
2100

"THE MATERIAL COULD HAVE BEEN A BYPRODUCT FROM any chip manufacturing process," Rubeo told Stoner over the secure video link as the others looked on in the trailer. "You will need more proof."

"I have people working on running down the ownership and digging through contracts," said Stoner. "What's important is that they could have made advanced chips there. These weren't for VCRs."

"Gallium arsenide is not wasted on entertainment applications."

"A company owned by a man named Chen Lee was apparently behind the factory when it was set up," said Stoner. "I'm looking into it right now, but I don't know what if anything we can run down. Chen is one of the most common names in Taiwan."

"Taiwan?" asked Rubeo.

"Yeah."

"Chen Lee is a prominent businessman—he hates the communists."

"They all do," said Stoner.

"Yes." The scientist scowled. "There's a Taiwanese scientist who's done considerable work on the mirroring system I believe was used in the intercepted transmissions. And he has a connection to Chen Lee, whom any Internet search will show is one of the most ardent anticommunists in Taiwan and a very rich, rich man."

"Is the clone the scientist's?"

"You're the investigator, not me, Mr. Stoner. Doing your legwork is getting a little tiresome."

"I'm sure it's appreciated," said Colonel Bastian.

"What's the scientist's name?" asked Stoner.

"Ai Hira Bai," said Rubeo. "He has not taught anywhere, or shown up at a conference, or published a paper, in at least eighteen months, perhaps more."

"Can you upload enough information for me to track him down?" said Stoner.

"Gladly."

"Bottom line here, Doc," said Colonel Bastian. "Could this Chen Lee guy build a Flighthawk?"

"It's not a Flighthawk," said Rubeo with pronounced disdain.

"Could Bai build something like we found?" asked Stoner.

"It depends entirely on his motivation and financing."

"What about the government?" asked Zen.

"No. If it was a government thing, I'd know about it," said Stoner. "Believe me. We've really checked into it. We're plugged into the Taiwanese military."

"I don't see a private company, or a couple of individuals doing this," said Alou. "What? Try to start a war between China and us? No way. Not without government backing."

"Some things are easier without the government involved," said Rubeo. "Much easier."

Dog glanced at his watch as Stoner and the scientist traded a few more barbs as well as ideas on where the UAV might have been built. The Taiwan connection was the overwhelming favorite, so much so that Dog knew he had to tell Jed what was going on. The others, meanwhile, seemed as if they were ready to pack it in for the night.

"All right, I'll tell you what," said Dog, interrupting them, "let's call it a day on this side. I'll talk to the NSC and tell them what we think. Ray, you and your people keep working on the data. Stoner—"

"There's a hundred people sifting the tea leaves back at Langley for us, Colonel," said the officer, referring to CIA headquarters. "We'll see if the NSA can come up with anything for us as well."

"Good," said Dog. "All right, let's—"

"Colonel, I'd like a word in private," said Rubeo before Dog could shut down the line.

"Well I'm out of here," laughed Zen. The others followed him from the trailer.

"Just you and me now, Doc," Dog said when they were gone. "What's up?"

"Jennifer Gleason has submitted her resignation," said Rubeo.

"She can't do that," said Dog.

"Well, she has a different opinion about that than you do."

"She can't leave," insisted Dog.

"Her contract—" started Rubeo.

"I understand she's not in uniform," said Dog. "I mean, she can't leave. We need her. And she'll screw herself, her career, I mean—"

"None of those things seem to be considerations," said Rubeo. "As I was starting to tell you, her contract states that she may return to teaching at any time with sixty days' notice, and she's submitted papers indicating that she wants to do that. It's not a formal resignation, but it's what she has to do to be in position to submit a formal resignation."

"Damn it Ray. God damn it."

Rubeo blinked at him. "Yes, Colonel. Damn it. Damn it all to hell."

Washington, D.C.
0915
(Brunei, 2115)

JED BARCLAY SLID INTO THE BACKSEAT OF THE CAR when the secure satellite phone he carried rang.

"Barclay," he said, swinging up the antenna so sharply that it cracked against the bulletproof glass of the limo.

"Jed, this Colonel Bastian. Can you talk?"

"Uh, yes, sir."

"We think the ghost clone may have been made by Taiwan, possibly by a private company. We're looking into it now."

"Taiwan?" Jed leaned back against the seat. "Taiwan?"

"That's what it looks like. We're not positive yet, though."

"I'm going to talk to the President about Taiwan," said Jed. "There's a high-level conference between the premier of Mainland China and the president of Taiwan next week. We're thinking of sending the vice president."

"I don't think that has anything to do with this," said Bastian. "This is just one little airplane."

"I don't think the President's going to agree," said Jed.

* * *

FORTIFIED BY ANTIBIOTICS AND A SHELF'S WORTH OF vitamins, Jed's boss walked shakily into the paneled conference room in the basement of the West Wing. Jed hovered nearby, ready to lend his arm or shoulder in case Philip Freeman suddenly ran out of energy.

Freeman's presence made Jed feel considerably more relaxed than he had been over the past few days; there'd be no need to speak, except to his boss. While Colonel Bastian's assessment that the Taiwanese were involved was bound to shock most of those at the meeting, Freeman would bear the brunt of the questions.

The President and most of the invited Cabinet members had already arrived, along with half of the service chiefs. They were already discussing the summit between China and Taiwan.

"We have to encourage the meeting, and the best way to do so is by sending the vice president," said Hartman, the secretary of state. "He's already in Japan. It won't take anything for him to go to Beijing."

"Too much too soon," said Chastain. "Especially since the Chinese are still blaming us for shooting their aircraft."

"The official protest has been withdrawn," said the secretary of state. "The rest is just for internal consumption. It's posturing."

"I'd like to show them posturing," said Balboa. He looked at Jed as he said it and winked.

"If we're not there, we run the risk of being left on the sidelines," said the secretary of state. "The vice president can say that he's going to Beijing to discuss the unfortunate crash of the Chinese aircraft in the South China Sea."

"Let's not do that," said Martindale. "If we go, we go. No baloney playing. Have we figured out what happened yet?"

All eyes turned to him.

"The Dreamland team has come up with a theory," said Jed. "But we need more information."

Jed could feel his face turning red as the others waited for him to continue. Jed glanced at his boss, who nodded. He'd already told Freeman in the car on the way over.

"It looks like Taiwan. Or actually, a private company working without the knowledge of the government," said Jed.

"Taiwan?" said Hartman.

"We just got the information on the way over," said Jed. "Colonel Bastian and the Dreamland team are looking for permission to enter the country to do more research."

"Taiwan? Not Mainland China?" asked Martindale.

"Taiwan does make sense," said Freeman, his voice raspy. "If it's one of the old hard-liners, not the new government."

"But a private company?" asked Martindale. "How? Who?"

"We're still trying to gather data," said Jed, "but the CIA expert working with Dreamland believes the plane was developed by a businessman who's at odds with the present government. The companies that seem to be responsible are owned by a man named Chen Lee. He's pretty old—he fought in Chiang Kai-shek's army. The embassy says he's one of a handful of hard-liners against the summit next week. Like I say, we're still gathering information. This is really new, as of a few hours ago."

"You sure this isn't something Bastian cooked up to make himself look good, young Jed?" asked Balboa.

"I don't think so, Admiral."

"Colonel Bastian's not like that," said Freeman.

"What's the status of the investigation into Dreamland?" asked Chastain.

"Unofficial investigation," said Jed.

"Yes?"

Jed looked to his boss and then the President before giving the unofficial findings of the AFOSI. "They can't rule it out, but everything points to no penetration."

"A weapon such as the Flighthawk in the hands of the Taiwanese—whether it's the government or not, makes no difference—is going to anger the Mainlanders," said Hartman. "It will make the situation extremely volatile."

"If they have it, how come we haven't figured it out until now?" asked Martindale.

Jed—one of the people responsible for figuring such things out—looked down toward the table before speaking.

"It may be that it's been developed entirely outside of the ordinary military channels," he said. "As a matter of fact, that seems most likely. Because otherwise, we'd have had indications. The Taiwan connection took the CIA totally by surprise."

"It takes the Air Force by surprise as well," said the defense secretary. It seemed to be a jab at the service chief, who hadn't offered anything in the discussion—a sound political move, in Jed's opinion.

"This is all very interesting, but it's not going to contribute anything to our decision on what to do about the summit," said Hartman.

The secretary of state got the discussion back on track, arguing for an American presence in the capital during the meeting. Chastain responded by pointing out that many of Taiwan's neighbors were taking a very cautious approach. Japan in particular had yet to weigh in on its opinion of the meeting, a clear sign that it viewed it with suspicion at best. There was also the danger that high-level U.S. presence in Beijing at the time of the meeting would raise expectations beyond a reasonable level.

As the debate continued, Jed watched President Martindale. His face gave no hint of which argument he agreed with. Jed knew from experience that he liked to gather as much information as possible before delivering a pronouncement. This often made for a fairly long fact-finding period, though once the President decided, he never wavered or second-guessed himself. Jed admired that; he himself often worried after he made a decision, and even something as simple as picking a tie might be revisited three or four times.

"The real question is whether rapprochement is in our interests or not," said Freeman. "At this point, I frankly feel the answer is not."

"Long term it is," said the secretary of state.

"I agree with the national security advisor," said Balboa.

Jed thought he ought to pull out his pocket calendar and record the date—the admiral and his boss rarely agreed on what to have for dinner, let alone anything substantive.

"I don't think we can actively discourage peace," said Chastain. "But I do argue for caution."

The President raised his hand.

"I think we have to encourage peace in Asia," said Martindale. "At this point, we want the dialogue to go ahead. Obviously, we want to monitor events there very, very closely. And we don't want any developments that would derail it."

There was more debate, but Jed could tell the President had already made up his mind. Martindale let everyone take one more shot at having his say, then ended the discussion for good.

"The vice president will arrange his schedule to visit Beijing on the first day of the conference," he said. "But he will not attend it, or offer any comment on it. He will visit the Chinese premier and the president of Taiwan privately. That is absolutely as far as we can go."

"It's pretty far," said Chastain.

"Anything else, gentlemen?" said the President, rising.

There was, of course, nothing else.

"Feeling better?" he asked the national security advisor as Freeman and Jed started to leave.

"Getting there," said Freeman. "No cigars for a while."

"Your wife must be glad of that," laughed Martindale. He turned to Jed. But instead of joking, his voice was once more dead serious. "I want you to tell Dreamland to nail this down."

"Yes, sir. But—"

"I don't like buts, Jed."

"Um, they're going to want to go in-country and look around," said Jed. "Colonel Bastian already suggested it."

"Tell them to do so," said Martindale. "Quietly. Very quietly."

"If the Taiwanese have such a weapon, what do we do?" asked Freeman.

"We worry about it when we're sure they have it," said Martindale.

IV

DUTY

Dreamland Visiting VIP Office
12 September 1997
1200

RUBEO LAID THE PRINTOUTS FLAT ON THE TABLE, PULL-ing the two pages close together so that the lines he had highlighted were next to each other.

"I don't expect you to understand," he told Cortend. "But to anyone with a modicum of knowledge of the systems involved, it's obvious what's being done. There's a repeater system that takes bits of captured information and rebroadcasts it. You can see here, here, and here. That's why the signal seems to be ours. It is ours. This"—he took the two sheets from the folder, laying them side by side—"shows the intercepts and our own flight communications from the other day. Incontrovertible. That word is in your vocabulary, is it not?"

Cortend glared at him. Rubeo realized that he had made exactly zero progress with the old witch.

Then again, he hadn't come here to convince her. He'd come for the satisfaction of showing her to her face that she was an idiot. And he had accomplished that.

"Now that I know what's going on, we can easily strip out the signals that are being beamed back, and then determine the actual signals. I would explain how we do it," he said, gathering up the pages, "but you don't have the clearance to hear it. Let alone the IQ to understand it."

He had nearly reached the door when Cortend spoke.

"Just a minute, Doctor," she said.

Rubeo couldn't resist one last look at her constipated face writhing in the torment of ignorance unmasked. He turned around. Cortend pointed at her two assistants, dismissing them with flicks of her finger. The lieutenants scurried away.

"You think I enjoy questioning the integrity of your people?" she said.

"In a word, yes."

Cortend said nothing for a moment. "My father's name was Harold Bernkie. Does that name mean anything to you?"

"Hardly," said Rubeo.

For the first time since she had come to the base, Cortend smiled. "It shouldn't. In the 1950s, he was a very promising scientist. And then his name was linked with the Communist Party. He was blacklisted and couldn't get work. He's my father, so obviously I think he was a genius, but of course that really isn't for me to say. I only know that he eventually became an electrician. A very good one, in my opinion, though I suppose that too is neither here nor there. This hasn't been a witch hunt. I've been extremely fair."

"That's a matter of opinion."

Cortend shook her head. "No. I believe that you will find that I have been thorough, that I have been a stickler for details, and I have pursued any and all leads. Those were and remain my orders. As far as your Miss Gleason goes, I never charged her with a crime or recommended any disciplinary action against her."

"That's because your investigation wasn't complete," said Rubeo. "Don't banter definitions around."

"You are a scientist. You're precise in your work. I am precise in mine," said Cortend. "No charges were filed against your coworker. I was here on an informal basis precisely to spare you and your people the ordeal of a full-blown inquiry. Believe me, it would have been ten times worse."

"I doubt that is possible."

Cortend took a long, labored breath. "I've been informed that there are explanations for what appeared to be omissions concerning the conferences. Given those explanations, I see no need to make any recommendation concerning her to the commander."

Rubeo wasn't sure exactly what to say. He remained angry—extremely angry. This idiot had cost him one of the top scientists in the world, who even now refused to get out of bed, claiming to be sick.

"The data that you have gathered would appear to exonerate Dreamland completely," said Cortend. "Coupled with the information about the aircraft's physical characteristics, it would appear very convincing."

"You're not going to imply that we created it," said Rubeo.

"I'm sure you're clever enough to do so," said Cortend. "But no, Doctor, I don't believe that for a moment. And more importantly, there is no evidence suggesting that you did. There is no evidence suggesting that anyone at Dreamland is anything less than a dedicated and patriotic American. Good day."

That was it? She was giving up?

She was giving up.

Truth and reason had won?

Truth and reason had *won*. The Inquisition was over.

Rubeo, unsure exactly what to say, turned and left the room.

Approaching Chiang Kai-shek Airport, Taipei
13 September 1997
0600

"ARE YOU AWAKE?"

Danny Freah floated for a moment, caught in dream limbo between sleep and waking. He saw his wife, he saw the hard-assed Colonel Cortend, he saw two brown eyes staring down at him asking whether he was awake.

"Yeah," he said, pushing up in the seat.

"The pilot is asking everyone to put their seat belts on," said the stewardess.

"Oh. Thanks." Danny smiled and pushed his head forward, as if trying to swim away from the back of the seat. Bits and pieces of the dream fluttered away, just out of reach of his conscious mind.

Jemma and Colonel Cortend—God, what a combination.

"It's beautiful from the air, isn't it?" said the woman next to him. Her name was Alice something-or-other, and she was a programmer for a computer firm who traveled a lot between LA and Asia.

No, she worked for a company that manufactured rubber boots. The programmer thing came from his dream.

"Yeah," said Danny, leaning forward to see past her. Their arms touched and he felt a shock go through his body; he jerked back, as if the touch had been something else.

"Temperature's only eighty degrees, Fahrenheit," said Alice. "Humidity is supposed to be pretty low. I don't remember the percentage."

"That's good."

Danny avoided her eyes, inexplicably feeling guilty about sitting next to her, as if he were somehow being disloyal to his wife.

He'd spoken only briefly to the woman before falling asleep—the civilian flight had proven to be among the most comfortable he'd ever taken—and their conversation had hardly been intimate: he'd given his basic cover story, claiming that he was working for a banking company as a security consultant, and then spoke of New York City as if he lived there.

Which he did, since his wife had their apartment there.

Alice was a middle-aged businesswoman, nice enough, but not really attractive to Danny. He was impressed that even though she was white, her voice didn't have the forced tone white strangers sometimes took with him, the "I'm really not a jerk and please let me prove it by being nice to you" tone that the best-intentioned stranger sometimes betrayed. But no way was he having sexual fantasies about her, not even if she had been ten years younger and maybe twenty-five pounds lighter.

So why was he feeling guilty about Jemma?

Because he'd changed his mind about leaving the Air Force to run for Congress?

He had changed his mind, hadn't he? Even though he hadn't really thought about it.

The plane rocked slightly as it settled into its final approach. Danny felt his neighbor's arm jostle against his and once more thought of his wife. He was still thinking of her a few minutes later when they parked at the terminal and passengers began disembarking. He waited for the others nearby to clear out, then rose and pulled open the overhead compartment where his suit jacket and carry-on were. He took out his seatmate's as well.

"Thanks. Don't forget, if you need a guide, give me a call," said Alice.

"Right," said Danny. He gestured toward his shirt pocket, remembering that he had put her card there hours ago. She gave him a smile, then bumped her way toward the front of the plane with her heavy carry-on.

Danny's civilian sport coat was a little tight at the shoulders, and he felt the squeeze as he waited in the terminal to complete the arrival processing. He eyed the line behind him as he approached the clerk, professional paranoia suddenly kicking in. By the time he made it through the passport check his heart had started to beat double-time, and he sensed he was being shadowed. He turned left in the large hallway, then saw the row of limo drivers holding signs up for arriving passengers.

And there was Liu, holding up his placard as if he were a driver.

"Mr. Freah?" asked Liu as Danny stood in front of him.

The sergeant was of Chinese extraction, but even Danny could tell that he looked different from the other drivers. He wore the right clothes, his short hair and smile seemed to fit, but there was something American about the way he filled the space— his shoulders rolled as he moved, as if he were a linebacker waiting for a blitz.

"This way," said the sergeant, starting to the left.

"Should have insisted he take your bag," said someone behind him.

It was Stoner.

"Hey," said Danny.

"If you guys are going to play spy, you got to work on the routine," said Stoner, moving ahead briskly.

Stoner had an overnight bag under his arm, as if he were an arriving traveler. In fact, Liu and Stoner had come up from Brunei the night before on a leased airliner, bringing along some of Dreamland's high-tech gear with them. They had landed at a military base, which allowed them to move their equipment in without much notice. Still, as a security precaution Liu had brought along only a few essential items, including a short-range communications unit that could upload surveillance information to Dreamland. Danny had more gear and men en route to Brunei in case things got more interesting.

The muggy outside air felt as if they'd stepped into a shower room, even though it was balmy by local standards. He followed as Liu and Stoner turned left, continuing past both the taxis and the rentals. A small blue Toyota darted through the lot and headed toward them as Liu stepped off the curb; Danny grabbed for his sergeant.

It was just their driver pulling up. Stoner smirked and got into the front seat; Danny and Liu took the back.

"Jack is from the American-Asian Business Coalition," Stoner told them. "That's where he learned to drive."

The driver, who looked no more than fourteen, turned and grinned. He seemed to be Chinese, though obviously in the employ of the CIA. Since America did not officially recognize Taiwan, there was no embassy; interests were handled at the American Institute. Danny gathered that the American-Asian Business Coalition was a "trade" organization that was one of several fronts used by the CIA in Taiwan.

"We have a few places to check out," Stoner said. "I'd like to get started right away."

"Fine with me," said Danny.

"Satellite transmitter is in the trunk," said Liu. "We ran a diagnostic on the way over. Sat phone connects without a problem."

"Good," said Danny. The phone and transmitter tied into the Dreamland system normally used by the Smart Helmets and Dreamland aircraft to communicate. The transmitter took information from a variety of sensors and sent it back to Dream Command for real-time analysis.

"Colonel Bastian is working on getting a Megafortress up here as part of the ASEAN exercises," added Liu. "They want to keep the cover story intact, so he sent us ahead while he worked on it."

"That's fine," said Danny. The captain smiled to himself, thinking there was little need for a Megafortress, though it was just like the colonel to line one up. No self-respecting zippersuit could stand to see an operation under way without air support.

Danny reached into the bag for the viewer he'd brought from Dreamland. Shaped like a large pair of opera glasses, the device could present different "slices" of heat at a depth up to roughly one hundred meters. The information from these views would be analyzed by specialists back at Dream Command, who could use them to draw a diagram of a building's interior and what was going on inside. But the device's sensor plane had to be kept cool for it to work properly; he slid it into a bag that looked like a collapsible lunch bag and twisted a plastic container at the bottom that released liquid nitrogen into the cooling cells.

Danny also had a Geiger counter and radiation analyzer, which measured alpha, beta, and gamma radiation and could identify fifty-five isotopes. He also had a number of self-activated bugs, video spy devices, and motion detectors.

"First target is near Sungshan, the domestic airport not far from here," said Stoner. "The others are in the south on the coast near Kaohisiung. We'll drive over to the site near the airport, look around. Then we'll arrange for a helicopter at the airport. All the easy spots have been looked at already by my associates, and I don't know how close we're going to get to the ones that are left on our list, so this may all take a while."

Taipei
0805

WITH EVERY SECOND THAT PASSED WAITING FOR THE elevator in the lobby of his grandfather's building, Chen Lo Fann felt the weight against his chest grow. He could not avoid his solemn duty to tell his grandfather that he had failed, even though the disappointment his grandfather would feel would surely hurt the old man as gravely as any injury he had ever felt.

Surely, his grandfather already knew that he had failed. The communists had not attacked the Americans or the ASEAN fleet, despite their rhetoric. Nor had they called off the summit.

The criminals were cowards at heart. That was why they picked on lesser nations instead of facing truly worthy opponents. Chen Lee no doubt knew this.

But that did not remove his grandson's duty to inform him.

Chen Lo Fann had rehearsed what to say for hours, thinking of it the whole way back to Taiwan aboard the helicopter, as if the right phrase might save him. But finally he'd conceded to himself that the words themselves were insignificant.

Professor Ai had taken the helicopter back with him, and offered to come along to talk to Chen Lee, perhaps thinking he could soften the blow. But Chen Lo Fann had politely declined. There were other things the professor must see to in Kaohisiung; facing the old man was Fann's duty.

The elevator opened. Chen Lo Fann stepped in.

He remembered jumping up to tap the button as a child. The memory pushed down against his shoulders as the car slowly made its way upward.

The secretaries stared at him as he got off. Chen Lo Fann lowered his gaze toward the carpet, walking the familiar steps to his grandfather's office suite. The two security guards stepped aside as he approached, as if they didn't want to be polluted with his failure.

It wasn't his failure, it was the communists'. And most especially the treacherous president's, their supposed leader. A coward, a quisling, a traitor.

Chen Lee's secretary nodded. He could proceed.

Chen Lo Fann went to the door to his grandfather's office, his hand hesitating on the knob. He opened it with a burst of resolve; he would face his grandfather like a man.

Chen Lee sat at his desk, his back to the door, staring out the window. Chen Lo Fann stepped forward, waiting for the old man to turn around. He waited for nearly five minutes, until the clock struck the quarter hour.

"My plan has failed, Grandfather," he said, no longer able to bear the weight on his chest. "The mongrels will not make war and the president will go ahead with his meeting."

The old man said nothing.

Chen thought of what to suggest. Assassination had been debated; as desperate as it was, perhaps it was the best option now. The only option.

But there would be other traitors. The people to strike were the communists, the usurpers. Chen had suggested bombing the capital with the UAV, but they did not possess a strong enough weapon to guarantee the death of all the thieves.

"Grandfather?" he said, when the old man failed to respond. "Grandfather?"

As unbearable as the weight had been before, now it increased ten times. Chen flew across the room, turning the chair roughly.

His grandfather's slender body slid from the chair into his arms. His pale skin was cold; the old man's heart had stopped more than an hour before.

Chen Lo Fann trembled as he put the old man back in his chair. There was a note on the desk, the figures drawn in Chen Lee's shaky hand.

"The weapons are in place," said the note.

Chen stared at the ideograms. He was not sure what weapons his grandfather was talking about, or even where they might be. Silently, he folded the paper and placed it back in his pocket. And then he went to find out.

Club Lion, Brunei
1205

ALL HIS LIFE, STARSHIP HAD BEEN ON TOP OF THE WAVE. He'd ridden it to the State Class A Football Championship in junior year as all-league quarterback; the next year he'd taken the state trophy in wrestling. The Academy—more success in football, of course, where his exploits against Notre Dame were still the talk of the place. Pilot training, F-15 squadron. The assignment to Dreamland was supposed to be another notch in the belt.

It was. But it wasn't going precisely as he had planned.

For one thing, he hadn't planned on joining the Flighthawk program—he'd been shooting for one of the manned fighter programs but discovered the only open pilot slot was in the Megafortress, and with all due respect to the monster craft, no amount of Dreamland gadgets could turn it into an exciting ride. He'd managed to finesse a slot with the Flighthawks and figured he'd be in a good position to transition eventually—though eventually might be far down the road.

But what Starship hadn't counted on was the pressure. Because even though he was good—better than good—he'd felt unbelievable stress ever since the start of the deployment. He wasn't sure why— was it because he was so far from the plane he was flying? Was it the fact that Kick was looking over his shoulder? Was he intimidated by Zen, a pilot so tough he could lose the use of his legs and still come back for more?

Or was it fear?

He slid another ten-dollar bill on the bar of the club.

Eating at the palace last night with Mack Smith had been a revelation. He'd thought the job proposal was complete BS, but the sultan turned out to be serious. He wanted to take Brunei into the twenty-first century—even beyond. He wanted frontline fighters and Megafortresses. Mack Smith could build an empire here.

And it looked like he was going to take the job.

If he did, Starship would be in line to help. Major Smith had said so. More than likely, much of the work at first would be staff BS and PR, but he would have the pull to fly whenever he wanted.

Those little trainer jobs they flew at first, but eventually, real planes.

A week ago, he'd have laughed out loud about the whole idea. But now he wasn't sure.

Starship took his drink and slid around in his seat to watch the girl dancing on the stage. The girl started to slide her skirt down.

Someone shook Starship from behind.

"What's the story?" he said angrily, turning.

"So this is where you're hiding," said Kick. "I can see why."

"Hey, roomie. Pull up a stool. How'd you find me?"

"Mack Smith suggested I look here."

"Yeah, good ol' Major Smith. Have a drink."

"Thanks but no thanks. Zen wants us ASAP."

"What for? It's our day off. Besides, we're still grounded, right? Because of the Chinese baloney?"

"Not anymore. Colonel Bastian arranged for *Pennsylvania* to fly up to Taiwan as part of the ASEAN exercises. You're supposed to leave right away."

"Damn," said Starship.

Kick stepped back. "I'll tell him I couldn't find you."

"Screw that," said Starship, sliding off the barstool.

"I'm serious, man. You can't fly."

"Better than you."

Kick looked at him. "Not at this moment."

"I can fly better than you in my sleep, Kick boy."

Taipei
1210

THE FIRST FACTORY STONER TOOK THEM TO LAY ABOUT a mile and a half from Sungshan airport, in a crowded district of warehouses and industrial buildings. The roads were so thick with traffic that it took hours to get to the facility itself; when they finally did they found their way blocked by uniformed employees. The men were polite—the driver pretended to be asking for directions and they answered helpfully—but there was no way past them.

Danny eyed the fence, which was topped with barbed wire; there were also video cameras. Besides the two men at the gate he saw another patrolling down the way.

He took out the IR device and slowly began scanning the building. A small wire connected to the side; it was an earphone that buzzed as soon as the reading was complete and logged. The data were ferried via a small antenna to the transmitter unit in the trunk, though at the moment they weren't broadcasting to Dreamland because of the small possibility that it might be detected.

Every time the machine buzzed in his ear, he pushed the small trigger button on the top between the two barrels; the IR sensors adjusted themselves and took another "bite" at the building. As it moved further inside, the buzzes started to be punctuated by clicks; it was having trouble seeing. Danny tried holding it at different angles and jostling it; finally he decided they had gotten everything they could.

"So?" asked Stoner as they drove away.

"We'll see what the techies say. They can construct a three-D model when they look it over," said Danny.

"That thing like a radar?" asked Stoner.

"No, it uses heat signatures so it can't be detected. We call in IR or infrared, but the techies say it has a somewhat wider band. The sensors are here." Danny pointed to the top rim of the glasses. "They have to be kept fairly cool to work right. But they have better range than the viewers on our Smart Helmets, and since there's no radio waves, there's nothing to be detected."

"I'd still like to get inside."

"Fine by me," said Danny.

"They make seats for aircraft," said Stoner. "I have somebody working on getting us in as buyers. But it's going to take a few days."

"Is it big enough?" asked Liu.

"Could be," said Danny. "We'll see what the tech people say."

"There's a rail line that runs from the back over to the airport," said Stoner. "Chun Sue owns some hangars there. That's one of the companies Chen Lee owns. As far as I know, only one is occupied. I figure we hit the empties first."

They uploaded the data on the way over. The Dreamland techies told Danny that he had only managed to see about eighty feet inside the building; a stock of insulation and fabric for the chairs blocked a deeper view. Everything they had been able to see was consistent with a seat factory—or something trying to look like one.

They didn't need the viewer in the airport; all the hangars were open and unguarded. Stoner had prepared a story—they were looking to lease a facility—but no one seemed to even notice they were there.

Danny took a small scoop and wad of plastic bags from the attaché case he'd brought, sampling some of the dust so the chemicals could be analyzed. He also took out the Geiger counter and took some readings; all were within background norms.

"Just a hangar," said Stoner, walking to sit on an old crate in the corner.

"What's the crate say?" Danny asked.

"It's the name of a fish company. Heavenly Fish, along those lines."

"Why would it be here?" Danny asked. He bent down to examine it.

"Shipped cargo in and out. Lost one of the crates," said Stoner.

"The crate wasn't used to carry fish. It's too clean."

Stoner shrugged.

Danny took a picture with his digital camera,

then took out his knife and took a sample of the wood where it had been worn down. He took his rad meter out again, but found nothing special. Finally, he planted a pair of the video camera bugs near the doorway.

The cams were about the size and shape of three-quarter-inch bolts, the kind that might be used to secure a part on a child's bicycle. There were two types, one with a wide-angle lens and the other more narrowly focused but able to work in near darkness. Each sent its signal to a transmitter the size of a nine-volt battery, which could be hidden anywhere within fifty feet of the cams. This transmitter in turn linked with a large base station—about the size of a cement block though nowhere near as heavy—that uploaded images either on command or in a random burst pattern that made it difficult to detect. The cameras and transmitters themselves used a similar random pattern with a very weak signal that would generally escape detection.

"You sure those things work?" asked Stoner as they got back in the car.

Danny turned to Liu, who gave him a thumbs-up. The sergeant was using his sat phone to talk to Dream Command, where the techies had just finished diagnostics on the gear, confirming there was a signal.

"Now I am," said the captain.

The hangar that housed the airplane was open, and the four Americans managed to walk right in. The building was about twice the size of the others, and the Boeing 767-200ER it housed filled only about a third of the massive space. The wings of the large airliner were covered with large sheets of rolled cardboard, and the place smelled of fresh paint.

A pair of Chun Sue employees came over and told them that the company airplane was undergoing refurbishment. The men were very polite, and seemed flattered by the praise Danny threw at the airplane, which in fact was a beautiful piece of machinery. The 767 typically cruised between 35,000 and 40,000 feet; this model, optimized for the long-distance flights common in Asia, could clock close to six thousand miles before having to hit the gas pumps.

The experts back in Dreamland noted one other interesting fact about the airplane as they briefed Danny through the headset connecting to his sat phone—it was a bit large for the airport, which was generally used by smaller jets and turboprops on local hops.

Danny took several photos with his small camera for them, and planted a pair of video cams near the entrance.

"Those suckers cost a fortune," he told Stoner as they left.

"The company is pretty rich," said Stoner. "You notice anything funny about the paint?"

"Besides the fact that the plane doesn't need painting?"

"The colors are used by the People's Xia Airlines."

"They own them too?"

"That's a Mainland airline," said Stoner. "They left off the symbols on the tail, but otherwise it's a ringer."

Brunei IAP, Field Seven
Dreamland Temporary Hangar
1312

ZEN TOOK ONE LOOK AT STARSHIP AND ROLLED HIS eyes.

"Where the hell did you find alcohol in Brunei?"

"Excuse me, sir?" said Starship.

If Zen had had any doubts about Starship's sobriety, the accent he put on "sir" would have dispelled them.

"Take the rest of the day off," he told the lieutenant. "You were due rest anyway. I shouldn't have called you back."

"I can fly, Zen. Major—I can fly."

"Go take a shower, Starship. That's an order."

Starship's face turned red. He spun on his heel and retreated from the hangar.

"You and me, Kick, let's go," said Zen, backing his wheelchair away so he could go and get his flight suit and other gear. "*Pennsylvania* is taking off in an hour. We're way behind schedule."

THEY LAUNCHED THE FLIGHTHAWK AS SOON AS THEY were over water. Zen took the first leg of the flight, checking on some of the merchant ships that lay in their path. He wanted Kick to take the last half of the flight so he'd have the experience of landing at Tainan Air Base, their destination on Taiwan.

"See the ship there, Kick?" he asked his nugget assistant, who was monitoring the flight from the second station.

"Yes, sir."

"Zero the cursor in, query it, get the registration data."

"Yes, sir."

"Relax, Kick, I'm not going to bite your head off. You don't have to say 'sir' every ten seconds."

"Yes, sir."

Zen laughed.

Both Kick and Starship were excellent pilots and Flighthawk operators, but both men tended to be nervous around him. Was it because he was in charge of the program and therefore had a huge amount to say over their futures?

Or was it the wheelchair?

When he first came from his accident, he would have automatically assumed the latter. Lately, though, he'd become more discerning, or at least willing to let the complicated attitudes people had toward him ride.

Most days, anyway.

The wheelchair could get in the way. It had with Fentress—but that was Zen's fault. He'd been jealous of the kid, or rather jealous of the fact that the kid could walk away from a session and he couldn't. He wasn't going to let that happen again.

"Got the data," said Kick.

"So? What do you think?" Zen asked.

The information was already on Zen's screen—the ship was a Malaysian freighter.

"Looks pretty straightforward. Carrying tea. My thinking is we go over low and slow, find out. No big deal."

"No big deal." Zen nudged the Flighthawk toward the ship. The computer already had a dotted line plotted for the recon run; he authorized the flight and gave control to C^3.

"You know how I got crippled?" he said to Kick.

"I heard some sort of accident."

"Mack Smith and I were having a mock dogfight with the Flighthawks. I got too close to one of them. Sawed me in half. I was below five hundred feet. A lot below, actually. I don't even remember bailing out."

Kick was silent. Finally, he said, "Sucks."

"Yeah, it does. But you move on. You have to."

"Yes, sir."

"Hey, you know, just call me Zen. You take the stick after this run, all right? I'm going to roll back on the deck there and grab myself a soda."

"I can get it."

Pity? Or just a young officer trying to please his superior.

Zen opted to believe it was the latter. He'd give the kid the benefit of the doubt until proven wrong. Same with Starship.

"That's okay, Kick. I want you to get as much practice in the air as possible. Okay?"

"Great," said the other pilot. "I appreciate it."

Kaohisiung
1650

THE ISLAND OF TAIWAN MEASURES ONLY 396 BY 144 kilometers. While Kaohisiung was on the opposite end of the country from Taipei where Danny and the rest of the team were, the flight south in a rented Sikorsky took less than an hour.

The first site they had to check was a large office building near the center of the city off Kusshan-1 Road. Danny took out his fancy opera glasses and slowly scanned the interior. Liu, once again acting as the liaison with the Dreamland team, declared the basement nearly empty; the only machinery on the floors above related either to the cooling system or to the elevators. Twenty-something stories filled with office workers and nothing more lethal than a letter opener.

Even so, Stoner and Danny went inside, going up to the fifteenth floor where a Taiwan magazine had its offices. They played tourist, Stoner claiming to work for a San Francisco publication Danny had never heard of but that somehow impressed the Taiwanese. After a few minutes it was clear to Danny that there was nothing of much interest here, and he practiced smiling and nodding. Stoner passed out a whole parcel of business cards; Danny realized from the looks he was getting that not having any was a serious faux pas.

"What's with the cards?" Danny asked as they took the elevator down.

"Considered polite to exchange them," said the CIA agent. "I have dozens for every occasion."

He showed a few to Danny. They declared he was a magazine editor, electronics equipment buyer, engineer, and American trade representative. The backs of the cards had the information in Chinese characters.

"You sure you're not schizophrenic?" said Danny, handing the cards back.

"Sometimes I wonder." Stoner pocketed the

cards. "Computer system is easy to access. They're networked with an Ethernet. We can get in if we want."

"You think it's worth it?"

"At the moment, no. But now we can come back and get in easily. Once the system is bugged, the NSA whizzes can get into the printing plant."

"Where's that?"

"Our next stop."

NEITHER THE PRINTING PLANT NOR THE WAREHOUSE they looked at seemed very promising; the printing plant was in fact used for printing, and the warehouse held vegetables. Stoner pushed on, aware that the last site on his list was the most promising—it had a pier on the harbor front and sprawled over nearly a hundred acres.

It was also well guarded by fences, men, and dogs.

"This would be a perfect place," said Danny, looking at the site through binoculars from a dock diagonally across the bay. "What the hell do they do there?"

"Recycle everything and anything," said Stoner. "Electronics mostly. That shed at the far left had car batteries. They strip away the outer casings, reuse the lead and the acid as well. Those drums there are filled with sulfuric acid."

"Lovely."

"Oh yeah. Real environmental operation."

Stoner pointed to two buildings at the right side of the facility, fenced off from the others by a double row of razor wire.

"That's where I think the operation might be, if it's here. There's a track up from the pier."

"Pier looks shaky," said Danny.

"Appearances can be deceiving. Can you get a scan?"

"We're too far for the viewer. We have to get a lot closer."

"Not a problem. We can get on that dock at night, go up to the fence. There's no guard on the water side."

"Not now, maybe," said Danny. "What about at night?"

"We'll have to find out," said Stoner. "But if they're not going to watch during the day, they probably won't at night."

"Man, I can smell the acid from here," said Danny.

"Yeah. We stay away from the damn battery shed if we can."

"I got to scan it."

"Your call." Stoner put down his glasses. "Hungry?"

"Starving."

"Let's go get some shrimp."

"I THOUGHT WE WERE GETTING SOMETHING TO EAT," said Liu when they stopped in front of the large warehouse building in the city's southwestern district.

"We are," said Stoner, getting out of the rental.

"This a restaurant?"

"In a way."

Danny, Liu, and the driver followed Stoner up a set of cement steps to the side of the large metal building, passing inside to a small corridor lit by several rows of fluorescent lights. Tekno-pop boomed from beyond the plasterboard wall, the bass so loud the cement floor shook.

A woman sat on a stool in front of a large opening at the end of the hallway; at first Danny thought they'd been taken into a carnival. Stoner said a few words, first in Mandarin Chinese and then in English, before handing over some of the local money; in return, the woman passed out several fishing poles, empty baskets, and kids' pails filled with what looked like small brown slugs.

"Bait," said Stoner, handing a pail to each man. "Liver. I think. She had trouble with my Mandarin and I couldn't quite get her Taiwanese."

"What is this?" asked Liu.

"We have to fish for our dinner," said Stoner.

The driver was smirking. Danny followed him inside, where a large pool of foul-smelling water was surrounded by pink lawn chairs, about a third of them filled by Taiwanese "fishermen." The water was filled with six-inch-long shrimp; the crustaceans were easy to hook, though pulling them out required a bit of wrist action. There were several ways to do this, which the nearby fishermen were eager to explain; Danny found his small basket quickly filling up with shrimp.

"On to the barbie," said Stoner when each of the party had caught about a dozen or so. The warehouse was studded with charcoal barbecues; Stoner showed them how to skewer the creatures, snap off their claws with a knife, and then roast them alive, or at least nearly alive.

They washed dinner down with cans of beer, bought from one of the vendors.

"Lovely," said Danny, eyeing his roasted dinner.

"It's really tasty," said Liu.

"So's burnt toast."

Stoner laughed, and got a few more ready for the grill.

Aboard *Penn*, over the South China Sea
1834

KICK HAD *HAWK ONE* RUNNING FIVE MILES AHEAD OF *Penn* and was just checking back with Major Alou about a contact when *Pennsylvania* was hailed by a flight of AIDC Ching-Kuos of the Chung-Kuo Kung Chuan—Republic of China Air Force, aka the Taiwan air force—patrolling the waters south of the island.

The AIDC Ching-Kuo came in two "flavors"— a single-seat tactical fighter, and a two-seat combat trainer. Developed with the help of Northrop and other U.S. manufacturers, the Ching-Kuo was a two-engine aircraft that might be favorably compared to a Northrop F-20 or advanced F-5E, able to top Mach 1.7 and with a combat radius of one thousand kilometers.

Major Alou altered the flight to the Megafortress, and Zen told Kick to let them know where he was as well. No sense surprising the allies, whose flight path would take them into visual range as they approached.

Both Taiwanese pilots spoke English very well,

though Kick struggled somewhat to make out the words through the accent and vagaries of radio transmission. The two CKKC aircraft were flying southward toward the Megafortress at roughly thirty thousand feet, about five thousand below *Penn*'s altitude.

Kick plotted out an intercept in his head, mocking up how he would handle the two planes if they were Mainland Chinese. His altitude and tiny size gave him a decent advantage; he saw himself tucking his wing, slashing into a front-quarter attack on the lead plane before he even knew Kick was there, then lashing back around to take out the trailer. A "normal" aircraft would find the maneuver difficult at best, but the small Flighthawk would have no trouble spinning back around for the second attack.

"Quite a plane!" exclaimed the CKKC leader, a Captain Hu, as they drew within visual distance.

"Thank you," answered Kick.

The CKKC pilot began peppering him with questions about the aircraft's performance. It soon became clear that he didn't realize it was a robot.

"What should I tell him?" he asked Zen.

"Tell him you're a UFO, recently enlisted in the U.S. Air Force," joked Zen.

"Um—"

"I'm just pulling your leg," said Zen. He clicked into the circuit and spoke to the CKKC pilot, giving some generic data that they were cleared to share. The existence of the U/MFs was no longer a secret, since they had seen action over the past year and even been written up in the aviation and general media.

"Wants to race you," laughed Zen.

"Race?"

"He'd probably win. The AIDC Ching-Kuo is a good aircraft, very capable. No match for a Flight-hawk, of course, but we won't tell him that." Zen's tone changed. "All right, we're about ten minutes from the coast. Best check with Major Alou about the landing details. I'm going to see if I can get ahold of Captain Freah and see how he's doing."

"Yes, sir," said Kick, wincing as the word "sir" left his mouth.

ZEN DOUBLE-CHECKED THE PLOTTED COURSE AS THEY headed toward the airfield. In general, he was pleased with Kick's flying. The lieutenant was still a few notches behind Starship, but he did have potential, and undoubtedly his skill would grow as he became more comfortable with the aircraft.

"Zen, got a second?" asked Alou over the interphone.

"Always for you, Merce," he laughed.

"Danny's got a little job lined up for tonight, couple of hours from once it's dark. Wondering if we can provide a little overhead reconnaissance."

"That's why we're here," said Zen.

"Okay. We'll go ahead and land and get refueled, find some grub. Think they do takeout here?"

Kaohisiung
2101

DANNY COULD SWIM PRETTY WELL, BUT THE MILE FROM their small motorboat to the pier was nonetheless a trial. The water stunk of oil and sewage. It felt like acid, boring its way past his wetsuit, through his skin, trying to disintegrate his bones. The wind whipped at the water and Danny lost his sense of direction; he knew he was moving forward, but it seemed as if his target kept moving away. By the time he finally drew within fifty yards of the pier, his shoulders were burning with the effort.

Odd sounds rushed into his ears, the whine of machinery and boats and other mechanical sounds jumbling with the lap of water against the docks. When he got near the end of the dock, he heard a sharp whistle and turned to find Stoner treading water a few feet away.

"How are you doing?" Stoner asked.

"I'm okay."

"There's a spot to get up on the shore over there, on the other side of the pier. A little dock they use for boats."

"I thought we were going up here," said Danny. "That was the plan."

"There's a light at the end of that wharf there. I saw it coming in. I'm afraid we'd cast shadows."

Danny grunted, and followed as Stoner slid under the pier. He brushed his leg unexpectedly against the side of one of the pilings, and even though he knew it was just part of the dock, he instantly thought of sharks.

Stoner had already climbed out of the water by the time Danny reached the incline, which was lined with rotting pieces of wood. He hoisted himself up and crawled on the planks, pushing up from the harbor.

"Don't get a splinter."

"No shit." Danny caught his breath a moment, then pulled up the waterproof sack he'd towed with him. He exchanged his flippers for a pair of sneakers, then took the viewer from its cooled bag. Stoner, meanwhile, was scouting on shore, viewing the facility from a pile of old ropes and tires.

Danny settled in next to him and trained the viewer on the general area, getting a lay-of-the-land picture for the specialists. Stoner pulled out a sat phone to talk to Dreamland, confirming that the device was working.

"Target buildings are that way," he said when Danny finished. "We go along that fence line right to the building. See the railroad track? We can walk right up it."

"Don't think the midnight express is running to-night?"

"Hope not," said Stoner.

Danny pulled out his sat phone and hooked in the headset so he could talk to Zen.

"Whip One to Hawk Eyes," said Danny. "Zen, how are we looking?"

"Twenty-twenty," replied the pilot. "Just making another pass now. We have you and the spook down near the wharf. Six guards, up near the road. Uh, looks like there's a couple in target building one, still just the one in building two."

"Thanks for the assist. We're going to get closer and use the viewer."

"Have fun. Hey, Liu told me you went shrimp fishing," added Zen.

"An experience, believe me."

"Beats McDonald's."

"Don't count on it."

Danny and Stoner climbed over an eight-foot fence to get to the railroad tracks, then walked along them to the razor wire fence separating the two buildings they wanted to inspect from the rest of the yard. Rather than climbing the fence as they had planned, Stoner led the way to a large yard on the other side of the tracks dominated by piles of discarded computers and electronics gear. The piles gave them a good vantage on the first building and a decent though slightly obstructed look at the second.

"About a million dollars' worth of computer parts here," said Stoner as Danny climbed the largest pile. The old PCs—some dated to the first IBM models—provided a surprisingly solid base for him to stand on.

"Just think of how much they cost new," said Danny, pulling up the viewer and getting to work.

Over the Southern Taiwan Strait
2115

ZEN DID AN INSTRUMENT CHECK ON THE FLIGHTHAWK as he looped south of the target area, confirming that the aircraft was in the green and in good shape. Zen had flown the U/MF so long now that he had an almost extrasensory feel for it; still, as he told his young charge sitting next to him, you couldn't take anything for granted.

"There were twelve people near the gate on

that last pass," said Kick as Zen finished his check. "That's six more than before."

"Uh-huh," said Zen. "Maybe we just missed them the last time."

"Might be. But it looks to me like they came with two more cars."

"Probably just a shift change," said Zen. "But let's take another look when we swing back."

**Kaohisiung
2117**

DANNY STEADIED THE VIEWER, COMPLETING THE LAST of the series. Stoner had gone down toward the buildings to do more reconnoitering; Danny packed the gear away and hooked back into the Dreamland circuit with his com device. Zen warned him a security patrol was approaching the area where they were.

"They're on the other side of the building," said Zen. "They have a pickup."

"Thanks," said Danny. He stared into the shadows at his left, waiting for Stoner to reappear. He missed his Smart Helmet—not only did it have an integrated night viewer with magnification, but he could have popped up a screen showing where his team member was. He planted a pair of his video "bugs" in the ref-use pile, then added the transmitter to the collection of discarded CPUs.

Damn thing looked right at home.

The Dreamland techies confirmed that the gear was on-line.

"So what's inside the buildings?"

"We're still analyzing it," said Charlie Tombs, who was back at Dreamland handling the data flow. "Go on and get out of there."

No shit, thought Danny, but before he could reply, bright light filled the overhead sky. A siren sounded and someone back by the building began shouting.

"Back to the water! Go!" yelled Stoner, running toward him.

"What the hell?" asked Danny.

"Go! Go!" said Stoner, and as if to punctuate his command an automatic weapon began firing from back by the warehouses.

Over the Southern Taiwan Strait
2119

ZEN HAD ALREADY STARTED TO BANK AWAY FROM THE target area when he saw the explosion. He tucked back eastward and almost immediately got a warning from the computer that he was flying at the edge of their control range.

"*Penn*, I need you closer to our target area," he said calmly.

"Hawk leader, we're trying. We have a request from an air traffic controller and—"

"I need you closer," insisted Zen. "Team may be under fire."

"Understood," said Alou.

Zen felt the big plane sway beneath him, lurching closer to the shoreline.

"The guards are coming around toward the dock area," said Kick, watching from the other station.

"Let's distract them," said Zen. He pushed the Flighthawk downward, diving toward the buildings from about eight thousand feet.

"How?" asked Kick.

"Like this," said Zen, starting to pickle the air-defense flares.

Kaohisiung
2120

AS THE LIGHT SHOW SPARKLED DIRECTLY OVER THE road at the front of the complex, Danny put his head down and ran for all he was worth back toward the dock. Stoner was waiting for him at the eight-foot fence, an M203 grenade launcher in his hand.

"You can't shoot that," Danny yelled at him. "We're under orders."

"It's smoke," said the CIA agent. "Fog up their night gear."

He pumped a few rounds into the area back by the computer piles, in effect laying out a curtain they could escape behind.

Danny felt his heart thump as they went over the fence and ran to the dock area. He stopped, pulling his flippers out of his pack, but then jumped into the water with his shoes, figuring it would be safer to change in the water. In his haste he fumbled with his gear and nearly lost one of the flippers; a mouthful of putrid water reminded him he wasn't a SEAL.

"Let's go," hissed Stoner.

"I am," said Danny, stroking out after him. He could hear voices on the shore, curses, he thought; something loud ripped behind him.

A machine gun?

"Our boat's coming in!" yelled Stoner.

The warning came just in time—Danny pushed himself back as the hull of the speedboat passed within a few yards. Water churned everywhere; there were more shouts; Danny felt himself being lifted out of the water and then flying away, hustled from an exploding typhoon.

"What the hell happened?" Sergeant Liu asked.

"One of the guards must have seen Captain Freah up on the pile," said Stoner. "He fired a flare."

"They were shooting at you," said Liu.

"Guess we found the right place, huh?" asked Danny, finally pushing himself upright. "Anybody got a towel?"

Over the Southern Taiwan Strait
2135

WHILE ZEN'S FLARES HAD SERVED THEIR PURPOSE IN momentarily distracting the guards from Danny and Stoner, they had also attracted the attention of the local authorities. The CKKC as well as the local police and harbor authorities were rushing to investigate; Zen and Major Alou discussed whether they should admit they'd launched the flares as a mistake during their flight. But it would be difficult to explain how the small incendiaries had managed to travel nearly twenty miles from where the Megafortress—clearly visible on radar—was flying, and for the time being at least it seemed better to say nothing.

By the time a CKKC controller came onto their frequency to ask for help searching for "possible communist intruders," Zen realized he'd blundered. They played through, joining a search off the coast.

"Want me to take the stick for a while?" asked Kick.

"Let me hold on to it," said Zen. Then he reconsidered—the kid needed the time a heck of a lot more than he did, and it wasn't like they were really going to encounter anyone.

"Yeah, good idea, Kick," he told him, and they initiated the swap.

The radar capabilities of *Pennsylvania* made it virtually impossible for an airplane to fly anywhere within two hundred miles of it without the EB-52 catching a whiff, but the CKKC pilots didn't know that. They assumed that the Megafortress was equipped similarly to regular B-52s, which of course had very good radar, but weren't outfitted as a mini-AWACS. Zen felt a bit embarrassed as the pilots swept southward; he realized now how seemingly innocent misunderstandings during the Cold War had nearly led to hostilities several times.

"Hawk leader, we have a contact on the surface that's not supposed to be there," said *Penn*'s copilot, Kevin McNamara. "We're wondering if you can check it out."

"Roger that," said Zen. The information was fed in from the Megafortress, indicating two small boats—or possibly submarines—thirty miles directly to the west. "Kick—hop to it."

"On it," said the pilot.

WHILE IT WAS PITCH BLACK OUTSIDE, THE FLIGHTHAWK visor gave Kick a view as detailed as he would have if it were high noon. Synthesized from its radar as well as IR and optical feeds, the screen showed the sky as a light gray and the water a deep blue; if he wanted, Kick could choose any of a dozen preset schemes or even customize it with a 64,000-color palette.

A bit too much choice as far as he was concerned, but what the hell.

Kick pushed forward in his seat. It was difficult to square the movements of the Megafortress with the path of the plane he was controlling. Most of Kick's airtime had been in the cockpit of A-10As. While the Hog—the popular, though unofficial nickname had been shortened from Warthog—wasn't particularly fast, it was highly maneuverable, and a Hog driver got used to taking g's real fast. But this was different, bizarre in a way—he pushed his stick left and slightly forward, and his stomach began to climb nearly straight up.

"I have a shadow on the surface," he told McNamara, the Megafortress copilot. "Feeding you visual."

The shadow lengthened into the thick thumb of a submarine. Upstairs on the flight deck, the copilot had taken the image and presented it to the onboard computers, which searched for identifying marks and then compared these to an onboard databank. In this case, the mast configuration, along with a small fin toward the bow of the craft and a rounded nub at the conning tower, told the computer the submarine was a Chinese diesel boat, a member of the Romeo class originally designed by the Russians in the late 1950s. Though competent, the sixty-man submarines were hardly technological marvels.

"Good work," Zen told Kick. "Look for the other further west."

"On it."

"I have a patrol vessel approaching from the east," said the copilot. "I'm handing off the information."

Kick changed his view to IR, thinking he could pick up the thermal trail of the submarine. But the change in the screen disoriented him.

"Use preset two," prompted Zen. "The IR takes the lower left window next to the sitrep and you still have your main view on top. Watch your altitude."

"Right," said Kick. He nudged upward and asked the computer for the proper screen configuration. As it came in he got a distance warning. He backed off the throttle slider so abruptly he nearly flamed the engines. Disoriented, he pulled up out of his search pattern, afraid he was going to stall the U/MF right into the waves.

"Go back again," said Zen.

"Okay," managed Kick.

"It's all right. You did all right. Best thing to do sometimes is just take a deep breath. The system throws a lot of information at you and you have to learn to process it."

"I'm all right," insisted Kick. He immediately regretted the sharp tone in his voice, but there was no way to take it back; instead, he concentrated on

getting himself back into position to resume the
search.

ZEN FOLDED HIS ARMS IN FRONT OF HIM, WATCHING THE
Flighthawk screens with one eye and Kick with the
other. The kid had just passed through a crisis, and
how he handled himself now was key. If he got himself back on the horse—put the Flighthawk back
into the search pattern, went after the other sub,
didn't fuck up worse—there'd be hope for him.

This was exactly the sort of experience that could
be the making of him. You had to fail, Zen thought;
you had to taste the bitterness of screwing up in
your mouth, and then get beyond it. And it was infinitely better to fail in little ways, as Kick just had,
than to wait for one big blowout failure to end all
failures as Zen had.

There was no way to teach that, no way to simulate it in exercises. Kick—and Starship, for that
matter—had to learn it for themselves. His job
was to somehow get them to the point where they
could.

"Team is recovered and heading back to the
hotel," reported Major Alou. "We can head back
whenever you want."

"Soon as Kick gets over that other contact, we
can head back for the barn," said Zen.

"Got it at two miles. It's diving," said the Flighthawk pilot.

The submarine was similar to the other one
they had seen. Data recorded, Alou set a course for
home.

"Keep your eye out for an unidentified aircraft firing flares over the city," added the pilot.

"If we see it, you'll be the first to know," said Zen.

Dreamland Control
0700

RUBEO STOOD BACK FROM THE COMPUTER SCREEN, rubbing his temple fiercely. They had taken all the inputs from Danny's viewer and compiled them into a model, supplementing them with information from the Flighthawk flyover and earlier satellite data.

"Problem, Doc?" asked Natalie Catsman.

"It's not an airplane."

Major Catsman looked at the three-dimensional mockup of Shed Building Two, which included legends showing items in the facility. The area next to the wall looked like a machine shop, with several stations set up that looked to contain presses and drills. Further back were large banks of some sort of computer equipment, though the Dreamland system could not render it with much precision.

"Recycling?" asked Catsman.

"You wouldn't need computer-controlled machinery for recycling," said Rubeo. "This material here. It's a portable wall. It's shielding."

"Shielding what?"

"Yes," said Rubeo. "This piece here came from a centrifuge. Or could have. They're making bombs here. I believe they're nuclear weapons."

Catsman, still new to Dreamland and the high-tech gear at its disposal, frowned as if she were over-whelmed.

"We need more data," said Rubeo. "But look at this."

He pulled up another screen filled with a row of numbers.

"The lottery?" Catsman laughed.

"Readings from Captain Freah's Geiger counter. They are above normal background levels. Material was taken through here, and there was an accidental spill. Small, but it contained minute traces of plutonium."

"We have to tell Colonel Bastian about this right away," said Catsman.

"Absolutely," said the scientist.

Brunei
2220

MONITORING THE OPERATION FROM THE DREAM COMmand trailer, Dog watched the fuss over the flares at the site and the subsequent patrols. Taiwan and Mainland China might be on the verge of historic discussions, but tensions were still very high—the wrong match at the wrong time, and they could just as well be exchanging gunfire as greetings. And war wouldn't be confined to the two Chinas. Units all across Asia had hiked their alert status.

Gradually, things ratcheted back down. As Dog waited for *Penn* to return to base, the screen flashed with an urgent, coded communication from Dream Command marked EYES ONLY. He punched in his password, and leaned to the eyepiece so the computer could confirm his identity by checking his irises. Natalie Catsman's face flashed on the screen.

"Colonel, the site that Captain Freah inspected today, we don't believe there is a UAV there, or any aircraft. It's only remotely possible that it's ever been there," said Catsman. "But—"

She stopped, turning around to someone in the situation room.

"But what?" said Dog.

"Shed Two appears to be a fabrication factory for bombs. Possibly nuclear," said Catsman.

"Nuclear?"

"Dr. Rubeo has someone with him who can explain."

Rubeo came on the screen, along with a physicist from one of Dreamland's weapons labs. Together, they gave the colonel a ten-minute executive summary of the types of machinery needed to construct a high-yield nuclear device, typically known as a neutron bomb.

"We're not sure of this, absolutely not sure yet," emphasized the physicist, Dylan Lyon. "Until we have direct access to the devices, there's no way of knowing for sure. However, combined with the plutonium reading—"

"Plutonium reading?" asked Dog.

Rubeo cut in, explaining what Danny's detector had picked up.

"Guys, bottom-line this for me," said Dog, cutting the scientist off as he began talking about sieverts and rad counts.

"Bottom line, you have an apparently private

company with the technology and the wherewithal to make a nuclear device," said Catsman. "And the company owner doesn't particularly like the Communist Chinese, or the current president of his own country."

Washington, D.C.
1100

JED BARCLAY HAD JUST STARTED TO SIFT THROUGH THE latest CIA briefing paper on South Asia when the secure phone in his small NSC cubicle buzzed.

"Jed, this is Colonel Bastian. We have to update the President."

Jed tried to work out where the nuclear material had come from as the colonel ran down the evidence the Dreamland team had passed along. Iran, North Korea, and Russia were the probable candidates, though none was a perfect fit.

Korea, probably. They were desperate for money and would sell to anyone.

Assuming there was a weapon. He cradled the phone as he spoke, quickly booting his personal computer into the restricted access intelligence network known as SpyNet and searching the Asian pages for anything new. The update was dominated by the arrival of the vice president in Beijing ahead of the summit.

"There hasn't been a threat," said Jed. "There'd be blackmail of some sort. If someone had a weapon and didn't want rapprochement, say, they'd threaten to use it."

"I think you're way too optimistic, Jed. I think these people might just go and blow people up. Forget about blackmail. They'd worry about the weapon being taken."

"Good point. I'm going to have to go to the boss right away on this. The whole NSC," said Jed. "I need everything you have."

"They're expecting your call at Dreamland. Major Catsman has a team assembled to brief you. Jed—I think if they do have a weapon, the summit will be an inviting target."

"I was just thinking that. It starts tomorrow."

"Exactly my point."

Dreamland, Computer Lab One
0900

RUBEO SLAMMED HIS HAND DOWN ON THE COUNTER area, barely missing the computer keyboard but upsetting the nearby cup, which shattered on the floor, sending a spray of hot coffee onto his pants.

"Figures," muttered the scientist.

"Problems, Ray?"

Rubeo turned and found Major Catsman with her arms folded in the doorway.

"Major."

"You all right, Ray?"

"Peachy."

Catsman smirked, then walked over to the pot of coffee on the nearby counter and helped herself. She made a face with her first sip.

"Wow," she said.

"Yes," muttered Rubeo, who had made the coffee himself. He might have the equivalent of several Ph.D.'s, but none was in home economics.

"Your people just finished briefing Mr. Barclay. Dylan was very good. Thank you."

"Yes," muttered Rubeo.

"They may want you to talk to the President himself."

"Fine."

"Problems?"

Rubeo liked Catsman; she was intelligent, quick on her feet, and unlike some of the career military people, pretty easygoing about working with civilian scientists. He had worked with her several years before on the Megafortresses prior to Major Cheshire's arrival. Still, Rubeo wasn't in the habit of sharing personnel concerns with bluesuits, with the exception of Colonel Bastian.

"There are always problems," he muttered.

"New theories on the ghost clone? Or the weapon?"

"I have plenty of theories," he said. "Putting them into action is the problem. I could use about twenty more people."

"Maybe Jennifer Gleason could help."

"Hmph," he said.

"Hmph?" said Catsman.

"Ms. Gleason is thinking about leaving us," said Rubeo, almost in spite of himself.

"But she was cleared by Danny, and Colonel Cortend."

"Yes, well, she's rethinking her future."

"Don't we need her here?"

Catsman might be a good officer to work for and with, but there was still a block there; she couldn't quite understand that dealing with geniuses wasn't like flipping on a computer. And Jennifer Gleason was a real genius.

Ironically, until this security blowup, she'd been among the least temperamental geniuses he knew.

Excluding himself, of course.

"Of course we need her," said Rubeo.

"Have you asked her to come back to duty?"

Rubeo realized that he hadn't *asked* her to come back. He'd just assumed that she would when she was ready.

"Want me to talk to her?" asked Catsman.

"No thank you, Major," snapped Rubeo, jumping up from the console.

He was actually surprised when Jennifer answered his loud rap on the door.

"It's me, Jennifer. I'd like to talk to you."

"Door isn't locked."

Rubeo put his hand to the knob hesitantly and turned it. Jennifer, dressed in a gray T-shirt and jeans, sat on the couch across from the entrance to her small apartment.

She looked different.

"What have you done to your hair?" asked Rubeo.

She touched the ragged edge above her right ear, smiling faintly. The jagged edges made it clear she had cut it herself.

"Latest look," she said.

"You look like Joan of Arc," he said.

"Maybe I'll have visions soon."

"Hmph." Rubeo felt his arms hanging awkwardly

by his sides. He shoved them into his pockets. "I've been working on an idea for tracking the clone and possibly taking it over. But there's so many systems involved, I'm having trouble pulling it together."

"Good," she said, making no move to get off the couch.

"I was wondering about your help."

A quizzical look crossed her face, as if she didn't understand the words.

"I'll help," she said, still making no move to get off the couch.

"Are you still going to leave?"

"I haven't made up my mind," she said.

Coming from anyone else, Rubeo would have interpreted the statement as hinting at blackmail. But Jennifer wasn't like that.

"Teaching—I don't think you should waste your time," he said.

Jennifer smiled. "Someone taught me."

"Well, yes. But in your case . . ."

"Let's go get some breakfast. Blue room?" she said, referring to one of the all-ranks messes.

"Fine," said Rubeo, following her out.

JENNIFER PICKED UP THE LONG STRIP OF BACON AND eased it into her mouth, savoring the salty tang. She hadn't eaten for days. She hadn't eaten bacon in months if not years; her breakfast ordinarily consisted of yogurt and an occasional oatmeal.

"Good?" said Rubeo, sitting across from her at the table.

"Delicious. Go on."

Rubeo wanted to use the electronic signal gathering capabilities of *Raven* to intercept the control frequencies used by the unmanned plane and take it over. *Raven* carried gear ordinarily used to jam radars, and they could link the Flighthawk control units into it to supply the proper code.

Couldn't they?

"Probably. Of course, if we interfere and don't get the encryption right, the UAV will probably go into native mode," observed Jennifer. The Flighthawks were programmed to act that way if interfered with. "The first thing you have to do is straighten out the hooks between C^3 and the *Raven* systems—that's a real tangle. I mean, you may not even be able to do it physically."

"I have Morris working on it."

"Morris?"

"Well, you weren't available," said Rubeo. "The team from the Signal Group is helping him."

Jennifer picked up another piece of bacon and stabbed it into one of her eggs. She scooped up the yolk with the bacon like a spoon and pushed it into her mouth.

"Have you tried checking the data against the NOSS system?" Jennifer asked. She was referring to a network of quasi-stationary Sigint satellites used to gather radio signals around the globe. The abbreviation stood for Naval Ocean Surveillance System.

"Why?"

"You could use that to track down whatever they're using as a base station. Then you'd know where they were operating from and you could physically take them out of the picture. All that data has to be available. You can backtrack from that. You really haven't done that yet?"

Rubeo frowned. He hadn't thought of it, but being Ray, he wasn't going to admit it.

Jennifer stood, then reached down and grabbed the bacon off her plate. "Let's get to work, Ray. What have you been doing for the past few days anyway?"

Taiwan
14 September 1997
0300

STONER DECIDED TO GO BACK TO TAIPEI; HE WANTED TO talk to his people back at Langley as well as see what else the local agents had dug up on Chen Lee and his companies. Though dead tired, Danny insisted on going along, and so he was awake when Dylan Lyon called him from Dreamland to tell him what his survey with the IR viewer had found. The physicist began grilling him about the site. Danny really couldn't supply much more information than what the sensors had already transmitted, but he answered their questions patiently, describing the exterior of the site and everything he'd seen.

Danny stayed on the phone as they switched from the helicopter to their rented car, and only concluded the conversation a few blocks from their destination. That gave him just enough time to call down to Brunei and tell Bison to get the team ready to move out; he anticipated Colonel Bastian would want another recon at the recycling plant, and this time he was going in with full gear.

Dog had already beaten him to it.

Stoner drove to a building owned by the American-Asian Business Coalition on Hsinyi Road not far from the American Institute, which handled American "concerns" in Taiwan on an officially unofficial basis. Despite the late hour, the coalition building was ablaze with lights, and Danny wondered if anyone in Taipei believed that the coalition was anything other than a front for the CIA.

Stoner led the way downstairs to a secure communications center. In contrast to the Dreamland facilities, the unit was primitive, amounting to a set of encrypted phones and two computer terminals that had access to a secure network. The decor wasn't even up to the command trailer's standards: The walls were paneled with a wood veneer so thin it looked like plastic; the industrial carpet on the floor was old and ragged.

Stoner pulled out a rolling chair from the conference table at the side of the room and swung it next to the desk with the phone bank. He swept his hand for Danny to take a seat, then made the connection back to Langley. When it went through, Stoner gestured for Danny to pick up a nearby phone. A case officer named James Pierce came on the line, updating them on information he'd gotten from Dreamland and the NSC liaison, Jed Barclay. That segued into a discussion of the capabilities of the government forces of Taiwan, and conflicting estimates of

Chen Lee, his business empire, and the possible capabilities of his companies.

"There are dissenting views," said Pierce. "But at this point, the best guess is that the government knows nothing about the UAV project. And if this is a nuke, they know nothing about it."

"You sure?" asked Danny.

"The real expert's sitting next to you," said Pierce, meaning Stoner. "But there are no intercepts from known CKKC units indicating any sort of operational control on the aircraft, let alone any indication of experimental work, no unit movement, nothing," said Pierce. "The NSA group working on it for us has gone over it pretty well. And as for nukes, forget it. We're pretty wired into the government; we'd know. Believe me."

Danny wasn't sure whether Pierce meant what he said literally or figuratively.

"The best evidence that they don't have one is a conversation three weeks ago between the president and the defense minister debating whether they should start a program and what it would cost," added Pierce. "It was partly that debate that led the president to make his overtures toward China."

Brunei
0600

DOG'S FOUR OR FIVE HOURS OF FITFUL SLEEP MADE HIM feel more tired than ever. He cut himself shaving, then burned his finger on the in-room coffeemaker.

His mood was so foul that even a message on his voice mail system at Dreamland that Cortend had returned to the Pentagon "and contemplated no formal report" failed to put a bounce in his step as he walked from his hotel room to his elevator. Instead, his brisk stalk warned off the security detail escorting him, even the normally loquacious Boston, heading the team. The men stood at stone attention during the brief ride to the lobby, fanning out as the door opened—as much to stay out of the boss's way as to protect him.

Miss Kelly, the State Department rep, was waiting near the door.

"Good morning, Colonel," she said. "Breakfast?"

"No thanks. I have to check in with my people," he told her.

"I wanted to apologize for being brusque the other day," she said.

"Not necessary," said Dog.

"I wonder if I could have a word," she said, touching his arm to stop him and then glancing at the bodyguard detail.

"Fire away," said Dog.

"The sultan would like a demonstration," said Miss Kelly. "He's heard so much about the Megafortress from his nephew, the prince—they would greatly appreciate a ride."

"I thought Mack was entertaining them," said Dog.

"He is," said Miss Kelly. "But he made it clear that a ride, uh, a flight, was up to you."

"I'll bet he did."

"He's looking for a liaison and has asked Major Smith if he might stay on."

"I have a mission here," said Dog, starting back into motion. "Mack can deal with him."

"I have a mission here as well," said Kelly, who had trouble keeping up in her heels. "I will call Washington."

"I'll give you a quarter."

THE COFFEE AT THE DREAMLAND COMMAND TRAILER had been made hours before, and to compare the burned-out dregs to crankcase sludge would have been to defame engine oil everywhere. Boston volunteered to make a fresh pot; Dog made a mental note to add a personal commendation to the sergeant's file at the earliest convenience.

He was on his second cup of coffee when Ray Rubeo's face snapped onto the screen from Dream Command. Rubeo's familiar frown was back, and even before the scientist stepped aside to reveal the others in the control room, Dog knew Jennifer was back.

But what in God's name had she done to her beautiful long hair?

"Good to see you back where you belong, Ms. Gleason," he said.

She didn't answer; it wasn't clear that she had even heard.

"We're sifting through a forest of radio transmissions," said Rubeo, giving the latest update. "We're still a distance from figuring it out."

"Anything new on the bomb factory?"

"The video cameras that were placed show nothing unusual," said Rubeo. "They've continued their standard security sweeps."

"We have to assume they know something's up," said Stoner, who was in Taipei. "But we do have people watching both on land and out in the harbor, and there's nothing out of the ordinary."

"Even if the assessment is right and they do have a bomb, we haven't found the delivery system yet," said Dog.

"Sure we have," said Jennifer. "The UAVs."

"They're not big enough," said Zen, who was on the circuit from *Penn*, on the ground in Taiwan.

"You're looking at their UAV as if it were a Flighthawk," Jennifer said. "It isn't. From the analysis that I've seen—and admittedly I've been out of the loop for a few days . . ."

She paused. Dog could see her frown.

"From what I've seen," she continued, "the ghost clone should be able to go further with a heavier payload. It's been used up until now for reconnaissance, but reengineering it for a different role is child's play. If I were building a long-range nuclear cruise missile, I'd start with an airframe like the ghost clone's. It's not quite as stealthy as a B-2, but it's damn close. And it's small to begin with."

"Then why not use a cruise missile?" asked Zen.

"It is a cruise missile," said Jennifer. "With longer range and a heavier payload. The thing is, if my technology isn't good enough to build a very small nuke, this may be easier."

"We are speculating," said Rubeo.

"Sometimes speculation isn't wrong," said Jennifer staring into the video camera.

Washington, D.C.
13 September 1997
2103

AFTER A LONG DAY OF MEETINGS, JED BARCLAY'S EYES felt as if they'd screwed themselves deep into his skull. The NSC had scheduled a meeting for ten P.M., but he and his boss had been summoned by the President to the White House for a private briefing ahead of the session. While not unprecedented, the move underlined how serious the situation was. The meeting in Beijing was now less than twenty-four hours away. The vice president had just arrived in the capital.

Jed and Philip Freeman were ushered up to the private quarters, where the President was changing after returning from an appearance in Bethesda. No matter how many times he came here, Jed still felt a feeling of awe. He was walking where Lincoln had walked, taking the same stairs Madison had used to look for his wife when the British were marching up the hill. They were shown to the East Sitting Hall near the Queen's Bedroom, one of Martindale's favorite conferencing spots. Jed pulled over the ornate wood chair so that it was catty-corner to the couch and opposite his boss's seat, anticipating that the President would sit on the couch. The drapes had been drawn across the large fan window that dominated the room; lamps on both sides of the couch cast a yellowish light around, reflecting in the chandelier above.

Jed closed his eyes for a moment, wondering what it would have been like a hundred and fifty years before. Lincoln strode through, looking for his clerk, calling him: "Nicolay! Nicolay!"

Mrs. Lincoln wandered behind him, fretting over her sick son Willie, not yet dead . . .

"Sleeping on us, Jed?" boomed the President, coming in.

"No way," said Jed, springing upright.

The President patted him gently on the back, pulling over his own seat rather than taking the sofa. His chief of staff and several other aides, along with members of the Secret Service, had trailed him to the end of the hall, standing back to give them a modicum of privacy.

"They have a bomb, or they may have a bomb?" asked the President, immediately cutting to the heart of the issue.

"We're not sure," said Freeman.

The folder in Jed's hands contained the latest estimate—it was really more like a guess—of what had happened, fingering Iran rather than Korea as the likely source. Small amounts of material—enough for one or two bombs—were possibly unaccounted for.

The estimate, courtesy of the CIA, was three sentences long. The argument that had led to those three sentences was continuing over at Langley.

"How can we be sure what they have?" asked Martindale.

"We have to go in and find out," said Freeman.

"Jed?"

"I would agree, sir. Dreamland—Colonel Bastian is preparing a plan to cover that contingency, if you order it."

Martindale nodded.

"I would note," said the national security advisor, "that at the moment there's no concrete evidence supporting the construction of a bomb. We have circumstantial findings only."

"Two weeks ago there was no evidence there was an advanced UAV," said the President. "Will Colonel Bastian have his plan ready for presentation at the NSC meeting?"

"I believe he will," said Jed.

"Good." Martindale got up. "Ties are getting better, Jed."

"Thank you, sir."

Dreamland Command Trailer, Brunei
14 September 1997
1103

THE BRIEFING WITH THE NSC WENT ABOUT AS WELL AS Dog had expected, meaning that it didn't go particularly well at all. A mission to inspect the site further was authorized, but most of the members of the NSC were skeptical that the weapon even existed. Dog couldn't really blame them; all he really had to go on was the fact that his scientists thought it was there, and while that was good enough for him, it wasn't particularly surprising that it wasn't good enough for Washington.

Dog's plan called for securing the site if a weapon was found. That, of course, would create real complications—Taiwan was an ally, but the operation, at least at present, was to be conducted without the country's government or military knowing about it. It had to be that way, since it wasn't yet clear what if any connections Chen might have that would tip him off.

Assuming that he did in fact have a weapon.

"Have you located their robot plane?" asked Admiral Balboa after Dog finished his briefing.

"We're still trying to figure it out."

"Thank you, Colonel. We'll take it from here," said Freeman. "Keep us advised."

The connection broke. Dog resisted the temptation to punch out the video tube. No matter what he did, it would never be enough for Balboa.

He got up, glancing at his watch. He needed to do about twenty million things, including get the latest Dreamland updates and prep a flight to Taiwan so he could support the mission.

But he also wanted to find out what the hell Mack was doing.

"Boston?"

"Yes, sir."

"Find Mack Smith and bring him to me. Fetch Lieutenant Andrews as well."

"On my way, sir."

MACK SMITH WAS ENJOYING YET ANOTHER RETELLING of his exploits when the beautiful if stuck-up Miss Kelly entered the reception hall, trailed by a member of the Whiplash security team. Though the tall, bulky sergeant wore civilian clothes, he was instantly recognizable as a Dreamland trooper by his swagger and bulk.

"Miss Kelly, a pleasure," said Mack. "Very sharp

suit, Sergeant," he added to her escort. "Boston, right?"

"Sir, Colonel Bastian wants to see you yesterday."

"If he wants to see me yesterday, he'll have to settle for videotape, won't he? Or maybe fly back to Dreamland. I think with the dateline it's yesterday there when it's today here."

"Yes, sir. I need Lieutenant Andrews as well."

"Starship," said Mack, calling over to the other end of the lounge. Starship emerged from the small pack of European women he had been fraternizing with. "The master beckons."

TWENTY MINUTES LATER, DOG INTERRUPTED HIS LATEST update from Ax to give Starship the sort of stare no lieutenant should ever have to endure from his commander.

It made an impression—for about half a second. Then the lieutenant's fighter jock smile returned.

"Where the hell have you been?" the colonel demanded.

"Sir, you had told me to, uh, see if there was anything Major Smith needed. And so I went to it."

"That was yesterday, Starship. Did you get that handle because your head was out in orbit?"

"Nah."

"Go get your gear, and get over with the Flighthawk personnel and make sure your aircraft is ready to fly."

"All right! Kick ass."

The lieutenant slapped his hands together, twisted on his heel, and practically ran from the trailer.

"As for you, Major, we're under a Whiplash order," Dog told Mack. "We have an operation tonight."

"Great." Mack stood, but then a quizzical look appeared on his face. "What am I flying?"

"Nothing. You're going to stay at the trailer to liaison with us."

"Liaison?" said Mack. "But—"

"We have some Air Force security police heading over from the Philippines to pull security, but they're not cleared to enter the trailer. You got that? It's just you. They have to take a leak, they have to go across the street."

"You want me to act as communications sergeant? I mean, all I'm doing is babysitting the gear?"

"You have the general idea, Mack. The security detail will be armed and under orders to shoot if there are any problems. Nobody in and out."

Mack's face had turned white.

"I'd like you in uniform before they get here," Dog added. "I believe you have about ten minutes."

Outside Taipei
1105

CHEN LO FANN HAD KNOWN THERE WERE ENOUGH parts for another UAV.

The bomb was another matter.

"It was created five years ago," explained Professor Ai. "Your grandfather foresaw the day when this would occur. The Russians were desperate, and opportunity presented itself. Even so, it has taken considerable work. The bomb has only been ready within the past month."

"Your visits to your aunt?"

"I regret that I found it necessary to lie to you," said Ai, bowing his head slightly as a gesture of remorse. Chen Lo Fann knew it was a sham, and said nothing.

"The bomb will kill the people in the target area, but not damage the buildings," said the scientist. Fann knew Ai was exaggerating slightly—buildings very close to the blast would be damaged and possibly destroyed by the neutron bomb his grandfather had had built. Still, unlike a "normal" atomic weapon, the large cylinder before him would cause relatively little damage to the capital.

Should he use it?

His concerns had nothing to do with the deaths the bomb would cause—he cared nothing for the communists, who clearly deserved to die. While undoubtedly many innocent victims would be caught up in their destruction, their deaths were completely justifiable, an honorable part of the necessary equation. Regrettable, lamentable—but necessary.

Chen's concern was with what would happen next. The communist military leaders who survived would no doubt wish for revenge.

Would the Americans step in and prevent it?

He was unsure.

And if they did, then what?

An uneasy truce? Things would continue as they had for the past fifty years.

That would be an even greater failure.

Perhaps he should wait, and try and build other bombs, enough to obliterate every last communist.

Chen Lo Fann thought of his grandfather, whose body he had just come from cremating.

The letter in the old man's desk—a letter Ai knew of, though he seemed not to have read—directed that the meeting between the two heads of state be stopped at all costs.

What was his duty as Chen Lee's grandson? Should he use the weapon as Lee clearly wished? Or should he choose his time?

Duty demanded he carry out his grandfather's wishes. The way was clear.

The endless surging of the universe, as he interpreted the Tao, or "way."

The way that can be spoken is not the true way.

Life and death were as one, different stages in the never-ending river. His grandfather's death, his own—these were meaningless. Duty was constant. Duty lasted longer than the poor clay and ashes of a single day.

"Prepare," he told Professor Ai. "We will strike during the meeting, as my grandfather wished."

Dreamland
2100

JENNIFER GOT UP FROM THE COMPUTER STATION AND bent her head straight back. Her vertebrae all seemed to crack at once. She felt a surge of energy, and if it weren't for the fact that they were close— very, very close—to a breakthrough, she would go for a run. Instead, she stretched and twisted her way across the lab to the coffee counter. A fresh pot had just finished sifting through into the carafe; she poured herself a cup and took a few slow sips.

Dog's voice had surprised her during the video conference earlier that morning; he seemed to have aged ten years since she'd last seen him.

Maybe that meant she was over him.

Good.

She went back to the computer, which had just finished running a search of an NSA database. The computer had deposited three lines of hexadecimals on her screen; not taking any chances, she recorded them on the blank yellow pad at the station, then entered each one into the second search program she and an assistant had customized earlier in the day. A set of computers across the country at Fort Meade, the NSA headquarters, began rumbling through a vast array of intercepted and logged transmissions, trying to match the scripts she'd just harvested. Six keystrokes later, a Navy computer began doing the same.

The screen flashed. It had found the radio.

Several radios.

"Oh," said Jennifer aloud to the empty lab. "Now I get it."

She picked up the phone to call Major Catsman, who was over in the Dreamland Command Center getting ready to update the Whiplash Force in Taiwan.

"I know how they do it," she said when the major came on the line. "Basically they're using buoys and a commercial satellite. I should be able to narrow down the ship, but I'm going to need some help from the Navy. High-level help. We have to tap into their collection of NOSS intercepts, the Sigint data they collect to track ship movements."

"Who do I talk to?" asked Catsman.

Hangar 43C, Taichung Air Base, Taiwan
1600

ROLLING TOWARD THE SMALL ROOM AT THE FAR END OF the hangar, Zen realized he hadn't spoken to his wife, Breanna, in more than two days. While she'd certainly understand, he felt a pang of guilt, and told himself he'd catch up with her as soon as he could.

Dog—just in from Brunei with *Penn* and the two Flighthawks—was already holding forth on the latest plan. Danny and Stoner had come down from Taipei, along with a driver and Sergeant Liu; the rest of his Whiplash team was due in a few hours, aboard Dreamland's souped-up MC-17, which was en route with one of the Ospreys tucked inside its cavernous tummy. A contingent of Marines from the Philippines was due to arrive at the airport no later than 2300; they would add a little more muscle to the assault.

Danny and Stoner had worked out a straightforward plan to secure the factory site at Kaohisiung. *Penn* would launch a laser-guided E-bomb at the start of the assault, wiping out all unshielded electronic devices at the target site. Whiplash would parachute in, secure the building, and hold it. The Marines would come in with the Osprey as well as some small boats, providing backup and extra security. The devices would be evacced out via the Osprey to this airport—the hangar area would be secured by more Marines—and then taken away by the MC-17 to Brunei.

Stoner would ride with the Marines in the Osprey, carrying backup detection gear and his own hot link back to Dream Command, where a team of experts would be providing real-time analysis of the data the assault team gathered. Major Alou and *Penn* would fly offshore, with two Flighthawks—one piloted by Starship, the other by Kick, providing cover. About the only difficulty Danny could see was persuading the Marines to take what was drawn up as the secondary role in the operation.

While the site was being secured, Zen and *Raven* would head south to observe the ship Dreamland had just tagged as the possible UAV operator. With the help of signal intelligence the Navy routinely collected as it tracked ships on the ocean, the Dreamland team had matched seemingly innocuous radio transmissions to those Jennifer Gleason had ID'd as belonging to the UAV control mechanism. The transmissions had been traced to the *Dragon Prince*, a small oil tanker. According to Jennifer's theory, it operated the UAV with the help of a network of buoys and a satellite, disguising transmissions to appear as routine navigational inquiries or as "junk" reflections from other systems. The latest intelligence, cobbled together from a variety of sources, showed that the ship was due in Kaohisiung harbor tomorrow.

Undoubtedly to get the bomb.

If the robot launched, Zen would destroy it. *Raven* had been tabbed for the mission because its computers had the UAV frequency data; Dog would take the helm.

The *Dragon Prince* would be apprehended by two U.S. Navy destroyers in international waters after the ground operation was under way. The ships were already en route, though they had not yet been informed of their exact mission or situation.

"Washington is worried about security concerns," explained Dog.

"That doesn't make sense," said Stoner. "The ship captains may not think it's a high priority. They ought to have the entire situation laid out for them."

"It's not my call," said Dog. Zen realized from the sharpness in Colonel Bastian's voice that he didn't agree with the decision, but was prepared to carry it out. "The concern is not only to preserve the element of surprise, but to keep the Mainland Chinese from finding out. If they knew there were nuclear devices on the island, they might use that as a pretext to launch an all-out attack."

Major Alou brought up a few practical issues about which non-Dreamland frequencies would be used during the operation, as well as the availability of refueling assets that were being chopped from Pacific Command. Zen found his mind drifting as the discussion slanted toward minutiae; he worried about Kick and Starship, who'd be working without a net.

And then he remembered he'd still forgotten to call his wife.

What was up with that?

He eyed his watch, waiting for the briefing to end.

Bright Memorial Hospital, Honolulu
1800
(Dreamland, 2100)

BREANNA STOCKARD HAD JUST FINISHED PACKING HER things when the phone on the bedstand rang. Thinking it was probably her mother—her mother had taken to calling her every hour on the hour— she blew off the first few rings. Finally, she reached for it, grabbing it just in time to hear whoever had been calling hanging up.

Probably Zen, she thought, instantly angry with herself for not picking up the phone. She took her bag and went out, glad to finally be out of the small whitewashed space.

As she rode the elevator downstairs, Breanna felt a surge of concern for her husband. She knew he'd deployed on a mission somewhere, but security concerns had prevented him or anyone else from saying exactly where he was or what he was doing. As a member of the military—not to mention the same elite unit—Breanna was expected to understand that there would be times when duty demanded she not speak to Zen. But it wasn't easy, just as it wasn't easy for the literally thousands of other men and women—and children—who found themselves in similar situations around the country. Breanna accepted this as a given, a part of her life. Even so, as she made her way to the elevator, she felt an undeniable ache, a longing to be near her husband.

The ache turned into something else in the elevator downstairs, something sharper, a jagged hole.

Fear. She was worried about him, afraid that something was going to happen.

She was sure of it. Convinced. Her hands began to tremble.

The door opened. Bree's mother stood a few feet away, talking to some other doctors. Breanna managed to bite the corner of her lip and pushed herself out of the elevator. She forced a smile and suffered through her mother's greeting and introductions, looking toward the floor not out of modesty as her mother bragged, but hiding the emotion suddenly washing through her. She signed herself out, the words on the papers at the desk invisible behind a thick fog.

Spotting a phone nearby, she gave in to the temptation to call Dreamland, even though she knew she wouldn't get Zen himself. She dialed the number, her finger sliding off the keys.

No one would be able to talk to her anyway. It was an open line. All she'd do was make other people nervous.

The phone rang and was answered before she could hang up.

"This is Breanna Stockard," she told the airman handling the phone. "I—"

"Captain, how are you?" said the operator, and before she knew it she was talking to Chief Master Sergeant Terrence "Ax" Gibbs.

"Everybody who's anybody is out seeing the world," Ax told her. "If you know what I mean."

The twinkle in the chief's eyes translated somehow into his voice. Breanna's apprehension didn't melt—it was too deep for that—but her hand stopped trembling and the ground beneath her feet felt solid again.

"Something up?" asked the chief.

"No, chief, thanks. I appreciate it."

"Sure I can't do anything for you?"

"You have, kinda," she said. "I'll be there tomorrow morning."

"Red carpet'll be waiting."

Taichung Air Base
2300

BOSTON HAD NEVER WORN ONE OF THE FOGSUITS before, and Sergeant Liu had to help him into it. Covered with a thin layer of LEDs, the suit was designed to emit light in a pattern that blended with the surroundings. In pitch black, of course, it was completely dark. But in a grayish setting it would appear gray, and on a splotchy brown background it would look splotchy brown. The technology was still being worked on at Dreamland, and the scientists predicted that within a few years, new versions would make foot soldiers practically invisible to the naked eye.

For now, they were just extremely hard to see, especially at dark.

Sergeant Liu unfurled the hood from the back of the suit, covering all but the visor area of Boston's helmet. The six Whiplash troopers looked like aliens, ready to take over the earth.

Or at least a small part of it.

"Check your tasers," said Liu.

Because of the political ramifications of operating without authorization in an allied country, the White House had ordered the Whiplash team to use nonlethal weapons "to the extent practical and possible" to take down the factory. Each team member carried a special Dreamland shotgun taser as his primary weapon. The gun looked like an Olin/HK CAWS RHINO (Repeating Hand-held Improved Non-rifled Ordnance) Special Forces shotgun with a large box in front of the trigger area. Traditional tasers fired two darts at a target that were connected to the weapon by a wire, allowing the shock to be administered. While potent, the need for the wire limited most tasers to relatively short range—fifteen yards was an industry standard. That was perfect for many police applications, but would put a Whiplash trooper at a severe disadvantage.

The Dreamland gun—officially known as T-3, though the troopers usually just called them tasers or sometimes phasers after the weapons used in the *Star Trek* sci-fi series—fired a shell containing two bullets that looked like the jacks used in a child's game, except that their points were considerably sharper. The bullets housed capacitors charged as the gun was fired; the shock when they contacted a target was enough to put down a horse.

While the weapon could fire its cartridges beyond a hundred yards, technical difficulties with the separation of the bullets meant the team had to decide between short or long-range cartridges, with effective ranges between five and fifty yards or forty and one hundred yards. In both cases, the bullets would not separate or set the charge properly before the minimum range, and beyond the maximum they tended to be wildly inaccurate. All team members carried clips packed with both sets of ammo, color-coded and notched so they were easily ID'd.

The team members also carried standard-issue M-4s—shortened M-16s favored by Airborne and SF troops—or MP-5s beneath their fogsuits; they were intended only as weapons of last resort.

"We're ready, Captain," said Liu over the shared team frequency in the Smart Helmet as the last trooper signaled he was good to go.

"Good." Captain Freah's rich baritone reverberated in Boston's helmet. "Now remember, the E-bomb will go off just as we hit the ground," he added. "It may not get everything, and they may start looking for us once their lights go out. Questions?"

Bison made a lame joke about plugging his taser into an outlet and charging the city for electricity.

"Any real questions?" asked the captain, and the silence told Boston they were ready to board the plane.

Aboard *Penn*, over the Taiwan Strait
2335

STARSHIP TOOK THE FLIGHTHAWK FROM THE COM-puter as the launch sequence completed, tucking the U/MF down toward the water as Kick authorized his own launch. It was damn good to be back in action.

He wasn't feeling any jitters, and the pressure wasn't even up to football game levels. The fact that Kick had his hands full with his own aircraft reassured him somehow.

Bottom line, Starship knew he was twice the pilot Kick was. Having his rival next to him in the Flighthawk bay flying his own aircraft seemed easier to deal with than having him hovering over his shoulder.

It didn't hurt either that Zen was off in the other plane.

"*Hawk One* is coming through 25,000 feet, on course and ready," he told *Penn*'s pilot, Major Alou. "Systems are solid. Instruments are in the green. I'm ready, Major."

"Roger that," said Alou, his voice so calm it sounded as if he were ready for a nap. "Preparing for alpha maneuver and launch on *Hawk Two*."

The big aircraft began to dip, sleighriding downhill as it fell into the launch maneuver for the other U/MF. The launch went perfectly; Starship saw his wingman pop onto the sitrep to the west, picking up speed as the computer and pilot double-checked their systems.

"As we drew it up, boys," said Major Alou. "Starship, you have the first run over the target area. Keep your altitude up; we don't want anyone hearing us. You ready?"

"Born ready," said the pilot, tacking onto his course back toward land.

Aboard Dreamland MC-17 *Quickmover*
over the Taiwan Strait
2355

DANNY FREAH WAITED UNTIL HE HAD THE INFRARED feed from the Flighthawk before clicking the bottom of the visor to get the computer-interpreted view from the Dreamland tactical computer system. Located deep in the computer bunkers below the Megafortress hangars, the computers were sifting through the data supplied by the camera and radar in *Hawk One*, interpolating it with what was already known about the site.

Building Two, their primary objective, was occupied by a single guard at the shore side of the compound. Another dozen men were nearby, in a building about a hundred yards away, most of them clumped in a basement suite they had identified as the security headquarters. The suite and its sensors would be blinded by the E-bomb, which would effectively fry any unshielded electronics within a half mile of its air-burst explosion. The bomb—actually a small laser-guided missile that could be controlled by Danny once launched—sat in *Penn*'s bomb bay, ready to go.

"All right, listen up, you can see the schematic," said Danny as the image of the site flashed into his team's helmets. "As we planned it. Liu and Boston on Shed One. My team has the security headquarters building. Bison and Reagan, you have the approach. Make sure the Marines don't kill us," he added, knowing it would get a laugh from his men.

Six Marines, all trained in SF warfare, were

jumping with the team to help take control of the perimeter. They too were armed with nonlethal weapons—Remington shotguns, equipped with crowd-control shells, along with M-4s as backups. Frankly, the hardest part of his job so far had been convincing the Marines they had to stay behind his guys once they got on the ground.

Two companies of Marines had squeezed aboard the Dreamland Osprey and would roar in once the Whiplash team was down. Four small boats sat about a mile offshore, filled with Marines, ready to race into the harbor. Danny had worked with a number of Marine units over the past few years and was confident that, despite a bit of jawing back and forth, they'd do as good a job as his troopers.

What he hadn't worked with before in combat was the fogsuit. It was a great idea in practice, certainly, and had done well during the exercises. But jumping from a large aircraft in the middle of the night was always a risky venture. If the bulky suit felt uncomfortable to him, he was sure it would feel uncomfortable to most if not all of the others.

And being uncomfortable was never good.

But it was too late to take them off. The light flashed. The ramp at the back of the aircraft cranked open. The wind howled.

"We're going," he told Major Alou aboard *Penn*.

"Missile launch is counting down," replied the pilot over the Dreamland circuit.

Bison, the jumpmaster, put up his fist.

"Let's go," Danny heard himself say.

Aboard *Raven*, over the Taiwan Strait
15 September 1997
0002

ZEN HAD SPLIT HIS LOWER CONTROL SCREEN IN HALF SO
he could see a sitrep feed from Dream Command
showing the assault. The screen was tiny, especially
in the helmet viewer, but he avoided the temptation
to make it his main view—he was controlling two
Flighthawks from the hold of the Megafortress,
orbiting *Dragon Prince*, and watching for signs of
activity. While the computer was presently doing
most of the work, Zen couldn't afford to let his attention stray too far from the controls.

"First wave is out of the plane," relayed Dog, who
was piloting the plane. "Looking good."

"Yeah."

"Merce is ready to go with the E-bomb."

"Roger that."

Zen checked his instruments, purposely trying
to draw his attention away from the other operation. His guys were good. They could handle it.

Best thing to do was let them.

"Hawk leader, you want to take a run over the
ship's deck?" asked Dog. "Get a real close-up and
see if we can spot the clone?"

Zen acknowledged, then took the helm of *Hawk
Three*—his U/MFs were designated *Three* and *Four*
to avoid confusion—and tucked toward the oil
tanker, which was about ten nautical miles from the
mouth of the Kaohisiung harbor.

The sitrep for the assault flickered.

"E-bomb went off as scheduled," said Dog. "The

power is gone in that part of the city. Everything's on schedule."

"Roger that," said Zen, forcing himself to concentrate on the task at hand.

On the Ground in Kaohisiung
0004

DANNY HIT THE ROOF OF THE BUILDING SQUARE IN THE middle, only a quarter meter from the point the computer had designated. With two quick snaps, he had unhooked his chute. He pressed the trigger on his taser lightly, activating its targeting mechanism. Its aimpoint appeared as a crisp red circle in his Smart Helmet visor. With the helmet's starscope vision showing him the night, there was no need to pop on the LED wristlight that was an integral part of the fogsuit; instead, he made his way to the end of the building above the door closest to the security headquarters. He saw the door open as he reached it. Kneeling, he waited as two of the company guards emerged from the building, each carrying a handgun. As the door started to close behind the men, he fired.

Vvvvrooop.

Vvvvrooop.

A net of blue light enveloped the men. Both Taiwanese spun slightly, stunned by the shock of electricity pulverizing every muscle and nerve in their bodies. Danny climbed over the edge of the roof and swung down, landing on his feet a few feet from the men he had downed. The shock had rendered them semiconscious. He kicked the guns away, then Danny took a small plastic canister from his pocket. It looked like a grenade with an extra-long spoon handle. He pulled the handle and tossed it between the men, stepping back as netting material expanded over them. The sticky material was not escape-proof, but it would easily hold them in place until the reinforcements arrived.

Egg Reagan, meanwhile, had come around the side of the building. He slapped what looked like the head of a plunger on the door; it was actually a man-portable radar unit similar to SoldierVision to help them see inside. Using the unit rather than their own Smart Helmets would prevent anyone from homing in on the source of the radio waves and targeting them. Egg strung a wire to the unit and stepped around the corner, viewing it in his helmet visor after attaching the wire at the back.

"Clear," said Egg.

The door was locked. Danny took out a Beretta loaded with metal slugs and fired point-blank through the mechanism.

"Still clear," said Egg.

"In."

The hall, dark because both the electricity and backup lighting had been knocked out by the E-bomb, made an L about twenty feet from the door. As they cleared the corner, the yellow beams of small flashlights danced at the far end.

"We'll zap them," said Danny. "I have the ones on the left. Wait as long as we can; get them all in view."

He edged toward the side of the hall as the first of the Taiwanese guards came around the corner.

As soon as one of the lights played across the floor near Egg, Danny opened up, firing two bursts in rapid succession. Three guards shot back against the wall of the hallway, literally blasted off their feet. But another man had been behind them; unharmed, he began to retreat. Danny and Egg gave chase, running for all they were worth down the hall. The bulk of their suits and gear slowed them down, however; by the time they reached the corner, the hall was empty.

"Fuck," said Egg.

"Yeah," said Danny. "Let's see if we can find this joker."

He tapped his Smart Helmet, activating the unit's penetrating radar mode. The mode emitted low-power radio waves that could penetrate walls roughly out to thirty feet. Their subject was nowhere in sight.

Danny flipped back into Dreamland connect mode, taking the display off the Flighthawk. But the U/MF was too far to the west to be of any use.

"Hawks, I need some coverage down here," he said. "On my building."

"Copy," said Kick, gunning the aircraft back.

Aboard *Penn*
0012

KICK HAD JUST STARTED THE FLIGHTHAWK BACK WHEN the Osprey veered across his path. He threw the small robot plane down hard toward the earth, realizing even as he did that he had overreacted. Curs-

ing, but only to himself, he came back with the
joystick control, trying to swoop level and get back
more or less on course. The robot fluttered slightly,
her airspeed plummeting.

"*Hawk Two*, looking for that view," said Captain
Freah in his ear.

"Yeah, roger that," said Kick. "We're working on
it. A lot of things going on up here."

Starship, whose aircraft was to the west covering the harbor approach to the complex, started to
interrupt. "You want me to—"

"I'm on it," insisted Kick, sliding his speed up.
The target building was now dead-on in his screen.
Kick let his speed continue to bleed off, determined
to provide a detailed view to the ground team.
The Osprey, meanwhile, began rotating its wings
upward, driving down toward a field near the road
to drop its men.

Someone shouted over the circuit—there were
people on the ground, near where the Osprey was
headed.

Several things happened at once—the chain gun
in the Osprey's nose rotated, Kick threw his Flighthawk down toward the spot, Danny Freah yelled a
warning and told the Osprey not to fire.

Kick struggled to keep his head clear, fighting the
black fuzz of confusion creeping up from behind his
neck.

"The boats," someone said, and whether it was
intended for him or not, Kick started to line up the
Flighthawk for a view of the harbor. But he was already crossing over the dock toward the water; he

accelerated and began banking to the south to try for another run.

On the Ground in Kaohisiung
0014

As soon as Danny saw the Taiwanese guards emerging from the buildings beyond the battery re-cycling shed in his sitrep window, he shouted at the Osprey pilots to back out. He saw the Osprey whip away just as one of the men began firing an auto-matic weapon. An instant later, Sergeant Geraldo Hernandez launched a stun grenade and then fired his taser, scattering the guards.

"Two of the fuckers down," said Hernandez.

It took Hernandez another sixty seconds to work around a pile of discarded metal before he could get close enough to take out the others. He popped a mesh grenade over the pile, then ran around the side and zapped them as they struggled.

"Osprey in," said Danny.

"Can I get my view of the building now?" he asked Kick after the Marines flooded out of Osprey.

"Roger that," said the Flighthawk pilot. "Two seconds away."

Danny toggled between an IR and a penetrat-ing radar view, preferring to see the details himself rather than using the synthesized and annotated image the computer provided.

"Freeze," he said, getting a good visual of the fa-cility. It looked like there was only one man here besides themselves; he was two corridors down to the right.

"With you," said Egg, following as Danny set out cautiously.

Aboard *Penn*
0015

STARSHIP SAW THE BOAT DARTING INTO THE HARBOR. He knew it wasn't theirs—the computer had the Marines dotted out with daggers—but he hesitated, as if his brain were trying to process the information and couldn't find the next branch in the logic tree.

Gun in the boat.

Big gun.

Something else.

"Company," he said finally. "I'm taking them out."

He leaned on the stick, starting the Flight-hawk downward. But then something tingled in his brain—the other half of the thought that had started a millisecond before. He pulled back, nailing the throttle slide to full just as the missile flared from the boat.

Missile.

They were gunning for the Osprey, coming in over his right shoulder.

"Flares!" he yelled, hitting his diversionary devices.

Ordinarily, he would have jinked away, ducking the surface-to-air missile that had just been launched, getting himself to safety. But something had pushed off the instinct for survival; something deeper took over—he kept the Flighthawk on her course, directly into the path of the oncoming missile.

The shoulder-launched SA-14 hurtled upward at something approaching Mach 1. Though primitive by Dreamland standards, the Russian-designed heat-seeking missile was nonetheless an effective weapon when properly handled. The sensor in its nose ignored the flares, sucking the heat signature of the large aircraft it had been aimed at. But then something juicier stuck itself in its face—the tailpipe of the Flighthawk, flashing within a few meters of the weapon. The missile jerked itself to the right, following the hot scent of its new target, but it couldn't quite keep up. Afraid that it would lose everything, it ignited its charge, sending a spray of shrapnel through the air.

Starship felt the small robot spinning to its left before he actually lost the U/MF; whatever sixth sense it was that helped him fly the plane knew he was down.

The last feed from the cam in the Flighthawk's nose showed the Osprey just a few yards off. The frame froze, as if the tiny aircraft wanted to show that its death had not been in vain.

"Nail the motherfuckers in the boat," Starship told Kick. "I'm outta the game."

On the Ground in Kaohisiung
0021

BOSTON'S VISOR PORTRAYED THE INTERIOR OF THE building in a ghostly gray. A door sat at the far end of the room, leading to a hallway. There was an office at the end outside the range of the helmets' low-power radar; two guards were holed up there, marked in the small sitrep view in the lower left-hand corner of the screen supplied by the Flighthawk sensors. The guard icons blinked steadily, indicating the view had not been updated in more than thirty seconds.

Sergeant Liu moved ahead stealthily. Boston saw a shadow in the hall and steadied his taser at the doorway.

"One coming," he told Liu.

"Wait," said the team leader, his voice so low Boston could hardly hear it. "We want both."

The Taiwanese guard appeared in the doorway, holding an M-16. Boston steadied his weapon, watching the man peer through the dark room. He seemed to know they were there somehow. Boston decided he could take no chances, and fired his weapon. The doorway burned blue and the guard fell to the ground. Liu dove through the doorway from the side, spinning left in the direction of the offices where the guards had been earlier. As he did, the sitrep updated itself as the Flighthawk flew overhead once more.

"Other guard's still in the office," Boston told Liu.

"Yeah," hissed the team leader, and Boston belatedly realized that Liu was now close enough for his helmet-borne radar to pick up the guard.

By the time Boston reached the hallway, Liu was next to the doorway. He reached inside his fogsuit and took out a small tube that looked a bit like an old-fashioned folding carpenter's ruler. He unfolded it, hooking a wire into one end and then pushing it around the corner.

The near-infrared view was capable of greater detail than the radar, and had the advantage of not giving off a detectable radio wave. Liu configured the feed so it could be shared by the team members; a small window at the right of Boston's visor opened and both men saw the guard inside, huddled behind a desk at the left of the room.

A Minimi machine gun sat on one side of the desktop; the guard was pounding a computer keyboard, possibly erasing information. The computer had obviously been hardened against electromagnetic pulses somehow.

"Flash-bang?" whispered Boston.

Too close to the door to risk speaking, Liu fisted a yes signal and Boston reached below his fogsuit for the grenade. He thumbed off the tape as he slipped forward, crawling along the floor and then sliding the grenade into the room.

Time altered its shape in the scant seconds before the grenade went off. Boston felt Liu move, then stop; things flew into fast-forward as the grenade flashed.

"In," said Liu, but by the time the word settled into Boston's skull, the guard at the computer was falling backward, zapped by the discharge of Liu's taser.

Boston ran to the computer.

"No. Check for explosives," said Liu. "I have the computer."

Boston clicked the bottom of his helmet visor, selecting a sniffer mode optimized for explosive materials such as C-4. The unit got two significant hits back in the main part of the building; the computer ID'd them as five-hundred pound bombs.

There ought to be more explosives, Boston thought—I'm not even picking up what would be used for the nuke.

"Boston," said a controller back at Dream Command. "If you guys are secure, we need you to use Probe I so we can locate the nuke. We haven't caught it yet."

Boston stepped out of his fogsuit and pulled out the probe, an ultra-sensitive ion detector that looked like a long wand from a vacuum cleaner and weighed a little more than three pounds. By the time he had the device out and working, Liu had slapped a special modem on the parallel port of the computer and began sending the contents of its hard drive back to Dreamland.

Boston walked slowly through the hall, passing his arm back and forth. The readings were being relayed directly back to Dreamland for analysis through his Smart Helmet system; he had no idea what the unit was picking up, only that his own Geiger counter had not detected radiation serious enough to warn him away.

Large metal-working machines dominated the left side of the room. Wooden boxes and other items were lined neatly on the other wall; most of the middle was empty.

"How we looking?" Boston asked the Dreamland people as he walked toward the area where the explosives sensor had found the two bombs. They were packed into slatted wooden crates, the sort that were used to ship vegetables back in the States. Boston thought these might be the nukes, but in fact they were a bit too small and filled with conventional explosives.

Sergeant Liu joined him when he was about three-fourths done.

"Marines are down," Liu told him. "We have to finish the sweep before they can come in. Find anything?"

"I don't know."

"They'll tell you. Keep at it. I'm going to go back up to the rooms in the front, make sure the data transfer is working. You okay?"

Boston nodded and kept moving forward with the probe.

Aboard *Penn*
0021

STARSHIP PULLED OFF HIS CONTROL HELMET AND stared at the white screen at the top of his station. He could see from the sitrep at the bottom of the screen that the Osprey was landing.

He rubbed his eyes, trying to get them to refocus and adjust to the darkened flight deck. Finally, he pulled on his headset.

"Shit. You did that on purpose?"

Kick.

Was that a legitimate question, or was he being an asshole?

Both, thought Starship, even though he knew he was being unfair.

"Yeah, on purpose. Otherwise they'd've gotten squashed," he said.

"I got the boat," said Kick. "Sank the mother-fucker."

"Good."

"You saved them," said Kick.

"I did," said Starship.

Kick said something to someone on the ground. Starship undid his restraints, stood up, flexed his back and legs, then sat back down. He clicked the radio into Zen's frequency to tell him what had happened.

"I heard already," said Zen before he got two words out of his mouth. "Good going. Watch Kick."

Starship grunted, then reached to change the resolution on his main screen. A shiver shook his upper body. His throat was dry, and he felt a thirst more powerful than any he'd ever felt before.

"Looking good," he told Kick. "Looking good."

On the Ground in Kaohisiung
0029

THE GOOD NEWS WAS THAT THE REST OF THE SITE WAS secure, with the Marines now arriving and holding positions around the perimeter. A computer shielded against electromagnetic pulses had been captured and was feeding itself to Dream Command.

The bad news was that preliminary data said there was no bomb here. They'd have to conduct a painstaking and no doubt time-consuming search, and hope that the local authorities took their time responding to the alarms that were now sounding about gunfire and explosions around the harbor.

But Danny had a more pressing problem to deal with: The man they had missed in the hallway earlier had barricaded himself inside a men's room. He was armed with at least two machine guns—Belgian Minimis, compact 5.56mm machine guns known to American troops as M249 Squad Automatic Weapons, or SAWs.

Egg and Danny watched him from around the corner of the closed door, thanks to the helmet radar. The image was sharp enough for Danny to see that the machine guns were special short-barrel versions equipped with belt feeds contained in compact boxes ahead of the trigger area. The box could hold a hundred bullets.

"He doesn't have a NOD," said Egg. A NOD or "night optical device," also known as night goggles, amplified available light or used the infrared spectrum to allow the wearer to see in the dark. "If we could get that door down, we could get in."

"Too risky," said Danny. "Those bullets can go through that wall like butter. Easier."

While they were wearing body armor, a hundred shots at very close range were bound to find something soft sooner or later. At this point, it was better to go a little slow rather than take any unnecessary risk.

Danny switched his helmet's com device to loudspeaker, and repeated the Mandarin word for surrender Dream Command had given him.

There was no response.

The language specialist at Dream Command

suggested they tell the man he was under arrest, and gave him the phrase, which was rather long. Danny tried it.

"Didn't work, Coach."

"Try Cantonese."

"Give me the words."

To Danny, the phrase sounded nearly identical to the Mandarin: "Nay in joy bee ku boh"—*néi yīn jōi bēi kùi bō.*

His pronunciation may not have been precise, and he couldn't quite master the up-and-down bounce of the tonal language, but the captain did a good enough job to get an answer: A dozen slugs from the Minimi splattered through the hallway.

"You had the wrong tense," said the translator. "That was *You have been arrested.*"

"Forget about it," said Danny.

"Let's just fucking take the bastard out," said Egg. "Demo the door."

"No. You got a flash-bang?" said Danny. "Let's see if we can make him use up his ammo."

Egg rolled the stun grenade down the hallway, hunkering down as the loud bang and flash filled the corridor. The Taiwanese guard immediately began to fire his weapon; if he didn't go through the entire box of slugs, he came pretty close. Danny waited until he stopped firing, then told Bison to toss another grenade. It bounced, rolled a bit, and then went off. Another fusillade of gunfire filled the hall.

Danny trained his taser on the doorway, expecting that the man would run out into the hall, tired of being toyed with. But the guard showed admirable restraint.

"Let's smoke him out," said Egg. "I'll go down and pop a smoke grenade in."

"Not yet," said Danny, fingering his own stun grenade. He set it, then underhanded it down the hall.

The grenade boomed and flashed, but this time the guard did nothing.

"Figured it out," said Danny.

"Or he's out of ammo."

Danny put the visor in radar mode and went down the hall, half walking, half crouching. The man was still there, still staring at the door. Danny took out the telescoping IR viewer, angling to get an idea of what was left of the door. The center had been shot out, but the frame and lower portion remained intact.

The man inside began firing again. Danny fell back as a slew of 5.56mm bullets laced up the corridor, the last few only inches away.

No one would blame him now for saying the hell with the damn nonlethal crap. One conventional grenade—he had two—and the SOB and his stinking machine guns would be history.

But he had his orders.

"We're going to use a variation of your plan," Danny told Egg. "Post a flash-bang. When it goes off, I'll toss in a smoke grenade. Nail the motherfucker with the tasers when he comes out."

"You going down that close?"

"Bullet holes show where he can reach."

"Damn, Cap. Be careful he doesn't shoot your hand off."

"Yeah," said Danny. "Let's go."

The grenade rolled down to the end of the hall. Danny pushed his head down, waiting. The helmet took some of the loud impact away, but the charge was still unsettling; he swung up and popped the grenade into the hole, slipping and losing his balance as he did.

A shadow moved behind the doorway.

Danny saw the barrel of the Minimi inches away.

He pressed the trigger on his taser just as the first bullet flew from the Belgian-made gun. Something smacked him hard against the leg—then everything went blue, and he smelled fire.

"Shit, shit," Egg cursed, running up. He fired his taser at the door two, three times without a target.

"He's down, he's down," said Danny, seeing on his visor that his shot had knocked the Taiwanese guard back into the room. "I'm all right. Chill."

BY THE TIME STONER GOT IN WITH THE MARINES, THE technical experts back at Dreamland had finished a preliminary analysis of Building Two. Aided by the data on the computer as well as their physical analysis, they had no doubt that one or two devices had been stored and probably assembled here.

They also had no doubt that the devices were no longer in the building.

The next logical place on the site was Building One, and Stoner sent a team inside with their rad meters and a video cam. But even before the feeds from their gear started back through the mobile transmitters, Stoner had climbed to the top of the administrative building, trying to figure out where else on the site the bomb might be.

"How you doing?" asked Danny Freah, clambering up behind him.

"I have a bad feeling about this."

"Yeah. I'm going to let Zen and Colonel Bastian know what's going on."

Stoner folded his arms, thinking.

"I say we stop that ship right away."

Dreamland Command Center
14 September 1997
0935

JENNIFER JOINED THE OTHERS IN THE COMMAND CENTER after pulling an all-nighter working with the computer team on a Trojan horse virus to take over the ghost clone's control system. Jennifer was convinced that the best bet was to simply block the communications, then try to insert some of the commands they'd intercepted. The problem was, they couldn't be sure what those commands were, which meant they might succeed in stopping the clone from doing what its masters wanted, but not be able to have the clone do what *they* wanted.

Jennifer took a seat at a station in the second row reserved for her use and began loading the necessary code into computer memory so it could be shipped out to Zen. As the CD-ROM spun, she popped open her notebook computer; she had some more code for the Flighthawk control computer aboard *Raven*, which would have to attempt the takeover.

"And?"

Jennifer looked up at Ray Rubeo, who was wearing his twenty-four-hours-with-no-sleep frown.

"And is a conjunction," said Jennifer. "You can't use it alone."

"Can we take over the clone?"

"Probably not," she said frankly.

Rubeo frowned.

"Yes. Come look at this," he told her, starting for one of the stations at the very front of the room, just below the large display screen. The bomb experts were reviewing coding from a computer at the Taiwan base.

"It's encrypted. We're working with the NSA on it," said one of the experts. "We're feeding it back and forth. There's a lot of technical data and inventory information. We want to see where to concentrate our resources; the encryption takes quite a while to get through."

"This block here is email," said Jennifer. "Look at the structure. Tell them to look for the dates and times."

"Why?" asked Rubeo.

"Maybe they're instructions on when to do something, like launch an attack."

"They may just be love notes," said Rubeo, scowling.

Even though he meant it as one of his acerbic remarks, the idea stung Jennifer.

"Maybe," she said, looking over to the screen where the decryptions were appearing.

Aboard *Raven*
15 September 1997
0040

ZEN HAD *HAWK FOUR* POSTED TO THE NORTH, READY to intercept the ghost clone if it got off. He swung *Hawk Three* down, readying a pass that would take him from bow to stern and give the people back at Dreamland a good view of the ship, which was about forty miles out of the harbor. The Navy destroyers, meanwhile, were still a good hour away to the south.

The E-bomb had successfully wiped out the radios back at the assault zone; *Raven*'s powerful sensors had not picked up any transmissions from the *Dragon Prince*. It seemed clear that the ship did not know what was going on; its speed was below ten knots. Except for its normal running lights, the deck and the area where it launched the ghost were dark.

Zen checked his speed, nudging off the throttle slightly as the ship grew in the screen. The HUD ladder notched downward; he dropped through five thousand feet. The Flighthawk engines were relatively quiet, but at this altitude the aircraft could be heard; Zen figured that was a reasonable trade-off for the better images the lower altitude would provide.

As he closed to five miles off the bow, the water on the starboard side of the boat bubbled. His first thought was that the crew aboard the *Dragon Prince* had thrown the robot aircraft overboard; a few seconds later another geyser appeared on the port side, and Zen finally realized what was going on.

"Submarines," he said over the Dreamland circuit. "Two of 'em. Those ours?"

Two people started to answer at once, and Dog said something over the interphone circuit. Zen kept *Hawk Three* on beam, riding in over the tanker.

There were people moving now aboard the ship. Something flashed at the stern—Zen saw a small rubber boat in the water near the bow.

"They're being boarded," he said. "The Chinese."

Aboard *Penn*
0041

AS SOON AS THE MARINES SECURED THE WHARF AREA, Kick took *Hawk One* over the water. He saw some flotsam where he'd sunk the boat earlier, and one body; as he began to bank for another run, he saw two small speedboats approaching from the distance. The dark, sleek hulls looked very much like Mark V Special Operations Crafts (also known as SOCs), used to land SEALs.

"Two un-ID'd boats," he said over the Dreamland circuit. He clicked into one of the frequencies the Marines were using. "I have two unidentified boats approaching from the harbor, moving at twenty-three knots, twenty-four. I want to make sure they're not ours."

"I'll work on it," interrupted Starship, buzzing in on the interphone circuit. "Take a pass and get some video back for Dreamland."

"Yeah, good thinking," said Kick. He pulled the

Flighthawk around, accelerating as he set up a pass that would take him across their bows.

STARSHIP HIT THE KEYBOARD PRESET AND BROUGHT UP the infrared on the approaching boats. The heat signal from the engines was baffled—these were not pleasure cruisers, and they certainly weren't Americans.

"I say we nail the mothers," he told Kick.

"Marines are checking with their captain. What's Dream Command say?"

"Screw Dreamland," said Starship. "They're scientists back there. Get these guys."

As he finished his sentence, a flare shot from the stern of one of the boats.

Not a flare—a shoulder-launched weapon.

KICK SAW THE MISSILE'S IGNITION AND KNEW IT WAS coming for him; as the thought formed in his head another jumped in—scumbag.

A jumble of other thoughts and images came in quick succession, the most important of which was the realization that the missile, fired at his nose, had no chance in hell of hitting him.

"Guns," he told the computer, activating the gun radar. The screen blinked red—he had the small boat's midsection fat in the claws of his targeting pipper.

The trigger on the Flighthawk stick had a long run, a precaution against it being fired accidentally. He nailed it all the way down, and a burst of 20mm shells punched a fat hole in the boat's midsection.

"Get the other mother," said Starship.

"Yeah, no shit," said Kick. He tried pirouetting the Flighthawk on her wing but had too much speed to get the right position; he had to nose down and bank around, far out of position and cursing himself for trying to do too much.

Not too much for the plane. He'd seen both Zen and Starship pull that hard a maneuver several times during various flight exercises. He didn't quite have the right feel for it; he wasn't really sure where the performance edge was, and maybe hesitated a little as he got near it.

Not a problem, he told himself. He didn't have to fly like Zen did, or even Starship. His job was to take the boat.

And that could be done very easily.

STARSHIP SNICKERED TO HIMSELF AS KICK TRIED TO get on the second boat in the first pass; it was obvious from the screen that he hadn't set himself up right for the hard slam downward that it would require to pirouette the Flighthawk back in that direction. Sure enough, Kick had to pull off and get into a wider approach.

Dream Command said something about the boat being ID'd as a Mainland commando group.

They had carte blanche to take it out.

About time, he thought.

"Sink the boats," said Colonel Bastian, breaking in from *Raven*. "Take them."

"Roger that," said Starship. "We're on it."

As he clicked off his mike, he realized he'd covered Kick's own acknowledgment.

"Sorry about that, roomie," he muttered as the cannon in the U/MF lit up.

Aboard *Raven*
0045

DOG STUDIED THE FEED ON THE SMALL VIDEO SCREEN as Zen finished his sweep. There was gunfire on the port side and stern of the *Dragon Prince*; two or more parties of commandos were aboard the ship. Most likely they had launched their operation from some distance away, and then waited for the submarines to close in before going aboard. The effort appeared coordinated with an attack on the Kaohisiung plant; fortunately, Dreamland's schedule had been a half hour ahead of the Mainlander's.

Dog had no trouble giving approval to take out the Chinese boats attacking Kaohisiung himself; it was necessary to protect his people and clearly authorized by his governing orders. The situation below, however, was not quite so clear-cut. The Navy destroyers that were supposed to assist had been authorized only to stop the ship, with the minimal amount of force required to make it comply.

Given the circumstances, however, Dog decided he had to take out the clone and the ship or the UAV would fall into communist hands.

"I can pepper the submarines with cannonfire," Zen told Dog. "Get them to back off until the destroyers get here."

"Negative, Hawk leader. It's too late for that. We're going to sink that ship. Stand off."

Dog told Delaney to open the bay doors.

"Bays," said the copilot, who functioned as a weapons officer in the slimmed-down crew structure.

The large rotating bomb rack in the bay of the aircraft spun around, preparing to launch one of the two Harpoon missiles aboard. While the AGM-84 (Block 1D) missile had been developed by the Navy, B-52s had actually carried the tried-and-true anti-ship missile for more than a decade. A noodge over twelve and a half feet long, the missile carried five hundred pounds of explosives in its nose. Designed as a fire-and-forget weapon that could be launched from at least seventy-five nautical miles away, the Harpoon would duck toward the waves and then skim the surface of the ocean, extremely hard to detect and even harder to stop.

"Ready to launch on your command," said Delaney.

"Jed Barclay in the Pentagon situation room for you," interrupted Major Catsman at Dream Command. "You want Channel Two. It's scrambled."

"Jed, make it quick," said Dog as the NSC aide's face flickered onto the com screen.

"Colonel, we're monitoring the situation here at the Pentagon."

"Then you know I have two Chinese submarines taking over the ship that controls the ghost clone," said Dog, trying in vain to muzzle his anger. "They have to be stopped now."

"Stand by," said Jed.

"What the hell?" said Delaney.

The defense secretary came on the line.

"Colonel, we don't want you to hit the Chinese submarines."

"Understood," said Dog. "That's why we have to strike right away."

Modern communications technology could be a blessing—he had a team of highly trained experts backing him up halfway across the globe at Dreamland. But it also gave the Washington types unprecedented ability to screw things up.

"We can't afford collateral damage," added Chastain.

"Look," said Dog, his patience nearly gone. "I have about thirty seconds to decide whether to try to sink the tanker or not. If the robot plane is aboard, the communist commandos will grab it."

"Colonel, we're on their radar," said Delaney, breaking in. "This may be some sort of unbriefed fire control radar—the computer is doping it out as an SA-6. Has to be a mistake . . ."

The SA-6 was a Russian-made ground-based antiaircraft missile; there was no way it could be aboard the Chinese submarine.

Then again, this wasn't a particularly good time to be wrong.

"You're cleared to take down the *Dragon Prince*," said the defense secretary.

"Fire the Harpoon," Dog told his copilot. Then reached to the panel and killed the connection to Dreamland—and the Pentagon. "Missile status?"

"I've gone to ECMs. Computer says those subs carry no missiles."

"Is it on the tanker?"

"Searching."

"Zen, can you get a look at the decks of those submarines?"

"Roger that," acknowledged the Flighthawk pilot.

"Watch out for the Harpoon," warned Delaney. "It's terminal."

"No shit," said Zen.

ZEN CHECKED *HAWK FOUR* AS HE BANKED *THREE* BACK toward the tanker, making sure the computer was doing a good job flying the robot. Systems green, course perfect—he jumped back into *Three*, zooming in toward the ship. The right side of the tanker flared.

"Harpoon hit," he told Dog.

"Negative!" said Delaney. "It's still en route."

Zen saw the shadow streaking toward the middle of the tanker at the bottom of his screen, then realized what had happened as the tanker exploded.

"I have a launch. The ghost clone is airborne!"

"Take it out," said Dog.

Dreamland
14 September 1997
0958

JENNIFER PUNCHED THE MIKE BUTTON AGAIN, TRYING to tell Zen that she was ready to upload the program. But they'd lost contact with the Megafortress.

Dog had punched it out, she knew, pissed at interference from the Pentagon people.

Just like him to shut off the rest of the world.

She slammed her hand down on the desk counter so hard it stung.

"Damn it," she shouted. "I want to upload!"

"The telemetry circuits are open," said Rubeo behind her, his voice soft and calm. "Go ahead. You don't need to talk to them until the program is ready to run."

Aboard *Raven*
15 September 1997
0058

ZEN SLAMMED THE THROTTLE AGAINST THE STOP, COAXing *Hawk Three* out past Mach 1. He glanced at the sitrep, making sure *Four* was positioned in case he couldn't catch up. C^3 began calculating moves to stop the aircraft, its silicone brain prioritizing them according to the likely shootdown percentage.

Catching the clone from behind with *Hawk Three* rated only fifth on the list, with a 65.3 percent shot.

Zen laughed at the computer.

"You just want all the glory, my friend," he said, momentarily baffling the verbal instruction interpreter circuits.

The clone had stopped accelerating. Its speed barely touched 200 knots. Zen gained rapidly and the targeting cue went to yellow as he started to close. But he had too much altitude and had to tug downward to get a better shot; his real danger was overshooting his target. One of the Elint operators upstairs started to tell him something, but just then the pipper went to red; Zen lit his cannon, riding a stream of hot lead down into the delta-winged air-craft.

The clone shot left, zigging desperately out of the way. But it was already too late for the robot; the right wing had been hit in three places and now cracked under the pressure of the turn. A large hunk of metal separated as the UAV jerked back north; before Zen could squeeze his trigger again, the air-plane exploded in a red fireball.

Dog was too busy getting the Megafortress north to keep up with the U/MFs so he didn't see the Harpoon's strike on the tanker. He heard his copilot's "Wha-hoo," however, along with his more sober and professional "Good splash" pronouncement a few seconds later. By then, Zen had taken out the ghost clone, which collapsed into the water in its own fireball.

"See if the experts back home can figure out if there was a bomb on it," Dog told Zen.

"Lost my link," said Zen.

Dog reached to the buttons and keyed it back, feeling somewhat sheepish. A cacophony of voices flooded into his ears over the circuit.

"We're talking first," he said, trying to clear the line and the confusion. "Splash one ghost clone. We have a good hit on the tanker, *Dragon Prince*. Returning to assess the damage now."

"Was the bomb aboard the UAV?" asked Cats-man, back in Dream Command.

"We're looking for your assessment," said Dog.

He noticed that the Pentagon people were quiet. He'd undoubtedly have to deal with them later.

They would not be pleased that he had killed the link.

So be it.

"Colonel, this is Danny Freah."

"Go ahead, Danny. How are we?"

"We have complete possession of the site. There are no nukes in Building Two or Building One. Repeat, we have found no devices."

"None? Did they have a bomb or not?"

"They do," said Stoner. "It must have been moved."

"It's possible it was aboard the ship already. We've just sent it and the ghost clone to the bottom," said Dog.

"I say we keep looking here," said Stoner.

"Authorities are approaching the gate," said Danny.

"Hold them off until you've completed a thorough search," said Dog. "Look under every pile of garbage there."

"That may take some time."

"Understood."

Chiang Kai-shek Airport, Hualin
0059

CHEN LO FANN STRAPPED HIMSELF INTO THE FIRST OFficer's seat of Island Flight A101, pulling on the headset. He had come from checking with Professor Ai in the back, making sure that the big jet was ready.

Discovering that the Americans had placed bugging devices in the hangar of his grandfather's 767-200ER had caused him to move up his plans. But otherwise it had not complicated things too badly—his grandfather had apparently foreseen the possibility that the first plane would be discovered, and so had prepared a nearly identical 767 with the necessary launch and control apparatus, storing it in Hualin. Chen Lee must have suspected something himself, since he had ordered the UAV and the weapon moved from Taipei twenty-four hours before. Most likely he was only concerned about the possibility that security would be increased at the international airport when the president took off, but it was a fortuitous move.

Fate favored his plan. It was a sign that Chen Lo Fann had made the right decision to honor his grandfather's wishes and fulfill his duty and destiny.

The only difficulty to be overcome was the length of the runway here. At roughly three thousand meters, it could not be called short. Nonetheless, it did present a challenge to the 767, which was not only fully loaded with fuel but had to take off with the UAV under its wing. Chen Lo Fann could not have gotten the plane up himself, and was only too glad to follow the exact command of the pilot in the captain's seat as they completed their checklist and prepared to taxi to the runway.

Chen's grandfather had disguised the aircraft well. It was a "combi" or combination passenger-cargo carrier; fake windows lined the fuselage, complete with lighting that helped simulate passengers moving around inside. The plane's path from the hangar was obscured from the tower; the presence of the UAV under the wing could not be detected until it was off.

And then it would be too late.

The tower granted clearance. Chen Lo Fann took a long breath. The plane turned from the ramp.

"Ready?" asked the captain.

"Absolutely," replied Chen, and the 767 began rumbling down the runway.

V

VAPORIZED

———

DOG DID EVERYTHING BUT CALL A TIME-OUT, TRYING TO settle his people down so the situation could be sorted out.

Besides a thorough search of the harbor site and a look at the sinking ship, they needed to review all the data gathered during the exchange. Dog quickly confirmed that this was going on, then went to Jed at the Pentagon. *Now* was the time for Washington involvement, he thought, though he was far too tactful to say that.

For now, anyway.

"Looking good, Colonel," said Jed. "We confirm the so-called ghost clone is down. *Dragon Prince* is split in half; bow is gone. Navy asset R-1 is arriving now."

R-1 was a specially equipped A-6 Intruder that carried a sensor array beneath its belly that would send live video (including near-infrared) back to the fleet, and from there back to the Tank. The destroyers, meanwhile, were close enough to see the flames from the stern section in the distance. "We're ready to alert the authorities," added Jed. "The ambassador is en route to the airport to meet with the Taiwan president."

"Why the airport?" asked Dog.

"The president pushed up his flight to Beijing," Jed said. "They're getting out early in case there are any protestors at the airport."

Dog's attention was diverted by the feed from *Hawk Three*, which showed that one of the Chinese submarines had begun to submerge.

"They don't look like they're carrying out rescue operations," Zen said. "They took in a few commandos, that's it. Other sub is still on the surface, but looks like they're bugging out too. Nothing big came aboard either one."

"Roger that. We're alerting the civil authorities," said Dog.

Dreamland
14 September 1997
1005

WITH THE CLONE DOWN, JENNIFER WENT BACK TO HELPing the team studying the data on the Taiwanese computer. She scrolled through the decrypted emails, trying to see if anything there might be useful.

The information had been translated by a computer program into English. It was not exactly perfect, but it saved considerable time and could highlight key words; anything of special interest could be reviewed by a language specialist, either at Dreamland or back East at the NSA.

Three emails spoke of packages, which an NSA analyst guessed meant bombs, though of course that was just speculation. The "meat" of the emails was simple:

Package checked
Package sent
Package 3468×499986767×69696969

The last string of numbers appeared to be part of the encryption that the computer couldn't unlock, though it was impossible to tell.

Jennifer began looking at more of the data on the computer. Apparently the men in the plant had initiated a scrubber program, and much of the drive had been erased. Danny's team had located other computers, but they seemed to have been hit by the E-bomb. Data on all of them might be recoverable, but they would have to be analyzed back at Dreamland.

Package checked and sent. Probably the bomb.

Or the UAV.

Or lettuce.

She got up and went to look at the station where they were analyzing the video from Zen's encounter with the UAV, checking pictures of the fuselage to see if a bomb had been carriaged below the fuselage. One of the technical experts had enhanced the image of the Taiwanese plane being launched from the ship; the image had been generated completely from radar, in some ways a more interesting technical feat than the creation of the UAV itself. Jennifer watched in fascination as the techie put the display into freeze-frame, then dialed in a program that analyzed the structure of the aircraft.

"Are those vertical tabs?" Jennifer asked, pointing at two bars that protruded from the area near the top of the wing root.

"Probably just weird radar echoes," said the engineer. The frame advanced; the pieces remained on the aircraft.

"If they weren't echoes, what would they be?" Jennifer asked.

"Hooks to recover the aircraft or hoist it onto the catapult."

"Or launch it from a plane," said Jennifer. "Like the U/MF-3 Flighthawk."

"Sure."

Jennifer went back to her station. An NSA analyst looking at the data had just sent an instant message suggesting the number stream after "package" in the third email might be a key for a code to activate the bomb. Jennifer called it back.

The repetition at the end of the number stream looked familiar, though by itself it seemed to mean nothing. She pulled over her laptop and brought up the code they had prepared for taking over the UAV.

There were similar sequences in the tail of the communications streams, though she had no idea what they stood for.

×69696969

A coincidence?

If the NSA analyst's guess was correct, then the intercepted communications might mean that the ghost clone had been carrying a nuke when they first encountered it.

But that was impossible—Jennifer turned to the screen on her right, clicking into the stored data to bring up the analysis prepared from the early intercepts. The performance seemed to rule out any bomb.

Unless the code unlocked something in the com stream. Maybe it was part of an encryption key.

What if the package was another UAV? Because maybe you'd want to know the key it used for communications.

Maybe. She needed to look through the rest of the data.

No time for that if there was another plane.

"Ray—I think there's another clone, another plane," she said aloud. "Look at this."

On the Ground in Kaohisiung
15 September 1997
0109

DANNY WATCHED THE MARINE TEAMS CHECKING IN with their captain, listening as they reviewed their findings. The men worked smoothly, running through the different piles of recycled material as if they'd done this sort of thing a million times before.

"We're getting some hits on one of the Geiger counters," the Marine captain told Danny. "In the battery section."

"Let me check it out," said Stoner.

"You have to get the protective gear on," said the Marine.

"Yeah," said the CIA officer, walking toward the shed anyway.

Danny shook his head, then went over to check with Liu and Boston in Shed One.

"Never been in a nuke factory before," said Liu as Danny poked his head through the hole at the back that the two troopers had cut for access.

"Looks more like a machine shop," said Danny.

"I thought it'd at least look like a science lab or something," said Boston. "We gonna glow when we get out of here?"

Danny laughed. They hadn't detected any serious radiation levels; a visit to the dentist posed a greater health threat.

A pair of Marines had begun carting out computer equipment. Boston, helping them, picked up a large memory unit and brought it out to the Osprey.

"The guys back at Dreamland say they assembled them right in this area here," said Liu. "Didn't even use a clean room."

Danny looked around the building. It *did* look like a machine shop. Not even—an empty shed with a few large machines, bunch of computers.

Was it that easy to build a bomb?

He began walking around the shed, wondering to himself how difficult his job might be in five or ten years. If a private company could build a nuke, when would some crazy fundamentalist in the Middle East do so?

There were crates against the wall, vegetable crates.

"Bomb squad took out two five-hundred-pounders," said Liu, referring to a small squad of demo experts tasked to deal with the weapons. "Said they didn't have fuses and couldn't go off, but nobody wanted to take any chances. Leave them for the authorities."

"They came in these boxes?" said Danny, pointing.

"Don't know. The boxes were there. I don't know if they were crating them. Couldn't figure it out."

"I saw some boxes like that in Taipei," said Danny. "In a hangar there."

"Just vegetable boxes. Bring lettuce and stuff around, like that."

"A lot of lettuce gets eaten in Taipei."

"Tons."

Danny flicked his com control to talk to Dreamland.

Aboard *Raven*
0120

WITH THE TAIWANESE AND AMERICAN AUTHORITIES NOW arriving on the scene of the sinking, *Raven* and its Flighthawks were reduced to the role of spectators. Zen let C³ take both Flighthawks in a general patrol pattern; it was the down part of the mission, and once he had his own aircraft squared away, he turned his attention to his two young protégés aboard *Penn*.

Zen shook his head as Starship and Kick engaged in some good-natured banter over how close the Chinese Communist missile had come to splashing the Osprey before Starship managed to get his Flighthawk in the way. The joking started a bit off-color and then went quite a bit further; about the only word that could be repeated in polite company was "road."

"All right guys, let's not forget we're working," Zen told them finally.

He felt more than a little proud, as if he were a high school basketball coach whose team had just won the championship. It wasn't that bad a metaphor, actually—they were clucking away like high school kids, their jokes on a sophomore's level.

At best.

"Check your fuel," he added. "I don't want you walking home."

Starship's retort was cut off by Dog on the interphone.

"Zen, I want you in on this. Go to the main Dreamland channel."

He clicked off without saying anything else to the two Flighthawk pilots, listening as Ray Rubeo detailed an argument for another UAV.

"We're trying to get a line on that plane," added Rubeo. "The surveillance equipment that Captain Freah placed shows the other still in the hangar."

"What plane?" asked Zen.

"Chen Lee's companies have two 767s. One is in Taipei on the ground but we're looking for another that they seem to have leased a few months back," explained Dog. "The UAV has handles that could be used for an air launch. We have someone en route to the airport to take a look at it."

"Let's get north," said Zen.

"My thoughts exactly," said Dog.

Aboard Island Flight A101
0130

FANN CHECKED THE COURSE MARKER. THE UAV HAD A range just over fifteen hundred miles, but that was without the extra weight of a bomb, and flying at medium to high altitude. Professor Ai had calculated that its fuel would take it roughly a thousand as presently configured. They were just approaching the thousand-mile mark now.

The longer they waited, the less possibility there was of the small plane running out of fuel. But it also increased the chance that they would be found.

He checked the map and his watch again. In less than two hours, Beijing would be destroyed.

No—the communists would be destroyed. The capital, *his* capital, would be intact.

He would return to Taipei, a hero.

And a criminal, in the eyes of the communists and their collaborators in the present government. Undoubtedly he would be killed. But death merely meant a change; it was no more permanent than life.

Waiting increased the chances of success, but it would also allow him to see the explosion. He would witness the moment of his grandfather's triumph with his own eyes.

"We are in range," said Ai.

"We will wait as long as possible. I calculate an optimum launch in twenty minutes," he told the scientists.

"The communists are reacting to action by the Americans. They are scrambling fighters, alerting their troops. I've seen the radar and radio intercepts and—"

"We will wait as long as possible."

Aboard *Raven*
0140

ACCORDING TO THE MANUAL, A "STOCK" B-52H COULD make 516 knots at altitude. B-52s had long ago ceased to be "stock," and in practice the typical Stratofortress's hull was so cluttered with add-ons and extra gear that even 500 knots in level flight could be more fantasy than reality.

Dreamland's EB-52s—which in most cases had started their lives as B-52Hs—contained no external blisters to slow them down. Thirty-something years of work on jet engine technology allowed their four power plants to do the work of the original eight more efficiently, and the use of more alloy and composites in the wing and tail structures did the same for the airfoil. In short, if an entry for the Megafortress's top speed were to be made in a reference book, it would be listed at close to 600 knots, along with an asterisk indicating that, depending on the configuration of the power plants and the load the massive plane carried, it might do considerably better.

Dog, with full military power selected, passed the 600-knot mark as he pushed northward through the Taiwan Strait, the two U/MF-3s leading the way.

Mainland China and Taiwan existed side by side in an intricate and highly charged relationship.

On the one hand, their governments considered each other bitter enemies. On the other, there was a myriad of commercial relationships between the pair. Among those relationships were regular flights from Taipei to a number of Mainland cities, most especially Shanghai.

Such flights might give cover to a 767 loaded with a UAV and nuclear device, Dog thought.

"*Raven* to Dream Command. Major Catsman, have we located that other 767 yet?"

"We're going over the airport right now," said Catsman. "We have CIA assets on the ground."

"Copy that."

Dog looked over at his fuel panel. They had about three more hours of flying time before nudging into the reserve cushion, depending on what twists and turns Dog took.

He brought up another set of instrument readings on the configurable screen, focusing on his aircraft's performance. *Raven* could have been used to set the benchmarks for a maintenance manual.

Come to think of it, it had.

"Danny, what's your situation?" he asked Captain Freah, bouncing back onto the Dreamland line.

"We're secure here. Still going over everything, but it looks about as clean as a diner an hour before the health department inspectors arrive. Authorities are at the gate," Danny added. "We're holding them off—got about another ten to fifteen minutes of searching to get through."

"Roger that."

On the Ground in Kaohisiung
0151

STONER SAW THE PANEL BEHIND THE VAT OF SULFURIC acid a second or two after the Marines did, and had to shout at them to keep back.

"Very good chance the sucker's booby-trapped," he told the two men, who unlike him were wearing special chem suits with breathers to protect them from the acidic fumes.

It wasn't that Stoner liked to take unnecessary risks; he knew people worked in this plant with the acid all the time, and figured his brief exposure was nothing like what they exposed themselves to.

Not that it was pleasant. He went to the floor panel and knelt down, instantly soaking his knees in the residue of a thousand car batteries. He could feel the material get sodden and start to tickle at his skin.

"Back," he told the Marines, pulling out a long knife.

One of the men began to object; if the panel was booby-trapped, they had a special squad trained to defuse it. But Stoner had already found two wires with his knife; he pulled them up gently, scraped some of the insulation off, then checked the current with a small meter the size of a pen top. A yellow light flashed on; he clipped another set of alligator clips to the wires and got a green.

"You're fucking lucky," said one of the Marines as he jimmied open the lock.

"How's that?"

"Could have just as easily blown when it was shorted."

"Well, only if my sensor here screwed up. It's all right—my guess is it's just an alarm and it was taken out by the E-bomb," said Stoner, shining around the flashlight. "There aren't any charges here."

He'd suspected that; the acid would have made keeping explosives here fairly dangerous, especially with people working all around the area. What he hadn't expected was that the panel led to a ladder, which disappeared downward.

"Come on," he told the Marines as he positioned his NOD monocle and pulled out his Beretta. "Cover me."

Aboard *Penn*
0200

KICK LEANED BACK AS THE COMPUTER TOOK THE Flighthawk further out into the harbor, still searching for any other Mainland boats or submarines. The Taiwanese port authorities, local police, and navy assets were all rushing to the area, and a search-and-rescue operation was under way. *Penn* had vectored in some of the SAR assets, but communication with the local units was torturous because of the different radio frequencies and, more importantly, accents. Still, several of the Mainlanders had already been recovered.

If he were in their place, he wouldn't want to be saved.

"Major Alou is asking you to check that merchant ship out, just about head on at two miles," relayed Starship.

"Yeah, roger that, thanks."

"Easy man, you're jerking your stick like you're muscling a Hog," added Starship. "This is fly by wire. Fly by *remote* wire."

"You know, Starship, I really don't need your help."

"Fuck yourself then."

"And fuck yourself back."

Starship laughed. Kick started to laugh too.

STARSHIP WATCHED THE SMALL TRAWLER GROW LARGE in the display. There were two or three people on deck, but the ship had no lights on at all.

He suspected the craft had launched the commandos they'd intercepted in the harbor. But they'd already run a check on the registry and found that it was owned by a company in the Philippines.

That would undoubtedly prove to be bogus, but at the moment there was nothing they could do about it.

Kick brought the Flighthawk across the bow in a gentle arc, still a bit unsure of himself as he flew. That was reassuring in a way. Kick would never be as good a pilot, even a remote pilot, as Starship; he could compare himself to Kick any time and know he was ahead.

It didn't take away the jitter he felt in his chest, though. And he was thirsty, very thirsty. And for something more than the bottled water in the galley fridge at the back of the compartment.

"See any antiair?" Kick asked.

"Negative."

"This has to be the ship. Think we ought to splash it?"

Starship looked at the shadow of the ship. They could say they saw someone with a shoulder-launched missile on deck—thought they saw someone.

Shoot out the rudder, stop the damn boat cold.

Be heroes.

That wasn't their job, though.

"I think we better tell Major Alou it's clean but suspicious," said Starship. "Get the Taiwan or Navy people on it."

"Yeah. Better. I'd love to nail the mother."

"You and me both."

On the Ground in Kaohisiung
0200

STONER COULD HEAR THE SOUND OF WATER DRIPPING in the distance as he walked down the hall the ladder had led down to. Six feet wide and seven feet high, the passage ran straight for about ten feet, then took a sharp turn to the right.

Stoner stopped at the corner, his hand on the smooth concrete. There could be anything around the bend.

One of the Marines stepped forward with his M-16. Stoner grabbed the man's shoulder, stopping him.

He wasn't going to let anyone else do his job.

"Just cover me," he said, and before the two Marines could stop him, Stoner had thrown himself onto the floor, sliding into the middle of the open space with his pistol ready.

The hallway was empty. It went on for about fifteen feet, then took another bend to the right. Stoner jumped up and scrambled down it.

The Marines were at most a half step behind him, their gear clacking as they whipped the noses of their rifles up and down across the space. One of the young men started forward. Stoner grabbed him.

"No—a motion detector. This bunker must've been shielded somehow against the E-bomb."

As he finished the sentence, the space behind them exploded.

Aboard *Raven*
0200

ZEN REQUESTED A REFUEL FOR *HAWK THREE* AS *RAVEN* neared the north end of the Taiwan Strait. Dog acknowledged and started backing down his speed—anything over 400 knots made for a very difficult tank, even when handled by the computer.

The Taiwan air force, officially known as Chung-kuo Kung Chuan or the Republic of China Air Force, had launched several patrols, including a full set of submarine hunters to chase the commando craft in the south. A Grumman E-2T radar plane, escorted by a group of F-5Es, was just taking up a station in the strait to the north, its radar sweeping the area for Mainland attackers.

The E-2Ts were essentially the same aircraft as the U.S. Navy's E-2C Hawkeye, extremely capable, fleet, airborne radar craft. The longish nose of the planes carried a forward-looking Litton AN-ALR-73 Passive Detection System antenna; three other antennas were stuffed into other locations in the plane. But the truly unique feature of the Hawkeye was its radardome, a twenty-four-foot flying saucer mounted over the wings and fuselage. The E-2T could find an airplane at roughly 260 nautical miles; the computers aboard allowed it to track at least six hundred air targets (later-model American planes could handle over two thousand). In practice, "only" forty or so intercepts could be controlled at one time; even so, that would allow one E-2T to nail more than half of the attack sorties in the Battle of Midway in one shot.

Zen listened to the *Raven* copilot exchange pleasantries with the Taiwanese as he came in for the refuel. The computer painted cues on the screen, making it unnecessary for the Megafortress to carry the director lights common on dedicated tankers like the KC-10. As the small robot closed, Zen turned the procedure over to C^3, which fought through the rough eddies of air rushing off the Megafortress's bulky body. As the robot plane slapped into the straw, the automated system aboard the Megafortress exchanged some code with the Flighthawk—the digital equivalent of "Fill 'er up"—and the jet fuel began to flow.

REFUEL COMPLETE, DOG CHECKED THEIR POSITION against the GPS screen and turned the helm over to his copilot so he could stretch his legs. But before he could unsnap his restraints, Major Catsman's overstressed voice came over the Dreamland channel.

"Colonel, we have an update on that leased 767 that Chen's company owned," said Major Catsman. "We're still trying to pull together information, but it was moved to Hualin two weeks ago. It underwent work there to one of the wings."

"Where is it now?"

"Unknown. We also think there may be another UAV but we haven't anything definitive. The thinking here is that the alterations to the wing would have been to air-launch the aircraft, or possibly to carry a bomb."

Major Catsman had already done some checking and narrowed down the possible suspects to three 767s.

"We should get the airports shut down," said Dog. "Let's get the Taiwan air force involved. I need a direct line to the general in charge. Can you set that up there?"

"Will do. Jed Barclay wants to talk to you in the meantime."

"And I want to talk to him," said Dog.

On the Ground in Kaohisiung
0205

STONER CLOSED HIS EYES AND PUSHED DOWN HIS head, knowing he was going to die but not wanting to give in. It seemed like a waste to go out here, when he hadn't even figured out what had happened to the bombs the bastards had made.

Dirt pushed into his pores. He couldn't hear and he couldn't see.

Poor fucking Marines. Poor Marines. Shit. He couldn't let those guys die.

He pushed up against the massive blocks that had smothered his head. They began to give way.

I'm like Samson, he thought. Where is this strength coming from?

A light flashed in his eyes. He blinked.

Was this what death felt like? Did God really send an angel out to get you?

There was a groan behind the light.

One of the Marines.

He wasn't dead. He wasn't even buried. One of the Marines had fallen on him, probably trying to protect him.

Idiot Marines, always trying to do their job.

The kid was breathing. Good. But the chamber was blocked off with rubble—he could see the pile reflected in the flashlight's shadow as the dust finally settled.

"Stoner," said the Marine with the light.

"Yeah, I'm here," said the CIA officer, dragging himself up. The NOD lay on the ground; he didn't even bother picking it up to see if it was working, turning on his wristlight instead.

"The charge was back in the main tunnel. It blew down the entrance."

Stoner stood. "Help him," he told the other Marine. "I'm going to see where this hole goes."

"You think we're trapped?" asked the Marine. There was no fear in his voice; he might have been asking about the daily special at a restaurant.

"If we are, Danny Freah'll get us out," said Stoner. He took his radio out and gave it to the Marine.

"Make sure Captain Freah knows we're here and take care of your buddy. I won't be long."

"Yes, sir."

Aboard *Raven*
0220

ZEN RAN *HAWK THREE* AHEAD OF *RAVEN*, CONCENTRATing on intercepting the first of the planes to be checked, a 767 supposedly chartered by an English tour group headed for China. The Boeing carried identification gear that could be queried to show its identity. As he drew close, Zen used the Ident gear; the registry jibed with the flight that had taken off. The gear was not foolproof, however, and they had to assume that anyone clever enough to manufacture the UAV and a nuclear device would have the wherewithal to fake an ID. Zen pushed the Flighthawk toward the aircraft, needing a visual to make sure the plane was in fact what it said it was.

The massive Boeing lumbered ten miles ahead, flying at 32,000 feet, about 5,000 below the tiny Flighthawk. Zen checked *Hawk Four* in the bottom screen—he'd had the computer take her in to be topped off, getting potential fuel problems out of the way—then nudged *Hawk Three*'s nose gently earthward so he could get a look under the 767's wings. He had to check his speed, however; *Raven* had slowed to complete the refuel, and he got a warning from C³ that the connection was about to break.

"Zen, be advised we have some communications

coming off the target plane indicating there are passengers aboard," said Wes Brown, one of the Elint operators. "Cell phone communications."

"Roger that," said Zen.

The infrared cameras on the Flighthawk synthesized an image for Zen in the main screen, gradually sharpening their focus as he pulled closer to the tail of the massive airliner.

Clean.

"They don't have a UAV," Zen told Dog.

"Copy that," said Colonel Bastian.

"Think they have a bomb aboard?" asked Zen.

"I doubt it, but the Taiwanese authorities are looking for a divert field so it can be inspected. Let 'em know you're there, see how they react."

Zen tucked his wing and slid away from the airplane, running down and then coming back up close to the cockpit area. As he rose, he contacted the pilot, asking him to identify himself. Though there was surprise in his voice, nothing the civilian captain said indicated he was flying anything but a charter packed with tourists. The sensors on the Flighthawk couldn't get a comprehensive read on the interior of the moving plane, but there were clearly passengers aboard.

"Taiwanese are sending two F-5s north for him," said Dog. "They're going to order him home."

"Roger that."

"I have our second target north at one hundred miles, making 400 knots. We'll take him next."

"Hawk leader," said Zen, acknowledging.

Pentagon, Washington, D.C.
1420

JED BARCLAY LISTENED AS THE SECRETARY OF DEFENSE and the secretary of state debated whether to inform the Communist Chinese of what was going on. The Mainlanders were already scrambling aircraft, probably in response to the Taiwan activity.

"They'll just shoot all the planes down," said Secretary of Defense Chastain. "I would."

"If a nuclear device is exploded in China, they will retaliate," answered Hartman.

"Not necessarily," said the defense secretary.

"That's what Chen Lee is counting on," said the secretary of state. "It's insanity."

Jed glanced at the video screen from the White House, where his boss was sitting with the President, listening to the debate. Before leaving to come over here, Jed had given Freeman a briefing paper from the CIA that argued that Mainland China would not nuke Taiwan; instead, they'd invade the island using conventional forces. An appendix to the paper suggested that the communists would threaten America with nuclear missiles if it interfered.

"Can we stop all of the aircraft that have taken off in the last hour before they're over China?" asked the President.

"We can get close," said Jed. "But there's no guarantee that we can stop them."

"We can shoot them down ourselves," suggested Hartman.

"In that case, I'd rather inform the Chinese and let them do it," said the President.

"Then they may consider it a first strike and retaliate," said Hartman. "They may obliterate Taiwan."

"We're not even sure that Chen launched his plane," noted Freeman. "Let's give the Dreamland people a little more time to work on it."

"The way the intercepts are lined up right now," said Jed, checking the feed from Dreamland that gave the planes' positions, "Colonel Bastian is going to fly into Chinese territory just off the coast to check that last flight."

"Then that's what they'll have to do," said the President.

Aboard *Raven*
0250

THERE WERE NOW FOUR DIFFERENT FLIGHTS OF INTERceptors within fifty miles of *Raven*, two from Mainland China and two from Taiwan. The Taiwan flights—all F-5Es—were out at the end of their normal operating radius and would have to return to base fairly soon. The Mainland interceptors were J-8s, grouped in twos and also getting close to bingo. A pair of JJ-2 "Midgets" ordinarily used for training and not particularly adept at night operations were also in the air over Wenzhou on the coast, but were probably not much of a threat to anyone but themselves. Dog's crew had its hands full sorting through the intercepted communications; Zen, meanwhile, pressed on toward the next craft they had been tasked to intercept, a 767 cargo craft.

"We're on the Chinese ground intercept radars,"

reported the copilot. "Tracking us. They'll vector the fighters at us any second."

Dog grunted in acknowledgment. A pair of spanking new Taiwanese Mirage 2000s had just selected afterburners, pushing their delta-winged airframes north to come up and take a look what was going on.

"Target plane is at ten miles," said Zen. "Ident checks. Hailing him."

One of the communist flights did the same to *Raven*, telling Dog he was violating Chinese airspace.

"Bullshit," said Delaney. "We're more than fifty miles off the coast."

"Standard Chinese practice," said Dog.

"Like I said, bullshit."

Dog answered that they were in international airspace and pursuing their flight plan. While true as far as it went, the statement was not particularly informative, and the Chinese pilot countered that the American plane had better turn around.

"What's his controller telling him?" Dog asked Wes, who was listening in on the frequency.

"Telling him to challenge us and take no nonsense or something along those lines," said Wes. The transmission was in Mandarin, but the computer gear aboard *Raven* included a competent on-the-fly translator.

"Activating his weapons radar," warned Delaney. "Asshole."

The J-8 challenging them was roughly fifty miles away, and flying a nearly parallel course—there was no way the aircraft could hit the Megafortress with anything but four-letter words.

"Want to go to ECMs?" asked the copilot.

"Let's not give him the satisfaction."

Sure enough, the communist pilot gave up a few seconds later, turning back toward his base on the Mainland.

THE 767 APPEARED ON ZEN'S SCREEN, A BLUR AT EIGHT miles away. While the ID checked out, the pilot had not answered Zen's hail.

The blur slowly drew into focus.

Was there something under the right wing?

Zen nudged the throttle for more speed, but got a warning from the computer that he was too far from *Raven*. He backed off, telling himself not to get too impatient. The two-engine plane slowly came into better focus.

The wing was clean.

Converting a civilian plane into a conventional bomber was not particularly difficult; a bomb bay could be cut into the floor in an afternoon with plenty of time left over for the crew to catch happy hour. Add some proper targeting gear, and the Boeing could be at least as accurate as the aircraft used in World War II. Of course, a 767 would never stand a chance against an interceptor or a ground-defense system—unless it had the element of surprise on its side.

"Wes, Target Two is not answering my hails," Zen told the op upstairs over the interphone. "Why don't you take a shot at it with the translator?"

"Doing so now, Zen."

Zen continued to fly toward the plane, trying to get a look at the body. If there were bottom-opening doors beneath the fuselage, they weren't obvious.

Unlike the 767 he had intercepted earlier, there were no cabin lights, even though he could see the outlines of windows.

"No answer," said Wes.

"Try all frequencies."

"I've tried every one known to man."

"Dog, I think we may have found our target," said Zen.

Dreamland
1155

JENNIFER TOOK A SIP OF HER DIET PEPSI AS SHE CONtinued to scan the NSA intercepts of telemetry being gathered in real time over the South China Sea by Elint satellites and an RC-135. She'd programmed the computer to tell her if anything came across similar to the segment from the email. Reams and reams of material were now being intercepted by satellite and listening stations all over the South China Sea, and even with the computer's help, looking for the UAV would be like searching for a needle in a haystack.

Zen had just pulled close to one of the 767 flights. It wasn't answering hails—this looked to be a good bet. She heard Colonel Bastian talking to the White House directly, asking for instructions.

They were going to tell him to shoot it down, she knew.

Jennifer reached to flick her hair back behind her ear, belatedly remembering she had cut it off.

Dog was telling Jed they had the plane.

Something in her reacted viciously to that. Anger at her lover, or ex-lover? She clicked on the circuit.

"Colonel, that's not the plane," she snapped.

"Jen?"

"That's not the plane," she insisted.

"You sure?"

She wasn't sure at all—logically, it probably was. But she insisted she was.

Why?

Jennifer wanted to argue with him. She wanted to tell him to screw off. And she wanted everyone to see her telling him off.

She wanted to be right, and she wanted everyone to know it.

But she wasn't, was she? Because it had to be the plane.

"Colonel Bastian, you are authorized to use all necessary force to terminate that flight if they won't turn back," said a deep, sonorous voice over the Dreamland Command frequency.

The President himself.

"It's not the right plane," Jennifer insisted. She slapped her computer keyboard, backing out from the intercept screen to the communications profiles stored earlier. The 767 had taken off from Taipei—they had some data from it somewhere in the vast storehouse of intercepts, didn't they?

"Jen, this is Colonel Bastian. Can you explain?"

Fuck yourself, thought Jennifer. She began paging through data.

"Major Catsman?" said Dog.

"Um, just a second, Colonel. Jennifer's working on something here."

Aboard *Raven*
0259

ZEN HAD THE PLANE FAT IN HIS TARGET SCREEN; TWO bursts from his cannon and it would go down. All he needed was an okay from Colonel Bastian.

A Chinese Chengdu J-7 was on a rough intercept from the northwest, its intentions unclear. It wouldn't be a factor for another two or three minutes, however; by then this should be over.

As he waited, Zen checked *Hawk Four*, flying a routine trail behind *Raven*. He decided to put it into a preset position ahead of *Raven* called Escort Two; the robot would fly seven miles ahead of the mother ship's left wingtip. That would give him a reasonable position to deal with the communist interceptor if it continued south and he was still hanging behind the 767.

C^3 acknowledged his command, whipping the tiny plane forward. When he'd first learned to handle the Flighthawks, Zen would have insisted on taking the plane himself. But he'd grown to trust the computer, and knew he could concentrate on *Hawk Three* and the 767.

"Hawk leader to *Raven*. Colonel, what's the story?"

"Dream Command is checking on something."

"That J-7 is going to afterburners," said Delaney.

"Coming for us?" asked Zen.

"We'll know in a minute," said Delaney.

Dreamland
1200

JENNIFER SAW IT ON THE SCREEN AS DOG NAGGED them again for an update. She pointed to the break in the transmission so Major Catsman could see as well.

"This back here is them saying they have radio trouble," said Jennifer. She paged back to the translation screen, trying to get the right place.

She couldn't find it, and for a moment she doubted herself, thought that her anger at him had made her unconscious mind invent it. She stabbed at the cursors.

Where is it? Where is it?

"Wait," said Catsman, grabbing her hand. "Calm down. Go back. Just relax. We have time."

Two backspaces.

"Colonel, it looks like the aircraft you're querying was having intermittent radio trouble shortly after takeoff. They may not be able to hear your hails. I'm not sure why they didn't turn back," said Catsman. "But maybe you can get their attention visually."

Jennifer pushed back from the screen. Tears were falling down her cheeks.

She hadn't invented it.

"Are you all right?" asked Catsman.

Slowly, she nodded.

The major put her hand on Jennifer's shoulder. "We won't shoot down the wrong plane. We won't."

Aboard *Raven*
0305

ZEN ACCELERATED OVER THE RIGHT WING OF THE 767, pushing past the cockpit. The pilot in the big jet did what any self-respecting pilot would do when a UFO blasted across his bow—he ducked.

And took the aircraft with him. Fortunately, the big jet was athletic enough to handle the violent jerk on her controls fairly calmly—if rolling through an invert can be considered calm.

"Getting some radio flickers but nothing intelligible," said Wes upstairs. "I think Jennifer's right—I think he's having radio problems and didn't realize it."

"Wouldn't he have checked in with civilian controllers?" Zen asked.

"Well, given the situation between the two Chinas, I wouldn't be surprised if he didn't talk to them at all, and vice versa. His flight plan has him heading for South Korea."

Whatever the situation, the 767's pilot appeared to realize he was in fact in trouble. Rather than coming back to his original course, he turned southward, as if he were heading back to Taiwan.

"Taiwan Mirages have him on their radar," said Dog. "They're going to hook up and escort him home."

"Roger that," said Zen. "But if he's not our guy, who is?"

On the Ground in Kaohisiung
0305

THE MARINE CAPTAIN WANTED TO BLOW THE BUNKER entrance with C-4, but Danny wouldn't let him.

"That'll kill them for sure," said Danny. "Best bet's to keep digging."

"Sooner or later they're going to run out of air," said the Marine. "We can't get those big blocks out of the way."

"Maybe we can get some earthmovers from the city," suggested Danny.

"God knows how long it'll take to get them here."

Danny stood back. Blowing the hole open looked like the only option—but it risked killing his men to save them. Even if they moved far from the entrance, the shock of the explosion might weaken the already damaged bunker.

The rest of the facility had now been searched; it seemed a good bet that the nuke was down there.

If they blew the concrete to bits, would they blow up the bomb as well?

No—because if it weren't safed against accidental explosions, it would have gone off already.

Assuming it was there.

Go with a minimum charge.

"Set up the explosives," Danny told the Marines reluctantly. "One of my men will help. Make sure the people inside know what we're doing. Yo, Boston. Get over here and put some of your demo training to work."

* * *

STONER PUSHED THROUGH THE DUST, THE DIM BEAM from the flashlight dancing against the walls. The path had taken two turns and gone down two flights of stairs, widening somewhat as it went.

The bunker had definitely been intended as more than a place to hide a nuke or two. As he walked, Stoner worried that he would run into guards. He'd retrieved his hideaway Glock from his leg—the Beretta had been lost in the blast—holding the gun in his hand. The flashlight was strapped to his wrist, casting the shadow of the gun ahead as he walked.

He walked slowly, stopping every second or third step, waiting, listening.

What was this place? he wondered. A cement hole in the ground, a hiding place?

He turned the corner and something flashed in his face. He fired his gun and felt incredibly cold.

Cement and the tang of gunpowder stung his eyes. No one was there—he'd tripped another EMP-shielded motion detector. He was at the entrance to a paneled room.

He took a step, then froze, belatedly thinking of booby traps.

Fortunately, there weren't any.

"My lucky fuckin' day," he said aloud.

The room itself was empty, except for a small couch. A Taiwanese flag hung on the wall. On the wall opposite it were some framed papers and scrolls. Most were in Chinese, but one was in Latin with a name written in Roman letters:

AI HIRA BAI

A diploma or certificate of some sort. He was in the professor's lair.

A door on his right was ajar, revealing a bathroom.

To the left, a set of steps led downward. Stoner walked to them. Another light came on, but this time he was prepared.

The steps led to a small office dominated by a wooden desk with a glass top. Beneath the glass was a map of Mainland China. He reached for the top drawer, opening it gently. It was empty, except for an envelope with Chinese characters on it. Stoner's ability to interpret ideographs was somewhat limited, but he thought the words meant "To the next generation."

BOSTON WATCHED THE MARINES SET THE CHARGES amid the rubble. The passage was blocked by an extremely large and thick piece of the wall; to get it out of the way they had to use considerable explosives. There was simply no way of knowing what other damage it might do.

"How we looking down there, Boston?" asked Captain Freah.

"Uh, the charges are just about set," the sergeant told him. "A good hunk of C-4."

"Understood. Make sure you're far enough away."

"Yeah."

"Something bothering you, Boston?"

"Uh—"

"Look, Sergeant, the thing about Whiplash is, you have an opinion, you share it. You got me? I didn't pick you to join the squad because I thought you were stupid. I want to know what the hell it is you're thinking. Talk to me."

Boston had been in the Air Force for a while, but no officer had ever spoken to him exactly like that. While there were definitely good officers around, the usual attitude toward NCOs and enlisted men in general edged more toward tolerance than partnership.

Was Freah different?

Maybe it was the fact that they were both black.

Or maybe what he and Colonel Bastian and the others said was true—Dreamland was a team effort.

"I have a weird, weird idea," offered Boston. "We could use that Osprey to pull some of these big suckers off. I saw this big crane helicopter do that once back home when this building—"

"Pull the charges out of there now," said Freah, cutting him off. "Next time you get an idea, Sergeant, you share it right away, you got me?"

"Damn straight, sir," said Boston. "Damn straight."

**Aboard *Raven*
0315**

Zen jumped into *Hawk Four* as the Chinese J-7 closed to within fifty miles of the Megafortress. The J-7 was essentially a MiG-21, with all the pluses and minuses of the venerable Russian design. Zen could take it in a heartbeat; as a matter of fact, the computer itself could handle the plane if pressed— C^3 had shot down almost enough MiGs to rate as a bona fide ace.

The Chinese pilot repeated roughly the same challenge the others had, telling *Raven* they were in sovereign airspace and to get his Yankee butt home. Zen laughed; Chinese pilots seemed to think they could make up for the shortcomings of their aircraft by boasting. As a class, they had to rate among the most cocksure flyboys in the world—which was saying quite a lot.

Dog gave a bland reply and held to his course.

They had one more aircraft to check out, another 767 whose flight plan said it was heading for Beijing. The ID had already checked out. *Hawk Four* was about forty miles behind it; overtaking it at the present speed would take nearly eighteen more minutes, by which time the plane would be nearing landfall just south of Shanghai.

"Controller's telling that J-7 to hang with us," said Wes. "He's got fuel problems, though."

"Any transmissions from the 767?" asked Zen.

"Negative."

"Zen, be advised we have a ground radar trying to track us," said the copilot. "You see that on your screen? Fan Song–style radar—getting some more action here."

"Just flashed in," said Zen as the icons indicating different ground intercept and guidance radars began to appear on his screens. The Fan Song radar was associated with Chinese V-75 SA-2 Guideline missiles, originally designed by Russia in the late 1950s but updated at regular intervals since. "Stealthy" did not mean "invisible"; the long-wave radar could detect the EB-52 at roughly ten miles. But unless the Megafortress had to fly directly over the site, it was unlikely to be successfully targeted. The Flighthawk was even more difficult to detect.

"We're out of their range," noted Delaney. "Fresh flight of Mirages en route from Taiwan coming up behind us, uh, should be on the radar in ten, a little less. Look here, J-7's turning around. Looks like the skies are friendly once more."

"Roger that," said Zen, jumping back into *Hawk Three* and pressing toward the 767.

On the Ground in Kaohisiung
0320

WHILE THE OSPREY WAS BROUGHT IN TO MOVE THE debris, Danny Freah went to the staging point down by the harbor to speak with one of the Taiwanese officers in charge of the forces there. By now the government had been informed by Washington that an operation was under way to apprehend terrorists pursuant to existing treaties, but details were still waiting Danny's completion, and in any event the Taiwan president had not yet been contacted.

The Taiwanese were angry but Danny wasn't ready to explain what was going on or turn over control. While there were now more than a dozen Marines at the entrance to the site, the Americans would soon be outgunned, and in any event were under orders not to use lethal force against their allies. So Danny tried an old politician's trick of diverting attention. He told the Taiwan officer in charge at the gate that the terrorists were probably Mainlanders and were suspected of having more forces in the harbor; they needed help checking the shorelines nearby. The officer retreated to consult his superiors; Danny also retreated, telling the Marines to appear as helpful as possible, but to stall before coming to find him.

Meanwhile, the Osprey hovered over the battery reclamation area. As powerful as the craft was, it hadn't been designed as an excavator. It groaned and ducked, power plants moaning. Trotting back toward the site, Danny realized he'd have to call it off before it became damaged. Before he could hit his com control, the tilt-wing aircraft lurched backward, then suddenly shot upward—the stone had broken free.

"All right, Boston, set the explosives up," he said, making his way back toward the area.

"No need to—we can get in. The Osprey pulled the block a couple of yards away."

There was a shout in the background.

"What's going on?" demanded Danny.

"Marines are okay. One with two broken legs swears he'll beat the crap out of anyone who tries helping him walk."

"Where's Stoner?"

"Inside somewhere. We're working on it."

Aboard *Raven*
0320

HAWK THREE NOTCHED FORTY THOUSAND FEET, SLOWLY but surely gaining on the 767. But this was another wild-goose chase, Zen realized; not only had the ID checked out but the pilot had spoken to controllers at the Shanghai airport. It was a combi flight, with a dozen passengers and cargo, and it would be landing in about fifteen minutes.

Two fresh Mirage 2000s had been scrambled northward from Taiwan. Bumped by their afterburners into Mach + territory, they would have the Boeing in sight about sixty seconds or so after Zen did. Their fly-by-wire controls and a subtle but significant change in the design's center of gravity made the planes much more maneuverable than the Mirage III they outwardly resembled. While Zen would still—rightly—prefer an F-15 in a dust-up, the ROC interceptors could definitely hold their own.

The same might be said—albeit much more grudgingly—for the Shenyang F-8IIMs now being vectored in to check out the Mirages by a ground control unit south of Shanghai. The Shenyangs were as fast as the Mirages and might be as maneuverable, though from what Zen had already seen of Mainland pilots, he doubted their ability to outfly their island rivals.

C³'s tactical section plotted their intercept—everybody was going within visual range at roughly the same time.

The computer blinked at him, as if asking: Want to see what would happen in a three-way brouhaha?

And then there was yet another J-7, now within three miles of *Hawk Four*, flying toward *Raven* from the northwest. He was now within radar-missile range of the Megafortress.

"*Raven*, what do you want me to do with that J-7?" Zen asked.

"Stay on his wing," said Dog. "He ought to be bingo soon."

"You want me to make him see me or not?" asked Zen. The radar in the J-7 was not adept enough to pick up the stealthy U/MF.

"Negative. No sense losing the element of surprise. He hasn't turned on his weapons. He's not much of a problem."

"Hawk leader," acknowledged Zen, somewhat disappointed that he couldn't scare the bejesus out of the fighter pilot. He put *Hawk Four* into a bank, turning parallel as the other plane approached. He would accelerate and ride about two miles behind the J-7 as it came in.

Or not—the fighter abruptly rolled its wing and turned toward the Mainland.

"Getting boring," Zen told Dog.

"Well, stay awake long enough to check out that 767," said Dog. "Then we can go home."

"Roger that. I think this has all been a wild-goose chase."

"Better than the alternative."

"WE'RE GETTING INTO OUR FUEL RESERVE," DELANEY told Dog on the flightdeck. "If we have to duck those idiot commies on the way back, we may run into trouble."

"How much time before Zen gets within viewing range?"

"Still a good eight minutes."

"That's not going to kill us."

"Famous last words. Those F-8s are coming hard."

"They'll probably turn around like everyone else."

"Says you."

"You sound like a pessimist, Mr. Delaney."

The copilot laughed. "Guess I am."

Dog checked in with Jed Barclay back in D.C. "We have one last flight to look at. IDs have come back good and it looks like it's clean. More than likely they never had a bomb to begin with."

"That's a relief," said Jed.

"Sure is," said Dog.

On the Ground in Kaohisiung
0330

STONER PAID NO ATTENTION TO THE NOISE IN THE HALL, figuring it was Danny coming for him. He continued to work at the documents; they were a kind of personal history, detailing Professor Ai's mother's flight from the Mainland.

Ai didn't want to take back China so much as destroy it. His mother had been accused of being a whore or traitor—the words weren't clear to him.

"Mr. Stoner," said one of the Whiplash troopers from down the hall.

"Yo!" yelled Stoner.

Boston trotted into the room, two Marines in tow.

Stoner looked up from the desk. "I need to talk to Captain Freah."

"Gotta come up to do it. We're not in line of sight, and we're too deep under the concrete for the sat transmission. That would be why your radio didn't work," the sergeant added.

Stoner smiled. He realized he hadn't even tried it.

"Mr. Stoner?"

"Yeah, I'm fine. Hang on a second. Let me finish this one section here. Then we gotta go find your boss. Quickly."

Aboard *Raven*
0330

WITH THE F-8IIS ON A NORTHERN INTERCEPT, ZEN turned *Hawk Four* onto their noses and changed *Hawk Three*'s course so he could fly by the 767 and continue out toward them. He was at 35,000 feet, about 8,000 higher than his target but lower than the Chinese Communist planes. He pushed his nose down slightly, figuring he would ride just above the airliner, close enough to get a good view but still give himself room to react to the Mainlanders.

The image of the 767 appeared in his screen, synthesized first by the long-range radar. He switched back to infrared, getting the now-familiar blur. The computer counted down the intercept in the lower left-hand side of the screen, time over miles. As he passed the five-mile mark, he saw the faint glow of the cabin lights.

"Looks like passengers aboard," he told Dog.

DOG ACKNOWLEDGED AND GLANCED AT DELANEY, WHO was already looking at him, probably ready with another warning about their dwindling fuel.

Before the copilot could do that, Danny Freah interrupted on the Dreamland Command frequency.

"Go ahead, Danny."

"I have Stoner here. He has more information."

There was a pause, some static on the line.

"Colonel, I found some sort of document here prepared by the man who did most of the work on the UAV and some weapons. They do have a nuke."

"You sure?"

"Oh yeah. It's not an ordinary nuke—it's a neutron bomb. A scientist named Ai Hira Bai developed it. I'm looking at what I guess you'd call kind of his life story. I haven't translated everything. It's kind of rambling about his past and family and the Japanese. He was close to Chen Lee, but apparently Chen Lee died."

"When?"

"Not clear. Recently, according to this. My guess is that if they have a bomb they'll try to detonate it over the capital, kill the Chinese leadership. They'll take out the leaders but spare the buildings. I'm pretty sure about that."

"Thanks for the advice," said Dog.

"One other thing—they have two bombs, not one."

"Two? You're sure?"

"The symbol for two happens to be one of the first things I ever learned," he said. "Looks like two missiles in a box. Yeah, I'm sure."

Aboard Island Flight A101
0331

PROFESSOR AI FELT THE SWEAT STARTING TO POUR down the back of his neck. He was not worried about death; he was concerned with failure. They must launch the dragon plane with its bomb now, or they would fail. The communists and the Americans were too close.

"It is time," he told Chen Lo Fann through the aircraft's radio. "We must act."

"Yes. Launch the plane."

Ai went through the procedure quickly, directing the pilot to begin his descent only a few seconds after he had ascertained all was ready.

The small UAV fell free of the wing. Ai's hands shook as he watched the plane's progress on his computer screen.

He tapped the command and severed the communications tie. The computer program aboard the UAV would carry it on its way.

Now he could carry out his own plan.

"Change course," he told the pilot, giving him new coordinates. Then he got up to go to the back of the aircraft.

"HE'S DIRECTING US TO SHANGHAI," THE PILOT TOLD Chen Lo Fann.

"Why?"

"He did not say."

Chen Lo Fann sat back a moment, trying to puzzle out what Ai was doing. The UAV had been programmed to fly to the capital on its own; it no longer needed guidance. But what was Ai up to?

And then Chen Lo Fann realized.

"There's another bomb on the plane," he told the pilot, unsnapping his restraints.

Aboard *Raven*
0332

THE WING OF THE PLANE SEEMED TO CATCH FIRE AS ZEN approached. The 767 bucked downward and then up, and his first thought was that it had been hit by a missile he hadn't seen.

Then he realized what was really going on.

"Hawk leader—we have a launch from the airliner," said Delaney, his voice about an octave higher than normal.

"Roger that," said Zen. He turned *Hawk Three* in the direction the 767 was flying. Mainland China lay in the distance, lights glittering in the dark night.

A small circle of red exhaust slid down through the left-hand quadrant of Zen's screen.

The clone?

Zen started to follow.

Aboard Island Flight A101
0334

CHEN FOUND PROFESSOR AI HUNCHED OVER A LARGE crate in the rear section of the aircraft behind the control deck for the UAV.

"Why didn't you tell me there was a second bomb?"

"Your grandfather forbade it."

"That's not true," said Chen Lo Fann. "My grandfather would not have done that."

"He didn't tell you about the first weapon," said Ai. "Or the UAV and this plane."

"But my grandfather would not have wanted to blow up Shanghai," said Chen Lo Fann. "Why do you?"

Ai Hira Bai didn't answer.

"Get away from the box," said Chen. "We will not attack Shanghai."

"If there is only one attack, the communists may not respond," said Ai. "This will guarantee war, and we will win."

"You want to destroy Shanghai. It's where your people come from, isn't it?"

Anger flashed in Ai's eyes, but he said nothing.

"Away from the box," said Chen. He took his hand out from behind his back, revealing the pistol he kept there.

"The city deserves to be destroyed," said Ai. "Everyone who collaborated with the communists deserves to be destroyed."

"Away from the box, or I will shoot you," said Chen.

Ai nodded his head, and started to get up. Too late, Chen realized he too had a pistol.

The bullet tore into Chen's left shoulder an instant before he fired his own weapon. For the first second, there was no pain. Surprised, Chen glanced at his arm, thinking Ai had somehow missed.

Then the pain came.

He fired again, but Ai had already collapsed. Chen took a step toward the scientist. The bullet had blown off a good part of his skull.

Pain seared Chen's body, and Chen felt what his grandfather had felt before he died of the heart attack. He slipped down to his knees, his good arm grabbing at the crate that held the nuclear weapon. There was a digital arming device at the front. It blinked at him. As Chen Lo Fann tried to focus on the digits and make out the control, the pain rushed across his body.

It's armed, he thought. Then he saw darkness and felt himself fall to the floor of the cabin.

Aboard *Raven*
0335

"F-8S THINK IT'S A MISSILE," SAID DELANEY.

"Is it?" Dog asked.

"Not sure."

"Can we get it with an AMRAAM-plus?"

"I can't get a lock."

"Get one."

"Yes, sir."

Dog leaned on the throttle slide, coaxing the power plants for more juice.

"Gonna screw up our fuel."

"Mind what you're doing," said Dog. "Zen, we're launching a Scorpion."

"Roger that."

"Bay," said the copilot. The plane shuddered as

the bomb bay door opened so the AMRAAM-plus could be fired.

"Locked—"

"Go!" said Dog.

Delaney launched. A second later, the Mainland planes turned sharply in front of them.

"They think we're firing at them. They have ECMs active," said Delaney. "That patrol plane over the mainland, fifty miles away—it's some sort of airborne AWACS type, jamming."

Dog ignored him. The techies liked to call the AMRAAM-plus guidance system "particularly robust," meaning it was hard to jam. But the distance was another matter. The target had been over forty miles away when the missile was launched. While the air-to-air missile could hit Mach 4, it was operating at the very edge of its effective range.

"Wes, hail the pilot," Dog said. "Tell him to turn around."

Delaney launched a second missile, then snugged the belly of the Megafortress. The 767 was now visible in *Raven*'s own infrared screen, a blur growing in the lower right-hand quadrant.

"Missile batteries coming up," said Delaney. "We're just about over their territory."

"Wes?"

"Not answering."

"Stand by."

Dog reached to the com panel to key in Jed Barclay. He wanted the President's direct command before proceeding. As he did, one of the equipment specialists behind Dog said something—the Taiwanese fighters were asking their base for permission to shoot down the 767.

And received it.

"Jed, here's our situation," he told the NSC op. "We think there are two bombs. If one is aboard the UAV, that leaves one for the 767."

"Understood, uh, the President is on the line."

"Colonel, stop him any way you can," said Martindale.

"Yes, sir. Zen?"

"Hawk leader."

Aboard Island Flight A101
0335

"HAVE YOU DONE YOUR DUTY?"

"Yes, Grandfather."

"Your lessons are complete?"

"Yes, Grandfather."

"Can you describe the Tao?"

The question shook Chen Lo Fann. He and his grandfather were in the midst of a large garden, with water burbling nearby. Chen was nine or ten.

"The Tao is the way," said Chen. "The world—our fate—everything together."

"The path we follow," said Chen Lee.

"Yes," said the boy.

"We will be reunited with our homeland someday," said the old man. "But the path is not a straight one. Remember that life and death are mere steps on the path, as stones next to each other in the garden."

The dream ended abruptly. Chen Lo Fann found himself staring at the bomb in the crate, numbers sliding away on the trigger device.

His grandfather had not wanted to blow up Shanghai; that was Professor Ai's doing.

The digits drained to 1:00, then 0:59.

It would blow up in less than a minute.

Should he let it? Ai's argument made some sense—two bombs would be impossible to ignore; the communists would have to respond.

But many innocent people would die.

Was Shanghai any different from Beijing?

Chen stared at the numbers.

:30

Bombing Shanghai was not his grandfather's will. Chen Lee had made no secret of where the bomb was to be exploded.

The plane veered sharply to the left, shuddering as it turned, losing altitude.

Chen reached for the control. One of the characters on the fifteen-button panel read "Abort."

He thought of his dream, but it provided no answers.

:10

If his grandfather had wanted to destroy Shanghai, he would have said so clearly, as he had made clear Beijing was his desired target.

:03

Chen Lo Fann reached to the device, ignoring the pain roaring in his chest and shoulder as he pushed the button.

Aboard *Raven*
0338

ZEN HAD THE FLIGHTHAWK CLOSING ON THE RIGHT wing of the 767, his targeting screen blinking yellow. He could see shadows through the windows of the plane, people moving around.

God, he thought, I'm going to kill dozens if not a hundred.

God.

What if there isn't a bomb in that plane?

Zen had killed a fair share of people in combat, but this felt very, very different. He had no proof that there was a bomb in the airplane; Stoner had told him he thought Chen had enough material for two weapons, but that didn't mean one was aboard the plane in front of him, or even that they had been made.

The windows seemed to grow, though this was an optical illusion. Zen pushed his nose down, the pipper just turning red.

He had his orders, lawful orders. They had come from the President himself.

What justification was that if he killed innocent men and women and children?

The pipper blinked. Zen pressed the trigger.

Three seconds later, his stream of bullets ignited one of the wing tanks of the 767.

"BOTH SCORPION AMRAAMS MISSED," SAID DELANEY. "I'm having trouble picking him up—the Chinese are jamming us, or trying to."

"Hang with it," said Dog. He checked the sitrep;

they were about thirty seconds from crossing into Chinese airspace; in fact, *Hawk Four* already had.

"Now that they know we're here, they're going to use our radar to home in on us," said Delaney. "If we turn it off, they'll have a much harder time finding us."

"Can we follow the UAV without the radar?" asked Dog.

"No. There's no signal coming from the ghost clone for us to follow," said Delaney.

"Then we're going to have to leave the radar on."

"Fan Song radar dead ahead," said Deci Gordon. "We're going to fly right over it. They'll see us."

"Jam it when it does," said Dog.

"Flight identified as Island Flight A101 is on fire and descending toward the ocean," reported Zen. His voice was as cold as the computer's synthesized tones.

"Can you get *Hawk Four* on the UAV?" asked Dog.

"Those F-8s are coming for us," warned Delaney.

"Zen, you're going to have to shoot down the UAV," repeated Dog.

"Roger that."

Dreamland
1240

JENNIFER STARED AT THE LARGE SCREEN AT THE FRONT of the room. The Megafortress and its two Flight-hawks were crossing into Chinese Mainland territory.

They were already being targeted by ground radars, surface-to-air missiles, interceptors—even a Megafortress couldn't survive the onslaught.

God, she thought, let him live. Let him live.

She did love him. Even if he had failed her, she did love him.

"Jen, this is Dog," he said to her.

"I love you," she said, thinking it was a dream.

"The programming you uploaded earlier. Can we use it?"

It wasn't a dream—he was talking to her. Jennifer felt her face flush deep red.

But there was no time to be embarrassed.

"You have to be within twenty miles. No, wait." Her mind wasn't clear. She shook her head, reached to pull her hair back behind her ear.

Nothing.

"The mother ship, you destroyed it. The UAV will be on its own. It'll default—we may not be able to take it over."

"How close do we have to be?"

"Twenty miles," said Jennifer. "But listen, if it's on default—it probably won't deviate from its course once it's set. But you can try it."

"Understood. Thanks," said Dog. "And I love you too."

Aboard *Raven*
0342

ZEN HAD TWO TASKS—PROTECT THE MEGAFORTRESS from the F-8s, and overtake the ghost clone.

Fortunately, he had two planes.

He let the computer take *Hawk Four* in pursuit of the UAV, using the information piped down to the computer from *Raven*'s sensors. In the meantime, he put *Hawk Three* on the noses of the two communist interceptors. They were swinging east to set up a rear-quarter attack, obviously planning on using their superior speed to close the gap behind the big American plane. Zen had to hang back and wait for them to get closer, his need to stay tethered to the Megafortress limiting his options. The Chinese defenses were handicapped by *Raven*'s near-stealth profile, but its need to use the powerful search radar to find the UAV, and the fact that it had to fly a more or less straight line, nearly canceled that advantage completely. Once they were in the general area of the Megafortress, the F-8s could use *Raven*'s radar as a beacon to show them where the plane was.

"Missiles!" said Delaney as the Chinese planes began to close in. A pair of radar homers had been kicked off from the lead F-8 at about thirty miles— probably too far to hit them, but they couldn't take a chance.

The Megafortress's ECM blared, not only killing the guidance systems in the missiles but giving the Shenyang pilots fits as well. Zen started an intercept that would allow him to slap the lead bandit with a cannon burst, then dip his wing and take on the wingmate.

The lead F-8 came on faster than he expected, its Liyang turbojet obviously feeling its oats. Zen got a shot, but just barely. The computer helped him put the bullets out in front of the Mainlander—in effect, the Chinese pilot ran into them. He got a hit, but it wasn't enough to stop the plane.

It was too late to worry about it. He tucked his wing, the targeting screen going yellow as the second F-8 flew into range.

"LEAD F-8 CLOSING. HE'S SETTING FOR HEAT-SEEKERS," warned Delaney.

"Stinger," said Dog calmly, referring to the airmine unit in the Megafortress's tail. A replacement for the tail cannon that had graced the original B-52, the Stinger spit out cylinders of tungsten-wrapped explosive. When the fuse in the airmines sensed a proximate object, they ignited their charges, sending a spray of hot metal into the air. The metal would shred a jet turbine as easily as a screwdriver puncturing a Dixie cup.

"Coming at us. Missile."

Dog hit his flares and jinked left, then right. Meanwhile, Delaney worked the Stinger. The combination of the F-8's speed and *Raven*'s evasive maneuvers kept the Mainlander from serious harm; on the other hand, his missile missed and his evasive actions took him temporarily out of the game.

"We have two AMRAAMs," said Delaney.

"Save 'em in case we need them to get the clone."

"Shit," said the copilot. "We've lost the UAV from the radar."

ZEN'S TARGETING CUE FRAMED THE COCKPIT OF THE F-8. He saw the outline of his opponent and thought of the people in the civilian jet he had just been ordered to shoot down.

He pressed his trigger, but he'd already blown the shot.

Zen kicked himself mentally, then checked the sitrep to line up for another shot.

He didn't have to—the Taiwanese Mirages were now in range of the F-8s. There was a whole lot of chatter in the air—two missiles were launched, then a third and a fourth. The Mainlanders decided the prudent thing to do was select afterburner and live for another day. They rode north, pursued by the ROC missiles.

A GROUND MISSILE BATTERY—A CHINESE HQ-9, roughly the equivalent of the long-range Russian SA-10 on which it was based—came on-line as *Raven* crossed over Chinese territory south of Shanghai.

"We're spiked," said Delaney, meaning that the ground radar had found and locked on the aircraft. It could launch a missile at any time.

"Break it," said Dog.

"Broke it," said Delaney. The copilot's voice had become hoarse.

"Good," said Dog. "You have the UAV?"

"Not on the scope. Negative."

"Wes?"

"No transmissions," said the specialist, who was monitoring the airwaves. "Chinese know we're here, though. About a million people gunning for us. Battery of FT-2000s antirad missiles trying to find us. Uh, some command problems there."

The FT-2000 homed in on ECMs and other electromagnetic radiation; it was a real threat to *Raven* since the best and possibly only way to defeat it would be to turn off the countermeasures and other gear. They had no decoys aboard.

"Is it up?" Dog asked.

"Doesn't appear to be."

"UAV?"

"They don't seem to see it. They think we're the threat."

"Do we have it?"

"Negative," said Wes.

"If it's going to Beijing, it's got a good distance to travel," said Delaney.

Dog remembered what Jennifer had said about the UAV—more than likely it would fly straight to its target, no fancy stuff in between. He plotted a line to Beijing on his multiuse display.

"If that's the way we're going, we'll never make it," said Delaney looking at the course he'd laid in.

"We better," said Dog.

Pentagon, Washington, D.C.
1545

JED BARCLAY LOOKED AT THE TABLE AS THE DEBATE continued on whether to alert the Chinese government to what exactly was going on. *Raven* had just crossed over land, so the incursion itself was evident, but the President's advisors weren't sure precisely what if anything to tell the Chinese.

The secretary of state argued that admitting the bomb existed would scuttle the summit before it started. The President asked if the UAV could be shot down without Chinese help.

Probably, thought Jed—but sooner or later the communists would take out *Raven*. If that happened first, and the UAV got away, they'd be blamed.

And that would undoubtedly lead to a full-scale nuclear exchange.

One of the Air Force experts was describing the radar and missile defenses in the corridor *Raven* had entered. He told the President that the Chinese ground defenses were not advanced enough to find, let alone track, the UAV or the Flighthawks. *Raven*'s onboard ECMs, however, should protect it from most of the missile systems.

Balboa wanted to declare *Raven* a renegade unit. It wasn't far from the truth, he argued.

Jed tried to speak but the words died in a mumbled stutter on his tongue.

"What do you think, Jed?" asked the President.

"I-I—"

"I think we can give them a few minutes more," interrupted the secretary of state. "They've never failed us before. This is Dreamland we're talking about."

"No!" His voice was so loud it echoed against the paneled walls of the sit room. Everyone around him stopped and looked at him.

"I'm sorry, but not even a Megafortress can survive the gauntlet around Beijing. The multilayered defenses, the f-fact they're flying in a straight line, and they're also low on fuel. It's not going to work. And the Taiwanese UAV—it's not as fast as the Flighthawk or the Megafortress but it has a good lead. It may take another twenty minutes to catch. We don't know what onb-b-board defenses it m-might have."

"What's your advice, Jed?" asked the President.

"Um, uh—"

Jed clenched his fist, trying to get the stutter to go away. "We have to tell the Chinese what's g-going on."

"That won't remove the risk to our people," said Chastain. "They still may be targeted."

"We have to tell them everything," said Jed. "They'll think we set this up otherwise."

He looked at the screen, trying to see his boss. What did he think?

Probably that Jed was a stuttering jerk.

"Jed's right," said Freeman.

"Make the connection," said the President.

Aboard *Raven*
0350

FROM THIRTY THOUSAND FEET, WITH NO CLOUDS AND A starlit night sky, the Chinese countryside looked remarkably peaceful. By day, the heavily populated eastern portions of the country bustled with a booming, rapidly changing economy, but at night the country still looked as it had fifty or sixty years before, largely rural though well populated.

But Zen wasn't relying merely on the optical feed. His screen was littered with purple blobs showing antiair radars, fingers grabbing for the stealthy little plane. The U/MF could zip right by them for the most part, its body too sleek to be picked up. Raven, however, had to fly a line directly through several of the blobs. It was making full use of its countermeasures to boink the radars. As of yet, no one had fired at them, but Zen knew that was only a matter of time.

A four-ship element of Su-27 fighters, purchased from Russia only a few months before, was bearing down on *Raven* from the north. Indeed, there were so many boogies in the air at the moment that Zen told the computer to show only those in the flight path or with a better than sixty percent chance of intercepting them.

The Taiwanese UAV had completely disappeared. Zen was sure it was still flying—he was convinced he'd have seen the crash. But where exactly it was, he couldn't say. The only thing they had to go on was Stoner's guess that it was headed toward Beijing, and Jennifer's belief that it would have to fly a fairly straight course once it was out of its mother ship's control.

"Pricks are calling us killers," said Wes on the interphone.

He was talking to Dog, but Zen couldn't help asking what he meant.

"Killer Fortress—they blame us for shooting down the SAR plane a few days ago. That's what the controllers are saying," said Wes. "They want us."

We ought to let the UAV blow up Beijing, Zen thought. These were the same bastards who had put his wife in the hospital, nearly killing her. The same bastards who had killed Fentress and the others. Let them all fry.

Zen tightened his grip on the Flighthawk stick. He nudged *Hawk Four* further east as a JJ-7, a version of the Chinese-developed MiG-21 ordinarily used as a trainer, darted toward *Raven*. It fired a heat-seeker from seven miles out—obviously the pilot's training hadn't gotten very far—then kept coming.

"Turn off," Zen told the pilot, speaking on his frequency in English. "If you don't, I'll nail you."

Whether the pilot heard or not, he kept coming. Zen's targeting screen went from yellow to red as the JJ-7 pulled to within three miles of the Megafortress. Zen pumped thirty rounds into the plane's engine.

Fifteen seconds later, the canopy blew off and the pilot hit the silk.

Zen gave the computer *Hawk Four*, telling it to fly back into the escort position. Then he jumped into *Three* . . .

. . . and saw the dim glow of the Taiwanese UAV's tailpipe fifteen miles ahead.

DOG SHOVED THE MEGAFORTRESS HARD RIGHT AS THE first wave of Chinese surface-to-air missiles climbed in the air ahead of them. The missiles were the Chinese equivalent of SA-6s and would be easily confused by *Raven*'s ECMs, but there were a half dozen of them, and with a warhead of just over 175 pounds, they couldn't be completely ignored. Delaney tracked them and pointed out another barrage of antiair a few miles ahead. Dog swung back west, zigging around the missiles.

"We're pretty visible up here," said the copilot. "One of their radar planes is on a line to the east. I don't think he sees us with his radar—I think he's homing in on ours."

"Can we get him with AMRAAM?" Dog asked.

"Sixty miles away," said Delaney.

That meant no. It also meant that it was too far for the Flighthawks.

"*Raven*, I have our target visually," said Zen. "He's in the weeds, maybe ten feet AGL. Ten miles and closing."

No wonder they hadn't found the UAV, Dog realized; it was so low to the ground the radar couldn't sort it out through the ground clutter—odd reflections of the radio waves off the terrain.

But flying that low also cut down on the UAV's speed.

"Intercept in four minutes, a bunch of seconds," added Zen.

"Are we close enough for Jen's takeover program?" Dog asked.

"Negative," said Zen. "It's thirty miles away total. I'll be close enough to shoot it down before you're in range."

"Missiles!" warned Delaney. "Breaking."

The copilot said something else, but Dog lost it. Both of the operators at the stations behind him were now spending their time jamming radars and communications systems in their path. Dog had two more antiair missiles left aboard; he wanted to reserve at least one for the UAV, in case the Flighthawks missed.

"Sukhois on our six at twenty miles and closing," said Delaney.

"When they're close enough, let them have it with the Stinger," said Dog.

"Yeah."

"Colonel, I'm going to put *Hawk Four* on that flight of J-8s coming at us from the west," said Zen.

Dog had to glance at the sitrep map to remind himself exactly which flight Zen was talking about. All of *Raven*'s high-tech gear and whiz-bang computers, ergonomic controls, and audiovisual doodads couldn't completely erase the limits of situational awareness. There were just too many threats for Dog to process everything at once.

"Go," he told Zen.

"I have to let the computer handle it. It's four on one—we may lose it."

"Our priority is the ghost clone," said Dog.

"Understood."

"FT-2000 in the air!" warned Delaney. "He's homing in on our ECMs."

"Can we break it?" asked Dog.

"Only if you want everything else they're firing to hit us."

THE FOUR CHINESE J-8 FIGHTERS CAME AT *RAVEN* IN A staggered line, each plane separated by about a mile and flying at different altitudes. The computer quickly recognized the pattern and calculated the best attack posture, prioritizing the targets in the order of the greatest threat to *Raven*. The strategy—a slashing attack that would take *Hawk Four* across the course of the flight and allow it to fire on at least two of the aircraft before maneuvering to catch a third from behind—was solid, and took into account the abilities of the enemy planes as well as the Flighthawk. It also gave the computer time to recover and change its strategy if the bandits drastically altered course and speed. The only problem with it was that by the time *Hawk Four* turned to catch the third plane, it would be out of communications range from *Raven*. Zen nonetheless approved the strategy as the best course, telling C^3 to stay in dogfight mode even if the connection snapped—otherwise *Hawk Four* would have defaulted back to escort and tried to find *Raven*.

"Go for it," he told the computer, using exactly the same tone he would have used for Kick or Starship.

The computer's verbal translation system had been "trained" to recognize much of Zen's slang, and took *Hawk Four* on the intercept.

Zen turned his full attention back to *Hawk Three*. The Taiwanese UAV was now just five miles ahead.

A warning flashed on his screen:

Connection loss in three seconds

TWO MORE MISSILES EXPLODED TO THE EAST OF *RAVEN*. Dog saw a pair of Su-27s heading in from the northeast, coming on at about ten degrees off his nose. They were at twenty miles, firing radar missiles.

"They're on us," said Delaney.

Dog hit his chaff, then jerked hard to beam the Doppler radar guiding the missiles. The maneuver would put the Megafortress at a right angle to the radar, temporarily confusing it.

"FT-2000 is changing course," reported Delaney. "It's going for one of the missiles that was just launched."

That's our one lucky break, thought Dog.

"*Raven*—I need you closer. I'm going to lose *Hawk Three*."

Dog jerked back toward the Flighthawk.

"*Raven*—you have to get closer."

"I'm working on it, Zen," said Dog. The throttle slide was at the last stop; he could hit the control with a sledge-hammer and the plane wouldn't go any faster. "Wes, see if you can reach any of these units. Tell them we're pursuing a cruise missile that's going to attack Beijing."

"But—"

"Do it, Wes," said Dog. "Deci, try the control program Ms. Gleason uploaded earlier. I know we're not in range yet but try it anyway."

Lieutenant Deci Gordon was the other electronics operator. While he could dupe Wes's controls, he was tasked at the moment to ID and fuzz radars.

"I have to clear the ECM board to load the program and use it. I won't be able to bounce the radars," explained the lieutenant.

"Do it."

"On it, sir."

ZEN CUT HIS SPEED, JUST BARELY KEEPING THE CONnection to *Hawk Three*. The Flighthawk was undoubtedly a good deal faster and more capable than the plane he was chasing, but it was *Raven*'s speed that counted, and the big airplane was already huffing and puffing. All he could do was sit and wait, hoping *Raven* would catch up—and that the flak dealer Delaney was now warning about wouldn't hit him in the meantime.

Maybe it would get the Taiwan plane at least.

Raven rocked up and down but stayed on its course. Zen cursed to himself, pushing forward against his restraint.

Come on, damn it. Come on!

He tried selecting *Hawk Four*, which had been out of contact since firing on the second fighter in the attack group. The feed from *Raven* showed where it was—about five miles out of range, launching an attack on one of the Chinese fighters.

It had already splashed two of the Sukhois. Not bad for a bunch of electrons.

Raven shuddered beneath him. Something had just hit the plane.

Stinking Chinese. They didn't deserve to be saved.

Come on, baby. Come on.

Something rumbled on Zen's right—shrapnel from a missile had taken a nick out of the EB-52. Zen felt himself sliding left, even though the Flighthawk remained level.

The targeting screen blinked yellow.

Ten more seconds and he'd be in range. He could see the fat belly of the Taiwanese bomb strapped to the fuselage of the UAV.

Raven stuttered in the air, her speed and altitude plummeting.

Nine seconds. Eight . . .

Connection loss in three seconds

"Dog! I need six seconds!"

* * *

ENGINE FOUR WAS GONE, AND THE OIL PRESSURE IN three was dropping. The computer helped Dog compensate as Delaney struggled with the defenses.

"I'm losing *Hawk Three*!" shouted Zen over the interphone.

The computer—prudently—wanted to shut down engine three. But Dog stayed with it, squeezing the last ounce of momentum forward, trying to keep close enough so Zen could complete the shoot-down.

Just wasn't going to happen. Even the Megafortress could not defy all the laws of physics at the same time. The EB-52 shuddered violently.

He was going to lose it.

They had to get closer to the Flighthawk, or the whole mission would have been a waste.

Dog pushed the nose of the big plane downward, picking up speed. They had a good deal of altitude to work with—but every foot made them more vulnerable to the air defenses.

"Missiles!" said Delaney. His overstressed rasp sounded like an old man's last gasp for air.

"Zen, I'm going to try and dive as close to *Hawk Three* as possible," said Dog. "After that, we may be bailing."

"Roger that," said Zen. "We need more speed—I don't have the Flighthawk."

"WES, CAN YOU TRY THAT PROGRAM JEN GAVE US again?" he said. "Just broadcast it?"

"I'm doing it," answered Deci Gordon.

The Flighthawk screen flickered.

"Control," said Zen.

Red pipper.

Yellow—no shot.

Zen pressed the trigger anyway.

Fire.

Fire.

Fire you goddamn son of a bitch.

DOG COULD SEE A PAIR OF FLAK GUNS STARTING TO fire off his right wing. The Megafortress was still too high to be hit—but it wouldn't be in about twenty seconds or so.

Come on, Zen, he thought. Come on.

ZEN LET OFF THE TRIGGER, SEEING THE BULLETS TRAIL far short of his target.

Beijing lay about a hundred miles away. The Taiwan UAV was going to make it.

The computer buzzed with a fuel warning and put a script up on the screen: He had ten minutes of flying time left at present speed.

Figures, he thought.

The targeting screen went yellow. The Megafortress shuddered, then started to yaw hard to his left.

Connection loss in three seconds

We're toast, he thought.

And then, either because its own programming called for it to pop up so it could detonate its bomb, or because of the program Jennifer had prepared, the UAV pulled its nose up. The maneuver made it lose speed. Zen's targeting pipper went red.

He fired.

He missed.

The ghost clone climbed off to his right.

"Sukhoi on our back, five miles, four," said Delaney.

"Stinger," said Dog.

"We're out of airmines."

"Flares."

"No more expendables."

"Can you launch an AMRAAM?" asked Dog, wrestling with the controls.

Delaney didn't waste his tortured throat. The question wasn't really serious—the AMRAAM-plus would have to go backward to do any good.

This was going to be it, thought Dog.

"Zen—we need you to take the target out now," he said calmly. "Crew, prepare to eject. Begin the self-destruct sequences on the gear."

The pregnant W danced upward and to the right. It must be answering Jennifer's control sequence somehow, thought Zen, trying to follow.

As he tucked his wing to the right, he got a yellow firing cue. And then a ball of red fire opened above him—shrapnel from a Chinese missile.

His screen blanked. *Hawk Three* was gone.

Zen pushed back in his seat, finally defeated.

Son of a bitch, he thought.

They were going out. That was going to be fun—he'd be dead meat wherever he landed.

No way. He'd go down with the plane.

Zen reached to pull his helmet off but then

stopped. *Hawk Four* had returned, flying off its left wing in Trail One, a preset position.

"*Four*," he told the computer.

The main screen came on, along with a warning—he had five more minutes of fuel.

At this point, that was like having a full tank.

Zen accelerated over the stricken Megafortress. The Taiwan UAV was five miles ahead, still climbing.

The pipper began to blink.

Red.

He pressed the trigger. The 20mm shells spit out in an arc, falling to the left of the target. He nudged his stick, moving the stream slowly slowly slowly.

He eased off the trigger, pushed the stick hard to the right, felt *Raven* lurch in the air, fired again.

The Taiwanese UAV erupted in a fireball.

"HE GOT IT! HE GOT IT!" SHOUTED DELANEY.

Dog, following his own self-destruct checklist, had wiped out the coding in the computer that helped him fly *Raven* and was too busy wrestling with the plane to answer.

He could fly with two engines, even if they were on the same side. What he couldn't continue to do, however, was duck enemy planes. And that Sukhoi behind was closing in for the kill.

"Dream Command, this is Dog—we have the clone down," he said. "Repeat, we have the clone down."

The answer came back broken up.

"We're hit pretty bad," added Dog. "We're into our destruct checklist on sensitive gear. Be advised we've told the Chinese that we were targeting a cruise missile bound for their capital."

Dog took a breath. He had gone against his orders to keep the mission secret, but in his judgment, the broadcast had made sense. Certainly the Chinese would find out about the attack at some point, and informing them now had been a valid attempt to save his people.

And screw anybody who second-guessed him.

"Dream?" he said, not hearing an answer.

"Washington is trying to contact the Chinese themselves and tell them what's going on," said Catsman through the static. Dog tried to ask for more details but got no response.

"Wes, have we wiped out all our radio antennas?" Dog asked over the interphone.

"Next thing on my list. I wait for your order unless, uh, unless it looks like you're not going to be giving it," said the lieutenant. Dog heard him mumbling to himself and punching his panel. "Colonel—the Chinese controllers are ordering their planes to stand down."

"They don't seem to be following orders," said Delaney as tracers flashed over their wing.

DOWNSTAIRS ON THE FLIGHTHAWK DECK, ZEN loosened his restraints. *Hawk Four* was low on fuel and now out of bullets, but it could still be of some use. He had the computer plot an intercept to the Su-27 behind them, and held on as it closed. The computer gave him two proximity warnings, then closed its eyes as the Flighthawk slammed into the front quarter of the Chinese plane.

But that was it. The fight was over. Four more planes were galloping in from the west, and two were closing ahead.

Zen initiated the self-destruct procedures. The first stage started a series of programs that wiped the drives and other memory devices. Then small charges began blowing up the Megafortress's side of C^3. The explosives were carefully calibrated to take out the circuitry but not damage the shell of the aircraft.

He took off his control helmet. The helmet was supposed to be physically destroyed with a small hatchet kept near the rear of the compartment. He had to lift himself from the ejection seat and get into his wheelchair to do that. He undid his restraints and pulled over the chair, wedging it into the space. As he pushed down to get in, the aircraft dropped twenty or more feet in an instant and he lost his balance, flopping back in the ejection seat rather than his chair.

So this was what it felt like to go down.

Zen remembered Stoner trying to tell him about the enemy he faced.

"They don't trust us," said Stoner.

Actually, he'd said that about Zen, hadn't he?

Zen scooped up his helmet and pulled it back on. "Dog—jettison our weapons and put the gear down."

"They'll shoot us for sure."

"No. They'll either accept our surrender, or they'll back off, thinking it's a trap," said Zen. "They will—they'll think it's a trap. They thought we lured their other planes close to us by making ourselves seem vulnerable and shot them down with a secret weapon. If we look defenseless, they'll hesitate. They're paranoid about us—they probably think we're broadcasting the orders from their controllers. It'll work. It's our only shot, one way or the other."

"THE SU-27 PILOTS STILL AREN'T RESPONDING," SAID Wes. "Their controllers are just about screaming at them."

Dog thought about what Zen had said.

If they put down their gear, dropped their weapons—would the Chinese figure they were surrendering and let them alone?

Maybe.

More likely, they'd think it was a trick.

But at this point, it didn't make much difference. One of the Chinese planes rode in over their wing, slowing down and hanging so close he could have hopped from his wing to *Raven's*.

"Open the bay," Dog told Delaney. "Eject the missiles. I'll get the gear down."

Delaney was too hoarse to argue. Dog lowered the gear, the plane objecting strongly. His airspeed dropped and he got a stall warning.

A fresh flood of tracers shot across their bow. The interceptors closed into tight formation all around them, adjusting their own speed as if they were flying an air show demonstration. Though they might have been temporarily confused, it was just a matter of time—seconds, really—before one of their bursts nailed them.

Dog reached over and hit their lights— everything, even the cockpit lights.

"Two on our tail, one on each wing," said Delaney, his voice a croak.

"Wave at 'em," Colonel Bastian said. "Show them we know they're there. Wave."

Dog turned to the cockpit window on his left and gave the high sign.

"Wave, Wes," said Dog. "Like we have the whole thing under control."

He waved again, then turned his attention back to the front of the plane. The tracers had stopped.

Was Zen right? Did the Chinese pilots think they were up to something? Had they heard the transmissions from the ground and finally decided to comply? Were they simply confused?

Or were they cats, taking a last moment to enjoy the fear of their prey before finishing him off?

"Wave, Wes. Smile at the bastards," said Dog.

"Uh."

"Wes?"

"The flight on our nose is asking for instructions," said the specialist. "Sir, uh, we're being asked our intentions."

"Honorable," said Dog. "Put me on their frequency."

EPILOGUE:

Heroes, after a Fashion

_____

IN THE BEST OF ALL WORLDS, DOG WOULD HAVE PREferred to be anywhere but Beijing.

In the worst of all worlds, he would also have preferred to be anywhere but Beijing.

But Beijing was where he was. And as an honored guest, to all forms and appearances.

A car stopped a few feet away from the building where he was standing with the Chinese officers who had met *Raven*. The American ambassador stepped from the plane, accompanied by a Chinese official. The ambassador stepped smartly to Dog, saluting first—Dog was a little taken aback, but gave the proper response—and then shaking his hand.

"A hell of a job," said the ambassador. "Washington's told me everything."

"Okay," said Dog, truly surprised as the ambassador grabbed him in a bear hug.

"Did the self-destruct go all right?" whispered the ambassador.

"Yes. Completely," said Dog. "The computers are completely fried."

"Excellent." He turned and smiled at the Chinese officials. "Washington will throw a ticker-tape parade for you."

The ambassador introduced the man who had come with him as the Chinese foreign minister. Dog tried to bow, though his back was a bit stiff from the flight and fatigue.

"You have saved Beijing," said the minister. "You are a hero."

Dog smiled weakly. A few weeks ago he'd thought he'd be ordered to bomb Beijing, not save it. But such were the twisted fates of war.

"They're having a ceremony to open the discussions between Taiwan and the Mainland," said the ambassador. "The Taiwanese president will thank you, and the Mainland premier may actually thank you too."

"I'd rather sleep," said Dog honestly.

The ambassador looked as if he were going to have a heart attack.

"But I'll do my duty," added the colonel.

"Good," said the ambassador, starting away.

Taiwan
1200

STARSHIP ROLLED OUT OF BED, EVEN THOUGH HE'D HAD less than four hours' sleep. He'd come to a decision about the Brunei offer.

No way would he take it. Major Smith would be disappointed, but that was too bad. He'd worked too long and too hard to get to Dreamland.

Granted, the assignment wasn't everything he thought it would be. But then, he wasn't everything he thought he was either.

He glanced at his watch. Noon. He could grab a beer, something to eat.

He'd be all right if he didn't drink too much.

It wouldn't matter today how much he drank. Major Alou said today was an *off* day. Off meant off. He'd give that to Alou—when he said off, he meant it. Not like Zen.

Zen and the others on *Raven* were being called heroes. Good, he thought; they deserved it. They were heroes.

He wasn't. But he had done his job, and because of that, an Osprey's worth of Marines and Air Force crewmen were alive.

He pulled on his pants. Maybe he'd see if Kick was awake.

Brunei
1235

MACK SMITH FLIPPED OFF THE TELEVISION, KILLING THE news broadcast just as it began showing the crowds in downtown Beijing cheering the arrival of the two Chinese leaders.

Or were they cheering for Lieutenant Colonel Tecumseh "Dog" Bastian, who had saved them from incineration a few hours ago?

Mack preferred to think it was the former—not that he didn't like Dog; on the contrary, he liked the colonel quite a bit. He had to—the colonel's blessing was needed for him to work out the arrangement as Brunei's new chief of the Air Force Command.

Chief of the Brunei Air Force Command. His

own title. At the moment, he was still technically a member of the U.S. Air Force on duty as Whiplash's political officer. But that was just a technicality—he already had his office, two floors of plush offices in the capital, complete with a lounge and an office for the chief that looked like a lounge.

No staff yet, but he'd take care of that this afternoon. Talk to Starship again, and maybe some of his old cronies. Paradise here, my friends—the babes are unbelievable, and boy do they put out.

Next order of business—purchasing twelve F-15s from America, along with six Megafortresses.

Mack didn't particularly want the Megafortresses himself, but the sultan insisted. And hey, it was his dough.

Getting the aircraft from America was probably going to take some heavy-duty diplomacy. Megafortresses had never been sold overseas. Even F-15s weren't sold to just anyone. In fact, only Japan, Israel, and Saudi Arabia currently had them.

Mack could fix that with a little charm in the right places. He was a born diplomat.

Secretary of state someday. Though personally he'd prefer defense.

Once they got the planes, they'd pull a few mods from the Dreamland playbook. Which meant he needed some brainpower as well.

And some mechanical monkeys. Not that he'd call them monkeys to their faces.

Chief of the Brunei Air Force Command Mack Smith. A boss in paradise—what more could he ask for?

Beijing
1240

THE HOTEL WHERE THE CHINESE HAD PUT UP THE
Dreamland crew was not exactly handicapped-
friendly, and Zen found himself having to ask two
of the staff to help him down the two steps from
the hallway to the lobby. As indignities went, it was
hardly the worst he'd ever suffered, but after struggling with the sink upstairs in his room and pushing
his way through the narrow maze they called a hallway, he was hardly in the best of all moods. And the
fact that he couldn't call the States from his room
didn't exactly calm his mood.

Nonetheless, he managed to ask for a phone
politely, explaining that he wanted to call home.
It took three tries—the hotel personnel all spoke
English, but his accent apparently was difficult for
them to decipher. Finally he managed to mime what
he wanted, and was led behind the desk to the man-
ager's own office. The door was just wide enough—
just—but Zen was used to that, and the man seemed
genuinely hospitable, anxious to do right by his
American visitor. He punched the buttons on the
phone to allow the international call, then waited to
make sure Zen had no problem connecting.

Zen used the "open" number for Dreamland,
which actually connected through Nellis Air Force
Base. It was highly likely, of course, that the conversation was being recorded, and so he had to be
careful exactly what he said. Still, he wanted to talk
to Bree.

"This is Major Stockard," he told the operator on duty who answered. "I'm looking for Captain Stockard."

"Yes, sir!" snapped the operator.

The line clicked, and a few seconds later, a male voice answered.

"Yeah?"

"Who's this?" asked Zen.

"Deke James. Who's this?"

"Zen Stockard."

"Why'd you wake me up for?" said James.

"I'm looking for my wife," said Zen.

"She ain't here."

Zen felt his jealousy spiking up—what the hell was James doing in their apartment?

"I want to talk to Bree," he said.

"Yeah?"

The line went dead. Zen held the phone out, confused and angry. Deke was one of the engineer dweebs on the Unmanned Bomber Project.

What the hell was he doing in their apartment?

He was just about to put the phone down and try again when someone suddenly picked up on the other end of the line.

"Major!"

"Ax?"

"What, you're away a few days and you forget who runs this place?" said Chief Master Sergeant Gibbs.

"How'd I get you?"

"Just lucky I guess. Deke James transferred you. Why'd you call him? What'd you do, wake him up?"

"I got the wrong number. What time is it there?"

"About 2100. He goes to bed early. Want to talk to your wife?"

"It'd be nice," said Zen.

"Hold the phone. And listen, Zen—you kicked butt big time. We're prouder than hell of you."

"Thanks, Chief."

Zen waited while the line once more went cold. Another voice picked up—male.

"Hey hero," said Greasy Hands Parsons.

"Grease—what the hell are you doing?"

"Partying with your wife," said Parsons. If Ax ran the administrative side of Dreamland—and he did—Greasy Hands essentially owned the planes. The chief master sergeant and Zen had known each other pretty much forever.

"She's okay to party?" said Zen.

"Better than ever," said the chief.

"Give me that phone," said Breanna in the background.

"Bree—"

"Jeff—"

Her voice was like a spell. He felt his body suddenly relax.

"You okay?" he asked.

"Am I okay?" she said. "I'm fine. How the hell are you?"

"Just tired. I want to see you."

She laughed. He could hear her talk to the room. "Hey, I got Zen on the phone—"

There was a general shout. Zen made out some congratulations from the assorted tumult.

"Where are you?" he asked, but Bree didn't hear. Someone took the phone from her.

"Zen?"

"Hey, Jennifer. How are you?"

"I'm okay," she said, with a tone that seemed to be meant to reassure herself as well as him. "Is Colonel Bastian there?"

"No, he's hooked up with some ceremonies and crap," said Zen.

"Tell him I said hello, okay?"

"I will. I think your program helped us nail the clone."

She didn't answer. Zen imagined seeing her turn red and push back her long, strawberry blond hair.

Breanna took the phone back. "So?" she asked.

"So what?"

"When you coming home?" Bree asked.

"Haven't figured that out yet."

"Well, get moving, Major. Get the lead out. Here, listen, everybody wants to say hello."

Zen didn't particularly want to talk to them, but somehow it felt as if it was his duty to. He leaned back in his wheelchair and listened as Breanna reminded them it was an open line.

Don't miss

the next thrilling chapter

of Dreamland

RAVEN STRIKE

Available now!

Southeastern Sudan, Africa

IT FELT AS IF GOD HIMSELF WERE HUNTING HIM, CIR-cling beyond the clouds, watching every movement. An angry, vengeful god, a god obsessed with obliterating him. It felt as if God had singled him out above all to be the focus of his persecution, the modern-day Job. Except that this Job must die, and die harshly, in bloody fire and unimaginable pain. To survive, this Job must do nothing less than outwit God.

Such thoughts would have been blasphemous to a believer, but Li Han did not believe in the Christian god, let alone the vengeful, twisted Allah his paymasters had created from their own misinterpretations of scripture. To Li Han, all conceptions of god were superstition, tales told to children to get them to bed at night. Li Han had no religion except survival, and no ambition beyond that.

Once, he had dreams. Once, he'd even had desires beyond staying alive.

He was going to be rich. He desired this so badly that he would do anything for it. And he had. Like a fool.

Too late, he learned that wealth and comfort were illusions. The simplest facts had taken so long to understand.

The pilotless aircraft droned above. Li Han could hear it above as he rested at the side of the mine shaft. He had constructed a passive radar device to tell him where the aircraft was, but it wasn't necessary now. All he needed were his ears.

Li Han waited as the engines grew louder. He saw it in his mind's eye as it came overhead. It was the shape of a dagger, sleeker than the UAVs he'd seen farther south, different than the one in Pakistan that had fired at his car but missed.

It was a special UAV. He flattered himself that the Americans had built it just for him.

The noise grew to its loudest—God's angry voice, calling him out.

He laughed.

The drone banked. The sound began to dim.

"You will go when I tell you," he said to the man standing near him.

The man nodded. He knew he was a decoy, knew even that he was very likely to die. And yet he stood there willingly, prepared to run, prepared to take the drone away.

Fool!

The sound lessened as the UAV banked toward the farthest edge of its track above.

"Now," whispered Li Han.

The man pulled the scarf over his head, pitched forward and left the cave.

Ethiopia, Africa

MELISSA ILSE FELT HER BREATH CATCH AS THE FIGURE emerged from the shadow of the hillside.

Mao Man, or an imposter?

Not for her to decide—Raven would make the call.

She watched the video feed change as the UAV's sensors locked onto the figure. His back was turned to the aircraft. The plane changed course slightly, angling so it could get a look at the man's face.

Melissa folded her arms to keep herself from interfering. This was the hardest part of the mission—to let Raven do its job on its own.

"Here we go," said Major Krock. The Air Force officer headed the team piloting the Predator UAV, which was flying with and helping monitor Raven. "Here he comes."

Melissa folded her arms. Even on good days she found Krock barely tolerable.

Four vehicles were parked along the hillside below. The figure kept his head down as he reached the dirt road where they were parked. Raven took data from its sensors, comparing what they gathered to its known profiles of the criminal the CIA had nicknamed Mao Man. The system began with the most basic measurements—gender, height, weight—then moved on to the more esoteric, measuring the figure's gait, the arc of his head movements. The computer could identify and sort over twelve hundred features, weighing each one according to a complicated algorithm. Using these data points, it then determined a "target match probability"; it would not strike unless that probability went over 98.875 percent.

It currently stood at 95.6.

Melissa watched the man on the ground reaching for the door handle of the vehicle. She could see the computer's calculations in real time if she wanted, pulling it up on her main monitor.

She didn't. What she wanted was for the operation to be over, to be successful—for Raven to prove itself. They'd been at this for over a month.

Nail him, she thought. *Let's go.*

Suddenly, the main video feed changed. Melissa looked over at the computer screen—target match probability had dropped below fifty percent.

A decoy?

There was another figure moving from the mine, scrambling down the hill.

Mao Man?

Raven wasn't sure. The computer learned from its mistakes, and having been hoodwinked just a few moments before, it would be doubly cautious now.

It was 87.4 percent.

Then 88.6.

It has to be him, she thought.

Nail him!

Come on, come on—kill the son of a bitch already!

Southeastern Sudan

Li Han heard the aircraft changing direction, its engines straining. He had counted on more time than this.

The motorcycle was twenty yards away. There was no sense running for it.

He stopped and turned, looking at the UAV tracking him. Its black skin stood out clearly in the blue sky. Barely a thousand feet away, it looked like a vulture, coming for its prey.

There was another nearby. This one was more common, a Predator.

Two aircraft. There was some consolation in that, he thought. He warranted more than the usual effort.

Western Ethiopia

A WARNING BUZZER SOUNDED AS THE COMPUTER CON-firmed Mao Man's identity. A missile had been launched from the interior of the mine he'd been using as cover.

The Raven immediately broke contact with its target. Flares fired from rear of the aircraft. The UAV shut off its engine and fell on its wing, sailing to the right to avoid the missile. Still without power, the UAV twisted on its back and folded into a three-quarter turn, clearing the area so quickly that the shoulder-launched SAM tracking it had no chance to react.

Instead, it locked on the heat signature of the flares. In a few moments it was past them, and real-izing it was about to miss, detonated its warhead. Shrapnel sprayed harmlessly in the air.

Raven had already computed a course back to Mao Man. Interestingly enough, the hostile action had no effect on its evaluation of the target. It re-mained locked at 98.2.

Melissa turned to the Predator screen to watch

the aircraft come around. There was a second SAM warning, this one from the Predator.

Then a proximity warning blared.

"Watch out!" Melissa yelled. "You're too close!"

But it was too late. A black tail filled the Predator screen. Then the video went blank.

Melissa looked back to the Raven panel. It was off-line.

Southeastern Sudan

LI HAN THREW HIMSELF TO THE GROUND, KNOWING HE was dead.

There was a loud explosion high above him—the missile fired from the cave.

Then a second sound, closer, though this one softer and longer, more a smack and a tear than a bang.

Another explosion, farther away from the others. A loud crack similar to the first sound.

Li Han lay on the ground for several seconds. He knew he wasn't dead, yet he didn't entirely believe it. The aircraft had been so very close to him this time. Finally he pushed up to his knees and turned around. The sky was empty; the aircraft that had been following him were gone.

Once more, Li Han had cheated the Americans. Or God. Or both.

He took a few steps toward the car, then stopped. The aircraft must have been hit by the missiles. If so, their parts would be nearby. There would certainly be something worth scrounging or selling.

One of the Brothers ran from the cave, yelling at him in Arabic. The Brothers—they were all members of a radical group that called itself the Sudan Brotherhood—used Arabic as their official language of choice. It was a difficult language for Li Han; he would have much preferred English.

But the gist of what the man was saying was easily deciphered: *Praise Allah that you are alive.*

You fool, thought Li Han. It was God who was trying to kill me.

"Where are the planes?" he said to the man in Arabic.

The brother shook his head. Li Han couldn't be sure if he didn't know or couldn't understand his Chinese-accented Arabic.

"The airplane," he said, using English, and held his hands out as if they were wings. The brother pointed toward the hills.

"Let us take a look," said Li Han.

The brother began to protest.

"Don't worry. The Americans never send three planes," said Li Han, starting away. "We are safe for a while."

CIA Headquarters Campus (Langley)
McLean, Virginia

JONATHON REID FROWNED AS SOON AS HE ENTERED the director's dining room. Reginald Harker was sitting at the far end of the table, holding his coffee cup out for the attendant.

Worse news: there was only one other place set.

When Reid had received the "invitation" to breakfast with CIA Director Herman Edmund, he assumed Edmund would actually be there.

As an old Agency hand, he should have known better. Reid's official title was Special Assistant to the Deputy Director Operations, CIA; in fact, he ran his own portfolio of projects at Edmund's behest. Officially "retired" and back on a contract basis, Reid was the grayest of grayhairs in the Agency.

"Jonathon." Harker nodded, but didn't rise.

Reid pulled out the chair opposite him and sat down. Harker had been with the CIA for a little over twenty years. In the old days, he'd been a Middle East expert, and had done his share of time in the region. Reid wasn't sure what he'd done in the interim, but at the moment he was a deputy in the action directorate, a covert ops supervisor in charge of restricted projects. Reid didn't know what they were; in fact, he didn't even know Harker's formal title. Titles often meant very little in their line of work.

"Just coffee," Reid told the attendant. "Black."

"I was glad you could make it," said Harker after the woman left.

"I was under the impression Herman would be here," said Reid.

"Very busy morning," said Harker.

"We have business, then?"

Harker made a face, then looked to the door as the attendant knocked. The woman had worked for the Agency for nearly forty-five years, and undoubtedly had forgotten more secrets than either man had ever been told. But neither Harker nor Reid spoke until she finished laying out Harker's meal and left a fresh pot of coffee for Reid.

"I understand you're working with the Office of Special Technology," said Harker finally. "Heading our half of it."

"*Mmmm*," said Reid noncommittally.

"We need help on an assignment."

"Who's 'we'?"

Harker put his elbows on the table and leaned forward over his untouched egg. This was all just show and posture—exactly the thing Reid hated about the Agency bureaucracy. The man obviously needed a favor. He should just come out and say it.

"I've been working directly under D-CIA," said Harker, meaning Edmund. "It's a special project."

"So far you've told me nothing."

Harker frowned, then changed tact. "I thought you were retiring, Jonathon."

"I am retired. Back on contract. At my pleasure."

Harker picked up his fork and took a mouthful of egg. Reid could now guess what was up: something Harker was in charge of had gone to crap, and he needed help from Whiplash.

"How is it?" asked Reid.

"Cold," said Harker, putting down his fork.

"So what went wrong?" said Reid finally.

"Why do you think something went wrong?"

"Reg, I have a lot of things to do today."

"We have a project called Raven," said Harker. "Have you heard of it?"

"No," said Reid.

"Well that's good, at least." Harker rubbed his

face. His fingers pushed so hard that they left white streaks on the skin. "It's a follow-on to the Predator program. In a sense. We lost one of the planes last night in Africa. We need to recover the wreckage. One of our agents is headed there now. We wondered—the director wondered—if it would be possible for Whiplash to back her up."

Brown Lake Test Area, Dreamland

CAPTAIN TURK MAKO STRETCHED HIS ARMS BACK AND rocked his shoulders, loosening his muscles before putting on the flight helmet for the Tigershark II. For all of its advanced electronics and carefully thought-out interface, the helmet had one serious shortcoming:

It was heavy, at least twice the weight of a regular flight helmet. And the high-speed maneuvers the Tigershark II specialized in didn't make it feel any lighter.

Then again, the brain bucket did keep the gray matter where it belonged.

"Ready, Captain?" asked Martha Albris, flight crew chief for the test mission.

Though standing next to him, Albris was using the Whiplash com system, and her voice was so loud in the helmet that it hurt Turk's eardrums. Turk put his hand over the ear area of his helmet and rotated his palm, manually adjusting the volume on the external microphone system. The helmet had several interfaces; besides voice, a number of controls were activated by external touch, including the audio volume. It was part of an intuitive control system aimed to make the Tigershark more an extension of the pilot's body rather than an aircraft.

Turk gave her a thumbs-up.

They walked together to the boarding ladder. The Tigershark II was a squat, sleek aircraft, small by conventional fighter standards. But then she wasn't a conventional fighter. She was designed to work with a fleet of unmanned aircraft, acting as both team leader and mother hen.

Turk went up the four steps of the ladder to a horizontal bridge, where he climbed off the grid-work and onto the seat of his airplane. He folded his legs down under the control panel and into the narrow tunnel beneath the nose of the plane, slipping into the airplane much like a foot into a loafer.

Albris bent over the platform to help him. As crew chiefs went, she was particularly pleasing to the eye, even in her one-piece coverall. Turk had actually never seen the civilian mechanics supervisor in anything but a coverall. Still, her freckled face and the slight scent of perfume sent his imagination soaring.

Maybe he'd look her up after the postflight debrief.

Turk's fantasies were interrupted by a black SUV that pulled across the front of the hangar, its blue emergency lights flashing. The passenger-side door opened and his boss, Breanna Stockard, emerged from the cab.

"Turk, I need to talk to you," she yelled. "There's been a change in plans."

Turk pulled himself back upright.

"Flight scrubbed, boss?" he asked. The helmet projected his voice across the hangar.

"The test flight is. But you're still going to fly."

"Really? Where to?"

"We'll discuss it inside," said Breanna.

BREANNA WATCHED TURK CLIMB OUT OF THE PLANE and run over to the truck. That was the great thing about Turk—he was enthusiastic no matter what.

"Another demo flight for visiting congressmen?" he asked.

"Not really," she said, turning toward the hangar. "We have to go downstairs to discuss it."

The Office of Special Technology used a small area in the Dreamland complex to house Tigershark and some related projects. Besides a pair of hangars, it "owned" an underground bunker and a support area there.

The Office of Special Technology was an outgrowth of several earlier programs that brought cutting-edge technology to the front lines. Most notable of these was Dreamland itself, which a decade and a half before had been run by Breanna's father, Tecumseh "Dog" Bastian. But the walk down the concrete ramp to the secure areas below held no special romance for Breanna; she'd long ago learned to steel herself off from any emotion where Dreamland was concerned.

"You're flying to Sudan," Breanna told Turk when they reached the secure area below. Once a medical test lab, the room was now used to brief missions. It was functionally the equivalent of a SCIF, or secure communications area, sealed against possible electronic eavesdropping.

Breanna walked to one of the computer terminals.

"Less than twelve hours ago, a UAV called Raven went down in a mountainous area in the southeast corner of Sudan, not far from Ethiopia," she said. "I have a map here."

"That's pretty far to get some pictures," said Turk, looking at the screen. "Going to be a long flight, even supersonic."

"It's not just a reconnaissance mission, Turk. Whiplash has been deployed. Our network satellite in that area is down for maintenance. It'll be at least forty-eight hours before we get the replacement moved into position."

"Gotcha."

Whiplash was the code name of a joint CIA–Defense Department project run by the Office of Special Technology. It combined a number of cutting-edge technologies with a specially trained covert action unit headed by Air Force colonel Danny Freah. Freah had helped pioneer the concept at Dreamland as a captain some fifteen years before. Now he was back as the leader of a new incarnation, working with special operators from a number of different military branches as well as the CIA.

Unlike the Dreamland version, the new Whiplash worked directly with the Central Intelligence Agency and included a number of CIA officers. The head of the Agency contingent was Nuri Abaajmed Lupo, a young covert agent who, by coincidence, had spent considerable time undercover in roughly the same area where the Raven UAV had gone down.

Nuri had been the first field agent to train with a highly integrated computer network developed for Whiplash. Officially known as the Massively Parallel Integrated Decision Complex or MY-PID, the network of interconnected computers and data interfaces, the system allowed him to access a wide range of information, from planted bugs to Agency data mining, instantaneously while he was in the field.

The high volume data streams traveled through a dedicated network of satellites. The amount of data involved and the limitations of the ground broadcasting system required that the satellites be within certain ranges for MY-PID to work. The Tigershark II could substitute as a relay station in an emergency.

"You're to contact Danny Freah when you arrive on station," Breanna continued. "We'll have updates to you while you're en route."

"All right, I guess."

"Problem, Captain?"

"No ma'am. Just figuring it out."

Turk folded his arms and stared at the screen. The target area in southeastern Sudan was some 13,750 kilometers away—roughly 7,500 nautical miles. Cruising in the vicinity of Mach 3, the Tigershark could cover that distance in the area of four hours. At that speed, though, it would run out of fuel somewhere over the Atlantic. He'd need to set up at least two refuels to be comfortable.

"The first tanker will meet you in the Caribbean," said Breanna. She tapped a password into the computer and a map appeared. "It's already being prepped. You fly south with it, then head across to the Med. A second tanker will come on station over Libya."

"How long do I stay on station?"

"As long as it takes. We'll find another tanker; you can just stay in transmission range if you have to refuel off the east coast of Africa. Obviously, you won't be able to provide any surveillance, but we'll have to make do until we get more gear there. Frankly, it doesn't seem like it'll even be necessary. The mission looks very straightforward."

Breanna double-tapped the screen, expanding the map area of southern Sudan. Next she opened a set of optical satellite images of the area, taken about an hour before the accident.

"This satellite will pass back over that area in three hours," she said. "It's possible that they'll find the wreckage before you arrive. If not, you're to use your sensors to assist in the search. All right?"

"Sure."

"Colonel Freah will have operational control."

Breanna looked up from the screen. The frown on Turk's face hadn't dissipated.

"What's wrong, Captain?"

"Nothing."

"Out with it."

"Tigershark's unarmed."

"And?"

"I could do a much better job with the gun."

The gun referred to was the experimental rail gun. The weapon was undergoing tests in a second aircraft, which was also housed at the leased Dreamland base.

"The weapon's not operational. And there shouldn't be any need for it." Breanna clicked on another folder. A set of images opened. "This is Raven. It's smaller than a Flighthawk or a Predator. It's armed with Hellfire missiles at the moment, but eventually it will be able to house a number of weapons."

"Looks more like a Tigershark than a Predator."

"It is. The contractor is the same for both systems." Breanna closed the file, returning to the map. "It was flying with a Predator, which also crashed. Danny will be working out of Ethiopia. You'll be able to land there in an emergency."

"I didn't think Ethiopia was an ally," said Turk.

"They're not."